ALSO BY JAN-PHILIPP SENDKER

The Art of Hearing Heartbeats
A Well-Tempered Heart
Whispering Shadows

The
LANGUAGE
of
SOLITUDE

A NOVEL

JAN-PHILIPP SENDKER

Translated by Christine Lo

37INK
—
ATRIA

NEW YORK LONDON TORONTO SYDNEY NEW DELHI

37INK

ATRIA

An Imprint of Simon & Schuster, Inc.
1230 Avenue of the Americas
New York, NY 10020

First 37 INK/Atria Books hardcover edition May 2017

37INK / ATRIA BOOKS and colophons are trademarks of Simon & Schuster, Inc.

For information about special discounts for bulk purchases, please contact Simon & Schuster Special Sales at 1-866-506-1949 or business@simonandschuster.com.

The Simon & Schuster Speakers Bureau can bring authors to your live event. For more information, or to book an event, contact the Simon & Schuster Speakers Bureau at 1-866-248-3049 or visit our website at www.simonspeakers.com.

Manufactured in the United States of America

10 9 8 7 6 5 4 3 2 1

Library of Congress Cataloging-in-Publication Data has been applied for.

ISBN 978-1-4767-9367-2
ISBN 978-1-4767-9369-6 (ebook)

For Anna, Florentine, Theresa, and Jonathan

The
LANGUAGE
of
SOLITUDE

PROLOGUE

I've ended up in hell. Not of my own making. Not my fault. I must have lost my way. There's no other explanation. At some point in the maze of life, I took the wrong turn without noticing. Wasn't paying attention, for once. Took the left instead of the right fork. Or the other way around. I saw no sign, nothing that could have been a warning to me. I simply walked on without stopping. Just like I've always done in my life. Onward. Always onward.

I am not alone here. Hell is a crowded place. That is not a comfort.

Life is falling away from me; with every breath there is less of it. Like an old ruin being cleared away. Stone by stone. Every day there is another piece missing.

My body has become a cave. It is dark inside, so dark that not a single ray of light reaches me. And cold. And damp. I am cold at night and cold in the daytime.

The world outside has been extinguished before my eyes. The colors disappeared first, from the house, the fields, the village. A life in black and white. Everything looked like it did in the old films that we used to love watching. Then the shapes went; everything went blurry around me; I was looking at the world through a wall of water. Soon after that the darkness fell.

I cannot taste anything.

I cannot smell anything.

Nothing is left of the order and the beauty that once surrounded me. Apart from you and the music. You keep me alive. I hear and see you all *day. Your tender hands with the long, slim fingers. Your laughing eyes. Your lips. The way you sit bent low over a bowl of rice. Without you I would not be able to bear the pain any longer.*

Musical scores also appear in the dark before my eyes. I see them quite clearly: five thin inky-black lines on a blossom-white piece of paper. Small black dots with strokes. Like tadpoles in a pond. Allegro. Moderato. Adagio. I listen to every note, the high and the low, the slow and the fast. I hear the little hammers striking the strings. I hear the lightest touch of the bow on the violin. Fugues, études, sonatas. I hear orchestras. The violinists, the wind section, the percussion section. I hear entire operas. Mimi, Alfredo, Figaro, and the Queen of the Night are my loyal companions. I came to them late, so have never been able get enough. The greed of the hungry. Forgive me. I have music in my head. It eases the pain. It chases away dark thoughts, as the wind hustles the clouds along in front of it on a fall day.

CAN YOU HEAR ME, DARLING?

Oh yes. I can't move. I can't reach my hand out to you whenever I want to; I can't turn my head toward you; I can't thank you, but I can hear you. Every step. Every sigh. Every sound. Every breath. When you do the dishes. Sweep the floor. Push a chair back. Empty the pan of my excrement into the toilet. When you lie next to me and give me some of your warmth. When I feel less cold. Like before. Those are the moments in which even a life like this one is worth living.

CAN YOU HEAR ME? WHERE ARE YOU?

There is nothing I wish for more than to be able to answer you. But I can't. I am trapped in this useless body. I want to pound my fists against the walls with all my might; I could scream as loudly as I wanted—no one would hear me down here. I . . . looooove . . . yoooou. Not so long ago I tried one more time to make the shapes with my lips, to put my tongue against the roof of my mouth, place it behind my teeth and push the air out. Just three words. Only three. You did not understand them. You brought your ear right up against my mouth and asked me to repeat what I had said. Shhhhhhh . . . shhhhhhh . . . shhhhhhhh. I couldn't get any further than that, no matter how often I tried. I had become a shhhhhhh. Just for a few hours. Then the silence finally captured me and led me away.

All that is left is the gurgling, the rattling breaths and the grunting that I now produce. What agony for me, when I love the human voice so.

Now my tongue lies useless in my mouth like a rotting old dumpling. My lips are dumb. But I feel your warm breath on my cheek when you carefully kiss me good-night. The unmistakable breath of my darling old husband. The breath of the life we have lived.

Though I have been in darkness for so long now, it is the nights that are the worst. It is the silence around me that I find difficult. The house and the village are suddenly silent. Now and then I hear a truck passing in the distance. A dog barks every so often. In the hours after midnight it is only the drawing of breath that binds me to the rest of the world.

They tell you that I am only an empty shell. A crumpled old doll with no soul. They let themselves be deceived by the way things look from the outside. As so often happens. As so many do. They wear uniforms, white coats; I know that, even though I can't see them. I can tell by their voices. The voices of people who wear uniforms, no matter the color, always sound the same. They know. They are sure. All the tests prove it. There is no hope. I do not hear any uncertainty in their voices. There is no hope. No hope. That is only possible in the realm of the dead, which is closed to us. Ah, all the things in our lives that we have to hear from men and women in uniform. Don't believe a word they say. They know nothing. They have no music in their heads.

No one must pity me. I don't want to complain. Not as long as you are with me. When I think about it properly, I am really only in the forecourt of hell. Hell for the living is reserved for lonely people. I am not one of them.

Not as long as I feel your breath at night.

You are someone who is hungry for love. This was the first time that a woman had said this to him. He did not know whether it was a criticism or a compliment. Aren't we all? he replied, without giving it great thought.

She smiled. Some are more so than others.

What about me? More or less?

More. More, more, more.

He took her in his arms. The delicate body that he was sometimes afraid he would crush. That could fill him with desire and render him helpless through long, sleepless nights like no one else in his life had done. He took a deep breath and closed his eyes.

More. More, more, more.

Hungry for love. There had been people in his life who would have meant to hurt him with these words. And there had been times when they would have succeeded. He would have taken the words as an insult, and rejected them as an outrageous accusation.

Not today. Although the words "hunger" and "love" did not fit together in his head. For him, at least with Christine in his arms, love was abundance, happiness, and fulfillment. Hunger, on the other hand, was a need. Hunger had to be satisfied, at any price if necessary. Hunger knew only oneself; love, only the other. People who were hungry were weak, but people who loved were strong. If hunger and love had anything in common, it was that they were both immeasurable.

He asked her what she had meant by it. If he should take her words as a complaint or a compliment.

Neither one nor the other, she said. It's just something I've realized.

They left it at that.

Maybe, he thought, she was right. Perhaps the previous three years had left deeper traces than he was aware of. Three years in which he had wished for nothing more than to be alone. Three years in which a day when he had not exchanged a word with a single person had been a good day. A period in which his world had shrunk to the size of one house and a small, barely inhabited island with no cars in the South China Sea. Maybe a person who had had to withdraw himself so much, who had lived in the past and on memories, who had loved nothing and no one on this earth more than someone dead, was a person who was in more trouble than Paul wanted to accept.

Hungry for love. It was the neediness in the description that he did not like, although he could not say exactly why. We are all needy, he wanted to say out loud, but he knew what Christine would say.

Some are more so than others.

What about me?

More. More, more, more.

He said nothing and kissed her on the forehead. He trailed his long fingers up her neck and massaged her head with gentle rhythmic motions. She closed her eyes, and he stroked her face and her mouth. He could feel that his touch was arousing her; he heard her breath quickening. Not a lot, but enough to show him that they would not stop. He kissed her on the throat, and she whispered that she wanted to make love to him. Here, on the terrace.

He heard the hum of the cicadas, the loud chirping of the birds, and, from a distance, the neighbors' voices, and wanted to say that someone might see them, shouldn't they go up to his bedroom instead? But she was kissing him so passionately and holding him so tight, showing him how much she desired him, here, now, that he said nothing.

She pulled one of the garden chairs over, pushed him down gently but firmly onto it, and straddled him.

She was wearing a skirt; she did not waste any time. She dictated the rhythm, and was more vigorous and abandoned in loving him than he had ever known her to be. At the end she let out a short cry, loud but not light and full of relief as usual. It was dark and deep, expelled with force, almost despairing. As though this were the last time.

They held each other tight for a long while, clinging to each other silently, listening to their breathing gradually returning to normal.

Before she got up, she took his head in her hands and looked him in the eyes. Did he know how much she loved him? What he meant to her? He nodded, a little surprised. Did he promise never to forget that?

He nodded again, too tired to ask any questions.

Later, when he brought her to the ferry, she was unnervingly quiet. It was a warm and humid tropical evening; they walked down the hill to Yung Shue Wan, and the bushes around them were full of rustling, chirping, and cheeping noises. He asked her what she was thinking.

Nothing in particular, she said.

Is everything okay?

She waved his question away.

They had to run the last few yards. Christine could not miss this ferry; she had promised her son and her mother to be home by dinnertime.

He hated rushing. The next ferry left in forty minutes, and Paul found it an intolerable imposition to be forced by a timetable into hurrying. He was often to be found walking in measured steps toward the quay while other passengers rushed past him panting, responding to the ringing that announced that the gates were slowly closing, leaving him the only one who missed the boat. Instead of cursing, he sat down calmly on a bench under the shade of the pine trees in front of the bookshop and gazed at the sea. Or he crouched by the edge of the water and looked at the spray beneath him. Even as a child he had liked to watch the drops of water moving through the air; he had been fascinated by how they separated themselves from the sea, took shape for a couple of seconds, whizzing through the air, before disappearing almost immediately into the expanse of the ocean. People were like these little drops of water, he had thought then, they rose from and disappeared into the same infinity they came from. They stopped existing but still remained part of the whole. Somehow this thought had been comforting to him as a ten-year-old. His father had liked it too, but he thought instead that people came to an end like drops of water falling onto a hot plate. They disappeared into nothing with a quick hiss. The young Paul had found that comparison anything but comforting.

He loved looking at the waves, the way they played with the fishing boats and lapped the rocks in front of him. He heard the voice of the sea. Sometimes he even missed the next ferry while he daydreamed away like this.

But you don't have a son waiting for you, Christine had said when he told her about this before.

No, he did not. His son was dead.

She had apologized immediately. She had only meant to say that he did not have any familial or professional obligations: no boss, no business partner insisting on punctuality, no one waiting for him apart from her. And, if there were any doubt about it, she would forgive him if he were late.

Christine said a hurried good-bye with a quick kiss. He watched her walk up the gangway without turning back to look at him, and she disappeared into the belly of the ship a few seconds later. He stood on the pier, waving in the darkness and watching the ferry until it disappeared around the tip of the island.

It was a dark evening. The sea was a deep black in front of him, and the lights of Cheung Chau and Lantau twinkled in the distance. A junk full of day-trippers hove into view, close to Lamma. He could hear the monotonous thump of its diesel engine, children shrieking and parents admonishing them. The sound of voices and laughter floated over from the seaside promenade in Yung Shue Wan. He strolled along the pier, relishing the mild, warm, and humid air, soft as silk. At the Green Cottage restaurant he got a table right by the water and ordered a freshly pressed apple, carrot, and ginger juice. He was the only lone diner. He missed Christine already, even though her ferry was only just arriving at Hong Kong harbor.

Four weeks ago he had sat at that very spot, looking at the fishing boats bobbing up and down on the water, the red lanterns reflecting in the sea, and wondered if Christine should move in with him. Her son could take the ferry to school, and she could take a slightly later ferry to work. There was enough space in the house. Square footage, at least, but would he be able to stand seeing another child in Justin's room? The idea of it was as terrible as it was tempting. An attempt at having a family, at age fifty-three, after the first one had failed.

The thought of it had stayed with him since, and he had wanted to talk about it with Christine today. But she had avoided his questions and had been very quiet all day, withdrawn. *Hungry for love.* What made her *think* that? He tried to remember how she had sounded when she said it. Tender, he thought at the time; now he began to doubt it.

She rang him every Sunday evening before she went to bed, to tell him she had arrived home safely, she had enjoyed the time with him, and that she missed him already. And he said that he felt exactly the same way. It was their Sunday ritual, and rituals had come to mean so much.

He paid attention to the little things now.

He had begun to pursue beauty into her hiding place. For the first time in his life.

The death of his son had been his teacher. A terrible, merciless teacher that had not forgiven any mistakes or tolerated any objections. Paul had learned one of the most important lessons in life from it: never to take anything for granted again.

He used to think that it was just a matter of course for babies to become children, children to grow into young people, and young people to become adults.

He had thought that bruises on a child's body came only from a fall or a push.

He had thought that children who fell ill got better.

The fragility of happiness.

The randomness of unhappiness.

Nothing was the matter, of course. Anyone who understood that—no, Paul thought, anyone who had experienced those banal words, so often said glibly, as an existential truth never, ever forgot it; he was an outsider forever, someone for whom home was an impossible concept. He could make plans, father children, buy houses, make decisions about the future, and know at the same time that he was submitting himself to an illusion, that the future was only a promise and that you could never rely on it, that security could never be permanent, but could exist only for short, infinitely precious moments.

Was all the happiness in this world not hanging from a thread stretched tight, to the breaking point? It was so thin that most people did not even notice it.

I'm sorry to have to tell you. With these words, the doctor had snipped Paul's thread. Forever and ever, as his son might have said. There was no going back. Paul had reconciled himself to this thought. Until he met Christine.

As if trusting was only for fools. As if we had a choice. Those were the first words she had said that he had remembered. He had not taken them seriously at first. He had been secretly a little amazed that a grown woman was so naïve. Until then, he had been convinced that being skeptical was very useful, that it protected us, and in sufficient measure, kept us from great disappointment. He knew they came from two very different worlds: Christine Wu, the dreamer, and Paul Leibovitz, the realist.

How was a person to trust when the most important thing in his life had been taken away? Overnight, through no fault of his own, and for no reason. Someone who had had to witness white blood cells multiplying relentlessly, watch their numbers rise and rise as no medicine in the world could stop them. What could he rely on now? What, Christine, what?

She had not answered this question with words. She had stayed by him even when he pushed her away. She had trusted him more than he had trusted himself. Trust can be infectious, she had warned him. And she had been right.

———

It was just after midnight. In Yung Shue Wan the voices of the evening had long died away and the lights of most of the restaurants had gone out. Lamma had given itself over to peace. Paul opened the large sliding door to the garden and stepped outside. How loud the night was in the tropics. The cicadas chirped away tirelessly and the shrill croaking of the toads in a nearby pond filled the air. The bush in front of him rustled loudly; probably a snake hunting down a rat. The bamboo canes bent slightly in the gentle breeze. He had listened to this regular creaking and groaning so often, and fallen asleep to it.

Christine would normally have rung him long before this time. To wish him good-night. He had checked several times that his telephone was switched on, that the volume was on, and that the battery did not need charging. He could not remember a Sunday when she had not called. Perhaps she had simply lain down on her bed for a moment and fallen asleep in exhaustion. He missed hearing her voice and had thought a few times about calling her. But that would not have been the same. He needed the gesture.

Hungry for love. Maybe she was right.

He decided to send her a text message.

My love, my darling,
Why have you not been in tou

No, he did not want to make any accusations.

My love, my darling,
Where are you? I was really looking forward to yo

Not even veiled ones.

My love, my darling,
Sleep well. Thank you for today. Thank you for everything.
I love you. More and more.

He hesitated. Added "I need you and I miss you." And deleted it. He did not want to sound needy.

Paul read his text message a few times. He was not used to writing text messages and did not want to risk any misunderstanding. Finally he sent it, switched his phone off, and immediately felt better. Tomorrow morning she would reply with a few tender lines, and the incident would be over.

It was a dreamless night. He slept well, longer than usual, and when he woke, his first thought was of Christine. What a gift it was to wake next to her while she was still sleeping. To feel the warmth of her body. Her regular breathing.

How little it took now to find happiness in its hiding place. How often we simply walk past it.

He reached for his phone next to the bed and switched it on. No new messages. Paul suddenly felt the same unease that had plagued him the previous night. It was too early, he told himself. At this hour she was taking a shower and getting ready for a long day in the office. She normally only texted him once she was on the MTR train on the way to Wan Chai.

He got up, tied the mosquito net in a knot, went down to the kitchen, and put some water on to boil for tea. The air had cooled only slightly during the night; the weather gauge by the window displayed 77 degrees Fahrenheit and 88 percent humidity, and it was not even eight a.m. yet. Paul had to hurry. The sun would be shining on the roof terrace shortly, and it would soon beat down so fiercely that he would have to seek protection from it, and be forced to do tai chi in the shade instead. The exercise always took exactly one hour. It helped him start the day after bad nights and gave him, at least for that hour, the feeling of almost cheerful ease.

Not today. His movements were imprecise and strangely clumsy; his hips were much too stiff and his shoulders tense. He even started the "single whip" and "white crane spreads wings" moves from the beginning, but was not able to achieve a harmonious flow of movements.

By evening he finally made contact with her. They spoke only briefly by phone. It was busier than usual in Christine's office, and in the evening her son had a high fever and needed his mother.

Of course Paul understood. She didn't have to explain or apologize.

On Tuesday morning came a text message; Christine told him that she would not be able to come to Lamma that Sunday. He rang her three times. All three conversations were unusually short. Their first call was cut short because a customer stuck at the airport in Jakarta was complaining, then Cathay Pacific was canceling flights, then Christine had the pediatrician on the other line. Each time, she did not call back as promised.

Her silence. Paul tried to ignore it. He cleaned the house even more thoroughly than usual. Dusted the books, wiped down the shelves, and mopped the floor. He rubbed the old Chinese wedding chest with new wax polish until it shone again. He cleared out the fridge and washed every compartment with soapy water. *Immune system weakened. Make sure everything is especially clean. In the whole house. A minor infection can be life-threatening.*

There are sentences, he thought, that follow us around all our lives. Justin would soon have been dead for four years. Nevertheless, to this day, Paul could not bear to have even the shadow of dirt in his house.

He went for a walk to Pak Kok, at the tip of the island. He left his phone at home. He did not want to be waiting for a phone call with every step he took.

He thought about the last two days and tried to think logically. What was he so upset about? That Christine had not found any time in the last forty-eight hours to exchange a few sentences with him in an unhurried way? It was unusual, but she was a very busy woman.

That her voice sounded less tender than it usually did? What was he? A teenager in love for the first time? He knew how much pressure she was under. Her mother made demands on her that he could not understand, but had to accept. The more he thought about it, the more he understood that it was not Christine who was making him feel insecure. He was the one doing it to himself.

She had asked him not long ago if he lived on Lamma in exile. The word had moved him strangely. "Exile." *Exilium* in Latin, if he remembered correctly. A sojourn in a strange place. Banishment. No, he had replied immediately. No one has banished me. He was not a refugee, not fleeing persecution. He could not be spending time in a strange place, because only people who had a home could do that. Paul did not have a home. His parents were dead. Nothing bound him to the country he had been born in. He remembered barely anything about Germany apart from the many ships in the harbor at Hamburg and, strangely, the deep and loud horn of the steamer that had brought them to America. His early years in Munich and his memories of his grandparents had faded with time.

He was an American citizen. His blue passport was proof of it. But it was a travel document, nothing more. After his mother died when he was nineteen, he had left the country forever. He did not have relatives anywhere in the world whom he knew personally.

Before, whenever people asked him, as they did from time to time, where his home was, he always said, On earth, more or less. Most of them thought he was joking.

He had lived in Hong Kong for over thirty years, but not in exile. If there was anywhere on this earth where he felt at ease, it was in this city. He was grateful to it. It had taken him in and never forced him to belong to any particular place. That suited him.

When he had told Christine what he was thinking, she had replied that she had not meant her question that way. She had been thinking more of how he had withdrawn after Justin's death. Had he voluntarily gone into exile because of it?

Paul had never asked himself this question; he owed it a reply.

A kind of self-imposed exile, fleeing life because he could not bear the pain and grief over his son? Perhaps. If that were so, then it was because of Christine that he had found his way back. Her patience, like an angel's, in the first few months. Her strength, which had borne with his moods. Her ability not to expect more than he could give.

She had brought him back to life and made him realize the simple truth of an old Chinese saying: "A human being alone is not a human being."

Was it any wonder that he was sometimes oversensitive in his reactions? He was surely not the first exile who found the return to a world that he had left, from one day to the next, difficult. There was a lot at stake. The short breath of happiness. As though fear needed a reason.

Once he returned from his walk, his cell phone showed a missed call. Christine. He called back but she didn't answer. A busy tone. He tried again, with no luck. She would see on her phone display that he had called. She would ring back as soon as she had time.

He circled the telephone the way Justin had done with a bar of chocolate that he was not allowed to have. He picked up a book and put it down again a few minutes later. He tried some music. Brahms didn't work. Neither did Beethoven. Puccini only intensified his longing.

He rang her shortly after eleven p.m. He wanted to sound relaxed. Calm, cheerful, casual, everything but hungry for love.

"Is something wrong?" she asked immediately.

"No. Why?"

"You sound so—"

"How do I sound?"

"Down."

He hated talking about important things with the small device pressed to his ear, asking questions and then hearing nothing but a hissing noise, not knowing when it would end. Waiting alone for answers that could be of meaning to him. He had to see who he was talking to in order to reassure himself that what was being said was reflected in the gestures and the body language, that it was consistent with what was in the person's eyes. How much simpler it was to tell untruths on the telephone. The wrong tone of voice or a tiny, unimportant misunderstanding was enough to unsettle him, to cause a moment of doubt that could flare quickly into an argument. For him, the telephone magnified a person's mood. It made the secure feel more certain and the fearful more frightened. Right now, he was one of the fearful. How was he to understand the harsh tone of her voice without being able to look into her eyes? He had no idea what to ask or what to say. "I just wanted to hear your voice," he said quietly.

"You woke me up."

"I'm sorry."

They were silent.

"Are you okay?" he asked.

"What do you mean?"

He wished he could hang up. Her words and her voice were making him feel the opposite of what he needed. If he weren't careful, the conversation would not end well. How sensitive needy people were. It was not her fault.

"We've barely spoken since Sunday. This morning I received a text message in which you simply—"

"Paul, you have no idea what I've had to deal with these last few days. Josh is sick and is ringing me five times a day. My mother has a pain in her chest and won't go to the hospital on her own for an examination. All hell has broken loose in the office. It's May and I'm almost twenty percent down for the first half of the year. Do you know what it means if we don't catch up?"

"I know, Christine. I just don't understand—"

"You have too much time on your hands. That's the problem," she interrupted again. "If I spent all day cleaning the house, cooking, and going for walks, I would also think stupid things."

What was he supposed to say to that?

"I'm sorry," she said after a long pause. "I didn't mean it that way."

"You don't have to apologize."

"I didn't mean to hurt you."

Paul felt empty and exhausted, as if they had fought for two hours. "You mean it's nothing more than that?"

"'More than that'?" Her voice sharpened again. "Haven't you heard what I said? That's all a great deal, if you ask me."

"Of course. That is all a great deal for you, but I didn't mean that."

"What, then?"

"I'm worried."

"About me?"

"Yes. About us."

She gave a deep sigh. "Paul, it's late. I can't sleep in tomorrow. My alarm is set for six thirty a.m. Could we talk about it another time?"

Now he could hear how tired she sounded. "Of course. But when?"

"Soon. Very soon."

"I love you. Sleep well."

"I love you too. Good-night."

"You too. Always and for—"

She had hung up the phone.

I love you too. That was all he had wanted to hear. Like a child.

Paul thought about Justin. *I love you.* He had said that to him every night after he turned off the light. *I love you too*, a tired child's voice had whispered back in the darkness.

She was absolutely right. He would go to Hong Kong tomorrow, ask her out to lunch, and apologize to her.

As if trusting was only for fools. As if we had a choice.

He would have liked to have fallen asleep with these comforting thoughts. Something kept him awake. A feeling that he did not dare himself to put into words.

She had hesitated for a moment. The office was very busy. It wasn't a good time. Tomorrow would be a better day. But when she heard that he was already on the ferry, she agreed. Paul went straight from the pier to the IFC mall to buy a small box of her favorite pralines and a deep-red long-stemmed rose.

They met in World Peace Café, a restaurant on Tai Wong Street East in Wan Chai. It was on the ground floor of a Buddhist center barely five minutes from Christine's office. They entered a high-ceilinged room with floor-to-ceiling windows. By Hong Kong standards, there was a wasteful amount of space between the tables. Three vegetarian dishes had been written on a chalkboard. Quiet jazz music came from the speakers on the wall, and several statues of Buddha, in different sizes, rested on the shelves around them. Every table had a small vase of flowers and a lit tea-light on it. It was the opposite of the crowded and noisy restaurants in which Christine normally had lunch.

Paul noticed she seemed uncomfortable.

"Do you not like it here?"

"I do, I do."

Her voice betrayed to him that she was not telling the truth.

"Should we go somewhere else?"

"No, no."

They ordered beet soup with tofu, two eggplant stews, water, tea, and a freshly pressed juice for Paul.

"The chef lives on Lamma," he said, to get her mind off things. "He told me that the waiters, cleaners, and kitchen staff are all volunteers."

"They must all have rich husbands," Christine said.

They sat opposite each other in silence, and he felt the inner unease rise again. Something was not quite right with her. She had managed to cover it up on the phone but not now, sitting opposite him. He saw it in her eyes. The way they avoided his, the way she stared down at the table or looked past him at the wall. He saw it in her face: the lips were too thin and the small lines around her mouth too deep. This was not the way she looked when she was well.

He was afraid to ask. He was afraid she would say that everything was fine. He did not want to be lied to.

"Christine?" He hoped that the way he said her name would be question enough.

She looked at him without replying.

As the seconds passed, the silence made him feel more and more uncomfortable. "What's wr—"

"Nothing," she interrupted, then paused. "No. Quite a lot." She took a deep breath, and buried her face in her hands. "I don't know how to explain it to you." She suddenly had tears in her eyes.

Was this the moment? Paul had the feeling that he had to hold on to something. He felt heavy, as if someone had put a leaden vest around him. Had she fallen in love with someone else? Had her husband returned? Or had she been to see a doctor and heard the terrible, comfortless words "I'm sorry to have to tell you . . ."?

"I need time," she said after a pause that seemed endless. "I need a little bit of space."

This sounds like the beginning of the end, Paul thought.

"What has happened between us?"

"Nothing."

"Nothing?" He had raised his voice. The diners at the other tables turned to look at him. "Four weeks ago we sat on my terrace and talked about whether we should move in together and now you suddenly need space. Why . . ." He wanted to get up and go to the ferry, to Lamma. Just get away.

"Please don't go," she said quietly, reaching for his hand.

Paul hesitated. He closed his eyes and tried to calm himself. He felt his heart racing.

"I love you, Paul." Her voice. Far away. Despairing. "It's not what you think."

"What do I think?"

"That I'm in love with another man."

He opened his eyes. "How do you know that?"

"Because that's always the first thought that comes to men."

He was silent for a moment. "With a woman?"

"No."

"Why are you saying that you need space then? Am I too much for you?"

She shook her head, saying nothing.

"Am I too hungry for love?"

"No." A smile flitted over her face.

"Why do you want more space then?"

"For your sake."

"For my sake?" He looked at her uncomprehendingly.

"I'm frightened, frightened that I could . . ." She didn't go on.

"Hurt me?" he said, finishing her sentence.

"No."

"Leave me?"

"No. Kill you."

"What did you say?" He thought he had misheard her.

She repeated the word.

Paul was on the verge of losing it.

"What do you mean by that?" he finally asked.

"Exactly what I said. I'm afraid I will kill you."

"What makes you think that?"

"It's a risk. I know it. Isn't that enough?"

"No. How do you know it?"

"Someone told me."

"Who?"

"An astrologer," she whispered.

"A what?"

"Must you shout? I went to see a fortune-teller. A Chinese astrologer. A man who can see the future. Call him what you will."

Paul could not suppress a laugh. The fear of the past few days, his insecurity, all because Christine had been to see an astrologer. He had lived in Asia for almost forty years, more than thirty of those in Hong Kong, and he knew how superstitious the people here were. Christine was no exception. She always wore something red: panties, stockings, or a scarf, or simply a thin strip of fabric around her ankle. She always had a small turquoise jade fish in her bag. In her tiny travel agency there was an altar on a sideboard; every morning, she lit incense sticks to it and made offerings of a couple of biscuits, a tangerine, or a banana. In February, at the beginning of the Chinese New Year, she had given Paul her new phone number and told him that those were her lucky numbers for the year. He had thought then that she probably visited a soothsayer from time to time, but had not asked about it. He would never have thought that she would ask for advice about her love for him.

"You can't be telling me that you love me less because I'm bringing you bad luck, can you?"

"I don't love you less. It's not about me, Paul. It's about you."

"How am I to understand this? Are you bringing me bad luck?"

She nodded and said nothing.

"I'm sorry, Christine, but this is ridiculous. How long have we known each other?"

"One year, three months, twelve days, and"—she looked at her watch—"twenty-two hours."

The waiter brought them tea, water, and the soup. They ignored him.

Paul kissed Christine's hand. "In that time I have felt happier than I have for a long, long time. The past few months have been some of the best of my life."

"It's not about the past. It's about the future."

"In which you'll be seized by insanity and murder me?" He had not meant to sound so smug.

"If you won't take me seriously we can't talk about this anymore."

"I'm taking you seriously."

"No you're not."

"I am. The person I can't take seriously is someone who claims to be able to predict the future."

"Why not?"

"Because . . . because I can't imagine the stars having any influence on our destinies."

"But I believe in it."

Paul took a deep breath and exhaled. He wished her bon appétit, took a couple of spoonfuls of soup, and wondered how he could end the conversation. He did not have the slightest desire to discuss superstition and horoscopes. But it was clearly important to Christine.

"What exactly did he say?" he asked finally. "What makes him think that you could kill me?"

"Do you really want to know?"

"I wouldn't ask otherwise."

She put her spoon down. "It's the year of the pig. He predicts that I will get a big surprise. That it will be a difficult year for me. For the business, and even more so for my personal life. That my mother will fall sick and that I will have problems with my son." She paused and gave him an expectant look.

"And?" Paul asked.

"And what? What do you mean? That has all come true!"

He wanted to say that you didn't have to be a fortune-teller to tell a woman in her early forties that her mother, who was at least sixty, if not older, would have health problems. And if this woman had a child, which Christine had probably told this man already, it was very probably going through puberty, or just about to. A time when all parents have trouble with their children.

"What did he say about your father?"

"That he is dead."

The waiter put the eggplant stew on the table and cleared away their half-eaten soup.

He would have liked to say to her that this statement had a high likelihood of being true, given the low life expectancy of men of that generation, but he hesitated, decided to simply nod instead, and said nothing.

Christine took his silence as an invitation to tell him more. "He said that a man would enter my life. This man would be very import-ant to me and would get closer and closer to me." She paused again and looked at him. Her voice had dropped to a whisper. Paul had to lean quite far across the table to hear the next few words she said.

"It will not be good for this man. He will not survive this year."

Paul shook his head. "That doesn't mean that you'll kill me."

"I didn't mean that I would murder you. It is being close to me that will kill you."

"How long is this supposed to last?"

"For the year of the pig, until the Chinese New Year, the next nine months."

Paul leaned back and gave Christine a long look. He wished he could laugh out loud. Or take her face in his hands and kiss her gently on the forehead in the hope that that would be the end of her fears. But the way she was looking at him, the way her dark-brown eyes rested on his, left no doubt that she was serious about this.

"I didn't go to one of those booths in Wong Tai Sin Temple and get my palm read for a hundred Hong Kong dollars," she said, as though she had not yet given up hope that she could convince him. "I went to Wong Kah Wei, one of the most highly respected fortune-tellers in Hong Kong. Every year, rich Europeans and Americans come to the city just to see him, and they pay a fortune for it. He even went to London once to give a member of the royal family a consultation. The only reason I can afford to see him is be-cause I've known him for a such long time I pay a special-reduced fee. I've recorded his entire forecast so that if I want to I can listen to it anytime and check if he was right."

"And if he isn't? Do you get your money back?"

It was not the right time to make jokes. She gave him a look of irritation and disappointment.

"Do you know the story of Oedipus?" he asked.

"No," she said curtly. She was clearly expecting him to make another joke.

"It's a Greek myth. A seer tells a king that his son will kill him and become a lover with his own mother. To prevent this, the king leaves his baby son out in the open to die, but a shepherd rescues the infant. Oedipus is brought up by a childless royal couple but leaves them when an oracle tells him that he will murder his father and marry his mother. On his journey he falls into a quarrel with an old man and kills him. That man is his father, the king of Thebes. Then Oedipus frees the city from a Sphinx and is given the hand of the king's widow as a reward. She is his mother. If the king had not listened to the fortune-teller, none of this would have happened. The prophecy was fulfilled because the king took it seriously and tried to prevent it from happening. I suggest that we ignore astrologer's forecast."

"You don't understand what I mean," she said, shaking her head. "Your story only confirms to me that each of us has a destiny that we can only avoid by making certain choices. Don't you believe that?"

"No."

"What do you believe in?"

He looked Christine in the eye. He wanted to say something quite spontaneous in reply, something humorous, in a final attempt to stop her taking the situation so seriously, but he couldn't think of anything. The longer the silence went on, the louder the question echoed in his mind: How should he, Paul Leibovitz, son of a German Catholic and an American Jew, raised in Munich and New York, unmarried, a member of no religion, in the fifty-fourth year of his life, having had many relationships of different depths and durations, and having experienced a failed marriage and the death of his child, reply? What did he believe in?

Paul said nothing.

Christine waited for a reply.

Justin had asked him once if he believed in God.

No, Paul had said. I believe in Miss Rumphius. A smile had flitted across his son's face. The story of Miss Rumphius had been Justin's favorite book for a long time. A little girl promises her grandpa to do something "to turn the world into a better place." When she is an old lady she remembers her promise and uses her savings to buy flower seeds, which she scatters on the ground. The next year, the first plants grow. She gathers their seeds and spreads them over a wider area, and soon the neighborhood is filled with a wonderful display of flowers.

You mean you believe in people who keep their promises?

Yes, Paul had said to his son. *And in people who do something to make the world a better place.* Justin had understood what he had meant. Christine, he feared, would think that he was not taking her seriously.

"I don't know what you want to hear," he said, avoiding a direct reply.

"I don't understand you. What's so difficult about my question?"

"Nothing. But the question of what the meaning of life is occurs more to teenagers, doesn't it?"

"Why should that be? It does no harm to take stock now and then."

"Okay." Paul took a deep breath. "I believe in music. In good food. In having a wonderful evening with you—"

"I'm not asking what makes you happy," she interrupted.

"Isn't that the same thing?"

"No." She rolled her yes and looked at her watch.

He hadn't meant to annoy her.

The more he tried to avoid her question, the more uncomfortable he felt. What did he believe in? Not in a god, whatever people wanted to call it. Not in a power that determines our fate. Not in destiny. If in anything at all, then in coincidence. In the arbitrariness of nature. In its unjustness. *I'm sorry to have to tell you.*

If Paul was being honest, he had no answer to Christine's question.

"I'll have to take my time to think over it," he said after a long pause. "Could I try to answer your question later?"

"Whenever."

"And you? What do you believe in? Apart from the stars."

"You know what I believe in. In feng shui. In yin and yang. In the power of harmony. I see life as a giant mobile on which different weights are hanging. They have to find their balance, otherwise things don't work. I believe in fate. I'm convinced that it wasn't just a coincidence that we met. It was destiny."

She looked at her watch again.

"I could tell you stories about my friends who were told the most astounding things by an astrologer that really came true. But I'm sorry, I just don't have the time to talk about Chinese astrology with you for the rest of the afternoon. If you want to convince yourself, call Master Wong." She took a pen out of her bag and wrote a telephone number on a napkin.

"You know his number by heart?" he asked, hoping that Christine wouldn't notice the hint of disbelief in his voice.

"I've been seeing him for years. Ask him whatever you like. He doesn't know anything about you. Maybe he can convince you."

She got ready to leave, but Paul stopped her.

"If I go to him and he tells me that it will be a good year for me, in which my body and soul will not be endangered in any way, what happens then?"

"I can't imagine that will happen."

"But if it does?"

"The we'll have to consult him once more together. Now I really must go."

She got up, took the box of pralines and the rose, and gave him a kiss. "I'll call you tonight. By the time Josh goes to bed. I promise."

Paul watched her leave. She turned back one more time at the door, blew him a kiss, and smiled briefly. He could not imagine not being able to see her for the next nine months. All because of a Chinese astrologer's prophecy. Because the pig wasn't compatible with the dragon. Or firewood should stay away from water. Or the horse

disrupted the flow of the rat. Nonsense. If a visit to Wong Kah Wei
was the only way to calm Christine down, then he could submit to
the mumbo jumbo.

He called the number. A woman's voice. No, Master Wong was
not free. Not today. Not tomorrow. The next available appointment
was in eight weeks. Paul switched to Cantonese, and a spirited bar-
gaining commenced, at the end of which he obtained an appointment for early that evening at three times the normal fee.

In his travels in the previous thirty years, Paul had visited sooth-
sayers, astrologers, and card-reading fortune-tellers, sometimes for
fun, sometimes out of boredom, or out of curiosity when someone
made an especially strong recommendation. In Sumatra, a blind seer
of ghosts had warned him never to travel by boat again. In Bangkok,
a former monk had been absolutely certain that the lines on his
palm showed that an opulent wedding with an Indian princess was
in store for him. A Chinese man in Kunming had prophesied great
wealth for him in his fortieth year. Paul had listened to all these
stories with amusement and not believed any of them. Quite rightly
too. He had not become a millionaire, had not become a member
of a royal family, loved traveling by boat, and had enjoyed the best
of health to that day. Of course, now and then he had heard tales of
friends who had been told things by a seer, fortune-teller, or palm
reader that had apparently come true just as predicted. Everyone
knew such stories from hearsay. Fairy tales, Paul thought. Stupid,
silly fairy tales.

He imagined Master Wong would be an old man with white
hair, living in a poky little place somewhere in the depths of Mong-
kok or Ma Tau Wai. Dim light from a single bulb hanging from the
ceiling and a few incense sticks burning in the corner, perhaps with
a crystal ball on the table and tarot cards on the side.

The master received his visitors on the eight floor of the Great
Wealth Building on Queen's Road Central, one of the most expensive addresses in Hong Kong. An elegantly dressed woman of
around fifty, Ms. Yiu, was at the reception desk. She asked Paul to
take a seat and disappeared into a small kitchen to make tea. The

office space was unusually large; a fountain pattered in a corner, and on the opposite wall tiny red fish swam in an impressive aquarium, while the shelves next to it displayed several antique Chinese clay statues. Paul could see the day's closing stock exchange figures for Hong Kong, Shenzhen, and Shanghai on Ms. Yiu's computer screen. There were plus signs flashing in front of the green numerals; it must have been a good day on the markets.

Suddenly the door opened and a small, gaunt man appeared, looking at Paul in silence. The man's face looked stern; at first glance, Paul felt that he was facing a bank official who would or would not grant him a loan.

"Master Wong?"

The man nodded and gestured to Paul to follow him into his office.

Stock exchange indices were also lit up on Master Wong's flat screen. In one corner of the room a set of gold golf clubs was propped against a bookshelf filled to bursting, and on the desk lay books, papers, pencils, a Montblanc fountain pen, and two news-papers, both open. The astrologer had clearly been poring over the results of yesterday's horse races in Happy Valley. Paul was just about to wonder what he had gotten himself into when he realized that the astrologer was speaking. His voice was quiet, almost a whisper, but it filled every corner of the room. It was firm and piercing, giving the man an almost mysterious authority that did not fit his outward appearance at all.

It was not a voice that one wanted to contradict.

"You know about Chinese horoscopes?" It sounded as though that was a precondition for the consultation.

"Yes."

"Then tell me what you want to know."

"What the months to come have in store for me. Whether the year of the pig holds dangers for me or whether it will be a good year."

"I believe this is about an investment? Property? The right time to invest?"

"No," Paul replied, annoyed. "Just in general."

"Then I need your date of birth. The place. And the exact time. Do you know the details?"

"But of course."

The man wrote everything down on a large sheet of paper. "I suggest that I tell you a few things about your past. If these things turn out to be correct, I will talk about your future. If I am wrong, then something is not right with my calculations. Then we will end the session. Of course you will not need to pay if that is the case. Is that all right with you?"

Paul nodded.

Master Wong started making his calculations. He stood up, fetched a thick, worn-looking book from the shelf, and looked inside it; he pulled out a second book to consult and made further notes. Paul had the feeling that Wong was growing more and more distant from him with every passing minute. He started to feel uneasy. He tried to stop himself from tapping his left foot by crossing his legs and crossed his arms behind his head.

After long minutes of silence the astrologer put his pen down and looked at him.

"You moved when you were a child."

Paul nodded. Many children did that, he thought, but he said nothing.

"Moved continent, even."

"That's right."

"You moved in early childhood."

"That's also right."

"Your relationship with your family was distant."

"Yes," Paul answered, his voice hoarse, his throat dry. He felt like a defendant in court, giving replies to a judge.

"Your parents are both dead."

"Correct."

"Your mother died young."

"Also correct."

Master Wong smiled briefly. "You don't have to confirm every piece of information. I'm not recording your personal details. All you have to do is tell me when I make a mistake." He paused briefly before continuing. "You married between your fortieth and fiftieth year."

Paul inclined his head in a nod.

"It was your first marriage."

"Yes," Paul said, as if in a trance.

"You are divorced. You have a child."

Paul shifted uneasily from side to side on his chair. He did not want to hear the rest.

"A son." The man paused for a long time. He consulted more books and scribbled something on a piece of paper, crossed through what he had written, and wrote something else beneath it. Paul could not decipher the Chinese characters upside down.

He wanted to say that he had heard enough, that everything the master had said was right, that he could talk about the future now, that he did not want to hear the next sentence. But no words passed his lips.

The astrologer lifted his head and looked him in the eye. "Your son is dead."

———

Paul sat at an outdoor food stall at the end of Stanley Street. It was hot, and his shirt clung to his chest. The sweat was dripping from his chin and trickling down his neck and back. Even his leather belt was damp. He had a plate of fried noodles and a cold beer in front of him. He was still in a daze. Even if he had wanted to, he could not believe the experience he had just had.

If a stranger had told him this had happened to him, Paul would not have believed a word of it. He wanted an explanation, but he had the feeling that he would not find one. Not now. He would have to search for it. For the second time that day he was in turmoil. Unsettled. Alone.

It had grown dark, and the foldaway tables and plastic stools around him were almost all occupied. Several cooks were preparing food in large woks. The smell of fried meat, garlic, and onions wafted over to him. All around were hissing sounds and rising steam, and now and then a rogue flame from the cooking fires flared high into the darkness. Four construction workers with bare torsos huddled at the table next to Paul, sizing him up. One of the men raised his glass and toasted him. Paul smiled briefly by way of thanks.

He pulled his tape recording of what the astrologer had said out of his bag, put it on the table, and wondered what to do with it.

Mr. Leibovitz, I'm warning you.

With regard to the future, Master Wong had at first spoken at length about what his Chinese clients were always most interested in: the financial outlook for the coming months. Paul's prospects on this front were not bright, but there was also no cause for special concern, though he was strongly advised not to make any high-risk investments that year. What the astrologer said was not very relevant to him, for he had invested his money in secure fixed-interest bonds; the income they yielded was not high, but he lived modestly, and it covered his needs. He had not touched his backup account for extraordinary expenses and emergencies in three years.

Wong had suddenly hesitated after that. He had made further calculations, flicked through two more volumes, and frowned as though he himself could not believe his own findings. He finally leaned back in his chair, peered over his glasses at Paul, crossed his arms across his chest, and said nothing for a long time.

Mr. Leibovitz, I'm warning you.

The principles of his profession forbade him to say everything that the constellations of stars told him. He would waive his fee under these special circumstances. Paul could go now.

Paul hesitated for a few seconds that seemed endless to him. He thought about the story of Oedipus and the power of the self-fulfilling prophecy. But then he immediately felt annoyed by that thought; it meant that he was giving this man's prophecy far too much importance. Of course he wanted to know everything—what he would do with the knowledge was another story altogether. He sat up straight in his chair and said that he had come to hear what the future held for him; he was a person who could deal with bad news—there had been enough of that in his life.

Wong looked at him intently. No.

In the end, it was Paul's stubborn refusal to leave the office before he had heard everything, or, more important, the determination he was displaying, that changed the astrologer's mind.

Listen to these sentences that I am trusting you with. They are only meant for your ears. Be careful with what you are hearing.

You will . . .

Three short sentences. Nothing more. An oracle that Paul had no idea what to do with. He had not believed any other prophecies before, but now he could not deny that he felt unsettled, no matter how hard he tried.

The biggest problem was Christine. She would ask questions. She would want to know what Master Wong had said, but she was not allowed to know. On no account. She would feel that her worst fears had been confirmed and reduce their contact to a minimum. He would have to calm her down with a plausible story. The prospect of having to lie to her made him feel even more uneasy.

He picked up the cassette and fingered it. It was tiny; one stamp of the heel on it would suffice. Or should he keep it, the way Christine kept hers? What for? He would not forget what he had heard about his future. He drank a mouthful of beer, used a toothpick to pull the brown tape out of the cassette, and unspooled it all. He grabbed the bundle of tape, got up, and threw it all in the trash can with the remains of his meal.

III

———

The letter lay between bills from PCCW Mobile and Hong Kong Electric. Christine marveled at the handwriting. Elegant, swooping script in black ink, written with a fine brush, more a piece of calligraphy than a mere address. No name or return address. She did not know anyone who could write such beautiful Chinese characters. The stamp: People's Republic of China. She tensed. The first glimmering, which she ignored. She decided to open the envelope anyway.

My dear Mei-mei,

Little sister. Her hands trembled. She lowered the piece of paper. Her brother was dead. Had died forty years ago. Of starvation. Of thirst. Or had dropped dead in a paddy field. Because his young body had not been able to bear the hardships of the harvest any longer. A victim of the Cultural Revolution. One of millions. Sent to the countryside when he was fourteen to learn from the farmers. By the command of a paranoid Great Chairman, whom nobody had dared to contradict. A sickly, weak young boy, ordered to go to the mountains of Sichuan Province because his father was said to belong to the clique of intellectuals. He had disappeared after that. He had no chance. How often had Christine heard those words from her mother's mouth when she was a child? Long Long is dead. He had no chance.

Everything rushed back in an instant: The warm and humid fall day in 1968. The flurry of loud footsteps in the hallway. The hysterical voices. The splintering of the door kicked in by the Red Guards. The fear of death on her father's face. Her brother, where was her brother? Why was he not with them? She did not see him in this picture. She saw her mother, the gaunt woman in her faded Mao suit. The terror on her face. She saw herself. Cowering under the table. The little girl who closed her eyes but opened them again, frightened and curious. Two, three quick, heavy steps. Her father perched on the windowsill. Like a big fat crow that was on the verge of spreading its wings. He jumped before she could grab him. The silence after.

An accident. That was the official version. Until today.

Soon after that, her brother was made to go to the countryside. A few months later, she and her mother escaped to Hong Kong. They swam until they had no more strength. Three of the people in their small group drowned. Coincidence saved them. Or fate, or the stars. Their time had not come yet, her mother later claimed. She had heard her pray in the water. She had not heard anything more about her brother since that time.

Who dared address her as little sister? She turned the page. On the reverse was his name: Wu Da Long. Big Dragon.

My dear Mei-mei,

How should I begin this letter? After so many years. You probably thought I was dead. And I was, or as good as. A slow dying, witnessed by an entire village. No longer one of the living, not yet one of the dead. A young girl brought me back. She is still my wife today. But I don't want to say too much about myself. I have started to chatter away like an old woman.

Do you remember me at all? They used to call me Long Long. But you were not even born yet. Later on you learned to walk holding my hand. You were so little. But healthy. I was always sick. A nimble girl with a parting in your hair, straight as a

*bamboo rod, two braids, right and left. That is how I picture you.
What do you look like now? Would we recognize each other if we
were face to face?*

What has happened to you? Are you married?

*Do you have a child? You wanted to be a doctor when you
were a little girl. A barefoot doctor. They used to walk from
village to village in the countryside back then, helping the sick.
You admired them very much. I'm sure you have fulfilled your
dream though perhaps not visiting your patients barefoot.*

*You are probably asking yourself why so many years had to
pass before I wrote you this letter. And you are right to do so.
There are, I assure you, many reasons. I will explain them to you
when, if, we meet again. For that is the request that this letter
brings: I would like to see you. As soon as possible. I am lucky to
be in good health now but who knows how much time anyone
has left? Apart from that, I now also—and I do not want to
hide that from you in this letter—find myself in the most serious
difficulty, through no fault of my own. To be clear: I need help,
urgently. Time is not on my side. You wish to know what this
is all about? I understand. Unfortunately the situation is so
complicated that I cannot explain it to you in a letter or on the
phone. Since it is impossible for me to travel, I must ask you,
though I do so reluctantly, to come to me. I live about three hours
away from Shanghai. I have a son, Xiao Hu, and a daughter,
Yin-Yin, in Shanghai. Yin-Yin will meet you at the airport
and bring you to us. She knows about this letter, and she will be
very happy, I need hardly say, to get to know her aunt. She is
a good girl. She is studying music at the conservatory and will
soon sit for her final exams. I know that this must all come as a
great surprise to you. I am asking a lot. I can do no more at the
moment than to ask for your understanding.*

*A final question: Is Mother still alive? If she is, which I of
course hope with all my heart, then I beg you not to tell her about
this letter. The joy at the news that I am alive would be clouded
by worries about my plight.*

I very much hope that this letter has not given you a shock. Will I hear from you soon?

Ge-Ge
Da Long

Then came an address and Yin-Yin's phone number.

Ge-ge. Big brother. Christine put the letter to one side. She picked up the envelope again, opened it once more, sniffed it, and ran her fingers over it. As though the folded paper could do what the words could not: bring her brother closer to her. While reading the letter, her agitation had given way to a strange feeling of inner peace. She was not sure if she could trust it.

Who was the man who had written these lines? Her brother? Probably, for who else in China could know the details of her childhood? But who was this person? What bound him to her?

She searched herself for an emotion. Was she happy? Touched? Feeling affectionate? What she found instead was a jumble of thoughts.

I need help, urgently. Her first thought was that he needed money. He was turning to his family after forty years because he needed money. *Since it is impossible for me to travel.* What did she expect from her? That she would take the next plane to Shanghai and hand him a briefcase full of banknotes? Why had she and her mother not heard from him for years? Why had he left them to believe that he was dead? Christine felt herself becoming angry. He would explain everything to her. She did not know if she wanted to hear his reasons.

Did she have a choice? To ignore the letter would be impossible. She could reply and ask him to explain himself. She could put him off. Or write to him and tell him that she was not a doctor, not living in a villa with an ocean view, but the manager of a pathetic little travel agency and did not know how she would pay the interest on her mortgage some months. Christine sensed that she had no feeling for how much obligation she had toward him.

She had no experience of sisterly love. It had been a long time since she had thought about him at all. He had become a stranger. In order to make up her mind, she had to meet him, and there was only one place in Hong Kong where that was possible: the Lower Ngau Tau Kok Estate.

———

The MTR station was full of people. All of them seemed to have a destination in mind, and were rushing toward the exits or the trains. Christine hesitated. When had she last been here? It must have been years ago. She had sometimes felt the desire to show her son this place, but had not been able to bring herself to do it. She looked across the platform and the train tracks to the apartment blocks. From here, they looked harmless, if not inviting. A dozen fifteen-story buildings, clad in blue-green concrete rather than multicolored tiles, with small windows. A housing project built in the early 1960s for the never-ending stream of refugees from China.

She took the stairs, not the escalator. It was important that she relive every moment.

She walked through an alley crowded with shops and restaurants and was soon at the bottom of one of the apartment blocks. Bare gray concrete walls, white fluorescent strip lighting on the ceiling, and wide stairs.

She climbed up to the fourth floor slowly. The corridors to the apartments led off to the left and right of the stairs, where the front doors were. She wanted to visit a small girl who had lived here for six years with her mother. In apartment number 444. An unlucky number that no one else had wanted. Mother had lacked the strength or the courage to ask for another.

Six years. In one hundred square feet. Four of them. Mother, daughter, a fat black crow that could not fly, and a ghost.

It had grown quiet. She heard a television and a radio, nothing else. She took a couple of steps toward the darkness. The doors had metal grilles in front of them. The stillness was unnerving. Christine inhaled and exhaled deeply. She walked farther into the darkness. The corridor must be six hundred feet long. Six hundred steps for a small child. She felt nausea rising. That was then. This is now. She repeated those words like a mantra until she was standing in front of apartment number 444. Someone had installed an iron grille in front of the door. It was ajar.

"Hello?" The silence swallowed her voice.

She knocked. No reply.

Christine opened the door gingerly. The room was unoccupied. Swept clean. Light cast by the streetlamps shone dimly through the window. The emptiness of the space made it even more unsettling— it made room for images she did not want to see.

A bunk bed fit in there. A foldaway table, on which she always caught her fingers, two collapsible stools, a couple of cardboard boxes. Their things were in plastic bags that hung from two washing lines strung across the room.

They were never on their own. They heard their neighbors' every word. Every quarrel, every crude expression, every mean word. Every tender one.

Her mother did not say much. It was as though she had left her voice in China. And her laugh. All of them had left something behind, and none of them spoke about it.

Sometimes she heard her mother sigh. She did not know why. Initially she thought it was because of her. She tried her best. The sighing grew more infrequent with time, but it never stopped completely.

Once she found a photo of her brother under her mother's pillow. Then she knew.

Most of the neighbors' rooms were bigger: 130, 160, or 200 square feet. Families with many children lived in them. The corridors were crammed with closets, chests of drawers, and boxes. Next to them sat children doing their homework while the elderly huddled in the rooms and played mahjong. It was often unbearably hot and humid. The air stayed still in the buildings even when all the windows and doors were open.

She had never heard anyone complain. People who had never known running water were happy to have a faucet, even if they had to share it with a dozen other families. People who had come from shacks and huts had no expectations. The refugees were the ones who had gotten off lightly; they needed very little.

Suddenly she remembered the candy man. Apartment 411. His blue shorts, on which you could see every stain. Especially the white ones. His pale legs and his sweat-soaked undershirt. One of the fingers on his left hand was missing, and he had a few teeth missing as well, though he wasn't old. Sometimes he gave the children candy. Wonderfully sweet, chewy candy that stuck to your teeth. But they still didn't like him. He was always in the places you didn't expect him to be. Especially in the dark. Buildings with too many nooks and crannies. Stairwells that were too dark for children's eyes. Corridors too long for kids' legs.

Once he came into her room with a bag of candy in his hand. He smiled. The gaps in his teeth looked like little caves. He was wearing his sweaty undershirt.

Where is your mother? he asked.

She's at work.

So late?

She works even later. It was the truth, and it was the wrong answer. She saw it in his eyes. They shone in a way that was wrong, totally wrong.

He bolted the door and switched off the light. He asked if she was frightened.

No, she lied.

He walked up to her and stood next to her. She could smell his undershirt and hear him breathing above her. A hot, excited breath that stank of cigarette smoke and, though she did not know it at the time, lust.

Open your mouth, he said, and she opened her mouth. A wonderfully sweet and chewy piece of candy slid in.

He was silent and she sucked the candy.

He took her hand and put something in it. A piece of flesh, soft and heavy. He moved her hand. It grew. In her hand. It grew hard and hot and moist.

He had a paper tissue with him and he wiped her hand clean. When he went, he put three candies on the table. These are for you, she heard him say in the darkness.

She threw up only after he had gone.

The stink and the stains. Her mother would not fail to notice them both. She must never find out what had happened. She wiped the table and mopped the floor in the whole room and crept into bed behind the cardboard boxes.

She lay mute in bed when her mother came home. Waited for her scream. She would see what had happened. As though the candy man were still standing next to her. As though his hot, excited breath that stank of cigarette smoke and lust still filled the room.

But the sounds were the same as usual. Her mother's sighs of exhaustion. Water boiling, the clatter of a teacup. Then she heard the sound of candy being sucked, and she retched again.

Her mother worked as a seamstress in a factory in Kowloon Bay. In the weeks that followed, whenever her mother was working the late shift or overtime, Christine found it more and more intolerable to have to go to bed on her own, so she walked to the big factory gate and waited there. Hearing the hum of four hundred sewing machines on the other side of the wall, she settled into a squatting position under the streetlamp. Streetlights were bright and kept away bad dreams. And sweating men. In the glare of the lights she fell asleep. She woke to the sound of her mother scolding her. What was she thinking? Sleeping on the street. Much too dangerous.

They had lived a nonlife. Mother and daughter, almost suffocated by unshed tears. Unspoken words. Unlived grief.

She had yearned for a big brother then. So much that it hurt. Not one who lay under her mother's pillow as a photograph. She had imagined how he would turn up at the door one day and say: Hello, Mei-mei, I'm here again. A strong and powerful young man, someone the blue shorts would be afraid of.

He had been a constant presence with them for the first few years. But not after that. The memories faded like a scrap of cloth in the sun. The stretches of time when she no longer thought about him grew longer and longer. Weeks, months, years. He disappeared without leaving any traces. As though she had never had a brother.

Now he was back. *My dear Mei-mei . . .*

She had only to open the door to him. But at what cost?

Christine had sworn to herself never to travel to the People's Republic of China. Not as long as the same party that had destroyed her family was still in power. The party that had turned a strong man into a boy whose frightened father had leaped from a window. That had taken her brother away. And her mother's laugh.

His attempts to change her mind had annoyed her. The Cultural Revolution was more than thirty years ago, he said. Even if what happened then still cast long shadows, she needn't be afraid. Tens of thousands of Hong Kongers crossed the border every day, to do business, as tourists, or to visit relatives, and they returned safe and sound.

What was she afraid of?

Christine didn't quite know, herself. She could not really explain it, but she had the feeling that a visit to China would be a step too far for her. That was then, this is now.

She had told Paul that she was not afraid, but that as long as the portrait of the Great Chairman hung above the entrance to the Forbidden City, as long the embalmed body of that murderer lay in a mausoleum on Tiananmen Square, as long as people waited in line to pay him their respects, she would not trust the Communist Party of China. Only when a huge memorial to the victims of the Communist Party stood there and the leaders of the party fell to their knees before it and asked for the people's forgiveness for the mistakes and errors the party had made and the millions of lives that these mistakes and errors had cost, only then would she be prepared to trust in this party, this leadership. She would wait patiently for that day. She had time—at least, she thought she did. But time had run out. Ge-ge needed help, urgently.

She felt a sense of duty and responsibility more than any sisterly love. The only trace her brother had left in her life was his absence.

Christine would go to him, but certainly not on her own.

Paul was the only person she wanted to go with her, but also the last person she wanted to ask. Not if the fortune-teller warned against it. Unlike Paul, she was convinced that Wong Kah Wei knew things that they had no idea about.

It was just after half-past eight; if she hurried, she could get the nine thirty ferry to Yung Shue Wan and come back on the last boat.

———

Paul was glad to hear her voice. Of course he had time to see her.

He was waiting at the pier, leaning against the railing in his white T-shirt, black flip-flops, and the light-colored knee-length shorts that she had given him not long before. The wind ruffled his curly gray hair. She was struck anew how hard it was for people to guess his age. The deep lines around his eyes and mouth and the gray hair indicated that this was someone who had passed his fiftieth year, but his trim and muscular frame with no hint of a belly was that of a younger man, and his laugh could have been a child's. She loved him for that too.

He waited until she was in front of him. A tender look from his melancholy deep-blue eyes. "Good evening, Miss Wu. What a nice surprise to be able to greet you here."

She noticed the red strip of fabric around his wrist immediately.

He stepped back from the railing, took her hand, and led her off the pier without saying anything more. The slapping sound of his flip-flops with every step. They turned off immediately after the pier and passed a small bookshop and a couple of tumbledown wooden shacks before walking up a hill. The path narrowed, and there were fewer and fewer streetlamps until there were none at all. But Paul had a flashlight with him and lit the way for her. They walked up the dirt track close together in single file. Twigs scratched Christine's calves, and she stumbled over tree roots several times. There was a rustling sound in the bushes, and she was afraid she might step on a snake. He led her to an outcrop of land where there was an octagonal viewing pavilion with a curved, Chinese-style roof. They sat down on a bench. Paul put his arm around her and switched the flashlight off. The night sky was dark and cloudless, full of stars. They were sitting directly above the sea. Under them, little waves crashed against the rocks, and it smelled of salt and fish. In the distance, they could hear the dull drone of engines from the cargo ships that were lying at anchor near the island. He stroked her hair. They sat in silence next to each other; his right leg jiggled up and down constantly. She was familiar with that. A nervous habit of his when he was tense.

"Now tell me, what did you absolutely have to tell me that made you come to Lamma late in the evening on a whim?" His voice sounded strained. He was not a good actor.

"I got a letter. From my brother."

She showed him the letter. The beam of the flashlight traveled across the paper. He sighed heavily and gave the envelope back to her. She waited, wondering how he would react. Instead of saying anything, he took her in his arms. She resisted at first. She wanted to talk. She wanted to hear his opinion. She wanted to be free of all the thoughts that had crowded her mind in the previous few hours. Then she felt her body relaxing, her head sliding from his shoulder to his lap. The way her body grew limp and gave up all resistance. The tears in her eyes. The essence of grief. Old unshed tears. Fat and ugly. Bitter to the taste, like cold tea left for too long. They swelled out of her like thick pus from an old wound. That was then. This is now. How much strength it took to keep them apart. Then and now. Like two colors that were trying hard to blend. As soon as her strength ebbed, they managed it: Then is now. Now is then.

She felt his hand in her hair, and she heard his voice whispering something she didn't understand. It didn't matter. The support in those words was enough for her. She had led a nonlife. Mama and Mei-mei. Not heard. Not comforted. Not caressed.

She buried her head deeper in his lap. She wanted to stay there until he got up, picked her up in his arms, and carried her to his house like a sleeping child. Laid her in bed. Put the blanket over her. Turned off the light.

Young tears followed the bitter old ones. They tasted different. Lighter, fresher, like saltwater.

Then even they ran dry. Christine lay quietly, listening to her breath.

He leaned over her and switched on his flashlight for a moment. "I thought you had fallen asleep."

"Almost," she said, sitting up.

"Have you phoned his daughter already?"

Christine shook her head. "I don't know what I should do."

"Why are you finding it so difficult to make a decision? Haven't you made your calculations?" His voice held a hint of a smile that she could not see in the darkness.

"Don't be that way," she replied, poking him in the stomach to show that she had understood his joke.

Making decisions, or rather the speed with which she and Paul made decisions, was one of the things they often argued about. In her eyes, Paul was someone who hesitated and dithered. A person who thought things through, swung from one option to the other, struggled with himself, and constantly tried to see a matter from all sides. He himself said he was someone who "weighed things up with a passion." We are the sum of our decisions, he said; that was why he was suspicious of people who always immediately knew what they wanted. Who instantly had an opinion on everything.

She was one of those people. But she did not regard indecisiveness as a strength. Once she had gone shopping with him in a big supermarket in Hong Kong, and had nearly gone crazy. Yogurt from Japan, Australia, New Zealand, Hong Kong, and Germany. With four different levels of fat content. Six different kinds of Camembert from three different countries, and regular mineral water from four continents. Hell for Paul Leibovitz. The range was so great that they had left the store after half an hour and picked up their groceries later on Lamma instead. Life was easier for him there: yogurt from Hong Kong. Two flavors, the same fat content.

She had tried several times to persuade him that most of these everyday decisions were not important, so it didn't make sense to spend too much time on them. For important things, Christine took a piece of paper and made a list of pros and cons. What was in favor, what was against? Advantages and disadvantages. All written down in two columns; at the end a line would be drawn and they would be added up. The question was always: What is this going to cost me? Credits and debits, a simple calculation. As soon as she had worked out the answer, the decision made itself.

Paul thought that was idiotic. The really important things in life could not be categorized as pluses or minuses. They were always a plus *and* a minus, and could not be definitively put in one column or the other.

She did not agree. Of course, lots of things had many advantages *and* disadvantages, but you had only to think things through consistently and honestly before you eventually knew what belonged where. To love a person *or* not. To be able to pay the interest on a home loan *or* not. Dead *or* alive.

He envied her, Paul had replied, and she had not known what he had meant by that.

Christine thought about her brother. "No," she said in a tired voice, "I haven't made my calculations."

"Then let me help you. On the 'pro' list, let's enter: 'Seeing a long-missed brother'; 'More family because of his wife and children.' But we'll have to put that in brackets because we don't know if they are nice people. They could appear on the list of minuses later." He said nothing for a moment. "I can't think of anything else right now. Let's move to the minus side. There we have: 'Costs money'; 'Takes time'; 'Takes energy'; 'Taking a risk,' because I don't know how much money, time, and energy it will take; 'Taking another risk,' because I don't know what he wants from me; 'Taking a third risk,' because I don't know how things will go for me in China. Christine, you don't need a mathematician to work that out. You're not going."

"Are you serious?" He was often able to confuse her; at times like this, she was not sure whether he meant what he was saying or not.

"I was just using your method. It really is quick. Impressive."

"But I can't just ignore his request. What do you think?"

"Why not? Did I forget something on the plus side? Shall we add it up again?"

"No, but—"

He interrupted her. "That's what I'm always trying to explain to you: the heart doesn't recognize credits or debits." After a pause, he added, "Or at least, it doesn't decide based on those criteria. It has its own."

Unfortunately, Christine thought. She did not think that the heart gave good advice. Her experiences of it had been bad. It was fickle and unreliable, easily swayed. Ignoring the results of the credit and debit tally had led her into making mistakes. Yet with Paul her heart had not been mistaken. From the very first moment she had been sure that there would be a balance of give and take. Her heart had not been put off even when her head had told her in the first few months that this unusual loner would disappoint her, that he was no longer capable of loving. The heart had known better, and it had been right.

His voice tore her back from her thoughts. "Of course you'll go to Shanghai. I'll even go with you."

"You know I won't allow that."

"And if I tell you that it won't be dangerous for me at all?"

"We're not having this discussion again."

Paul fell silent and took several deep breaths. She saw his outline in the darkness, his chest rising and sinking as though he were out of breath. She had the feeling that many unsaid things were piling up between them.

He picked up the flashlight and shined it in his own face. "Look at me. I too have something to tell you."

She knew him well enough to realize that he was trying to sound cheerful and relaxed, but the strain and tension he was feeling were unmistakable.

"I'm listening," she said, curious and cautious at the same time.

"I went to see Master Wong."

"I don't believe it. When?"

"Yesterday evening. After we talked," he said, switching off the light once more.

"How did you get an appointment so quickly?"

"It was all down to the fee."

"What did he say?"

"That the tiger will eat the dog. And that the owl will soon fall from the tree."

"Stop it!" she said angrily. "The Chinese don't have an owl in their zodiac. And neither one of us is a tiger or a dog."

"Alas. You found me out. He told me that I had nothing to worry about. The year of the pig won't be a bad year for me."

She took the flashlight, switched it on, and shined it on his face, looking closely at him. His eyes seemed bluer than usual. They blinked in the beam of the light. He gazed past her into the darkness. Were his lips trembling, or was she imagining it? "You're making that up."

"No."

"I thought you didn't believe in astrology."

"I don't."

"Why did you go to see him then?"

"For your peace of mind. And mine. I couldn't bear the thought of not seeing you for nine months."

She had hoped to find an answer in his eyes, in the lines around his mouth. She did not believe him, though she couldn't say why. "Do you have the recording? I want to hear exactly what he said."

"Christine. Since when have you started interrogating me? He said quite clearly that I'm not in danger, no matter who I spend the next few months with. Isn't that enough?"

She thought for a moment. "What did he tell you about your past?"

"That I had been married and divorced. That my parents were no longer alive. That I had had a son."

His voice sounded hoarse and exhausted. He swallowed a few times and cleared his throat. His long nose seemed more pointed than usual.

"I don't know if I should believe you."

"Call him."

"He wouldn't tell me anything."

"As if trusting was only for fools. Who said that?"

"Paul! I'm being serious."

"So am I."

She had no choice but to trust him, she knew that. Trust and hope. There was no alternative. Nevertheless, something in her resisted.

"Why are you wearing that red strip of cloth around your wrist?"

"It was Master Wong's idea. Always wear something red to bring me more luck this year. I thought it couldn't hurt."

"Any other advice?"

"He recommended that I avoid water, which is difficult since I live on an island. Jade will help me. Red protects me. Three is a threat. I won't become rich in the year of the pig. More is my lucky number."

"More?"

"More. Like many. Often. Not enough. Never enough."

He made her laugh more than all the men before him together had. She loved him for that too.

His right leg jiggled up and down violently, as if it were transmitting a Morse code message.

"Are you all right?" she asked.

"Yes, why?"

"Your leg."

He laid a hand on his knee and held it still. "Better like that?"

They saw the last ferry from Hong Kong appear at the end of the island.

"If we hurry you'll still catch it," he said, standing up.

"I thought you never ran to catch ferries or buses."

"I'll make an exception today for you."

She sat listening to the whispering of the sea. "I want to stay with you."

IV

They had arranged to meet at six at the departure gate. It was tight timing—the gate would close ten minutes after that—but Christine had said that it was impossible for her to leave the office earlier. She had booked the China Southern flight at half-past six and reserved seats; she would come to the airport directly from town.

Nine minutes after the hour he was the second-to-last passenger to board the plane. The airline staff cast a questioning glance at him just as Christine hurried down the corridor. She apologized, and he could see the shadows under her eyes through her makeup, which she was sweating through.

Row nine, a good number, he thought. There was no more space in the overhead compartment for her hand luggage.

His seat was confining. The pocket in the seat in front of his had a deep tear in it. One of the reading lights in the row in front of his was not working. Small things like this that no one else probably cared about indicated to Paul the level of the plane's maintenance. Not good signs. He looked out the window, uneasy.

They approached the runway. Christine fetched a small case from her bag and gave it to him. Inside was a deep-red jade amulet in the shape of a small dragon, his zodiac animal. It hung from a reddish-brown leather strap, but was barely larger than his thumbnail, and was so finely carved and so thin that it seemed almost transparent when he held it up to the light. Although he did not know much about jade, he knew immediately that it was old and probably quite precious.

"Red and made of jade. Like Master Wong recommended," she said. "You know what the dragon means to us: it has protective powers and it's a symbol of luck. It can make itself invisible and lives in the sky, the sea, the rivers, and the rain; it's even in the mist. He will look after you."

"It's so beautiful. Thank you so much." He gave her a kiss. "Where did you get it?"

"From my mother. She gave it to me many years ago. It was my father's."

Paul started. "Your father? It didn't bring him any luck."

"He didn't wear it. My father rejected Chinese astrology, which he thought was stupid and superstitious. He got this from his father, who believed strongly in the influence of the stars and was a dragon like you."

"Did it help him?"

"I think so. He lived to an old age."

"How old?"

"He died at eighty-four in an attempt to swim across a river that was too wide. His body was never found."

"That doesn't say much for the protective power of this amulet."

"It was at home. He forgot it that day."

"That's a family myth!"

"No. Otherwise we wouldn't have it any longer."

The engines grew louder and they were pressed down into their seats. Christine took his hand; he didn't know if she was feeling unwell or if she could feel his unease. They looked out the window. The lights on the runway whizzed by more and more quickly, and Paul felt the nose of the airplane lift and the air currents suddenly lift them into the sky, as though they were sitting in an elevator. It was a cloudless evening; stars were twinkling above, and beneath them lay the darkness of the South China Sea, on which so many ships shone, as if someone had shaken out a sack of small diamonds onto a black felt cloth. Paul recognized the outline of Lamma; behind it glowed the huge sea of the lights of Hong Kong.

He hung the amulet around his neck, tucked it under his T-shirt, and was surprised at how pleasantly warm it felt against his skin.

Christine had fallen asleep. He lifted her head gently and put a pillow under it, spread a blanket over her knees, switched off the reading light, and gently leaned her seat back. He envied her ability to sleep anywhere, from the MTR to a taxi or a ferry. He would have liked to discuss the coming two days with her then. What exactly had Yin-Yin said when Christine had called her? Had she given any hint of what her father's problems were? Did Yin-Yin not know what they were, or did she not want to say? These were questions that Christine probably had no answers to, but he would have felt better if he had been able to talk to her about them. In the past few days everything had happened much too quickly. Flights and hotels had been booked, visas arranged, and Christine had also had to arrange for someone to cover for her in the office and to look after her son. Paul was used to living at a different speed.

She woke from her sleep only when they left cruising altitude.

"I'm sorry," she said, and yawned. "I was exhausted."

"You didn't miss much."

She sat up, stretched, and tied her hair up in a ponytail. She looked like a young girl when she did this.

"How are you feeling?"

She looked at him and smiled. "Do you mean if I'm still tired?"

"No, are you anxious? Frightened? Looking forward to it? If—"

"I know what you mean," she said, interrupting. She hesitated before replying. "You ask strange questions sometimes."

"What do you mean by that?"

"No Chinese man would ask me that. At least none that I know."

"Why not?"

She shrugged. "I don't know. Maybe because we don't place so much importance on words. Maybe because it doesn't occur to us. Maybe because we think that the other person will say what they're thinking without being asked if they want us to know."

"But will you tell me anyway?" he asked, unsure of whether to take her last sentence as a criticism.

"Gladly." She thought for a moment. "How do I feel? To be honest, I don't really know. A little of all those things, I suspect."

"Which do you feel the most?"

"Nothing stands out, if you really want to know. I'm not fearful for my own safety, at least, not as long as you're with me. I'm anxious because I don't know what's waiting for us, what difficulties Da Long is in, and if we can help him. Yes, anxious, but not in an unpleasant way. Am I looking forward to it?" She looked at him as though he knew the answer to her question. "Probably, but not because I anticipate something happy will occur. I'm not meeting a brother that I last saw ten years ago. I'm meeting a stranger who I know is my brother, and his family. That is something quite different, if you understand what I mean."

Paul nodded.

"And," she continued, "I'll admit that it's good to know that we'll be on our way back to Hong Kong in forty-eight hours."

The pilot brought the plane back to the ground with an extraordinarily soft landing. They were among the last people to leave the plane. Christine was clearly reluctant to hurry, quite unlike her usual self. The nearer they came to the immigration-control counters, the slower she walked.

The tension in her face. They stood in silence in the line in front of the counters. Paul tried to lift her spirits with a smile, but Christine did not react. Her gaze wandered over the hall; she examined the other passengers and scanned the ceilings for cameras and looked at the young man in the blue uniform whom she was going to have to show her passport to in a moment. As though she were entering an enemy country. She wanted to go first so that Paul could come and help her if there was a problem.

The official was not interested in her fears. He merely looked up briefly, checked her papers, and gave her the passport back. It also took Paul less than a minute to pass through immigration. Their small wheeled suitcases were already on the luggage belt, and the customs official waved them through without asking to see them.

The arrivals hall was full of people waiting. Christine had asked Yin-Yin not to pick them up from the airport. They would take a taxi to their hotel and meet her there tomorrow morning at eight. Paul and Christine made their way through the crowd, which was lined up like an honor guard; although no one was waiting for them, both had the feeling that dozens of pairs of eyes were staring at them and observing them. Christine's steps faltered and Paul pushed her gently toward the exit.

Outside it was warmer than in Hong Kong, but not as humid. Of all the taxis in the line, they got one in which the air-conditioning was broken. Even with the windows open, the car stank of stale cigarette smoke. Paul sank deep into the saggy backseat; he could feel every spring in it. A picture of Mao—bringer of luck—dangled from the rearview mirror, and the taxi driver sucked at a butted-out cigarette. They turned onto a highway, and the driver accelerated as if they were in a car chase. He changed lanes constantly, always afraid of not being in the fastest-moving lane. Paul asked him to drive more slowly; he nodded, muttered a few words that Paul did not understand, and put his foot on the gas again.

Christine seemed not to notice all this. She sat behind the driver and looked out the window. Since they had passed immigration she had not said anything, and had reacted to what Paul said with only a nod, if she noticed at all. He could not read the expression on her face. The anxiety she had felt before they passed the border control had given way to a strange passivity that Paul did not recognize in her. He would have liked to ask her what was going through her head, but he had the feeling he would not receive a reply, so he said nothing. He had resolved not to make any demands on her in the next two days but to stay in the background, observe things, listen carefully, and be there for her when she needed him.

He took her hand, and she let him do so without looking at him. The ring of a cell phone brought her out of her reverie. She picked up her phone and looked at the numbers on the screen in the weak light from the streetlamps whizzing by overhead. She let it ring.

"Shall I answer it?" Paul asked.

She hesitated, shook her head, and put the phone back in her bag.

They sped down a six-lane flyover; in the darkness, new high-rise buildings stretched out before Paul as far as his eye could see. He saw the outline of Pudong appear on the horizon. The nearer they came, the more overwhelming the sight. Paul remembered his first visit to Shanghai. Where there were skyscrapers today, there had been corn and rice fields then, and pigs wallowing in mud. The forty-story buildings had been built almost up to the edge of the road on both sides. Paul could see through a few windows into the apartments; he guessed that the highway they were entering the city on was about as high as the eighth story. Christine was still sitting mute next to him, looking out the window. He was not sure if she was taking anything in at all.

Paul knew the Astor House Hotel from his earlier travels. It was on the other side of Suzhou Creek at the end of the Bund, a massive neoclassical building that had been one of the best addresses in town before the revolution. While he filled in forms at the reception desk, Christine looked at the photos of the former guests: Albert Einstein, Bertrand Russell, Zhou Enlai, and Charlie Chaplin gazed earnestly from the walls.

Their room was almost half as big as Christine's entire apartment in Hong Kong. He guessed the ceilings must have been about sixteen feet high; the walls were partly paneled in dark teak, and the old parquet floor creaked with every step. The extravagant lavishness of a time long gone, Paul thought. He fell exhausted onto the bed while Christine undressed. She disappeared into the bathroom and appeared shortly after, standing naked in front of him. It was the first time that he had seen her naked and not desired her immediately. Her thin, though muscular, arms and legs, her jutting pelvic bones over which her skin was stretched, her full breasts. A wonderful sight, but not erotic in the least. The shocking fragility of the human body; its vulnerability. Its longing for protection, for tenderness. Its neediness.

She crept into bed. He undressed quickly and lay down next to her; she nestled close to him, lay her head on his chest, and whispered, "Hold me tight. Hold me very tight."

He put his arms around her, stroked her neck, and did not dare to move until he finally heard the familiar sound of her breathing in her sleep.

———

The next morning, when they stepped into the hotel lobby at exactly eight a.m., a tall young woman, unusually beautiful, was waiting. She greeted them with a shy smile.

Christine sized up Yin-Yin. At first glance she could see no resemblance. Neither to her nor to her mother, Yin-Yin's grandmother. They were both small, while Yin-Yin was tall and had the pale skin and high cheekbones that were typical of northern Chinese. Her arms were notably long and toned. She was wearing tight-fitting jeans and a green T-shirt with Chinese characters on it. She had put her hair up, and two small gemstones glittered in her ears.

Only her eyes unsettled Christine. In them lay a long shadow, and the more she looked into them the more she was reminded of the photo of her brother that her mother had kept. Yin-Yin said something, but Christine was barely listening. She had the feeling that a black-and-white photo had started speaking.

V

Every misfortune sends its messengers. We have only to pay attention in order to recognize them. They like to deceive us, and often come in strange clothing. They outwitted me.

It started with my right thumb. Suddenly it was gone. I lay down for a nap after a lunch of noodle soup, and when I woke it was no longer there. To be precise, I could still see my thumb, but I could no longer feel it. It did not move. I pinched it and felt no pain. A couple of hours later my index finger and ring finger had also disappeared. They were there again in the evening.

I didn't think too much of it when the teacup slipped from my grasp the next morning. It slid out of my hand, and I looked on and could do nothing about it. The buttons on my jacket. They wouldn't go through the holes that I normally pushed through every day. The jars filled with tea, herbs, or spices in the kitchen. I couldn't unscrew their lids. The fingers of both hands, these sinewy, bony limbs that had given me good service for decades, were suddenly seized with a mysterious numbness.

The change of seasons, I thought. The winter had been long and cold and damp, and crept deep into my bones, and the brief spring had come upon us from one day to the next. The tiredness, the exhaustion. The aching limbs. The spring, what else? I did not want to make too much of it, at fifty-eight years of age.

No longer young.

Not yet old.

But a vulnerable age.

Two days later, I could no longer lift the rice bowl. I could not hold the chopsticks. I felt helpless, like a child, and claimed not to be hungry.

Then the ground began to sway. The street through the village, still just about flat, swung to the left sometimes, then to the right. The path across the courtyard was full of hills and hollows. I could no longer walk; I staggered through the village like a drunkard.

I, who had never been able to sit still, who was always finding out what had to be done, what had to be taken care of, for whom nothing could happen quickly enough, behaved as though I had discovered slowness. Everything about me was in the grip of a terrible sluggishness. They way I moved. The way I walked. The way I talked. When I spoke, it sounded as though I had just climbed four flights of stairs and was completely out of breath from it. I . . . don't . . . know . . . what . . . is . . . wrong . . . with . . . me. I swallowed some sounds and stretched others out much longer than necessary. Wwwwooooldd . . . yyyou . . . liiiike . . . tttoffu . . . fooor . . . ddinnerrr? I heard myself speak and felt embarrassed. My body, which I had never paid much attention to in my life, which I had always been able to rely on, was failing me.

The next day Chouchou went crazy. Our big black cat, who had lived loyally with us for ten years. He stood in front of the house, arched his back, suddenly twitched his legs and jerked his bottom up in the air, trying to stand on his forepaws. He was trying to do a cat handstand! My poor Chouchou, what's wrong with you? What are you doing? He didn't react to my voice but fell over onto his front, rolled over, and lay on the ground with his legs pedaling away furiously as though the devil had possessed him. I was afraid that he had rabies, and did not dare touch him. After a minute, he jumped up and started running around the courtyard. He raced around in circles, pursued by a demon or an invisible ghost; what else could have roused such fear in him? Still running, he changed his direction and darted sideways like a hare, at some point running against the wall of the house with all his might. Chouchou must have gone blind and lost his mind. He tumbled backward, fell over, got up, rotated several times on his own axis, and then charged straight against the wall on the other side of the courtyard. Chouchou, I cried desperately, stop it! Calm yourself. But the attack had not come to an end; he shot across the court-

yard and crashed into the fountain, the steps, and the pile of wood until he fell to the ground stunned. When it was nearly evening, the terrible sequence repeated itself. The next morning we found him dead in the fountain. He must have jumped in during an evening frenzy. As though he had wanted to bring his suffering to an end.

Two days later, the trembling started. I gripped the wooden spoon with my whole hand in order not to drop it. I raised it to my mouth, and when it reached my lips there wasn't a drop of soup left on it.

You were in town or in the fields so I was able to keep it from you until now.

When we saw the doctor everything was as it had always been. My fingers obeyed me once more. The ground was even, and the world did not sway. The sluggishness was a distant memory. Hello, doctor, how are you? My husband brought me to see you.

How lovely my voice suddenly sounded again. I relished every tone, every word, every sentence.

The doctor couldn't find anything wrong. No fever. Normal pulse and blood pressure. No coating on the tongue. The spring; what else could it be? When we were back in the village, the cramps started. I twitched and shivered like Chouchou had done a few days before, and if I had had the strength, I would have run against the wall with all my might.

Misfortune had sent its messengers.

Now it had come itself.

VI

She had been naïve. Thoughtless. Since she had decided to travel to Shanghai, Christine had been caught up with arranging the journey. She had sought out the cheapest flights and had booked the hotel in Shanghai, thought up a story to tell Josh and her mother, and trained someone to cover for her in the office. She had been so focused on taking care of everything that had to be arranged, on organizing details, on doing everything necessary, that she had lost sight of the essentials.

As she had so often in her life.

She had been so busy that she had not given any thought to the reason for her journey and what the meeting with her brother would mean to her. She had come completely unprepared. She had avoided Paul's question on the plane. And now this young woman was standing in front of her and claiming to be her niece.

The voice was quiet but not tentative. Yin-Yin led them to a VW Passat that was waiting for them in front of the hotel. She introduced a friend who was visiting his parents near Yiwu and was being so kind as to give them a lift.

They sat in silence in the car. The young man at the steering wheel concentrated on the traffic. Yin-Yin stared out the window from the passenger seat in front. Paul inspected the interior of the car and did not take his eyes off the speedometer.

Christine would have liked to ask her niece about the cause of the sadness in her eyes. She would have liked to know how her brother was, and how his wife was, and what Da Long had told his daughter about his family and why he had taken almost forty years to get in touch with them. She would have liked to know what kind of person her brother was. A good father or a bad one? Bad tempered and irritable, or peaceful and relaxed? So many questions. How was she to get close to this unknown life? Christine did not know, so instead of randomly making a start by asking one question that would lead to another and another, she said nothing at all.

Paul made an effort to help her, perhaps because he could no longer stand the silence in the car.

"Do you live in Shanghai?" he asked, in English.

"Yes." Yin-Yin's reply was brief but not unfriendly.

"What do you do?"

"I'm a music student."

"Do you want to teach?"

"No. I'm studying the violin at the conservatory. I would like to play in an orchestra. But I'm afraid I didn't pass the entrance test for the Shanghai Symphony last year. I'll have a second chance in four weeks. I'll have to practice a lot before that."

Christine joined in. "A musician? There hasn't been one in our family before." It was a statement, not a question, but she expected a reply nonetheless. "Where does your talent come from? Is my brother at all musical?" What a strange question, she thought. She disliked having to ask her niece about her brother's abilities. As though it was her fault that she did not know.

"A little," Yin-Yin said, smiling briefly. "He plays the harmonica very well. The musical talent really comes from my mother. She's a music teacher and would have liked to be a singer. She had a beautiful voice."

"Had? Is she dead?" Christine asked, as horrified as though she was asking after a good friend of hers.

"No." Yin-Yin took a couple of deep breaths before she continued. "But she no longer sings."

Silence.

"You're not an only child, are you?" Paul asked. He didn't want to let the conversation die away.

"No. I have an older brother."

"What does he do?"

"He lives in Shanghai too, and is a manager with China Life, the insurance company."

"Will we get to meet him?"

"I don't think so."

Christine started. A harsh note had entered Yin-Yin's voice, which had been friendly up to that point.

Silence filled the car again. A big ugly silence that was born of speechlessness, not of wordless rapport, which Paul and Christine shared.

Christine leaned back and looked out the window. Even though the car was traveling fast, she had the feeling that it was barely moving. The city looked the same everywhere: high-rise building next to high-rise building like trees in a forest, broken up only by cranes and construction sites on which new tower blocks were being built. After a while, the number of tall buildings decreased and the number of construction sites increased.

When the first few paddy fields appeared, they had been traveling in the car for almost two hours. The expressway now snaked through a hilly gray-green landscape, dotted with railroad embankments, newly built highways, and bridges. It was a strange area, no longer the city, but also not the countryside. She saw blocks of housing that had clearly been finished, but seemed empty. She saw half-finished buildings, shells that were already starting to fall apart. Wide roads that suddenly came to an end. Bridge posts without the bridges. As far as she could tell, many of the towns that they passed consisted mainly of factories and the workers' housing. Was this the face of the new China that she had read and heard about so much in Hong Kong?

Not beautiful.

Not ugly.

A densely populated but at the same time faceless, repellent landscape.

"We'll be there in around an hour. My parents live in a village near Yiwu. Do you know it?" Yin-Yin asked.

"No," Paul replied.

"We've booked a hotel room there for you. It's an interesting place."

"How so?"

"When we moved there twenty years ago it was a small town with thirty thousand inhabitants, but now almost seven hundred thousand people live there. I went to school there, but now I'm always getting lost in the city. A friend of mine went to America for three years and when he came back recently he could no longer find his home. He knew it was still standing but he just couldn't find it. He got out the taxi and got lost for two hours in the part of town he had grown up in. He couldn't recognize a thing in the neighborhood. Not a single building or street. After just three years! It's strange when something seems very familiar and is also totally different, if you know what I mean."

Paul nodded.

Christine slid to and fro on the backseat restlessly. She did not want to hear about cities growing or about strangers who could no longer find their homes. She wanted to know what was waiting for her. "Yin-Yin, can you tell me why your father sent me his letter?"

Paul turned to look at her, astonished.

Yin-Yin looked into the rearview mirror, and their gazes met there for a moment.

"You're his sister."

"I've been that for forty-two years." She immediately regretted saying that. What right had she to speak in such a sharp tone to her niece? "I'd like to know what kind of help he needs," she added in a conciliatory manner.

"He hasn't discussed it with me."

She was lying and was not even trying to hide it. Before Christine could reply, Paul leaned over to her and whispered in Cantonese, "Christine, you don't have to wait much longer. We'll find out soon."

Shortly after, they turned off the highway and arrived in a valley that stretched out before them. They drove a few miles on a country road and turned off again, this time onto a narrow road bordered by fields. It was so bumpy that they were able to proceed only at a walking pace. The expressway appeared again in front of them, spanning the valley on its tall columns. Beyond it was a village. The road ended on a sandy patch of ground at the edge of it. The driver turned off the engine.

"We have to walk the last thousand feet," Yin-Yin said. "The paths in the village are too narrow for cars."

Paul got out and looked around him. Christine would have liked to stay where she was, but he walked around to her side of the car and opened her door. She saw in his eyes that he was just as lost for words and confounded as she was. Yin-Yin's friend unloaded their luggage and said good-bye; he had to drive on to his parents' place; a taxi would take them to the hotel in the evening; he would come tomorrow afternoon to drive them to the airport. As Paul picked up the small suitcase, Christine watched the cloud of dust that rose behind the car. She felt left behind. Abandoned. Despite Paul. Even if she wanted to, she could not leave this place now without any help.

A barking dog ran up to them and stood about six feet away, barking so ferociously that he seemed on the verge of choking. He doesn't bite, Yin-Yin said, but Christine did not let the dog out of her sight. A gust of wind swept across the square, whirling up a cloud of brown sand; two plastic bags danced through the air like oversize butterflies until they glided gently to the ground in the shadow of a wall. The sun was almost vertically overhead; it was oppressively hot; and the glare of the light was so intense that it burned the eyes. Christine put on her sunglasses.

They crossed the square and turned into a long treeless alley. Two old men were sitting on wooden stools in front of a house, wearing white undershirts soaked through with sweat that clung to their torsos. They fanned themselves with faded paper fans and stared at Yin-Yin, Christine, and Paul. The looks they gave them were singular. Not friendly. Not hostile. Oddly flat, empty, practically soulless.

A woman with a bundle of brushwood on her back walked past them with uneven steps; she was bent so far over that she did not even look up when she approached them. The village was strangely silent; most of the houses looked unoccupied. They heard neither voices nor any other sounds apart from the wind and the noise from the highway. A lifeless, colorless world in which only different shades of gray-brown seemed to exist. They saw two women sitting by a gateway filling wonton dumplings with practiced movements. Their hair and their faces were as gray as the earth.

Christine's sense of unease grew, but she relaxed a bit when Yin-Yin stopped in front of a white-tiled wall and opened the heavy wooden gate in the round entrance. Christine and Paul followed her into a courtyard with a fountain in the middle. There were logs piled up against one wall and a couple of trees in a corner, leaves covered with brown dust. The courtyard surrounded a two-story house tiled in white all over, with a roof covered in red glazed tiles. It was the best-looking building in the village.

They heard the click of the gate closing.

"Papa," Yin-Yin called. "We're here."

Christine had not expected him to look so old. Worn out. Exhausted. Tired of life, she thought. He could just as easily have been her mother's brother. There were barely over ten years between her and him. China years. He had lived China years while she had lived Hong Kong years. They were not the same thing. They were neighbors on the map of the world, only a pinhead's distance apart. Hong Kong to Sichuan, Hong Kong to Shanghai; barely three hours by plane or a day and a night by train, but time had been reckoned differently in their lives. China years left deep traces. China years were voracious. Wore you down and devoured you.

She searched his face for the features in the photo of her brother that had lain for years under her mother's pillow. Life had not been kind; it had wiped away every trace of that boy from the face of the man standing across from her. The serious but curious and lively eyes of the child had turned into watchful, dark grown-up eyes, in which the same worry she had seen in his daughter's gaze shimmered, as though grief were hereditary in this family. The clear skin of before was now marked by deep furrows in his forehead and cheeks, and his bushy eyebrows were threaded with gray. The tiny mole on his chin had grown to the size of a fingernail, with long black hairs sprouting from it. It was a sad and careworn face, but not one that moved anything in her.

And he was short too, much shorter than she had imagined him to be.

She searched for similarities. There was a yellowed family photo, the only one, which showed her with her parents. All four of them were standing next to each other; father and mother in dark-blue Mao suits, looking grimly into the camera as if they had a premonition of the misfortune about to befall them. Her father was tall and slim but broad-shouldered; he had the typical build of the northern Chinese. Da Long had nothing of that. He had the full lips and the short stature of people from Sichuan Province; both from their mother. She could see no other physical similarities between him and her parents.

They stood facing each other in silence. Eye to eye. Motionless. She did not feel any impulse to hug him. He smiled awkwardly. He had two teeth missing.

"M-m-mei-mei." His voice was pleasant. Unusually soft and resonant; a voice that you liked to listen to. *Mei-mei*. Little sister. "X-x-xiao Hong." Her Chinese name: "Little Red." She wondered how anyone could have given their daughter such a name in all earnestness, but that seemed to have been a popular name in the People's Republic in the year she was born. He said it differently from the way her mother had; she had always said it with a slight hiss, as though she had never liked the name. Da Long said it in a gentler tone that was almost a little tender.

He continued talking, and she noticed that he had a speech impediment; her brother repeated the first syllable of each sentence as if he had a stammer. Her gaze wandered away to Yin-Yin and Paul before returning to him. He couldn't be serious. This could not be happening. Mandarin. What else? She felt completely shaken. She had lost sight of the basics. How were they to make themselves understood to each other? Her brother spoke Mandarin, which Christine understood only fragments of. She had been five years old when she had left this country, which sent children to their deaths and turned fathers into birds without wings; she had left everything behind: her father's ashes, the memories, her language. She had embraced Hong Kong and taken another name, a Western one that she liked better than her Chinese name, and had started speaking Cantonese, as her mother had. Brother and sister no longer spoke the same language; they had no words for each other that they could understand. She shook her head in disbelief. Asked if he spoke Cantonese. He shook his head, deeply embarrassed, as if it were his fault. English? No.

Paul saved her. He introduced himself politely and said, first in excellent Mandarin, then in Cantonese, that it was good when a brother and sister could still learn from each other when they were older, especially a language, and then he offered his services in the meantime as a translator.

Da Long looked at the tall foreigner in amazement, then a smile of relief fluttered across his face. He nodded repeatedly, thanked them formally for their visit, and stressed that it was a great joy for him, for the entire family, to see his sister again after so many years. He felt honored by the visit and hoped the journey had not been too difficult, and that the stars were aligned for their visit. He apologized for the poverty of the surroundings he was welcoming them in, and was relieved that Yin-Yin had brought them here safely, for as the Chinese saying went, "A man is never more likely to get lost than when he thinks he knows the way."

Christine had tried but failed to grasp the meanings of a few words, so she had to wait for Paul to translate the greeting. As she listened to him, she had the feeling that it was not only the sounds of her brother's language that were unfamiliar to her.

Da Long invited them into the house. They stepped into a large, dim room with very little furniture. Dark fabric hung over the windows as protection against the sun. Next to the front door was a table with four stools; on it was a plate of cookies, a bowl of candy, a teapot, and four cups. On the other side of the room was a black leatherette couch opposite a big television, and in the corner were a nightstand and a bed. It was warm in the room but not too hot, and it smelled like a hospital. There was someone lying in the bed. A woman.

Da Long said nothing to them about who she was, nor did he attempt to show them around. He simply invited them to take a seat. Yin-Yin poured them tea and passed the cookies around. Christine's brother laughed clumsily and pushed the bowl of candy over to her. "F-f-or you. Your favorite sweets."

Paul translated.

She gazed in wonder at the small pieces of candy wrapped in blue-and-white paper with a rabbit on each one. Her favorite sweets? Those were the black square pralines from Godiva; covered in divine dark chocolate and filled with dark, but not overly sweet, nougat; she let them melt slowly on her tongue in order to savor them longer.

Da Long noticed her uncertainty and added, "W-w-white Rabbit candy. You used to love it. Do you remember?"

She did not understand a word. It was terrible. She cast a what-did-he-say look at Paul. He repeated Da Long's words in Cantonese.

She shook her head.

Her brother turned to Paul as though there must have been a mistake in the translation. "W-w-hite Rabbit," he said again.

No, no memories. Not of white rabbits.

Suddenly she heard a kind of grunting noise that rose to a brief caterwaul before it subsided. Yin-Yin got up, went over to the bed, and wiped the sick woman's forehead with a damp cloth. She fetched a glass of water, lifted the woman's head, gave her a sip or two, kneeled down next to her, and took her hand. There was a small stereo on the nightstand. Yin-Yin put a CD in, and the sounds of a violin and piano started.

"Min Fang. My wife," Da Long said abruptly.

She had understood the name. And *tai-tai*. His wife.

"What is wrong with her?" Christine asked, enunciating every word clearly in the hope that he would understand her.

"Sh-sh-she is sick. Th-th-the music calms her."

"What illness does she have?"

"The doctors don't know exactly. At first they thought she had epilepsy. Then they said it was a stroke. Or several strokes. They say there is no hope." He paused and then continued. "B-b-but I don't believe them. Not the doctors here."

Christine cast Paul a look to ask for help. She guessed what was coming.

"Is that the reason for our visit?" she asked quietly.

Her brother nodded without looking at her.

"You think that I, Mei-mei, the little barefoot doctor, can help her?"

He nodded again.

"Da Long." She found it difficult to keep talking. "I'm sorry. I am not a doctor."

"N-n-no?" He was still not looking at her. His head was lowered, as though he had known. She was not a doctor.

"No. I was . . . Things were very difficult . . . when we arrived in Hong Kong . . ." It was impossible to speak in coherent sentences. How could she explain it to him? The dreams of a child. They were no more. "I didn't study medicine," she said at last. "I'm a travel agent."

"A-a-a travel agent? Y-y-you don't like White Rabbit sweets anymore and you're a travel agent," he said, as if to himself.

She wanted to take his hand in hers, but did not dare to. "When did your wife fall ill?"

Instead of replying, he looked down at her fingers and swayed his upper body back and forth repeatedly.

Yin-Yin replied for her father. "Not long ago. It's been just over two months. She was always completely healthy before that. I can't remember my mother ever being sick. Not even with a cold. Then suddenly from one day to the next—"

Da Long interrupted his daughter. "I-i-it started with the shivering," he said. "And with balance problems. She was unsteady on her feet. When I asked if anything was wrong, she said it was nothing. She was fine. Nothing to worry about. Two days later I could barely understand what she was saying. She spoke very slowly, stretching her vowels. That evening she could no longer hold her chopsticks, and the rice bowl slipped from her hands. The next morning I took her to the doctor in the town. She was suddenly well again and relaxed as she had always been. We had just arrived home when she was seized with terrible cramps. Her whole body was shaking. She was screaming with pain. She fell to the ground and rolled around in agony while I, I stood by and could do nothing to help her."

Da Long fell silent. He had been speaking quickly. Paul had barely been able to keep up with the translating. Christine realized that her brother's speech impediment fell away the longer he talked.

Yin-Yin poured more tea, and Da Long continued speaking. "H-h-her limbs had grown numb. I took her to the hospital in Yiwu in a taxi. She lay there for three weeks while the doctors did every possible test. She was given different medicines, but her condition only grew worse. She could no longer speak. She could no longer see. She could no longer move. The doctors said she could also no longer hear, but I don't believe that. At some point they said they could no longer do anything for her. It was a matter of long-term care. They had no space for that in the hospital. I was to take her back home. They brought her here in an ambulance and laid her down here in bed. They gave up on her. Can you imagine that, Mei-mei? Giving up on a person who was still drawing breath? I'm not giving up, I told them. I'm not giving up on my wife. The doctors said I was mad. They were sorry, and it was a terrible case of bad luck, but I had to be realistic. All the tests proved that there was no solution. No hope. But, little sister, a loving heart never gives up. Never. A loving heart does not even accept death. Min Fang eats. She drinks. She digests her food. She lives! Why should she not speak and see again one day? Who can say that she won't? They don't even know exactly what she is suffering from, so how can they be sure that she will never recover her health? Do you understand? What nonsense!" he said, slapping his palm down on the table. He had worked himself up into such a frenzy that he was short of breath, and only gradually managed to calm himself down. He leaned across the table as if he wanted to let her in on a secret. "I-I-I don't trust them. I don't believe in their tests. I was sure that you had become a doctor. How silly of me. I was convinced that you worked in one of the modern hospitals in Hong Kong. I hoped you could help us . . ."

"I'm sorry. I wish I could. Are there no good doctors here?"

From the look he gave her, she could see what a stupid question that was.

"Have you tried Shanghai?" Paul asked. "There are surely highly qualified neurologists there."

"D-d-definitely. But we can't afford to pay them," Da Long replied. "Besides, it's too late. Everything happened so quickly. How am I supposed to bring her to Shanghai in this state? And even if we managed it, the doctors said that with the test results from here, no hospital would take her. A hopeless case."

They heard the quiet grunting again. Da Long got up hurriedly, and Paul and Christine followed him.

It was not a pretty sight. Min Fang lay stretched out on her back, her gaze fixed on the ceiling, her mouth half open, her face distorted in a grotesque grimace. Her fingers were twisted and stiff—like large crow's feet, Christine thought. She could not imagine what kind of woman Min Fang had been a few weeks earlier. Attractive or ugly, graceful or clumsy, fat or thin; the illness had turned her into a helpless heap of a human being. Da Long sat on the side of the bed and stroked his wife's face, looking at her. Christine heard a hissing sound. Da Long switched the music off and held his ear very close to her mouth. A distant rattling. Like a sound from another world. He stayed close to her mouth, as though he just had to be patient enough.

"She's trying to say something and I can't understand her." He turned to them and said again, "I just can't understand her. After nearly forty years. How can that be? My own wife."

The despair in his voice moved Christine. She reached for Paul's hand behind her back.

An unpleasant smell rose from under the blanket.

"I have to clean her up," Da Long said, wiping his face with his hand. "Yin-Yin, perhaps you can show them the village in the meantime. It won't take long."

Paul and Yin-Yin walked toward the square that the car had dropped them off in. Christine followed a few feet behind. She did not feel like talking. She felt exhausted. Her head was heavy and she wished she could lie down. She wondered how she could help her brother, but she could not think of anything. She was not a doctor. She did not know any neurologists in Hong Kong whom she could ask for advice. She did not have enough money to fly in the best doctors to treat her brother's wife. She could try researching on the Internet, but for what? They didn't even have a diagnosis. She did not know much about medicine, but the father of a friend of hers had had a severe stroke the previous year, and her friend had told her about similar symptoms and episodes. Maybe there were drugs that could alleviate Min Fang's suffering, if it was not too late already. But if she was being honest with herself, she did not think that anything else could help this crippled, blind, and probably mute woman.

A loving heart never gives up. A loving heart does not even accept death. That sounded beautiful, but she doubted her brother was right.

Christine had lost sight of Paul and Yin-Yin. She came to a fork in the way, hesitated, and took the left-hand path. She was suddenly in a narrow, shaded cul-de-sac. She heard voices from a television turned up loud from one house and the clatter of pots and pans from another. A gray-haired woman dressed entirely in black was sitting in front of a doorway on a rusty wheelchair. Spit was dribbling from her half-open mouth down her chin and falling into her lap in long strings. The fingers of her left hand were gnarled, and her right arm jerked uncontrollably. She had heard the footsteps, and turned her head very slowly. Before their eyes could meet, Christine turned and hurried away, finding Paul and Yin-Yin, who had been looking for her, after a few steps. Christine told them about the sick woman she had seen.

"That's Mrs. Ma," her niece said. "She's a friend of my mother's. She had a stroke a few days before her, but she's doing better. As far as I know she can no longer speak properly and is partially lame, but compared to my mother she's been lucky."

They crossed the sandy square, walked down the road for a little while, and turned onto a footpath over the fields that led to the top of the hill. The expressway sliced the valley into two parts; the fields looked neglected; the farmers had probably given up on cultivating them long ago. In the distance they could see factories, housing settlements, and a railway line. It was so hot that they had to rest in the shade of a pine tree.

"I wanted to show you this view," Yin-Yin said. "This used to be our playground. When we were little there were many children in the village; there was even a school. We used to play outside every day. In the fields, in the woods, in the ponds. I learned to swim in a pond full of fish on the other side of the valley. Then the first few factories arrived. The expressway cut through the valley. The young people all moved to the cities, to Yiwu, Shanghai, Xiamen, Shenzhen. You can see what is left. In a few years it will all be gone. The entire village. The plans have been finalized."

"The entire village?" Christine asked, astonished.

"Yes. Any of the old folk who are still alive will be allocated an apartment on the outskirts of Yiwu. I stood at this spot with my brother three weeks ago. He was fine with it. We have our memories, he said, and the village wasn't worth keeping. Ramshackle old houses and homes with no air-conditioning; too hot in the summer and too cold and damp in the winter. Those things won't be a problem in the new homes with air-conditioning and heating, and there will be shops and doctor's clinics nearby. The move will be a good example of China's progress. He's probably right."

"What's your brother's name?"

"Wu Xiao Hu. We call him Xiao Hu, Little Tiger. He's four years older than me, born in 1974, the year of the tiger."

"Are you close?"

"Yes," Yin-Yin said. "We're very different though. People who know us both can't believe that we're brother and sister."

"How is he different from you?" Paul asked.

"He was always a top student. Very diligent, very ambitious. I was slow and dreamy. When we played in the river he used to build dams to hold back the water while I stared at the fish. I hate confrontations, but he doesn't avoid them. I'm not interested in politics, but he is, extremely. I've wanted to be a musician since I was little, while he wanted to be a member of the Communist Party of China. We've both got what we wanted. But I must admit that I'm not as successful a musician as he is in the party. He accuses me of not being ambitious enough. Maybe he's right. But I respect him a great deal. He's a good brother and a good person."

"Why isn't he here today?"

Yin-Yin looked down at the ground and shoved a bit of dirt into a little pile with the tip of one foot. "Papa and him don't get along too well."

"Why not?" Christine asked.

"I don't know exactly. It was different before. I used to be jealous of Xiao Hu. He was the firstborn! The son. Papa did lots of stuff with him and even took the time to help him with his schoolwork. He never once did that with me. Xiao Hu was meant to come top of class, and he did. Papa was always very proud of him. My little tiger will grow up to be a big one, he often said."

"When did things change?"

"Last year, practically overnight. They had a big fight. They didn't speak to each other for months, and Xiao Hu refused to visit my parents. Mama was desperately unhappy about it. She tried to mediate, and they did eventually start talking to each other, at least. But it's no longer the way it used to be. My brother is very hard on Papa. And I also get the feeling that Papa is uncomfortable with Little Tiger, as though he is scared of him."

"Why should he be frightened of him? What did they quarrel about in the first place?" Christine wondered out loud.

"I have no idea. I was in Shanghai at the time, and neither of them will tell me what it was about."

"They haven't given you the slightest clue?"

"No. And on top of that, they got into another argument two weeks ago over Mama. My brother is on the doctors' side. He thinks there's no point hoping for her to recover. He wants to try to find a hospital or a nursing facility for her to stay in. His salary from the party could make it possible. Papa won't hear of it. I think that when Xiao Hu refused to back down, Papa threw him out. Since then they haven't been speaking to each other."

"And you? Whose side are you on?"

Yin-Yin cast her aunt a blank look. "On my father's, of course."

"You think that your mother will recover?" Paul asked in amazement.

"I don't know about that. I'm not a doctor. But if my father wants to care for her at home, then we have to accept that and help him with it. I am his daughter; his wishes matter to me. After my second audition for the symphony orchestra I'll take time off and move back home to the village for at least three months to help him." She looked at her watch. "There's not much else to see here. I think we can make our way back now."

Da Long was waiting in front of the house. He was sitting on a bench in the shade, smoking. Paul crouched down next to him. A fat gray rat scurried across the courtyard. Da Long watched it until it disappeared under the pile of wood. "Ever since the cats died the rats have been plaguing us again," he said.

"The cats died?" Paul asked, curious.

"I don't know. We had a dozen cats in the village. They all died last month. Ours fell into the fountain and drowned. Other cats got cramps and died, foaming at the mouth. Probably a virus or rabies. Who can find out what it was? Our neighbor called the police, but they said it wasn't their responsibility. Then someone contacted the health authorities. They said the same thing. No one wants to know. Who cares about our cats?"

They went into the house. Da Long had cooked a noodle broth

with chicken and wonton dumplings. They sat around the table and
started eating without saying another word. Christine found the
silence uncomfortable. Did they have nothing to say to each other
after forty years? She wanted to make a start, so she began describ-
ing her life in Hong Kong. She talked about the first few years after
they fled there, about the one hundred square feet in Lower Ngau
Tau Kok Estate. About Mama's work as a seamstress. Not about
tears unshed. Not about things unsaid. And also not about men in
blue shorts on which you could see every stain.

Her brother listened while he slurped away and smacked his
lips. Without asking any questions. She was not sure if he was
paying attention to her. She told him about her tourism degree in
Vancouver, about her son, Josh, her wedding, and the failure of her
marriage. He carried on eating, nodding from time to time, spat a
bit of gristle out onto the table, and turned away once, quickly, to
blow his nose loudly. Christine watched him. A small old man bent
over his soup, sunk in his own little world. She felt that her brother
had been taken from her for the second time. They had nothing in
common. No roots. No memories. No worries about their parents.
They did not even speak the same language. There was no "do you
remember?" Not with him. Now was all there was, and she would
have been glad not to have had it.

She waited. She waited for him to say something about himself,
for him to ask a question, to show interest. But Da Long yawned,
said nothing, and poked away between his teeth with a wooden
toothpick.

She wondered if she should simply ask him something. Where
did you meet Min Fang? How did you get back to the city? What
did you train as? What did you work as? Did he want to be asked
or did he not want to share his life with her if he could help it?
In his letter he had started with such a familiar tone—where
was that now? Was the memory of how she had learned to walk
holding his hand a trick to move her? Had she been summoned
there only in the hope that she could do something for his sick
wife? Now that he knew he was mistaken, was she to go again, the

sooner the better? The longer the silence dragged on, the angrier she became.

"Why didn't you try to find Mama and me earlier?"

A difficult question. *Why didn't* you *try?* Most of the time, when we ask questions like these, we could just as easily ask them of ourselves: Why didn't *I*? But Da Long didn't try to fob her off that way. "Th-th-they were difficult times," he said. "Dangerous times. It was a black mark to have relatives in Hong Kong or anywhere abroad. Many people had to go to prison for that. Or to the labor camps. Because a few crazy people in their families had swum to Hong Kong. What could they have done about it? But that was how it was then. They could easily have declared me an enemy of the state or a counterrevolutionary. When the party told me that the two of you had escaped to Hong Kong, I had to write a five-page letter denouncing you. I cursed you as traitors, bourgeois vermin, class enemies, and dissociated myself from Mama and you, whom I called miserable wretches, forever."

"That was a long time ago." What right had she to accuse him?

"That's right." He was silent. Christine did not know if he was finding this conversation uncomfortable or if he was searching for an explanation himself. "We were too caught up with our lives. We moved from Sichuan to the coast, then shortly after that to this village. The children had to get used to a new place twice and we had to adjust to our new work. Min Fang gave a few small concerts and the time passed. Before we knew it, another year had passed. You know how it is. Apart from that, I had no idea where to look for you. For a long time I thought you had migrated to Australia or America after Hong Kong." He looked at Paul, and then at his sister, as though he wanted to make sure that his words were reaching her.

In his eyes she saw the question that she did not want to hear: And you? Did *you* try to look for *me*?

"It was the same for us," Christine said. "We were convinced that you hadn't survived the Cultural Revolution. Mama tried everything, but all her attempts to find out about what happened to you didn't lead very far."

Paul translated what she said. As he spoke slowly, brother and sister exchanged a long look for the first time. Christine was not telling the truth, only a part of it, and she suspected that it was no different for Da Long. They both knew that they were lying, and they both needed to forgive each other. This, Christine thought, is how secrets that are passed from one generation to another are born. This is how families bury their demons. With things unsaid, half truths, with unprocessed grief. Until they rise again. Bigger, more alive, and more powerful.

In reality, she had not spoken about her brother to her mother since she was a child. Even in their one hundred square feet, with his photo under a pillow, she could not remember having had a significant conversation about Da Long. Why not? Why had Mother not tried to find her son? Why had she assumed that Da Long had died in the chaos of the Cultural Revolution? Had she any information, witnesses, or other sources that Christine knew nothing about? How could someone not say anything about a person for nearly forty years? Because she did not want to be reminded of him? Because the pain was unbearable? The pain of loss? Or something else? She too had never asked about him, let alone searched for him. She had settled into a new city, into her life without a brother. But was there something that her mother and Da Long shared that she did not know about? She could ask him now, but did not dare to. Not now, not today. She had to ask her mother first.

Paul broke the silence. He asked about the music that was playing in the background. Christine was not interested in that, but it did her good to hear his voice. It was Mozart, violin sonatas. An amateur recording from the conservatory, with Yin-Yin on the violin. Da Long was convinced that it helped his wife to hear it. Let the doctors think what they may. Paul praised Yin-Yin's playing, and they started talking about music, about violin pieces by Brahms, Bruch, and Mendelssohn, names that meant nothing to Christine, about Chinese composers that Paul had not heard of. Da Long got up, fetched a harmonica, and started playing it. He closed his eyes, and his cheeks puffed out as he played, swaying his head in time. Paul clapped. It was the first time that Christine had seen Yin-Yin and her father smile. Her thoughts slid away from her as if from someone on the verge of falling asleep. She felt as if she did not belong there, as if she was sitting with them at the table but separated by an invisible wall. She could barely wait for the taxi to come and take them to the hotel.

In the car she realized how much the past few hours had taken their toll on her. Her head was pounding, and her shoulders were so tense that even Paul's tentative attempts to massage them hurt. She leaned against his shoulder, and he put his arms around her. She hoped he would say something, ask her a few questions that might help her bring some order to her thoughts and feelings.

After a few minutes, they had reached the outskirts of Yiwu, and were only able to proceed at a snail's pace because the road was jammed with a long line of trucks. It was no different with the traffic coming from the other direction. A convoy of yellow, red, blue, green, and brown container trucks was traveling in both directions through the country.

Paul whispered in her ear. "A little of everything?"

It took her a couple of seconds to understand what he meant. She loved him for saying things like this.

"A little of everything. I wish it were so simple. I don't know what I'm supposed to think."

"That's not what I want to know."

"What, then?"

"How you're feeling."

"I feel empty. Powerless. A little numb. Can you understand that?"

"I wouldn't have understood anything else."

She lifted her head. She thought about Min Fang, and shuddered.

"What's wrong."

"I was thinking about my sister-in-law. Awful. It doesn't look like anyone can help her now, can they?"

"No. But I understand your brother. A loving heart never gives up. He's right."

Christine wondered if she should say she disagreed, but she stayed silent.

"I like him," Paul said. "Do you?"

Christine thought for a long moment. "I don't know. I certainly feel sorry for him." After a pause, she added, "There were moments when I felt that you were visiting a friend and that I was accompanying you, not the other way around."

"Why?" he asked, surprised.

"Didn't you notice how little he looked at me?"

"Yes, I did. But it's often like that when you're talking to someone through an interpreter."

"I can't remember him asking me a single question, can you?"

"No."

"He didn't even ask about our mother once."

"He has other things to worry about."

"That's true. But I still felt very distant from him. I can't claim to have the feeling that I've found my missing brother today. Is that terrible?"

Paul leaned over and smiled at her. "What would you like to hear from me?"

"That it's not terrible. That I don't have to have a bad conscience."

"Do you have one?"

"A little."

"I would too."

Christine flinched. "Why? Must I?"

"No, of course not. But since when has the state of our conscience depended on whether there is an objective reason for it? Your mother escaped to Hong Kong with you, not with him. None of you had a choice. Life has been good to you. Less good to him. That is not your fault and also not his failure."

"What is it, then?"

"It's fate, isn't it? Do you think your mother really looked for him?"

"No. At least, she never told me anything about it."

"Strange, don't you think?"

"Yes, very."

"What would have stopped her?"

Christine did not have an answer.

"Have you ever asked her about it?"

"No."

"Why not?"

"No idea. We didn't talk about my father or my brother. Like I told you on the plane, Chinese people don't ask too many questions. I figured she would talk to me about it if she wanted me to know."

Christine found the silence between her and her mother more than strange now. She felt ashamed. She felt complicit without knowing what or whom she and her mother had been united against.

Three-quarters of an hour later, the taxi dropped them in front of the Grand Emperor, which Yin-Yin had told them was the best hotel in town. There were Mercedes and Audi limousines parked in the driveway, and an exclusive four-wheel-drive vehicle was drawn up right in front of the entrance. A bellhop took their small cases from them eagerly, and two doormen held the doors open for them. Giant chandeliers that Christine had never seen the likes of even in Hong Kong glittered in the lobby, and the white marbled floor was inlaid with eight bars of gold under a layer of thick glass. But they had barely left the lobby before they found themselves in the shabbiest luxury hotel that Christine had ever seen. It was as though they had stepped behind the stage set at a theater. The carpet in the corridor was worn and covered in stains from cigarettes and spilled drinks, and the walls had scuff marks and unsightly bulges of wallpaper.

Their room smelled strongly of cleaning products. Christine noticed a drop of liquid on the bedspread. She pulled it back to check if at least the sheets were clean.

"It's just for one night," Paul said, as though he had guessed her thoughts.

She drew the curtains back. The large windowpanes were covered in a gray film; behind them was a view of the gray city and factory chimneys belching gray plumes into the sky. She drew the curtains again.

They were too exhausted to go to the restaurant. Paul ordered fried noodles, rice, and eggplant with minced pork. Soon they were sitting on the edge of the bed eating while channel surfing among Qing dynasty soap operas, acrobatics shows, a singing competition featuring contestants with no talent whatsoever, and the stock exchange updates running on three of the channels simultaneously. The food was lukewarm and dripping with grease. After a few bites they put their plates down and stared at the images flickering in front of them.

"I want to sleep with you," Christine said suddenly, turning the television off. She hadn't meant it to sound like an order.

Paul slid further into the middle of the bed and pulled the blanket over their heads. "Are you sure?" he asked quietly.

"Yes," she whispered.

He touched her with his fingertips, gliding up and down her back, and licked her ear playfully; he was tender, as if it were the first time. What he aroused in her was much more than lust. She wanted to feel him in her, to hold him tight. Forever and ever. Melting together. He was not to move, but simply stay inside her. The pounding of their hearts. The weight of the world on her body.

VII

Paul tossed and turned in bed. The air was too cold and dry, and the air conditioner hummed noisily. Next to him, the red digits of the alarm clock glowed fiercely in the darkness: 2:45.

It was the thought of the cats that kept him awake. He stared into the darkness and tried to remember the details: Dead cats. Frenzied cats. When he had worked in Hong Kong as a journalist, he had once researched a story on cats for an American magazine. They had died in excruciating circumstances. That was at least thirty years ago. Paul no longer remembered either the name of the publication or the name of the place, and he could not recall what had been wrong with the animals that died. The only thing that remained was the image of a cat that had charged into a wall in broad daylight with its eyes open. Paul got up, felt his way to a chair, grabbed his clothes, entered the bathroom and got dressed, and went down to the lobby. It was still incredibly busy there. Three women at the reception desk were taking care of new arrivals, and a group of businesspeople were talking about which sauna they should go to. Sitting on the sofa were two women in miniskirts, who sized Paul up thoroughly.

The concierge was sorry to report that the business center was closed and only opened at seven a.m. He could have a massage; massages were available around the clock. There were computers with Internet access in every room; he didn't have to go to the business center for that. But Paul did not want to wake Christine up. After a brief discussion and a tip of fifty yuan, he found himself sitting in the empty office of the shift manager, putting different searches into the computer. Cat frenzy. Cat illnesses. Cats and health. Cats and rabies. He tried a Chinese search engine and found interesting stuff about the trade in cats and cat breeding, also the best cat recipes from Guangdong Province, but nothing that was useful to him. He switched to Google and got millions of hits. He found a few vague trails and a couple of pieces of the puzzle, but they still didn't make sense together. The longer he searched, the more convinced he was that the answer to the question of how a healthy woman in her late fifties could turn into a lame, blind, and mute being in a couple of days was hidden somewhere in the labyrinth of information. Paul tapped away at the keyboard more and more furiously and waited impatiently for the sites to load before moving on quickly. If he could just remember the name of the town he had written that story on back then. He had not visited it in person; he had conducted his research only on the phone, through interviews, and by using archival material before writing his article; he had not followed up on the story, and had eventually forgotten about it. Annoyed and frustrated, he finally gave up after two hours. Maybe he was deceiving himself after all. Maybe the doctors were right. A severe stroke. Hopeless. Even if he found something, what did the frenzy of the cats have to do with the lame, blind, and mute Min Fang?

He went back to their room. Christine was sleeping on his side of the bed, half covered by the blanket and curled up like a child. He felt drained but not tired; on the contrary, he was filled with an inner unease that made sleep impossible. He opened the curtains a crack and stood at the window. The streets were empty, and it had started raining. The white, red, and yellow neon lights were reflected in the puddles on the street and the roofs; drops of rain splattered against the window and ran down the glass in crazy zigzag lines. The sun would rise in about an hour.

Paul thought about Da Long. Christine's brother had moved him, right from the moment he saw him. His clumsiness. His embarrassed smile when he saw his sister. The formal greetings. The way he stammered at the beginning of every sentence. The shyness in his manner. He was either not able to or did not want to cover up his uncertainty.

Paul thought about the loud, rasping breath of the sick woman, her blank gaze at the ceiling, her stiff body. He thought about the colorful little rain boots in the hall of his house in Lamma. The raincoat in the closet. The marks on the door frame indicating the growth of a child, slowly fading. The strength of memory. It caused him physical pain that coursed through his body in waves. It had been weeks, months perhaps, since he had felt such pain. It came in surges, set off by a thought, a few words, the sight of a toy, a child, or a sick person. It came unannounced and with all its might, and it would never stop. That was fine the way it was. The never-ending pain of loss. The price of living.

Da Long's dark-brown, deep-set eyes. Their gazes had often met while Paul had translated for him; their eyes had rested on each other, sized up, and probed.

What must he have felt when he realized that his sister was not able to help him? Did he curse the moment he sat down to write to ask for her help? It must have been a huge effort for him, after nearly forty years. What had stopped him and his mother from searching for each other for so long? His excuse was just as flimsy as his sister's. There were no families without secrets.

A loving heart never gives up. A loving heart does not even accept death. He knew that to Christine, her brother's words must have seemed unbelievably corny and banal, but not to him. Anyone who had sat by the bedside of a loved one who was dying knew that some truths were so simple that people barely dared to say them, and forgot them again much too quickly.

He was overcome by an indescribable longing for Christine. He undressed quickly, lay down next to her, curled himself around her back, and put a hand carefully under her breasts. In a matter of minutes the warmth of her body helped him drift off to sleep.

Yin-Yin came to meet them at the village square. She looked despondent. She greeted them briefly without looking them in the eyes, and led them through the village without saying anything.

The atmosphere in the house was heavy. Da Long was even quieter than he had been the day before. He too seemed to have had a sleepless night. The lines in his face were deeper, and his eyes looked smaller; he seemed restless and agitated. Min Fang groaned loudly at intervals. Da Long sprang up and hurried over to her every time. But even when she was quiet he kept getting up from the table and going over to the bed to sit beside her, talk to her, wet her lips and face, and turn the music up or down.

"Did something happen during the night? Has she grown worse?" Paul asked.

"No, but my father is very angry," Yin-Yin said.

"Why?"

"My brother rang last night. He's spoken to a doctor, a neurologist, in Shanghai, who will be coming on Tuesday to examine my mother."

"But that's good," Christine said.

"Papa doesn't like it. He's afraid that it's just my brother's way of putting more pressure on him. Another doctor who will say there is no hope. Another person who will say that a nursing home would be the best thing for my mother."

"If he's a specialist, he might be able to help," Paul interjected.

"Maybe. That's why Papa agreed. But he doesn't trust him."

Da Long came back to the table and sat down with them. He drummed his fingers on the wooden surface, and his gaze wandered from Paul to Christine and back again as if he were asking himself what these two strangers were doing in his house.

"Da Long, would it be helpful if I were here on Tuesday when the doctor came?" Paul surprised himself with his own question. The words had simply come out of him without any thought. He did not want this despairing man who was clinging onto hope to be alone with a strange doctor. He knew what it was like. He knew the helplessness, the strain. He thought about all the conversations that he had had with doctors. *Is there no doubt about the diagnosis? Leukemia? What did the oncologists suggest? What side effects would the chemotherapy have?* The doctors had answered all their questions patiently. Paul had concentrated on everything they said, but just a few hours later he was no longer sure if he remembered it all correctly. He began taking notes during these conversations, and he and his wife agreed never to have a discussion with a doctor on their own. Four ears hear more and four eyes see more than two, he had always said to Meredith.

Christine saw the look of amazement on her brother's face and immediately wanted to know what Paul had said. He gestured to her to be patient for a moment; he wanted to hear Da Long's reply first before he translated for her.

"What did you say?" she repeated in a whisper.

"Just a second."

Before she could insist, her brother replied. "If it's not too inconvenient for you, I would be incredibly grateful. Four ears hear more than two."

"Then I'd be happy to stay," Paul said, turning to Christine. "I asked him if he would find it helpful if I was here on Tuesday."

She gave him a troubled look. "Are you serious?"

"Yes."

"What made you think of that? I have to go back to Hong Kong today."

"I know. I'll take you to the airport and stay with you till you go through immigration. Don't worry."

"It's not that," she said indignantly.

"What then?"

"That you've made a decision like that without talking to me about it first."

"Christine. The idea came to me on the spur of the moment. I'm not staying here for fun. I'm trying to help your brother!"

"I don't care about that. We could at least have walked out into the courtyard to talk it over for a few minutes. How on earth will you help him anyway? Since when do you know about anything medical?"

He had never seen her so worked up. He wanted to tell her about his discussions with doctors, about the loneliness of those moments, but there was so much anger and rage in her eyes that he stayed silent instead. She seemed to be trying to tell him this: This is not my brother who you are helping. This is a stranger whom I just happen to share my parents with.

The next couple of hours were difficult. Da Long sat on his wife's bed or clattered about in the kitchen. Yin-Yin tried valiantly to keep up a conversation with them. She told them a bit about her mother and her wonderful voice, about the little recitals they used to give together, about her studies, and about Shanghai. She did not ask any questions.

Christine found it difficult to suppress her fury. It was clear that she would prefer to be on her way to Hong Kong sooner rather than later, and when Yin-Yin offered to take her to the airport, as she had to be back in Shanghai that day anyway, Christine didn't hesitate.

Paul took a bottle of beer out of the minibar and emptied it in three gulps. He switched off the light on the nightstand, lay on the bed, and put his arms behind his head. The flicker of neon lights lit up the room at regular intervals.

The telephone rang. It was Christine calling from Hong Kong. She had landed and was at home. She had called to wish him goodnight. She had thought over his decision and she respected it now, even though she did not know what Paul could do without a medical background. But she apologized for being angry anyway. It was an overreaction, no question about that. The last two days had stretched her beyond her limits. She had not liked the thought of having to travel back to Hong Kong without him at all. She was sorry.

The memories came back slowly. Paul went over to the computer and sat down without switching on the light. The faint light-blue glow from the screen was enough to illuminate the keyboard. He entered a key phrase that he remembered from that time, and the very first click took him to a useful website; the next got him even further. And further. Every link got him closer to what he suspected. Suddenly he could go no further. The website of the *New York Times*, whose archive he wanted to access, was blocked. So was the BBC website. He tried the *Washington Times*, the *Post*, but no luck. Paul thought about how he could get around the Chinese censorship of the Internet. He tried other ways around it, but the media websites were still blocked; the connection failed every couple of minutes and then Internet access failed altogether. His attempts to restore it were unsuccessful.

He rang the concierge. He could not explain why Paul's Internet connection was down. No other guests had complained. The shift manager's computer was available for use. Paul felt a sense of unease; he hesitated and turned down the offer.

———

Breakfast was pathetic. The fish was swimming in a greasy sauce, and the rice congee tasted of nothing. The wontons were lukewarm and hard and dry at the edges. Even the tea was bitter. Paul left the food, fetched a yogurt, a couple of slices of watermelon, and a banana from the buffet table, and ordered a fresh pot of jasmine tea. He walked back to the farthest corner of the icy-cold, windowless room and thought about what he should do. He had actually planned to look around this strange city, one that had expanded so quickly that people returning after some time away could no longer find their own homes, but his head was still full of the whirl of contradictory stories that he had found in just one hour on the Internet the previous night. Could there really be a connection between the agonizing death of the cat and Min Fang's suffering? If so, what was it that connected the two? If it were some mysterious virus, how had they been infected, and how great was the chance of infection for the other people in the village? Could he, who was neither a doctor nor a chemist or a toxicologist, find answers to these questions? He had learned how to research things as a journalist; he could try to gather evidence and information. If his initial suspicion was confirmed, surely the Chinese authorities would take an interest. It wouldn't just be about the lives of cats then.

He had nothing to lose, apart from one day.

After breakfast, Paul bought a notebook, a ballpoint pen, and, after a moment's hesitation, a cheap, compact digital camera. If he found anything suspicious, he wanted to document it.

———

The taxi driver dropped him off in the village square just before eleven a.m. and promised to pick him up around six p.m., at the very latest at dusk. He gave him his cell phone number just in case. It was oppressively hot; there wasn't a cloud in the sky. The village seemed even more abandoned than it had on the previous two days. The heat kept all the inhabitants in their houses. Even the dog that had barked so furiously the day before yesterday was now lying in the shade of a building, and simply raised its head wearily at the sight of a stranger.

During the taxi ride, Paul had remembered the sick woman whom Christine had stumbled across in one of the side streets. He set out to look for her. He wanted to speak to her or to her family before he went to see Da Long.

The layout of the village was more complicated than it had seemed at first. He turned off the narrow road a few times, stepped through a rotting wooden gate, and stumbled into an empty court-yard that was connected to two others by a concealed path. The network of courtyards was as complex as the tunnels of a labyrinth. The single-story houses were of very basic build; Paul could see common Chinese architectural embellishments on only a few of the doors and windows. Everything seemed to indicate that the farmers here had always been quite poor. An abandoned bamboo chair, broken straw baskets, a tattered red lantern hanging over a door; these were the only signs of people living here. When Paul entered yet another unfamiliar courtyard a few minutes later, he had no idea where he was.

"*Ni hao*," he called, loud and clear, but the only reply he got was a silence that seemed hostile. He stood there for a moment, undecided about what to do, until he suddenly became aware of cooking smells.

He turned and followed the aroma, which led him down the very next alleyway. Once again, he called "*Ni hao*" loud and clear.

The head of an old man appeared in a doorway, staring at him suspiciously.

"What do you want?"

"Excuse me for disturbing you. I'm looking for Mrs. Ma," Paul said in his best Mandarin.

"Who are you?" the old man asked, unimpressed.

"A friend of Da Long's and his family."

The old man stepped out. His face was pockmarked, and he was wearing a faded, worn blue Mao suit; he had the sturdy build of a farmer. He was holding a wooden spoon in his hand. The frames of his large spectacles were held together on both sides with brown elastic bands, and there was a crack across the whole of the left-hand lens.

"Mrs. Ma is my wife. What do you want from her?" he snapped, putting both hands on his hips.

"Just to ask her a few questions."

"If you're a friend of Da Long's, you should know that she can no longer speak," the man said, starting to turn away.

"Perhaps you could answer a few questions?"

The old man gave him a suspicious look. "Are you a doctor?"

"No."

"Then get lost."

"But I could still possibly help you."

"No one can help us."

"I'm interested in your wife's illness."

"Go away now."

"Don't you find it strange that Min Fang and your wife both fell ill at the same time?" Paul said in a friendly manner, as though he had not heard the man.

"You forgot about Mrs. Zhuo," the old man added with a sarcastic edge to his voice.

"Who?"

"Mrs. Zhuo. The wife of Da Long's neighbor. You're supposed to be a friend of the family and you don't know about that? Who the hell are you?"

"The husband of Da Long's sister."

"Da Long doesn't have a sister."

"I'm sorry, that was meant as a joke," Paul stammered awkwardly. "I'm a friend of Yin-Yin's. I live in Shanghai. We play music together."

"Why are you interested in my wife's illness then?"

"Yin-Yin told me about it. I mean, about her mother and her mother's friend."

"What about it? What's it got to do with you, since you're not a doctor?"

Paul ignored the question. "Two women, three, in fact, fall sick in this village at the same time. Doesn't that seem strange to you?"

"No. There's a curse on this village."

Paul started. "What do you mean?"

"Three strokes in two weeks. I call that cruel fate."

"How do you know that they were strokes?"

"That's what the doctors told us. Are you trying to tell me that you know better than them?"

"No. But I'd still like to know if your wife's sickness started in the same way as Min Fang's did."

The old man hesitated. Paul had clearly succeeded in making him a little less suspicious. "The same way. She dropped the tea caddy. Numb in the left hand."

"At the same time?"

"A few days earlier."

"And then?"

"She found it more and more difficult to talk. Our son just happened to be here and we took her to People's Hospital Number Two in Yiwu straightaway. She got worse and worse by the hour. The doctors couldn't do anything. But we count ourselves lucky. Min Fang got it much worse."

When Paul heard oil spitting inside the house, he knew that it was a matter of seconds before the man would break off the conversation and hurry back to his wok. Then he wouldn't get a single word more out of him.

"Do you have cats?"

"Two. They died miserable deaths. Why are you asking about them?"

"The Wus also had a cat."

"So? The Zhuo family didn't have one. Does that help us at all?"

"May I ask what your wife liked eating?"

Mr. Ma thought a moment, unsure about whether to finally end this exchange. "Whatever there was to eat," he said coldly. "Or does it look like we have much choice here?"

"No," Paul said quietly. "Rice and vegetables, then?"

"Yes."

"No cats?"

"Cats? Are you one of those crazy animal rights people?" The man's voice was indignant. "They eat cats in the south. In Guang-dong Province. But not here!"

"I'm sorry. I didn't meant to insult you. I have absolutely nothing against eating cats—"

"They don't taste good," the man interrupted. "What else do you want to know?"

"May I ask where your wife is?"

"In the house."

"May I see her?"

Mr. Ma gave him a fierce look. "You want to come into my house?"

"I just want to see if—"

"No. That's enough. Leave us alone."

"Would it be possible for me just to take a quick photo of her?"

"A photo? She's not a tourist attraction. Go to hell, whoever you are," the old man said furiously, moving forward and waving the wooden spoon at him aggressively.

Paul flinched and took a step back, even though he was at least a head taller. He had nothing to counter the man's firmness. He apologized a few times and hurried out of the alley with quick steps.

Da Long was in the courtyard, bent over a deep wooden washtub in the middle of a mountain of laundry, washing a bedsheet. He lifted it up high, looked at the several yellow stains and two brown stains, each the size of a palm, on the light-colored material, tipped a bit more detergent powder into the water, and scrubbed away at the sheet until the stains were mere shadows. He put the sheet aside and dunked some gray pajama bottoms into the soapy water.

He looked up briefly when his visitor stepped through the gate, but didn't seem too surprised to see him. Paul thought he even saw the hint of a smile on Da Long's weary face.

"How are you?" was all he said in greeting.

Christine would probably have been irritated or disappointed by such a cool reception, but not Paul. He knew that for a person who was fighting for his child's or his wife's life, there were only two kinds of people: those who were or could be helpful or useful, and the others. All his attention went to the first sort of person; he ignored the rest.

"It's hot today," Paul said in reply.

"Mm," Da Long murmured as he rubbed the pajama bottoms together.

"Do you have to do the laundry every day?" Paul asked, trying to start a conversation.

"Nearly."

Paul helped him wring the laundry out. "I thought I would come and visit rather than spend the day sitting around in Yiwu."

Da Long nodded and hung the laundry on a clothesline that was strung across the courtyard.

"Yin-Yin told us yesterday that Mrs. Ma, Min Fang's friend, also had a stroke. I met Mrs. Ma's husband on my way here."

"Uh-huh." Da Long had nothing more to say. He clearly had no idea what Paul was getting at. Paul didn't know himself.

"It's strange, isn't it? Two friends, two strokes, within two weeks."

Da Long poured the dirty soapy water out of the washtub, ignoring him. Paul had the feeling that, this morning, he was one of the people whom Da Long thought could not be of any use.

"Tell me, are there any people in this village who eat cats?"

"I don't think so. Chicken, woodlice, and fish, yes, but no dogs or cats," Da Long said, lighting a cigarette.

Paul sat on the steps leading into the house, feeling at a loss. Perhaps he was on the completely wrong track. Perhaps the cats had nothing to do with the sickness. But what else did Mrs. Ma and Min Fang have in common? They drank the same water and ate rice and vegetables from the same fields, but so did the whole village. Suddenly he remembered the name of the place he had been racking his brains to recall for the last two days. A fishing village in Japan. Why hadn't it come to him sooner? He got the pen and notebook out of his backpack and wrote it down.

"Did you say fish?"

Da Long sucked at the cigarette stub between his lips and nodded. "Min Fang and Mrs. Ma often went fishing together."

"Where?"

"At the lake."

"You didn't go?"

"Hardly ever."

"And your neighbors, the Zhuos?"

Da Long shook his head.

Paul thought for a minute. "What did you do with the fish?"

"Ate them, of course."

"How far is the lake from the village?"

"Forty-five minutes on foot. It takes longer to get back. On good days the buckets were heavy with fish."

"Is it easy to find it?"

"You go down the alleyway in front of the house, straight down. After about two hundred yards you get to the end of the village and it becomes a footpath. Just keep walking and you'll eventually see it."

"Is it in an industrial area?"

Da Long smiled. "Quite the opposite. There's nothing but fields and a few bamboo groves all around. Why are you interested in the lake?"

"Just asking. I like fishing too."

"Try your luck if you like. Min Fang's fishing rod is right there next to the house."

Paul filled his water bottle, borrowed a faded old Mao cap from Da Long to protect him from the sun, and set off.

He followed the path that Da Long had described, and in half an hour, he found himself on the brow of a ridge of hills. In the valley before him was a lake that snaked through the landscape almost like a wide river. Paul guessed it was a good two miles long and two or three hundred yards wide. There were reeds growing almost all around the edge of the lake. Paul left the path and climbed the down the steep hill to the water. He found a gray-brown liquid that had a shimmering silver-blue film over it in places. There were patches of red, yellow, blue, and white everywhere by the lake, plastic bags that the wind had blown into the reeds. Paul trudged through the long grass. After a few steps there was such a peculiar crunching underfoot that it gave him goose bumps. He had stumbled across a family of ducks, all dead. Paul could make out the carcasses of the mother duck and four young ones; he had stepped on the bones of the fifth. Not far away lay the carcass of a bird. And another. A little farther away, he saw the skeleton of a larger animal, probably a dog. Paul took a few deep breaths. The air was filled with the sweetish smell of decay. He cleared his way through a bamboo grove, picked up a broken-off bamboo rod, and went over to the water, pushing it into various places in the reed beds without really knowing what he was looking for. He felt more and more uneasy with each passing minute, and he gradually began to feel that he had been mistaken that morning. There was more at stake than a wasted day. He emptied his water bottle, put his hand into the water, and grabbed some mud, which he put into the bottle. Then he held it in the lake until it was full. He didn't know exactly why he was doing this, but it was the only thing he could think of.

The ground by the lake grew more and more marshy and difficult to walk on. After half an hour he had reached a bend from which he could see to the end of the lake. There he saw a factory with two high chimneys, out of which white smoke was rising. He tried to walk on farther, but every step made a loud squelching noise and he kept sinking to his ankles, deeper and deeper into the sludge. Eventually he gave up and turned back. The bank on the other side looked better, but it was too late for that now. He had to speak to Da Long urgently.

About an hour later, he was back in Da Long's courtyard, using some water from the fountain to clean his shoes. Suddenly the loud groaning of someone who was straining beyond human limits sounded from inside the house.

"I'm back. Can I help you?" Paul called out, hurrying in.

Da Long stood by his wife's bed, holding her right leg in his hand, trying to bend it. There was a mixture of shame and relief in his eyes.

"M-m-maybe," he said, completely out of breath. "Th-th-the doctors said that I should move her limbs for a few minutes twice a day, otherwise she would get completely stiff. But her muscles are getting more and more rigid. Today is especially bad. Could you try?"

Paul stood on the other side of the bed and lifted Min Fang's left leg carefully. It was thin and pale, and so light that it made him feel nauseated. It made him think about his son. He too had been horribly emaciated in the final weeks of his life: his skin had grown paler and paler from day to day, and the blue veins beneath it had shown so clearly that his skin seemed transparent. The eight-year-old body had been so light that Paul had had no problems lifting it with one arm. It was no longer the weight of life, Paul had thought then, it was the weight of death that he held in his hands. He hesitated.

"Y-y-you have to try to bend the knee and push the thigh b-b-backwards, ten times in a row."

Paul took a firmer hold and tried to bend Min Fang's leg and push it toward her stomach. Da Long was right. Even though her leg was thin, it was much more difficult to bend than he had imagined. He had to use so much force that he was worried he would break her bones. Min Fang groaned quietly each time.

"I-I-I don't know if it hurts her," Da Long said. "But the doctors say it has to be done."

After Paul had managed ten bends he put her leg down, walked around to the other side of the bed, and rested for a bit.

"Da Long, tell me, how many sick people are there in the village?"

"N-n-no idea. At our age everyone is sick in one way or another, aren't they? Why are you asking?"

Paul nodded and started on Min Fang's right leg.

"Didn't you catch any fish?" Da Long asked.

Paul shook his head. "No. I didn't even try. To be honest, it didn't look very inviting."

"Why not?"

"There were more than a dozen animal carcasses around. Ducks. Birds. There were only skeletons left of some others. I couldn't tell what they were."

Da Long did not react.

"There were lots of dead fish in the lake. Is that normal?"

"Min Fang told me about it. She said it had grown worse in the last few months."

"But she kept on fishing there?"

"She said the fish didn't taste any different than before."

Paul did not know if he should ask the next question. After a while he said, "What kind of factory is that at the end of the lake?" hoping to sound casual.

"What factory?"

"At the far end of the lake I saw two chimneys with smoke rising, a few buildings, and a wall."

"Oh, that one. It's been there so long that I completely forgot about it. It's become a part of the landscape. Golden Dragon. It produces cough syrup, cough lozenges, and all kinds of teas to relieve colds."

"Are you sure? How do you know that?"

He shrugged as if to say that everyone who lived there knew that.

Paul looked at him carefully. Why should this tortured man lie to him? But this was China; his friend Zhang used to say that since the Cultural Revolution all Chinese were suspicious of one another. Distrust had become such a part of society's fabric that even after three decades of traveling and working in China, Paul found it often hard to tell whom he could believe and whom not.

"How long have you been eating fish from the lake?"

"I've no idea. For years. Min Fang loves fish. All kinds. And it costs nothing."

Paul was confused by the answers. If there was something wrong with the fish, why was it only the women who were falling ill? Mrs. Zhuo went along to the lake only rarely; what was she ill with? How was it that the other villagers, who had fished there more often, had stayed well until now?

"And you?"

"I don't," Da Long said.

"Didn't you just say that you ate the fish she caught?"

"Min Fang does. I don't. I'm allergic. I get a red rash all over my body."

Paul was so surprised that he nearly dropped Min Fang's leg. "Does Mrs. Ma's husband get it too?" he asked, struggling to conceal his excitement.

"No. But he hates fish. Doesn't touch it."

"What did you do with the rest of the fish that Min Fang caught?"

"If there was any left, we sold it for a few yuan in the village. We didn't get much for it. The cats got the rest."

Paul thought for a moment. "The Zhuos were regular customers, yes?"

"The best. How did you know that?"

"I guessed."

He carefully laid Min Fang's leg back on the blanket and wiped the sweat away from his forehead. The fish. It had been no more than a suspicion until now, even though it became more and more certain with everything that Paul found out. What could be so toxic in them that their consumption brought people to the verge of death?

Da Long sat at the end of the bed and massaged his wife's feet. Paul stood by the nightstand and watched him massage her heels, the balls of her feet, and every single toe with concentration and care. Min Fang's breathing was labored and rattling.

"Can you give her some water? It's next to you. I think she's thirsty," Da Long said.

Paul put his hand carefully under Min Fang's head, lifted it a little, put the glass to her lips, and let some water trickle into her mouth clumsily.

"Be careful," Da Long warned. "She mustn't choke."

Paul had been much too quick with the water. Min Fang could not swallow quickly enough, so most of it ran out of the corners of her mouth and down her chin and throat, or trickled onto her pajamas. Paul could see her body struggling, then she suddenly began to cough and gag. Just a little at first, then more and more violently. She was choking. Paul tried to lift her upper body upright, but it got stiffer and stiffer and was almost impossible to move. Da Long rushed over to help, and both of them tried to get her to sit up. He slapped his wife hard on the back and screamed, "Min Fang! Min Fang!"

Her coughing fit worsened with every second. Her pale face grew red; she was struggling for air.

"Please! Min Fang, breathe. Breathe. Breathe. Please. Please," he pleaded. Da Long's voice was full of fear and chilled Paul to the bone.

The soothsayer's prediction darted into Paul's mind. The first sentence had been: *You will take life.*

Not *kill*, not *murder*, but *take life.*

Paul started panicking. A rigid human body was having a seizure in his arms, gasping for air and struggling for its life. It was his fault. One glass of water. *Water.* He had been told to stay away from water. Through his carelessness, the first part of the prophecy would come true.

Da Long grabbed ahold of his wife, put his arms around her torso from behind, and pressed hard several times on her stomach and chest. They waited. Time stood still. No longer one of the living, not yet one of the dead. After a few endless seconds her coughing grew less frequent, she stopped retching, and they heard her draw breath again. Before long, her breathing had stabilized.

Paul staggered over to the sofa, completely exhausted.

"Y-y-you're trembling all over," Da Long said. "Sit down. I'll get some water."

"I'm terribly sorry," Paul whispered. "It was my fault. I wasn't being careful."

"N-n-no," Da Long said, trying to calm him. "She often chokes, even with me. But it's not been so bad before. We were lucky." He looked at Paul for a long moment, then added, "You were just almost as frightened as I was. Is everything all right? You don't look well."

Paul emptied a glass of water in one gulp. "Thank you. I'll be fine in a moment."

Da Long sat down next to him on the sofa. He was trembling too. His shirt was soaked with sweat and clung to his chest; his full lips had compressed themselves into two narrow lines; his left eye was twitching uncontrollably. They huddled next to each other in silence, each absorbed in his own memories. Paul stared at the digital clock beneath the television. The glow of the light and the reliable way in which the three followed the two and the four the three soothed him.

Da Long was the first to emerge from his thoughts. "Where did you learn to speak Chinese so well?"

"I've lived in Hong Kong for over thirty years," Paul said, turning to him. "I learned Cantonese there. I've liked Mandarin ever since I was a child. I traveled in China a great deal in the eighties and nineties. That's how I learned my Mandarin."

"What did you do in China?"

Paul hesitated. Would Da Long get suspicious when he found out that he was sitting here with a former journalist?

"I was a reporter for American and British newspapers and also for publications in China." When Da Long did not react, he added, "Later on, I was an interpreter and adviser to Western companies who wanted to invest in China."

"And now?"

"You mean, what I do, or how I make a living?"

"Isn't that the same thing?"

"Not for me."

"Then you must be very rich."

"What makes you think that?"

"Only rich people make this distinction."

Paul wanted to object, to tell him that he was wrong, but then he realized where he was. From Da Long's perspective, he was really an extremely wealthy man. A question of perspective. "I live from the returns on my savings. I live simply. In Hong Kong no one would call me rich. In China yes."

"And what do you do?"

No one had asked him this question for a long time.

"What do I do . . . ?" Where to start? "I had a son. He died. Since then . . ." Paul did not know how he should put it in words. "Since then . . . since then, I don't do much."

Da Long looked at him for a long time. There was no suspicion in his look, more wonder and curiosity, perhaps respect too, but Paul did not know him well enough to be certain. His face had stopped twitching, and his lips were no longer drawn thin.

"When a person's true self has not emerged, it will surely do so during the mourning period."

"Who said that?"

"Confucius."

Paul closed his eyes. An inner voice repeated the words; he let his head fall back on the leatherette couch. If this statement by the Chinese philosopher was right, when he looked back on what had unfolded in the last three years, he had to ask himself what kind of person he was. Someone who could not let go? Who enjoyed wallowing in self-pity? Someone who knew no limits?

No limits to his ability to grieve.

No limits to his ability to isolate himself.

No limits to his fear, to his rage, to his longing.

No limits to his ability to love.

He had always been comfortable with extremes. He had left home at nineteen after his mother had taken her own life, and had never seen his father again. He had left the country he was a citizen of, according to his passport, and had returned only once, for his father's funeral. He had lost his last job as a reporter for an American magazine because he had poured his beer over the visiting chief editor during an argument at the Foreign Correspondents' Club. After that he had never written a line as a journalist again. After the birth of his son, he had wanted to be a father to the exclusion of all else; he turned down commissions and job offers and cared for the child while his wife pursued her career at the bank.

He did not know a middle way. Hungry for love. Hungry for life.

Maybe, he thought, he had withdrawn not so much from life after Justin's death as from the community. Perhaps his true self had chosen the isolation of those years because it was able to emerge only that way, in that period of time. What was closer to living than to press up against oneself and look one's own truth in the eye?

"I've never thought about it that way. Confucius may be right."

"Then you really must be rich." When Da Long saw that Paul did not understand what he meant, he added, "Anyone whose true self emerges is rich, isn't he?" Da Long smiled mischievously. He got up, went to the kitchen, and returned a few minutes later with a pot of tea, two cups, and a bowl of roasted watermelon seeds.

"And you?" Paul asked.

"I'm an engineer. After the Cultural Revolution I went to college and worked first in a military factory in Sichuan, then for a company in Yiwu that manufactured tools. I took early retirement a year ago."

"And?"

"There's no and."

Paul leaned his head to one side and gave him a look of disbelief. "That must be the short version."

"You'll get the details another time," Da Long said firmly, but not in an unfriendly way.

Paul wondered for a moment if he should ask Da Long about Christine, but decided in the end that the reasons for the silence in the Wu family were none of his business. If Da Long wanted to, he would tell him about it at some point.

He remembered the fortune-teller's words instead. "Do you believe in Chinese astrology?"

"What makes you ask that?"

"Just wondered."

Just wondered? A questioning look.

"The short version of my reply. You'll get the details another time," Paul said.

Da Long smiled. "When two people have the same sense of humor, the house of friendship stands on good foundations."

"Confucius?"

"No. Da Long."

It was the first time that Paul had seen him laugh heartily.

"I think that there are lots of things between heaven and earth that we can't explain but that are true all the same. Whether astrology is one of those things, I cannot say." Da Long looked at the clock and stood up. "I have to prepare a lotion for Min Fang."

Paul followed him into the tiny kitchen, where Da Long fetched an old kitchen scale and carefully adjusted the weights. He took a handful of herbs out of a porcelain jar and weighed out fifty grams of it. He did the same with dried roots, leaves, mushrooms, and various unidentifiable animal body parts. Then he poured everything into a pot full of water and brought it to the boil, stirring all the time. Soon steam rose from the pot; it smelled unpleasant and stung the nostrils.

"A Chinese doctor prescribed this mixture. I have to rub it into her limbs three times a day. It's supposed to help relax the cramping of her muscles."

He poured the brew into a bowl and back into the pot again, repeating the procedure until it had cooled a little. Then he went to the bed, pushed the blankets aside, carefully rolled Min Fang's pajama pants up, wet a cloth with the black liquid, and started rubbing it against her legs with slow, rhythmic movements. Next came the arms. Then Da Long brushed his wife's hair, trimmed her toenails and fingernails, laid her back on the bed, and massaged her feet. While he was doing all this they did not exchange a word. Paul was not even sure if Da Long was still aware of his presence. Suddenly there was a sound of gas passing through. A brown stain spread on the bed linen. Da Long sighed briefly.

"Can I help you?" Paul asked, knowing that his offer didn't sound convincing.

Da Long gave him a long look and, to his relief, shook his head. It was clear that he would prefer to be alone.

Paul took his leave and promised to be back the next day at eleven on the dot. He went in search of his taxi.

What do you believe in? He thought about Justin, about Christine's question, and about her brother. Maybe, Paul thought, he would now say to his son and to her that he believed in human beings. In some of them, at least.

———

Back in Yiwu, he hurried to eat in a Hunanese restaurant opposite the hotel. He ordered "Chairman Mao's Favorite," pork with a thick rind and chunks of fat as big as his thumb, in a thick sweet-and-spicy sauce. He downed his beer quickly and was back in his room at the computer in less than half an hour. It would be a short night. There were 221,284 hits under the name of the Japanese fishing village. Paul crawled his way thought the endless World Wide Web, going deeper into the universe of letters, images, and numbers with each link. He made notes, compared figures, searched through archives, read scientific papers, and wrote emails to Christine and his friend Zhang in Shenzhen. Zhang had been made the head of the homicide department in Shenzhen the previous year after a corruption scandal, and he had been so busy lately that the two men had hardly seen each other. The last time he had visited Paul on Lamma, a few weeks earlier, they had cooked a meal together and promised again to meet more often. Now

Paul urgently needed a contact in Shanghai from him. He would text him by tomorrow morning at the latest. He could count on Zhang.

Paul made a few calls to a professor at Mainz University, and had a long conversation with another in San Diego. He had gathered enough information for the next two or three days. After everything that he had read and learned, the diagnosis of a stroke in Min Fang's case had to be wrong. Was it deliberate or due to incompetence? Shortly after five a.m., Paul finally went to bed. He switched off the light, exhausted, and fell into a deep, dreamless sleep.

Da Long was incredibly tense. He paced the house restlessly, unable to be still for even a moment. The twitch in his left eye was back, and he stammered even more while speaking than he had done during the reunion with his sister. Paul tried to distract him by asking a few questions, but received only monosyllabic replies. He sat on the couch, drinking tea and eating roasted pumpkin seeds, wary of being drawn into Da Long's agitation. The fear, the panic attacks before consultations with doctors. The ever-present desire for a miracle. The disappointments. The hope that kept resurfacing. He would never forget any of that. As though it were yesterday.

Dr. Zhou stepped into the courtyard at half-past eleven as arranged. He was a tall, gaunt man, wearing rimless spectacles, and even without speaking, he radiated calm and professional authority. He looked to Paul to be in his late thirties. He greeted them briefly, not in an unfriendly fashion, but with few words, sticking to the minimum. It was clear from his manner that by paying this visit he was doing a friend or acquaintance a not inconsiderable favor, one that he most probably expected to be returned.

He listened respectfully but impatiently to Da Long's description of the first symptoms of the illness and how it progressed. Then he took a small flashlight, a small hammer, a tongue depressor, and an ophthalmoscope out of his bag and went over to the bed. Da Long and Paul followed him.

"How are you?" he asked Min Fang, not expecting a reply.

"Can you tell me what your name is?" He felt her neck, pulled her eyelids up, and peered at her eyes.

"Are you in pain?" Dr. Zhou opened her mouth carefully with a wooden stick, turned her head from one side to the other, lifted it slightly, and held it in his hand for a moment, as though he were feeling how heavy a fruit was. He lifted her arm and bent it until her fingers touched her chest, then laid it back on the blanket. Paul could see that Da Long was watching every movement keenly, and could guess what he was thinking: the desire for a miracle outweighed the suspicion. A loving heart. Exploitable, easily led astray. Defenseless against the promise of hope.

"Is anyone there? Can you hear me?" The doctor walked around the bed, testing the reflexes in her knees and feet with the small hammer. He wrinkled his brow in a worried way and asked to see the documentation from the hospital. Da Long passed him a big brown envelope. Dr. Zhou opened it, took the test results and the CAT scans out, and held the images against the light, looking at each one of them in turn for a long time with great concentration. He put them aside, skimmed the written findings and the list of medications administered, looked at results of the tests on the blood, cerebrospinal fluid, and electrical activity in the brain, and finally put everything back in the envelope.

Da Long looked at him expectantly.

"Your wife is suffering from an irreversible, aggressive degenerative disease of the brain."

I'm sorry to have to tell you. Da Long said nothing, and Paul could see that he was not in the position to ask any questions. This was why Paul had stayed.

"How do you know that?" Paul asked.

"Because from everything that I see, a stroke is completely out of the question. There is also no indication of a tumor in the scans. The symptoms and the way the illness progressed are clear. Is there any hereditary disease in this woman's family that affects the brain?"

Da Long shook his head slightly. He reached out to lean on a chair, then sat down.

"To be absolutely sure, we have to get an MRI scan. But that can only be done in Shanghai. It's very expensive and not necessary. It will only confirm my diagnosis, not help your wife. Recovery is out of the question. The brain has been irreversibly damaged. No treatment or medication in the world can bring her back."

"Are you quite positive?" Paul asked.

"Yes, completely."

Paul found the certainty in Dr. Zhou's manner more and more jarring. The doctors who had treated his son in Hong Kong, especially Dr. Li, the oncologist, had been older; they knew that the human being was a mystery that had to be treated with respect, humility even, in full knowledge that every answer led only to new questions. There was not a hint of that in Dr. Zhou.

Dr. Zhou continued. "It's difficult to make a prognosis. She could live on for several years in this condition or die in two weeks."

"Might there be other medications that—"

"No," the neurologist interrupted him. "You can give her something for her cramps and some pain relief, but you're doing that already. Of course, there's the matter of whether this is the right place for her. But that is a decision for the family, not a medical one, if you understand what I mean."

"What awareness does she have of her surroundings?"

"None."

"Will she get worse?"

"From a neurological point of view, it can hardly get worse. Inflammation of the lungs is a problem; of the skin too. Her husband must take care that she doesn't get bedsores. I can't tell you anything more than that."

Paul couldn't think of any other questions. He looked at Da Long, who was staring into space expressionlessly.

Dr. Zhou packed his things, politely declined an invitation to stay for lunch, and spared them platitudes, like how sorry he was not to be able to give them a better diagnosis. It was clear to see that he wanted to get back to Shanghai as quickly as possible.

Da Long walked the doctor and Paul out into the courtyard.

Pretending to have forgotten something, Paul darted back into the house. He went over to Min Fang's bed, pulled a clump of gray and black hair out of the hairbrush on the nightstand, tucked it into an envelope that he had brought from the hotel, and put it in his backpack.

He found it difficult to leave Da Long on his own, but he had to be back in Shanghai by five p.m., and Dr. Zhou had offered to give him a lift. Paul was sure that he and Da Long would see each other again—if his hunch was right, probably in a few days. A brief good-bye, and a promise to be in touch with Da Long from Shanghai before he flew back to Hong Kong.

Dr. Zhou drove a black Audi, a model favored by senior party cadres. The car was so new that the interior still smelled of rubber, plastic, and glue. He drove it quickly and skillfully down the narrow roads and wove his way between the container trucks on the highway so speedily that it was like taking part in a car rally.

Paul held on tight to the door handle and slid uneasily from side to side in his seat. "Great car. What's the horsepower?" he asked, hoping to strike up a conversation, though he could not be less interested in cars.

"No idea. It's my wife's car," Zhou replied.

"Is she also a doctor?"

"No. A Realtor. Doctors can't afford Audis. They drive Passats."

"Which hospital are you at?"

"People's Hospital Number One."

"Are you a good friend of Da Long's son?"

"Yes. We have known each other for a couple of years. He bought two apartments from my wife. We see each other often."

"I thought he worked for an insurance firm," Paul said, curious.

"He does. He made a lot of money on the stock market and invested in property."

"Did he tell you that two other older women in the village fell ill with the same symptoms?"

"No." Zhou did not sound as though he wanted to turn around on the spot to go back to examine them.

"It's strange, isn't it?"

"Since I didn't see them, I can't say if there are similarities. To be honest, it sounds unlikely."

"How do people get neurological diseases like that?"

The doctor shrugged. "Hard to say. Possibly something genetic that Da Long doesn't know anything about. If we were in England and if Mrs. Wu worked in an abattoir or ate a lot of meat, I wouldn't rule out mad cow disease. But BSE doesn't exist in China."

"Can cats carry the virus?"

A shake of the head.

"And fish?"

Dr. Zhou laughed out loud. "How should fish carry mad cow disease? It's not called that for nothing."

"Could it be something quite different? Poisoning, for example?"

"Are you a family friend or a detective?"

Paul ignored the question. "Yes or no?"

"I'm not a toxicologist, but there are certainly nerve poisons that can have those effects. But why would the old man want to poison his wife, and with what?"

Paul's gaze fell on the clock on the dashboard. If they didn't get stuck in traffic, he would get to the laboratory that his friend Zhang had found to do the tests for him before it closed. And with any luck, he would have an answer to this and other entirely different questions in no more than forty-eight hours.

VIII

The meeting of Death's companions is drawing to a close. Da Long can hardly sit still. On the stage, a group of young girls in green uniforms is performing the dance of loyalty in honor of the Great Chairman. A man steps up to the podium, takes ahold of the microphone, and raises his voice. It is a powerful, vigorous voice, one that knows neither doubt nor moderation. It accuses. It makes demands. It threatens. The man hurls the sounds at them; he spits them out, hard, aggressive noises that fly over their heads like the cracks of a whip, punctuated by silences that increase the tension.

Da Long is among the hundreds of boys and girls squatting in long rows on the ground, listening intently. They don't miss a thing; they clamor to turn the words into actions, waving their red books in the air and jumping up after the last sentence. They are indignant, full of rage. They shout loudly as one and stream into the street, forming groups, each of which is allocated two leaders and at least six strong young men. They swarm the length and the breadth of the city. No one will escape them today.

They are young; some barely more than twelve years old, but their faces are solemn; everything childlike has vanished from their eyes.

They are at war. At war against the old world. At war against old ways of thinking. Old culture. Old ways of doing things. Old habits.

They know their orders: stamp out the old, find the enemies. Enemies of the revolution. Enemies of the Great Helmsman. Who are everywhere. In the schools, in the factories, in the universities. In the home next door. In the families. Their own too.

"A revolution," the man on the podium had declared, "is not the same as asking people to dinner or asking them to write an essay or paint a picture or do some delicate handiwork; it cannot be something so measured or noble. A revolution is an uprising, an act of violence, with which one class overthrows another."

A revolution was not for doubters. A revolution recognized only two sorts of people: winners and losers. Da Long does not want to belong to the losers. He has seen what happens to them.

He walks down the main street with his group. They pass the office of the City Committee, and after a few minutes they are in front of the building they have been looking for. A building like any other. The plaster is crumbling from its gray façade, and laundry is hanging out to dry from the windows. In the communal kitchen on the ground floor, an old woman is chopping spring onions; she freezes with fear when she sees the Red Guards approach.

Da Long stays in the hallway while the others storm up the stairs. He hears the pounding of their footsteps on the wooden steps. He hears them hammering on a few doors, the way they keep running upstairs, higher and higher, in search of their victim. He knows what will happen any moment; he's witnessed it firsthand often enough. They will hunt the enemy down in his hiding place. They will sweep the books from the shelves, take them out from under the bed, behind the closet, or under the floorboards if necessary. They will find the radio and destroy it, and the little altar and the handwritten notes on the works of Confucius. They will interrogate the wife and child, and they will not believe their lies. They will beat the man and the woman too, if they do not confess to the crimes he has committed. If they try to deny what cannot be denied.

They will drag him down the stairs, by the hair if needed, so that a people's tribunal can sentence him. Every class enemy gets the punishment that he deserves.

It is pleasantly cool and dim on the ground floor. In the hallway, there are bicycles propped up against the wall, and under the stairs is a wheelbarrow with leftover lumps of coal; the door into the court-yard is at the end of the corridor. It is open, and light falls through it into the hallway. He knows this hallway. He knows it like no other. He walks toward the courtyard. With careful little steps. He goes further and stops at the doorway. He can still hear the voices from the top floor. They fill the whole house. They fill the whole courtyard. They fill his whole body. But they calm him too, because they prove that he is not alone.

Then it is quiet. And even more quiet. A quick intake of breath that signals something cataclysmic. A dull thud. In the courtyard, right in front of his feet, lies a human being. Strangely twisted. A dark red liquid is trickling out of the mouth, flowing over the paving stones, and seeping into the gaps between them. It is a man. It is his father.

One of twelve enemies of the Great Proletarian Cultural Revolu-tion who died violent deaths in those few hours in his city. Two were beaten to death. Four jumped from roofs or out of windows. One hanged himself. One drowned himself. One was run over by a bus while trying to flee. One of them burned to death in the flames of a library from which he was trying to save an armful of books. One of them broke his neck when his strength gave out and he lost his balance and toppled from the stage onto the street after ten hours of standing and waiting with his hands tied behind his back and a placard around his neck with the words I AM AN INCORRIGIBLE COUNTERREVOLUTIONARY on it.

The memory of that day does not occupy Da Long's thoughts for long. There are more important things than family. The good of the party. The bloody battles between rival Red Guards. The times they live in demand sacrifices from everyone. To mourn that day would be a sign of decadent bourgeois thinking. A revolution cannot be a measured or a noble thing.

"Hard times create hard men," President Zhou Enlai declares. Or is it the other way around: Hard men create hard times?

Many years later, Da Long will sit with Min Fang in a hut in the mountains of Sichuan, listening to the snow fall outside. It is dark and bitterly cold; she sings and recites poems to him. He will always remember a chapter from the *Dao De Jing* by Laozi:

The human being, when he is born,
is soft and weak,
and when he dies
is rigid and strong.
Plants are born
soft and tender,
and when they die,
are withered and stiff.
Therefore those who are rigid and strong
are Death's companions.
The soft and weak
are Life's companions.

Old wisdom. Classical Chinese wisdom, over two thousand years old. He listened to the lines and remembered the voices in the courtyard. The intake of breath that signaled something cataclysmic. The cold breath of death.

If anyone had shown him the poem before or if he had stumbled across it by chance in one of his parents' books or in a book at school, it would not have meant anything to him. Old culture. Old habits. He would have torn it up or burned it, and denounced the owner.

They had been Death's companions.

Hard times create hard people.

————

Half a year after his father's death, he was sent to a far-flung corner of Sichuan Province for further training as a revolutionary. The party had decided to send the "young intellectuals" from the towns and cities, all those in high school and college, and all children of college graduates, to the countryside en masse. At fourteen he was actually still too young, but he volunteered, and because he had already shown impressive proof of his revolutionary fervor as a young Red Guard, he was allowed to become one of the youngest to follow Mao's marching orders. He did not ask himself what Mao Zedong's aim was with this movement, if it represented Mao's intent to disperse the Red Guards, who had become more and more powerful and difficult for him to control, or if it was Mao's final attempt to realize his dream of the "new man." There had been only one answer for him: the Great Chairman was trying to create a purer, better human being, and Da Long was part of the privileged generation that Mao had designated for this fate.

Along with eight hundred other young people, Da Long arrived in a village about two days' journey on foot from the nearest town. The first thing they saw was white columns of smoke that rose almost vertically into the skies. Before them, in the middle of a craggy, green mountainous landscape, was a collection of gray-brown shacks and houses spreading out from both banks of a river. Terraced fields surrounded the plain.

They were shown to a hut on the edge of the village. It had neither electricity nor running water. The walls of the hut were made of earth, rocks, and straw; stalks of straw were still sticking out in places. There was only one big room, with two raised brick platforms to sleep on; a fire could be lit under them so that the inhabitants wouldn't freeze on cold winter nights.

The villagers were farmers who grew rice, corn, and vegetables. Da Long admired them from the start, and could hardly wait to learn from them. To his astonishment, he realized that the farmers, surly and suspicious people, did not welcome them with open arms, but had a hostile attitude to them. This was especially true of the party secretary, a short, sturdy man with hands like spades, a sharp, piercing gaze, and a long scar on his right cheek. He had survived various political purges unscathed and ruled the community like his own little fiefdom. He did not like any of these young people. To him they were nothing but parasites, weak city folk, the spoiled offspring of the intelligentsia, whom he despised. Whom did Mao have to thank for victory in the People's Revolution? he asked the new arrivals at every opportunity. He left them in no doubt that there was only one answer to this question: the farmers. Not the college students, not the teachers, merchants, or workers. The farmers—men like him.

He disliked Da Long most of all. He thought he was a smart-ass, a typical city kid. Physically weak, clumsy with his hands, and not up to hard manual labor. He was annoyed by the excessive zeal that Da Long, trying to make up for his physical deficiencies, showed at the daily meetings to study the words of the Great Chairman. It gave him pleasure to show everyone in the village that this weakling, who considered himself a young fighter of the revolution, could not adequately complete his tasks. He gave him the heaviest baskets to carry, sent him on the most difficult treks to the most out-of-the-way fields, and made him dig deep ditches until he collapsed with exhaustion and had to be carried back to the hut by the others on piggyback. Even then, when Da Long was recovering on the thin straw bedding, he did not doubt the "revolutionary-spirited countryside dwellers."

The rest of the group soon noticed whom the party secretary had it especially in for, so they limited their contact with Da Long to the strictly necessary. As though he had an infectious disease.

New people, same old behavior.

Two weeks after the Chinese New Year, the party secretary stormed into the hut and planted himself ominously in front of Da Long's straw sleeping space. Where was his little red book with the words of Mao? he asked in a cutting tone.

In my jacket, Da Long replied, jumping up to get it.

Is that so, the man huffed, pulling a dog-eared and filthy book out of his coat pocket, holding it before his nose, and turning the pages with relish. Almost every page was stained with wet patches or muddy black smears, and even the red cover was barely recognizable under brownish-black mud. He had found it lying in the dirt near the river. In the mud! He concluded by flipping the cover open. There were two characters written on it: Da Long.

It must have slipped out of my pocket, Da Long stammered. There was no other explanation.

Don't lie to me, you miserable little rascal, the man shouted, coming so near him that Da Long could feel the warm cigarette stink of his breath in his face. This won't be the end of it, he added, his voice quivering with rage, before turning on his heel and stamping out into the cold.

Two hours later, Da Long found himself sitting opposite not only the party secretary and his two deputies but also the party leaders from the district capital, who were on an inspection tour of the region and just happened to be in the village for two days.

The wet and muddy book was passed from hand to hand to be leafed through and inspected with disapproving looks. The pitiful state of the volume was a clear sign of the young Red Guard's disrespect for the political leadership. Did he have anything to say in his defense?

Da Long said nothing, and they repeated their question. Harsh, brusque voices.

Da Long wanted to reply. He took a deep breath, opened his mouth, and lifted his tongue to the roof of his mouth, but expelled the air without producing any sound that could be understood. He looked into the serious faces of the comrades in front of him. It was a matter of carelessness, an accident, inexcusable, yes, but not deliberate. Nevertheless, he was ready to admit to anything they accused him of and to accept any punishment. Who was he to resist the will of the party? He couldn't help thinking of his father, who was like a fat moth swooping in and setting on his thoughts at this moment. How must he have felt when he heard the Red Guards storming up the stairs? He could not have expected them, or he would have destroyed the papers hidden under the floorboards in the kitchen long ago. Had he any idea who could have betrayed him? What had his final thoughts been?

Da Long was silent for a long time. When his speech finally returned to him he stuttered and spoke in fragments. He repeated vowels involuntarily and struggled to produce the simplest sounds;

he tried with all his might to control his speaking, but he had to make several attempts before he could pronounce the most basic words. Da Long had started stammering.

The party leaders from the city stared at him in amazement. Was this lout pretending, or was he really not able to speak properly? When his speaking did not improve after several minutes, they realized that it wasn't an act, and merely gave him a long and insistent lecture on how to take care of the most precious words that Chinese wisdom had produced in five thousand years of history, the most precious words it would ever produce.

The functionaries left the village, but the stammer stayed. It made him even more of an outsider, one who now often worked alone in the fields and did not exchange a word with another human being for entire days.

A few months after that, eight young people from Chengdu, the capital of the province, arrived. One of them was Min Fang. She was four years older than Da Long and was the daughter of a music teacher and a doctor. This fact, along with her habit of constantly singing or humming songs that neither the farmers nor their leader knew, quickly made her an outsider, though that hardly seemed to bother her.

She was tall and sturdily built, and treated the stammering Da Long like a younger brother who had been a cause of worry to his parents all his life, and whom she had had to take care of from an early age.

She helped him when he collapsed once again during the harvest and the farmers wanted to leave him lying on the ground. She was with him when he fell ill with a lung infection the following winter, dangling between life and death for many days and nights. No longer one of the living, not yet one of the dead. She brought his fever down with cold compresses; she rubbed herbal concoctions into his chest and back. When life finally gained the upper hand and the hunger returned, she shared her thin rice gruel with him so that he would regain his strength more quickly.

She dared to defend him when the party secretary announced at a meeting that Da Long's mother and sister had fled to Hong Kong, and that this was further proof of his dubious class background, which should be punished with additional shifts at work.

They spent more and more time together, planting rice in the water-soaked earth shoulder to shoulder, harvesting the same fields, washing their clothes in the river together; each volunteered to join the other in the long journey on foot to the nearest town when something was needed urgently. Big sister. Little brother. Hand in hand.

She listened patiently to him when it took him several attempts to finish a sentence. She assured him that he had all the time in the world, even when he seemed to be stammering out the same meaningless sounds over and over again. He trusted her; gradually, in her presence, the words began to come more easily.

At some stage, something in him changed. He began to notice whom Min Fang spoke to and for how long, whom she smiled at, and whom she offered to help. His heart began to pound more fiercely when he saw her. He was suddenly impatient to see her, and felt restless when she turned up late to work in the field. He realized how beautiful she was. It was such a sudden discovery to him that it was as if he were seeing her for the first time. The little dimples in her cheeks when she laughed. Her big light-brown eyes that could shine so bright. Her long black hair that she wore in two thick braids, her strong arms and legs, which rippled with muscle when she lifted the heavy baskets filled to the brim with rice. Her firm breasts, which he could see when she bent low in front of him while planting rice, the memory of which kept him awake with excitement at night when he lay on the straw.

He had started to love her without realizing it.

She did not reject his courtship, but she set the pace at which they grew closer. Sometimes she avoided him, sometimes she teased him, and sometimes she allowed him a furtive kiss. Clumsy and careful. He did not detect the slightest uncertainty in her. It was as if she had seen this coming for a long time.

On one of their marches to their town, on one of the dreadful sweltering summer nights in Sichuan when even the animals cannot sleep, the younger brother became a lover.

It remained their secret for more than two years, carefully tended in dark moonless nights in the fields, in the woods, in rain shelters. When they were not alone, it was expressed in brief glances of longing, in tender touches that appeared accidental. Two years in which not a day passed that they did not see each other. In which the stammer grew less pronounced with every passing week until it disappeared altogether. For the first time in his life, Da Long had something that belonged only to him, that he did not want to share with anyone else; he, who had not distinguished the words "mine" and "yours" until then.

It remained their secret until the son of the party secretary saw them making love in a field instead of weeding, and told his father everything. The very next day, the party secretary called a gathering of the Committee for the Defense of the Revolution, as well as the rest of the village. They met in a large circle in the square at the end of the bridge where the rice was normally laid out to dry. In the middle were Min Fang and Da Long on two wooden stools. The Party Secretary stood in front, inviting the comrades to criticize them. Person after person stepped forward and poured scorn on their heads. Breaking the laws of the village and of the party. Undermining public morality. Their addiction to pleasure. Their profligacy. Their bourgeois egoism, which put their own lust over the common good.

After a dozen tirades that seemed never-ending, they were to admit their guilt and practice self-criticism. Da Long would have done it if he had understood why he should. He owed his life to Min Fang. Why should he have to justify himself? For having stopped stammering with her help? For desiring her? For loving her? For wishing that she could become his wife tomorrow, even though marriage was only permitted from the age of twenty-five, and he still had six years to wait? Was that why he was sitting there on this stool letting himself be cursed as a mangy cur, vermin, and unscrupulous riffraff?

No. A loud, clear, and firm no. Not said out loud yet, but sounding unmistakably within him.

It was the tentative beginning of his own Cultural Revolution, not the great proletarian one, but a small and quiet one. One that took place not on the streets but in the heart. One that damaged no human beings, only the immovability of his belief in the mighty words of the Great Chairman. In mighty words altogether. It would be a long path, his personal Long March, but even that had begun with a first step.

Da Long wanted to stand up; he prayed that his voice would not let him down this time. How credible could an accused person be if he stammered while defending himself? He wanted to fight back, to reject all the accusations as false; he could think of nothing else. Then he heard Min Fang speaking hesitantly.

Yes, they had made a mistake. Yes, they had been frivolous and dissolute. Yes, they had let themselves be carried away by lust and not shown the proper class consciousness. They deserved the comrades' scorn. The fault was not Da Long's but hers alone.

When he tried to interrupt her she hissed at him to be quiet.

She was four years older, Min Fang said, and she should have known better. She had let herself be overcome by short-lived romantic feelings, which, in the words of the Great Helmsman, were well known to be as fleeting as the light of a candle in a storm. She lacked discipline and self-control; this was a result of her decadent bourgeois upbringing by a doctor and a teacher. A music teacher! That was why she was here. To learn from the revolutionary farmers. To become a reliable servant of the party. Her mistakes would only spur her on to work more and to be harder on herself. She was prepared not to exchange a single word with Da Long for the next six months, to ignore him like a horse ignores flies. She was ready to accept any punishment that the Committee for the Defense of Revolution decreed, but she pleaded that they be given another chance. A revolutionary does not fall from heaven, Mao Zedong said; a young revolutionary makes mistakes in his youth. A young revolutionary gets things wrong. That is why he needs the help and the guiding hand of the older and experienced comrades. He is shaped by them, just as the glowing iron is formed by the hammer. She did not want to ask for mercy or forgiveness. Only for the firm, shaping hand of the revolution.

Da Long kept his head lowered; he stared at his knees and barely dared to move. He did not know what to think of her self-criticism. What were those strange Mao quotes that he had never heard of? He hoped that she hadn't been foolhardy enough to simply make them up. If they caught her doing that, he would never see her again. Why was she distancing herself from him so severely? Did she fear the rage of the people so much?

Min Fang's speech did not fall short of its intended effect. The indignant muttering in the village had been silenced; even the party secretary looked thoughtful. He announced that the committee would withdraw for a consultation and make its decision known the next day.

The next morning, he declared that Min Fang and Da Long would have to write detailed self-criticisms, that they were to be given extra shifts, and that they would be in different work units for the next six months; any contact between them in this period was strictly forbidden.

Those six months were the longest of Da Long's life. He saw Min Fang working in other fields from a distance. He sat in the communal kitchen for meals with her but was not allowed to say a word to her. She treated him as if he were invisible. Not a glance, not a gesture, not a smile. He was alone with his insecurity and the question of why she was turning her back on him so fully. The longer he thought about it, the clearer it was to him that there was only one answer: she no longer loved him. Romantic feelings were as fleeting as the light of a candle in a storm, she had said.

Almost two months passed before he finally got a message from her. A small, crumpled note in a short length of bamboo that he found in one of his socks one morning.

He who does not trust enough,
is not to be trusted.
He who does not know eternity,
does harm for no reason.
He who knows eternity is patient,
To be patient is to be impartial.
To be impartial is to be all-embracing.
To be all-embracing is to be heavenly.
To be heavenly is to love.

—Laozi

He was not sure if he fully understood everything she meant to say to him with these lines, but he could be sure of one thing—she loved him. What did these six months matter? Only to those who did not know eternity! Now it was just a question of tenacity and self-discipline, and those qualities he possessed, as long as they were not undermined by suspicion.

Only much later, when he heard stories of Red Guards who had fallen in love and made the mistake of not being willing to self-criticize and distance themselves from each other, leading to them being separated and sent to distant corners of the country, only meeting again, if at all, many years later, did he understand what she had done for him, for them both.

Nearly nine months after they were allowed to resume contact with each other, Min Fang fell pregnant. They knew that she would be forced to have an abortion, by violent means if necessary, but she succeeded in hiding her growing belly under the baggy work clothing until it was too late for that. They went to see the party secretary and asked for a special permit to get married.

He fixed them with his cold, hard gaze for a long moment. Da Long had the feeling that he now knew this man well enough to be able to read his expression. After more than eight years of permanent revolution, endless self-criticisms, and trials, the party secretary was tired. He was thinking about the bother it could cause him to

separate the couple, to hold a tribunal, and to banish the woman
to the city. He was wondering if he might even get the blame if
the scandal became public, if he might be accused of neglecting
his duties. Da Long and Min Fang had speculated that he did not
have anything to gain by bringing charges against them, that he was
sufficiently worn out to take the path of least resistance.

They were right. One week later they were allowed to get married, and two months later, their son, Xiao Hu, Little Tiger, was
born.

———

The sun had set a long time ago. From the courtyard, only darkness
came through the windows now. A little lamp next to Min Fang's
bed was the only light in the room. Da Long had been pacing up
and down in the half darkness for hours. He did not know why all
these memories had suddenly returned.

The day his father died. He did not often think about it. There
had been times in his life when the memory of it seemed to have
been extinguished, but recently it had been recurring often. It must
be age, he thought. The memories appeared like trees in wreaths of
thick mist, clearly visible one moment, then gone again in the next.
It was strange, but he could not think of his father's death in the past
tense, only in the present. He *hears* screams from the top floor. Not
heard. A human being *lies* in front of him. Not *lay*.

It must be because of his sister. She had brought the images back.
It had been a mistake to turn to her in the first place. He had been
stupid and naïve. He had made himself look ridiculous. He had
guessed the truth, but had not wanted to leave any stone unturned.
His sister was not a doctor. She had no money. She could not help
him. The rest did not interest him.

She had told him a little about herself; it had been difficult for
her, and he had found it difficult to follow her. She had expected him
to ask questions; he had not failed to notice that, but he could not.
This was about his wife's life. There was no space inside him for new
stories. Another time. Maybe.

Who could help him now? Dr. Zhou's diagnosis had been as definitive as that of the doctors in Yiwu. Was that it?

Da Long stood still, took a few deep breaths, held his breath, and listened. Even the roar of the highway could no longer be heard. *Hopeless.* The silence in the room was deceptive; he could hear it quite well. The table and the chairs, the walls, and the couch had started speaking, and were whispering just one word: *Hopeless.*

He was on the verge of losing his mind. He was hearing voices where there were none; he had even started stuttering again. He went to Min Fang, felt her forehead with his lips to see if she had a fever, dissolved the two tablets to ease cramping that she had to take in some water every evening, and gave it to her in tiny sips. He looked in the pile of CDs for something suitable and chose the second movement of Schubert's Violin Quintet in C Major. One of her favorite pieces. Yin-Yin had recorded it with four classmates shortly after her mother had fallen ill. Da Long pushed his wife gently to one side of the bed, lay down next to her, switched off the light, and switched on the CD player. Tears came to his eyes every time he heard the first sounds of Yin-Yin's violin on this recording. He had never heard her play like this. Even though he was not the musical expert in the family, he could tell the difference in her playing. Her touch was so gentle and the sounds came from such fathomless depth and with such power that Da Long hardly dared to breathe. It was as though she were playing with all her might against the slow death of her mother.

He heard a quiet groan next to him. Was she in pain, or was she trying to say something to him? It sounded as though she was trying to hum something deep in her throat. How could the doctors claim that there was no light burning in her? Just because some instrument or another displayed wavy lines that were not the same as those of a healthy person. As though the inner life of a person could really be measured. As though we could express what goes on in a brain, a heart, and a soul in numbers, graphs, or tables. What do the healthy know about the world in which the sick live? What do the sighted know about the blind? The well fed about the hungry? What do we know about ourselves?

Da Long laid his head gently between her shoulder and her neck. She had started to smell different. That slightly sweet and sharp typical Min Fang smell, which he had fallen asleep next to every night and had woken up next to every morning for almost forty years, was beginning to fade. She is dying, Da Long thought. A little more with every breath, and he could do nothing to stop it. He wanted to hold her tight, to cling to her. This woman to whom he owed everything.

IX

Xiao Hu was not the kind of person who lingered long over bad news. He regarded his life as too short and too busy, his time as too precious, to spend much time on it. He believed that those who focused on problems saw problems everywhere; those who concentrated on solutions saw solutions. He behaved the same way with good news and bad news. He was convinced that this attitude was one of the reasons he had been practically untouched by negative events and influences through the years, and would remain so in the future. Apart from two exceptions. One of them was his mother's illness.

What his friend the neurologist Zhou had reported to him from his trip to Yiwu had not been a surprise, but the diagnosis had upset him nevertheless, and he did not manage to get it out of his mind for at least a couple of hours. Mama was lost. The light in her snuffed out. She would not come back again.

Xiao Hu sat on the twenty-first floor of the China Life building in Pudong and tried to concentrate. He had to prepare for a meeting of the legal department, which he had been head of for six months, but his thoughts kept sliding off in all kinds of different directions. He looked around his new office, which was bigger than the apartment he had spent his childhood in with Yin-Yin and their parents. That was not even including the adjoining bedroom, which came with his position, and in which his predecessor had slept with all the secretaries in the department. A city landscape stretched out on the other side of the floor-to-ceiling windows; a shiver still passed down his back at the sight of it. Roads, highways, and high-rise buildings as far as he could see. Directly in front of him was the new symbol of Shanghai, the mighty Pearl TV Tower. On the far left was the tallest building in China, the elegant Jin Mao skyscraper. If he stepped right up to the window, he could look directly into the construction sites on which half a dozen further skyscrapers were being constructed at breathtaking speed, a new floor every week. Growth knew no bounds. Not in this city.

On a clear day you could see the tops of the skyscrapers on People's Square glinting in the sun on the other side of the Huangpu River. Not today. Today a gray-brown bell of haze and exhaust fumes hung over the city; even the tower of the Peace Hotel on the Bund could be seen only in outline.

There were two telephones and two computer screens on his desk; one of them showed live information from the Shanghai stock exchange. Alibaba had gone up. Sino Chemical too. PetroChina too. China Mobile by almost 10 percent. On paper, Xiao Hu had grown richer by almost 50,000 renminbi in the last twenty-four hours.

A few notes from Beethoven's Ninth Symphony startled him. It took him a few seconds to find his iPhone among his papers. It was Zhou again.

"I'm sorry. Am I disturbing you?" It was not Zhou's style to wait for an answer. "I totally forgot to tell you something. The Westerner made a strange observation on the way back from Yiwu. He wanted to know if your mother could have been poisoned."

"Poisoned?" Xiao Hu's first thought was that this was an inappropriate joke, but Zhou tended to have a black sense of humor. What an absurd thought. "What made him think that?"

"No idea."

"Did he say poisoned by whom?"

"No. Surely only your father would come into question?"

"That's out of the question," Xiao Hu said firmly. After a brief pause, he added somewhat uncertainly, "Did the symptoms indicate poisoning?"

"Not directly. The brain is damaged. There can be many reasons for that. Maybe poison too. But why should your—"

Xiao Hu interrupted him. "Absolute nonsense! Don't waste any thought on it. Tell me instead if we're meeting for dinner this weekend."

"Sure."

The matter was laid to rest for the moment, and it was much too busy in the office for Xiao Hu to give it much thought. There was one meeting after another, and in the evening, a dinner with clients, followed by drinks in a karaoke bar. Only when Xiao Hu was in bed and unable to sleep did he remember Zhou's phone call. Was it possible that Da Long was responsible for the slow death of his mother? He believed his father capable of many things, almost anything, really. But the murder of his wife? He tried to think of a motive, but he couldn't think of even a shadow of a possible reason or provocation. Unless his family was threatened by another secret; but he thought that was impossible. No, the thought of it was absurd. He had been deceived by his father once, but on this point he was as certain as it was possible to be about another human being.

Why on earth had Paul Leibovitz asked such a question? What indications or observations at his parents' house had led him to have such a thought? Why had he stayed on in Yiwu in the first place instead of flying back to Hong Kong? He would know soon enough. They had arranged to meet after Yin-Yin's performance the next evening, and speak to him then. He held fast to this thought until his eyes closed.

———

His sister's concert took place at 9 Dongping Lu, an old villa that belonged to the conservatory. It was in the French concession, which had been governed by France in the time between 1840 and World War II, when the Americans, the British, the Japanese, and the French had, to all intents and purposes, divided the city among them. Even though that was a shameful period in recent Chinese history, he liked what the Allies, the French in particular, had left behind in terms of architecture and town planning. Entire districts full of *lilong* alleyway communities. Small parks and gardens. Art deco villas and art nouveau buildings. Boulevards of plane trees like the ones he saw in photographs of cities in the South of France. The building on Dongping Lu was one of those constructed in a French style, with its many turrets and bay windows; he recognized it from Yin-Yin's previous concerts. The mansion had been built in the 1930s; the stately driveway, the elegant hall, the old parquet floor, and the walls paneled in dark wood—that was all that was left of the bygone splendor.

The room next to the entrance that served as an auditorium was so full that there were crowds standing behind the last row of seats, right up to the wall. Xiao Hu was happy for his sister that there were so many people there. In the first row, he saw Johann Sebastian Weidenfeller, Yin-Yin's German boyfriend, who had reserved a place for him. Paul Leibovitz was in the next seat, and he introduced himself briefly before the musicians stepped onto the small stage.

Yin-Yin wore a full-length cheongsam in red silk, in a contemporary cut; her shoulders were bare and the collar was buttoned up; the material clung to her skin and the slit in the side of the dress went up way above her knees. Xiao Hu was struck anew by his sister's beauty.

They began with a Mozart violin sonata. In the first five minutes three cell phones rang; one of them was his, but neither Yin-Yin nor the pianist let it disturb them. Xiao Hu closed his eyes and tried to concentrate on the violin and the piano. He had his mother to thank for his love of music; she had patiently taught him how to read music, trained his ear, and given him an enduring interest in Western classical music, which he had far too little opportunity to cultivate in his life now. So he was especially happy to be able to hear his sister perform. Her playing had always been technically highly accomplished, but it had now acquired expressiveness and passion. It was incomprehensible to him that the symphony orchestra had rejected her after her first audition. He envied Yin-Yin and her gift, even though she didn't believe he did. He would have liked to have become a musician himself, but he lacked real talent. And, for quite some time now, the stillness.

As the second Mozart sonata began, the background noise of his thoughts began to drown out the sounds of the violin and the piano. The more peaceful it was around him, the louder the clamor within him grew. It was a nonstop stream of thoughts, plans, associations, and voices coursing through his head. It started in the morning even before he opened his eyes and abated only late in the evenings, enabling him to rest for a few hours. He thought about Alibaba, about his share options, and whether he should exercise them. About his father. About his mother. About the nights when he had lain in bed in the darkness hearing only her singing and the breathing of his sister sleeping beside him. About the comfort of hearing her voice. About an old kitchen table that his mother had sat at in a dim light, wrapping his tattered schoolbooks carefully in old newspaper. He thought about his chances of being transferred to Beijing and about the young woman whom he had fucked twice after the visit to the karaoke bar.

Yin-Yin had told him that there were days when she heard only music in her head and hours in which she thought about nothing at all. Emptiness. Quiet. Unimaginable for Xiao Hu. Horrible. He loved this stream of thoughts in his head, even if he sometimes found it a strain. If stillness was the price for a career as a musician, he did not want to swap places with her.

They waited in front of the villa while Yin-Yin changed. Leibovitz was standing a couple of feet away under a streetlamp, taking a telephone call. Yin-Yin had described him as a peaceful and friendly person. Now he was pacing up and down beneath the light talking in a firm and serious voice. Xiao Hu had no idea what he ought to think of this man. He was not wearing a suit, but a pair of faded jeans and a white short-sleeved shirt. His curly gray hair was so long that he could have tied it back in a ponytail. His body was so fit and toned that it probably made him look younger than he was. His eyes had disconcerted Xiao Hu the most. Paul Leibovitz's gaze was not one of those fleeting, quick ones that looked elsewhere immediately; it had rested on Xiao Hu for so long that he had turned away, unnerved. When Yin-Yin appeared, Paul Leibovitz ended his call, looked more relaxed, and walked over to them.

His sister had reserved a table at Simply Thai, a couple of buildings away. They took their seats in a tiny garden, ordered immediately because they were hungry, and drank a toast. Then they fell into a silence that Xiao Hu soon found uncomfortable. Yin-Yin was exhausted from her concert, and Johann Sebastian Weidenfeller, unusually, seemed not to know what to say. Leibovitz was quiet, waiting.

Weidenfeller found it difficult to tolerate silences. "Have you been to Shanghai before?" he finally said.

Paul nodded.

"Has it changed much since your last visit?"

"No."

"When were you last here?"

"Ten years ago."

Weidenfeller laughed in a pained way.

Paul Leibovitz spread his napkin out and leaned over the table; his eyes wandered from Xiao Hu to Yin-Yin and back again. "I have to tell you both something," he said in a quiet voice. "It's about your mother."

All three of them looked at him, curious.

"She's not suffering from a disease of the nervous system. She's been poisoned."

Yin-Yin looked as though she had been abruptly torn away from the sonata playing in her head. Xiao Hu looked at Paul Leibovitz without saying anything.

It was Weidenfeller who broke the silence again. "What makes you think that?"

"I sent her hair for analysis. The laboratory rang me after the concert. She's suffering from severe mercury poisoning. It's a thousand times over the permitted levels in the US and in Europe. It's practically a miracle that she's still alive."

Xiao Hu was having trouble thinking straight. Who did this man think he was to interfere with their family affairs? What had made him take a hair sample from his mother without asking and send it to a laboratory for analysis without getting anyone's permission?

"Did my aunt ask you to make investigations?" Xiao Hu asked in a sharp tone.

"No," Paul said calmly. "I thought you would be interested to learn what your mother is really suffering from."

Arrogant asshole. Xiao Hu was just able to swallow the words. He started to speak, but his sister gestured curtly to him to stop. "Our father is not a murderer," she said, with a cold look at Leibovitz.

"I'm not saying that he is. You're misunderstanding me. The fish poisoned her. The fish poisoned your cat. The fish turned Mrs. Ma into a cripple, and Mrs. Zhuo too."

"Which fish?" Xiao Hu asked in disbelief.

"The fish from the lake near your village."

"How do you know that?" Xiao Hu's voice had grown sharp again. He didn't believe a word this man was saying. "Are you a doctor? A chemist? A toxicologist?"

"None of those things," Paul replied. "I used to be a journalist, and covered a story on cats a long time ago, who died miserable deaths like your cat. They were suffering from Minamata disease, just like their owners. I remembered the story and became suspicious."

"What is Minamata disease?" Yin-Yin wanted to know.

"It's named after a bay in Japan. A chemical company dumped its waste in the sea there in the 1950s; it included methylmercury, which was concentrated in the aquatic flora and fauna that the fish consumed in large amounts. More than two thousand people died of the disease; many more fell ill, and women gave birth to disabled babies. It was one of the greatest environmental disasters of the previous century, and has now been almost completely forgotten."

"Why should our mother, of all people—"

Paul interrupted Yin-Yin. "The symptoms are exactly the same. I spent hours on the Internet researching it over the past few days. I've had conversations on the phone with scientists in the US and in

Germany. The mercury content in your mother's hair. Mrs. Ma and Mrs. Zhuo falling ill at the same time with the typical symptoms of the disease. All that fish. There is no other explanation."

"How could the poison have entered the lake?"

The voice of his sister sounded like she was beginning to believe in the far-fetched story.

"Golden Dragon," Paul said immediately, as though he had been waiting for the question.

"They make cough syrup, lozenges, and herbal teas for colds. Highly dangerous stuff," Xiao Hu said sarcastically.

"Supposedly. That's what your father told me too. But the factory belongs to the Sanlitun chemical company, and according to its website, that produces not just harmless syrups but also many things whose production can harm the environment. Polyvinylchloride, for example, known as PVC. In PVC production certain processes can use mercury chloride. That is transformed by microorganisms in the water into methylmercury, which is highly toxic."

"But the factory in our village produces cough syrup," Xiao Hu said loudly. "Didn't you hear what I said?"

"How do you know that?"

"E-e-everyone in the village knows that." Xiao Hu had started stuttering in agitation. Terrible. Like his father.

"They could have changed production locations within the company in the last few years. It must be possible to find that out."

The waiter brought them two chicken curries, a glass noodle salad, a papaya salad, and a second round of beers. No one touched the food.

"Assuming you're right, would that mean that my mother can be cured?" Yin-Yin asked calmly.

Paul shook his head.

"Is there no cure for mercury poisoning?"

"For an acute case, yes, but not at this stage."

"Why," Xiao Hu asked, "do we have to find out the cause of our mother's illness if it will not make her better again? It really doesn't matter then."

Paul Leibovitz felt himself about to lose his composure for the first time. "Are you serious?" He was so worked up that he even changed to a more formal form of address.

"Yes."

"If what I suspect is true, then we're talking about a crime. You don't understand the impact of this."

"I do, very well—that's why I'm being careful," Xiao Hu replied in a cutting tone. "I'm afraid you're misjudging the situation."

Yin-Yin tried to smooth over the escalating quarrel. "But many people in the village have eaten fish from the lake. Why have only our mother, Mrs. Ma, and Mrs. Zhuo fallen ill?"

Paul looked at her in surprise. "Are you quite sure that there are no more cases in the village of illnesses that have been diagnosed as strokes, Parkinson's, or other diseases?"

"No, of course I'm not," she said thoughtfully.

"Then we have to investigate."

"You want to what?" Xiao Hu asked, agitated.

"Investigate. How many victims there are."

"What for?"

"Are you really so cynical, or are you just pretending?" Paul cast him a look that wavered between indignation and contempt.

"I'm not cynical," Xiao Hu objected. "I'm pragmatic. That's a big difference. At least in China."

Weidenfeller, who had been listening to the exchange in silence until now, joined in. "Mr. Leibovitz, how many times have you been to China?"

Paul rolled his eyes in response.

"I suspect this is not your first time," Weidenfeller said, not letting himself be put off. "Yin-Yin told me that you speak excellent Cantonese. Your Mandarin is perfect, as far as I can tell from this conversation. Then you must know too that there are different laws here from those in the West. You're not seriously trying to lift the lid on a possible environmental scandal, are you?"

"No. I would merely like to know if Min Fang has been the victim of a mysterious illness or a crime. Wouldn't you?"

"No. Only if there would be a different outcome for her as a result."

Xiao Hu also shook his head. "No."

"What would my mother get from it?" Yin-Yin asked, her voice so low that she had to repeat herself.

Paul folded his napkin calmly, put it down on the table, and stood up. "Then I'm afraid we have nothing more to say to each other. Good-bye," he said in a friendly voice before pushing his chair away from the table, turning, and walking away.

He left a heavy silence behind him, one that even Weidenfeller did not wish to break. Yin-Yin sank deeper into her chair and closed her eyes. Xiao Hu sipped his beer thoughtfully, helped himself to rice and curry, and started eating.

"And if he's right?" Yin-Yin asked.

"It won't help Mama, didn't you hear that?" Xiao Hu replied with his mouth full.

"And what about the other people in the village? Shouldn't we at least warn them?"

Xiao Hu continued eating and said nothing.

"Does anyone still go fishing in that lake?" Weidenfeller asked.

Yin-Yin shrugged. "No idea." She stirred her glass noodle salad with her chopsticks and put them away again without tasting it. "Assuming that what he says is right, doesn't Sanlitun have to pay compensation to Mama and Papa?"

Xiao Hu sat bent over his curry, gnawing at a chicken bone, and cast his sister a serious look over the top of his glasses. "You'd better not even think about that," he retorted, spitting a piece of bone onto his plate.

"Why not?"

"Little sister, do you know what Sanlitun is?"

"A chemicals firm?"

"No. It's *the* chemicals firm, at least in Zhejiang Province, and if I'm not mistaken, it's one of the ten largest in China. We can go to my place after dinner and search the Internet to see who's on the management board and what connections they have to Beijing. You don't want to get involved with them."

"But—"

"My little sister," he said, his tone swinging between indulgence and warning. "I studied law for five years. I can tell you exactly what will happen if we try to fight for compensation. We won't even find a lawyer in Yiwu who will take the case on."

"Maybe in Shanghai," Yin-Yin interjected.

"I don't think so. But even if someone were crazy enough to represent us, not a single court in the province would be prepared to even hear our case."

"But if one did?"

"Even if I were wrong and a judge was brave enough to hear the case, there isn't the slightest chance of winning. We would have one lawyer, and Sanlitun would have a whole legal department. The burden of proof would be on us. We would have to prove that there is poison in the water, that Sanlitun is without a doubt the only source of the poison in the water, and that this poison caused Mama's illness. It wouldn't be a matter of suspecting or believing but of scientific proof! Even if we could prove that, which I doubt, think about what it would cost. And even if all the facts were established and all the information, figures, and witness statements were in our favor, we would still have no chance. The provincial government and definitely the cadres in Beijing are behind Sanlitun. Who will be behind us?"

He looked her straight in the eye to lend his words even more weight. "No one. Did you hear me? No one. Don't even begin to think about it." He pushed his empty plate to the middle of the table, helped himself to a toothpick, and began to pick out the bits of chicken stuck between his teeth.

"Papa could travel to Beijing and submit a petition," his sister suggested in a hesitant voice.

"And we can visit him in a labor camp after that. Great idea." He shook his head violently. "Stop that. We had better think about how we can care for Mama instead. Papa can't do it."

———

They walked up Fenyang Lu in silence and turned onto Donghu Lu, which took them to Changle Lu. There were not many cars in these small streets. People were sitting in the courtyards and outside their houses, enjoying the mild evening air. Xiao Hu saw two old men sitting on tiny bamboo stools, playing chess. Next to them, a gray-haired woman in pajamas was fanning herself and sizing up every passerby with keen eyes. Xiao Hu guessed that she must have watched over the whole block for the authorities before. At the next crossing, a man with oil-smeared hands was repairing a punctured bicycle tire; there was a toolbox and a pail of water next to him. They said good-bye on Changle Lu. Weidenfeller took a taxi and Yin-Yin went home on her own.

Xiao Hu looked at her as she disappeared among the plane trees without turning back. He worried about his sister. Mama's illness had changed her. She was even paler than usual and had lost weight. He had not seen her laugh for weeks. There was tension between her and Weidenfeller; he had sensed that at their previous meetings, and both of them had confirmed this to him in the last few days. Now the conversation with Leibovitz was an additional burden. Yin-Yin had been deeply affected by it; he could tell by the look in her eyes, and her voice, which had grown more and more strained as the evening progressed. She couldn't hide anything from him; he knew her too well. She had understood his argument but had not completely accepted it; he could tell from the way she had said good-bye. She had been brief, almost curt. He felt sorry; he had not wanted to anger her. Xiao Hu wondered if he had been too harsh, whether he should call her the next day and tell her that they were not so different after all, even though he might have sounded heartless and cynical. She mustn't think that he didn't feel the same way as she did. If Sanlitun was responsible for Mama's illness, he would be as horrified as his sister was. It would be a crime that ought to be punished. If this was happening in America, there would be lines of lawyers offering their services to fight for damages. And not only for Mama and Papa. If Leibovitz was right, more people in the village had been affected, and perhaps others in the area too. There would be a class action suit and compensation payments in the millions. An outcry in the media. The people responsible would be brought to justice. In

America. Not in China. He and Yin-Yin could be angry about that, disappointed, sad, whatever they wanted, but they could not change things. It was that simple. Getting worked up about it was a waste of time and energy. Which you really could spend on better things in Shanghai. She must understand that, surely.

He would have liked to call her immediately to make sure that they basically agreed on this. She was not only his sister but also his friend and closest confidante, and on no account did he want to quarrel with her over Mama's illness. But it was way past midnight. He would get in touch the next morning and ask her to lunch or dinner.

x
─────────

Christine felt horribly sick. She tried to take deep, calm breaths in
and out as she explained patiently to a brazen customer on the telephone why a free upgrade to business class was not possible, gesturing to an intern at the same time to show her where the application
forms for a visa to China were. She put down the phone and hoped
she would make it to the toilet in time. She had to hold on to the
shelf holding the travel brochures in order not to lose her balance,
and she was just able to kick the door closed behind her with her
heel before she threw up into the toilet bowl.

Christine had been suffering from this awful nausea for days,
along with pounding headaches, spells of dizziness, and a feeling of
total exhaustion. She fell asleep in front of the television at night,
and in the morning Tita Ness, the Filipina housemaid, had to wake
her up, because although she had heard the alarm ring, she'd fallen
asleep again immediately. Twice she had stayed in bed longer and
come to the office only later in the morning. She intended to go to
the doctor that afternoon. For the first time in years. She was not the
kind of person who worried about her health, her own, her son's, or
her mother's. Quite the opposite of Paul, who got worried over even
a tiny bruise, who noticed when her face was pale, and who regularly
inspected the few moles she had with care. You don't understand,
he said gruffly when she made fun of him. Christine believed that
no one and nothing could change the course of fate. A life that
had come to an end was finished. Time was up. The end. That was

sad, painful, and unfair. Call it what it you will, but it could not be changed. So, to Paul's consternation, she had only the recommended routine medical examinations on an irregular basis, and with no great belief in them. Fatalists were no good at prevention.

She wished Paul were with her now. Yesterday he had sounded very mysterious on the phone, but he'd promised to tell her more today. Now she could not reach him on his cell phone and would have to wait until he called her that evening from his hotel.

A disgusting sour taste rose from her stomach. She brushed her teeth thoroughly. The intern cleared the armchair that had been buried under catalogs and made an herbal tea for her. Christine sat down gratefully and closed her eyes for a moment. The phone rang: one of her last big clients, who wanted to speak to her urgently. She was glad for the distraction.

———

That evening, as she did almost every day she did not spend with Paul, she sat with her mother in front of the television. Her mother had moved into a small apartment three floors below her six months ago, and was constantly in and out of her home. Josh was busy with a new computer game in his room, Tita Ness was ironing in the bedroom, and Pearl TV was showing a Ming dynasty soap opera. They ate together, staring silently at the screen. Sometimes they exchanged no more than a few words on evenings like these. Her mother did not ask any questions, and Christine doubted that she listened properly when she, Josh, or Tita said anything to her. Christine poked at her rice without any appetite, watched her mother from the corner of her eye, and wondered how she would take care of her if business at World Wide Travel continued to be as bad as it was. The monthly life insurance payments were not even enough for the rent, and her mother did not get a pension. Christine had to pay for everything else. There would probably be no choice then but to share an apartment again; she would have to let Tita Ness go and ask her mother to take care of Josh and the household. This thought did not fill her with pleasure, but neither did it make her feel particularly unhappy. It was children's duty to take care of their parents, regardless of whether it suited them. It was a waste of time to complain about that. She wondered if moving to Lamma could be an alternative. It would be the best solution financially, but despite Paul's familiarity with the Chinese language, culture, and mentality, she feared that living with her, Josh, and her mother under one roof would stretch even his abilities to integrate.

"Mama?" Her mother was not listening to her. She was immersed in a world of intrigues, jealously, and revenge in a Ming courtyard, and Christine did not have the strength to raise her voice. Once again, she could not bring herself to tell her mother about Da Long and her trip to Shanghai. She should take care of herself, the doctor had said. Work less, not stress herself, rest more. He would have the results of the blood test in two days, then he would know more. A conversation with her mother about her brother was the opposite of what she needed now. Her mother's questions. The tears, shed or unshed. The mystery of why Mama had not searched for Da Long. She did not feel strong enough right then to find out about family secrets. There was no hurry. Not after forty years.

Paul's telephone call woke her. She was lying on the sofa in front of the television, which was still on. It was just before midnight. He sounded worked up; it took her some time to understand what he was telling her. Dead fish and cats. Japan, Minamata, mercury. Her sister-in-law had apparently been poisoned.

"Isn't it possible that the laboratory made a mistake?" she asked disbelievingly.

"I can't imagine they did," Paul said.

"You're in Shanghai, don't forget. Who knows if they even have the necessary equipment?"

"Christine! They have the fastest train in the world here now, the tallest building in China, and God knows what else. So they can definitely prove the mercury content in a hair sample. Apart from that, as far as I know, it's not a complicated test," he said. But he could not quash her doubts.

She thought hard. "If you're right, would that mean that Min Fang could be cured?"

"No, for heaven's sake!" he shouted, so angrily that she flinched and held the phone a few inches away from her ear. She had never heard him so agitated before.

"I'm sorry, it was just a question," she replied, irritated. "Why are you getting so worked up?"

"Because your nephew and your niece also wanted to know that. Because they lost interest in the whole thing once they found out that it didn't mean their mother could be cured."

"And what don't you understand about that?"

She heard Paul taking a deep breath, about to start speaking, but then he just exhaled in a quiet sigh, as if he were pulling himself together in order not to strike the wrong note again. "If what I suspect is true," he said, still irritated, "this is not just about Min Fang. The whole village, and probably other villages too, are at risk. Something has to be done."

Christine gave a deep sigh. He was, and was still, a Westerner, she thought, no matter how well he spoke Chinese, how long he had lived in Hong Kong, or how much he tried to understand the way the Chinese thought and behaved. There were limits to how much a person could understand about another culture, even if Christine didn't quite know where they were, who set them, or whether they were fixed or movable. Paul had clearly reached those limits now. "You know China and the Chinese so well; why are you getting worked up about this?" she asked in a conciliatory tone. "My mother has been living in Hong Kong for over forty years, and she's still afraid of the authorities. I don't know what would have to happen before she went to the police for anything. She would never take someone to court, because she doesn't trust any state prosecutors or judges. A few months ago a policeman came to her front door because he had a perfectly harmless message for her neighbor. It took her days to get over the shock. Her fear of everything to do with the authorities runs so deep. And that's someone who has spent over half her life in Hong Kong. What do you expect from Yin-Yin and her brother; what's he called again?"

"Xiao Hu." Paul paused for a long time. "I expect them not to stand by doing nothing while people are poisoned. Is that too much to expect?" He sounded calmer now, but she still found his self-righteousness unsettling.

"No. Or maybe yes. I don't know. I have no idea what I would do."

"If you saw someone in Hong Kong pouring poison into a reservoir of drinking water, you would definitely do something, wouldn't you?"

"Yes, in Hong Kong. But I don't know what I would do in China. Go to the police? Employ a lawyer? Say nothing? No idea. Anyway, are you quite sure about it?" She felt another wave of nausea rising.

"Yes," he replied in a defiant tone.

Christine wondered if he was really serious about this. She did not know Paul as an angry, self-righteous person. "Really?" she replied, surprised. The nausea grew worse. Whatever she did, she mustn't throw up on the couch.

"No, of course not!" Paul blurted out. "Who do you think I am? But we're not at that point yet. I just wanted to try to gather as much information as possible so that we know where we are with this. Then we can decide whether to get the authorities involved, to get a lawyer, or to do nothing at all. But they're not even interested in that. I can't understand it." His voice was quiet now, and he sounded resigned and full of doubt.

Christine could not stand it any longer. She stood up. "It's not your job to get any more involved in this. Remember what happened with Michael Owen. You were lucky with that. It could have played out very differently. And your friend Zhang, the only person who helped you then and who could perhaps help you now, is in Shenzhen. That's a long way away."

"I know," he said in a despondent tone.

"When are you coming back? I miss you," she whispered, trying to keep him from noticing how sick she was suddenly feeling.

"As soon as I can get a flight. I'm hoping that will be tomorrow, or Saturday at the latest."

"Take care of yourself. Don't do anything stupid, promise?" She walked toward the bathroom, holding the phone. "Sleep well now. I love you." She lifted the toilet lid.

"I love you too. Good-night."

"Good-night." She pressed the red button and felt the rice and vegetables spurting out of her in a gush at the same time.

———————

XI

Yin-Yin opened the apartment door carefully and crept in. Her roommate, Lu, who had a cold, was already asleep. She heard her light snoring through the bedroom door, which was ajar. Yin-Yin went to her room and opened the window. Warm early-summer air flowed in; it smelled of sautéed garlic and onions. Someone was still cooking a meal this late at night. Not a day passed that she was not grateful for the apartment, which she had shared with Lu for six months. It was in one of Shanghai's *lilong* housing developments, on the upper floor of a two-story building whose architect must have been influenced by the art deco style. The neighborhood felt almost like a village; the residents knew each other, children played bad-minton or basketball in the alleys, elderly people sat in front of the building shooting the breeze, and Yin-Yin was woken in the morn-ing by birdsong. Now she could hear the hum of air conditioners outside, the muffled voices of the next-door neighbors, and, from the floor below, the suppressed moans of Mrs. Teng, who made love with her husband almost every night at this time. Beneath all these sounds lay the dull roar of the big city like a carpet; it was a little quieter in the few hours after midnight, but never quite died down; it often helped Yin-Yin fall asleep.

She took the cheongsam out of her bag and hung the dress up on a hanger, smoothing it out. As she undressed, she looked in the mirror, and got a shock. She had always been glad not to be a skinny woman; she liked the proportions of her body, with its prominent bosom and bottom. But now her hip bones were jutting out and her legs were thin; even her breasts, which had been full and firm not long ago, were smaller now and had begun drooping a little.

Yin-Yin sat down on her bed, put her arms around her knees, looked up at the night sky lit up in silvery white, and felt glad that she was alone. Sebastian had wanted to come home with her, but she had no desire to sleep with him tonight or to listen to a lecture about China's legal system or the naïveté of people like Paul Leibovitz. If there was anything about Sebastian that she disliked, it was the way he analyzed and discussed everything down to the last detail. Every feeling had to be named, every thought had to be expressed in words. He stopped only when he believed that they were in agreement, and he often didn't notice that she frequently gave in because she found his lecturing wearisome and wanted to be left in peace. He was the first boyfriend she had had who was not from China, and she wondered if this love of talking was typical of just him or if everyone in the West prized words so much.

Tonight she had to be alone in order to think properly.

Yin-Yin felt incredibly relieved that she had made it through the concert. She had started planning it six months ago in honor of her parents, especially her mother, who had taken on all kinds of extra work in school to pay for her daughter's studies, and who had constantly encouraged her in her violin playing without ever pressuring her. Who had taught her to believe in herself, who loved her enough to let her go. Her parents had planned to come to Shanghai for the first time in many years for this concert.

Her hands had trembled during the first notes; the movement of the bow had been unsteady. She had closed her eyes briefly and had seen not the notes, but the face of her mother instead. The crooked hands, the empty stare at the ceiling. Only the mysterious power of the music had brought her back to the moment. She had trusted herself to first Mozart's, then Beethoven's notes, which had swept her into a world in which her mother's illness no longer mattered.

She thought about the conversation with Paul Leibovitz and her brother. What Xiao Hu said had affected her, not because he had lied or been hurtful, but because of the coldness of his tone, even if he had not meant it that way. Or at least she hoped not. She remembered the baby rabbit that they had once found as children. It was lying in a hollow in the ground, sick; it could no longer move its hind legs. It was an animal condemned to death, who would either starve to death in the next few hours, days perhaps, or fall victim to a bird of prey. Yin-Yin had been paralyzed with shock and pity, but Xiao Hu had picked up a stone and slung it at the animal. He was not used to killing. The rabbit squeaked. It struggled. She turned away, unable to do anything. He continued throwing stones until the guts spilled out of the little belly and the animal no longer moved.

He threw up in a field after that.

She thought he was cruel and repellent; he thought she was a coward. He said that he had felt just as sorry for the rabbit as she had, if not more. That was precisely why he had put it out of its misery. What was the use of pity if no action was taken as a result?

After that, a shadow had darkened the relationship between them for a long time. He had become a bit of a stranger to her. She could see that in some way he had been right, but there was something within her that resisted his cold logic, something that she could not find the right words for.

Why was she thinking of the day the rabbit died, right then? Her brother did not love their mother any less than she did, but the lack of emotion with which he had described the situation she was in had reminded Yin-Yin of that afternoon. She felt tears rising, and she no longer had the strength to fight them. She had been brave for weeks. Had gone home nearly every weekend. Had cared for her mother. Had supported her father. Suppressed her tears. She buried her head under her pillow and cried. Mama was gone. Nothing in the world would bring her back. She longed for her mother's voice. The familiar sound, the warmth in it. Her smell, her laugh. Gone. Lost forever.

When she had calmed down a little she got up, put on a long undershirt, went to the kitchen, and made some tea. She heard Paul's words again: *Your mother was poisoned.* Like something said in a film. She repeated the words in her head several times. Whispered them out loud. *Poisoned.* No, things were not as simple as they had seemed at the Thai restaurant. Was the question of who was guilty really only important if Mama could be saved as a result? The longer she thought about it, the more uncertain Yin-Yin became. Apart from that, there was the second point on which her opinion was different from her brother's: Why shouldn't Sanlitun help them if the company had really caused the illnesses of Mama, Mrs. Ma, and Mrs. Zhuo? It wouldn't take a great deal of money to pay for better care for them. It was not a crime to ask for compensation; the worst that could happen was that they would say no.

She wondered if she should call Paul Leibovitz. She had grown to like him over the two days in Yiwu. She was grateful that he had stayed with her father, and she had been glad when he rang yesterday and accepted the invitation to her concert. She was sorry that she had upset him with her reaction in the restaurant, but what had he expected? Simple gratitude for his help? She did not think that he was so naïve.

It was just before three in the morning when she picked up the phone.

"Paul Leibovitz speaking." His voice did not sound as though she had woken him.

"I'm sorry to disturb you in the middle of the night, but I was afraid that you would be taking an early-morning flight to Hong Kong."

"That's what I plan to do," he said coldly.

"I've thought about our discussions, and wanted to ask if you would come with me to see my parents in Yiwu today."

"What for?" He was still annoyed, and was not bothering to hide his feelings.

"To talk to my father. I don't know if he will believe me, and how he will react. You'll be able to explain things better, and besides . . ." She paused.

"Besides?"

"Besides, I thought that if we had the time, we could ask around the village to find out who else has fallen sick in the last few months."

"Yin-Yin, no matter what we find out, it won't make your mother well again."

"I know."

"You said that you weren't interested in anything else."

Was he being annoying or self-righteous? "Do you hold that against us?" she retorted indignantly. "Our first thoughts are for ourselves and our mother. Is that a bad thing?"

"If I'm right, then this is not just about your family."

Yin-Yin felt herself getting angry. "Are you so sure you would have behaved differently if you had been in our position?"

He said nothing.

"You have no right to accuse us of anything."

Still no reply.

"I say this to you honestly: Even if I could, I don't want to expose some environmental scandal. I don't want to fight a large chemical company. If your suspicions are right, then I simply hope that the authorities fence off the lake and that Sanlitun pays us a small compensation of its own accord, without a court case. That would make life a little easier for my parents. I'm not interested in the rest." She paused for a moment before she repeated her request. "Will you come with me later today or not?"

"Yes," he said without hesitation.

————

When Yin-Yin woke in the gray light of morning she was unsure for the first few seconds if she had dreamed the conversation with Paul or if it had really happened. She immediately felt her head pounding. A bad sign. She had this kind of headache only when she was extremely tired or anxious. Her brother would be very angry with her, and would not speak to her for days. There were not many situations in which she acted against his advice and actively defied him. She felt like canceling the trip, but it would be an embarrassing loss of face in front of Paul Leibovitz. She had to see her father anyway, and Leibovitz would be a great help with talking to him. The rest could wait.

Paul had organized a car and a driver. They met just after nine in the morning on Yanan Xi Lu in front of the Hilton Hotel and traveled on the highway toward Yiwu. Paul looked tired. There were shadows under his eyes, and he yawned often.

"Christine sends her greetings," he said, as though he was trying to be conciliatory after the previous night's conversation.

"Thank you. She's probably not very happy that you're traveling to Yiwu again with me, and staying on in Shanghai."

"No, she's not."

"Have you told her about the laboratory test results?"

"The gist of it."

"What did she say?"

"She can't believe it; she thinks the laboratory made a mistake." Before Yin-Yin could reply he added, "That was a very beautiful concert yesterday evening."

"I'm glad to hear that."

"I especially liked the Beethoven sonata."

"Thank you."

"Did you play it for your mother?"

"What makes you think that?" she asked, astounded.

He shrugged. "I don't know. Just a feeling. I've heard it played often, but rarely with such intensity. But maybe it's just me. I thought about her many times during the concert."

"I dedicated the whole evening to my mother," Yin-Yin said quietly, aware once more of why she was sitting in the car on the way to Yiwu.

"What does your boyfriend do? What was his name again?"

"Johann Sebastian Weidenfeller. He's a manager with a German pharmaceuticals firm and is head of the Shanghai and South China office."

"With a name like that he must know something about music."

"Yes. His father is a professor at a conservatory."

"How long has he lived in China?" Paul asked.

"For almost ten years. He spent a year in Nanjing while he was at college as well."

"How long have you known each other?"

"Almost two years. We met in the Hyatt Hotel. I used to play regularly in the hotel lounge."

"How long have you been together?"

"Hmm. Well, you could say that Sebastian didn't waste any time," she said with an embarrassed smile.

"That's the impression he gives."

"You don't like him?"

"No," he said matter-of-factly.

"But you don't know him at all."

"I do," Paul shot back in a decided tone.

"Have you met before?" Yin-Yin asked in surprise.

"No. I don't know him personally, but I know people like him."

"Are you always so quick to judge?"

"Not really. Christine actually thinks that I take far too much time to do so. But with some people I don't need long to form an opinion of them."

What a strange person, Yin-Yin thought. He surprised her with his sensitivity one moment, then with his heavy-handed judgments the next. She wanted to ask Paul exactly what he had against her boyfriend, but decided against it at the last moment. What could he possibly say to her apart from giving his superficial impressions of Sebastian? She did not want to ask him to expand on his presumptuous statement by asking more questions.

"I'm sorry," Paul said after a pause. "I didn't mean to hurt you. I'm sure he has many good qualities." When Yin-Yin did not react, he added, "He must have, if you love him."

She looked out the window without really seeing anything. At some point her eyes fell shut and she slept until the driver woke her to ask for directions shortly before they arrived.

————

Da Long listened to Paul's detailed report without any reaction at first. After a few minutes his left eye started twitching, and he pressed his lips together with such force that they remained white and bloodless for some seconds after he released them again.

When Paul had finished talking, Da Long said nothing for such a long time that Yin-Yin grew frightened.

"Papa?" she said carefully, after some time.

He nodded. "Are you sure?"

"The laboratory's findings are clear," Paul replied calmly. "I can't think of any other way that so much mercury could get into Min Fang's body."

Da Long shook his head helplessly. "H-h-how could that happen? It must have been an accident, mustn't it?" His words sounded more like a plea, an entreaty, than a mere question.

"Probably."

"D-d-do you think they didn't notice?"

"I can't imagine so, with that amount."

"W-w-why did no one warn us? Why did they let us carry on fishing there?"

His stammer, the disbelieving look, full of questions. Yin-Yin felt the pressure of tears in her eyes. Her father looked as despairing as he had on the day her mother had been taken to the hospital, a little man, collapsed into himself, defenseless as a child. It hurt.

"Do you know who else in the village has fallen sick in the last few months?" she asked.

He looked at her in surprise. "N-n-no. Since Mama fell ill I've barely been out. And we hardly get any visitors. If you want to find out about that, you'll have to go from house to house in the village. Start with the Zhangs. I often saw their daughter at the lake. The Jiangs too. And the Guos. Mama used to talk about them often."

Yin-Yin wondered if it would be better to go on her own. A Westerner by her side could make people suspicious and make the neighbors more reluctant than usual to open up about their private lives. She wanted to start with the Zhangs, without Paul, and see how far she got. She had played with Feng, the daughter, often as a child, but they had grown apart after school.

The Zhangs lived at the far, more populated end of the village. Yin-Yin had not been there for years. It looked just as she remembered it, though: wooden benches by some of the front doors, red lanterns hanging from some of the houses, and laundry lines full of shirts and trousers in front of others. Chickens pecked in the sand for grain between the buildings. A man was squatting in one corner, blowing continuously at a pile of glowing coals, sweet potatoes cooking on a metal sheet on top. When he heard her approach he looked up; his left eye was milky white and the other eye was missing; the eyelid hung loosely like a scrap of cloth. The image of the animal carcasses by the lake that Paul had described flashed into Yin-Yin's head, and she thought about the dead cats. She walked into the small square with the dried-up well in the middle. Four old men and women whom she did not know were sitting in the shade cast by a wall; they watched her as she approached. When she looked at them more closely she noticed that two of them were staring past her with fixed expressions. She was not sure if they were aware of anything at all. Their hands were trembling. No one returned her greeting. She repeated her "*ni hao*" but they remained silent.

The village in which she had spent most of her childhood and youth began to seem stranger to her with each passing minute. Yin-Yin was relieved when she finally found Mrs. Zhang, who recognized her immediately.

"Yin-Yin! Have you eaten? Come in. Sit down. How are you?"

Mrs. Zhang was a small, plump woman with red cheeks who had always had time and a smile for the children of the village. She offered Yin-Yin a chair, and they both sat down at the kitchen table. Gradually the memories returned. The cold and damp winter afternoons that she had spent sitting in front of the stove wrapped in blankets. The delicious pancakes that Mrs. Zhang had made; the rare smell of roasted chestnuts.

"How is your mother?" Mrs. Zhang wanted to know. She put a plateful of biscuits, a thermos of tea, and two cups on the table.

"Not well."

"I heard what happened. I'm so terribly sorry."

Yin-Yin nibbled a biscuit. It was stale and dry, and tasted as dusty as the roasted silkworms that her father sometimes served. "Are you all well, though?"

"I'm fine. My husband too."

"And Feng?" Yin-Yin asked, sounding relieved. Maybe it was just coincidence after all, and Paul's suspicion was unfounded.

Mrs. Zhang sighed. "We're worried about Feng."

"Why? Where does she live now?"

"She lived with us until just before her son was born. Now she lives with her husband in Guangdong Province."

"I didn't even know that she had a child," Yin-Yin said, surprised. "Who looks after the boy?"

"He's dead. He died a week after he was born." Mrs. Zhang wiped tears from her eyes. "Our only grandchild. He was born a cripple. I was there for his birth in the hospital; I saw him. He looked terrible. Like a . . ." She trailed off and started crying.

Yin-Yin took her hand. She felt sorry that she had asked her question. "I'm sorry. No one told me."

"It's okay. You have your own troubles."

"What was wrong with Feng's son?"

"He was born blind and deaf. His heart was much too big and his hands and feet were deformed. The birth was difficult. Feng won't be able to have any more children now," Mrs. Zhang said, her voice growing unsteady again. She swallowed a few times before she continued. "Things like that happen, the doctors said. It's fate. Just like the Bases' daughter. The only two young women who stayed on in the village gave birth to cripples. There's a curse on this place, Yin-Yin, I'm telling you. You did the right thing to go away early."

"What happened to the Bases' grandchild?" Yin-Yin asked cautiously.

"It's a girl. She's blind and was also born with a heart defect, but has survived, so far, anyway. Didn't you know that?"

Yin-Yin shook her head. "I don't know the Bases at all. They only moved here when I had already gone to Shanghai. Which house do they live in?"

"They live with their daughter and the child in Yiwu now. Near the People's Hospital Number Two. I heard that the little one often has to go to the hospital."

"Were Feng and the Bases' daughter good friends?"

"Not very close."

Yiwu felt nausea rising and her heart racing. Just like in the few minutes before an examination at the conservatory or an audition for an orchestra. She no longer doubted that Paul's theory was right; she only wondered if she wanted to know everything. The more people the poison in the lake had victimized, the lower the chances were of some small damages being paid. Sanlitun would never admit to the wrongdoing and pay compensation to the whole village. What was the use of knowledge if they could do nothing with it? She was a young woman dreaming of a career as a musician—not a career, really; all she wanted was to play in an orchestra and live modestly from her music. She did not need to own an apartment or a car. She didn't want much. If she met the right man, she would want to have a child and bring it up in the hope that it would have a life no worse than her own. She did not want to concern herself with toxic chemicals in a lake. She did not want to find out any more about poisoned fish, dead cats, and crippled newborn babies. She didn't even want to know how the poison had come to be in the water; whether it was an accident, an oversight, or a coldly deliberate action. She did not want to know who was responsible. She did not have what it took to be a hero.

"I'm very sorry," she said, standing up. "I hope Feng gets well soon."

———

Paul and her father sat quietly on the small veranda while Yin-Yin told them what she had found out, in a breathless rush.

"Could the mercury also have something to do with the deformed babies?" she asked Paul.

He nodded. "It's one of the poisons that can penetrate the placenta and damage the embryo. That happened in Japan too. I read through everything again."

"H-h-how did the mercury end up in the ocean then?" Da Long asked.

"Chisso, a Japanese chemicals firm, dumped it there over several years."

"I-i-it wasn't an accident?" her father asked, astounded.

"No."

"Th-th-they knew what they were doing?"

"Yes. The connection between the poison and the sick and dying wasn't immediately clear, but even after the tests had proved it, they continued pouring mercury into the sea for years."

Da Long's interest in the Minamata disaster grew with every sentence. He was sitting up straight and listening carefully. "What did the fishermen do?"

"They sued Chisso."

"And then?"

"The case dragged on for years."

"Were people punished at the end?"

"Not as far as I know. But the company had to pay damages."

"H-h-how much?"

"Many, many millions. Nearly a hundred million US dollars, if I'm not mistaken."

The father looked at his daughter expectantly.

She did not feel like talking. She wanted to go back to Shanghai. She wanted to practice for the symphony orchestra audition.

Da Long stood up. "I'll look for a lawyer, then."

Yin-Yin cast a shocked look at Paul. "You what?"

"I'll sue them. If they are guilty of causing Mama's illness, then they must be punished."

"But, Papa, what do you imagine will happen?"

"I'll find a lawyer who will represent me."

"Xiao Hu says that will be impossible. No one will take this case. It's much too dangerous."

"What does your brother know about it?" he said angrily.

"Papa!" she protested. "He's a lawyer."

"I don't care. I'll find one."

"Sanlitun is a big company. We can't win in a case against them," she said, repeating her brother's words.

"Maybe not," he murmured, barely audible. "But we must try. Let them see, we're not going to be pressured."

"Do you know a lawyer in Yiwu?" Paul whispered to her.

"How would I know any lawyers?" she replied curtly. "I know a journalist who works for the *People's Daily* in Yiwu."

"How do you know him?"

"He's a friend. We were in the same class."

"Maybe he can help us?"

"How?"

Paul ignored her question. "Can you ask him if we could meet him for dinner this evening?"

Yin-Yin hesitated. She did not know where Paul Leibovitz was heading with this.

"Come on." It sounded like a plea.

"What is he supposed to help us with?" she asked suspiciously.

"To find a lawyer. If you want to get compensation for your mother, you have to get a lawyer. To threaten to take them to court, not necessarily to really do so. Otherwise Sanlitun will never take you seriously."

She hesitated for a long moment.

———

They met Wang Cai Hua in a modest noodle-soup-and-dumpling restaurant near his office. He was on the late shift and did not have much time; they were the only diners. He was tall and thin and wore a white shirt and jeans; a few golden highlights glinted in his black hair. Yin-Yin was glad to see him; he had been one of the top students and at the same time the class clown, taking neither the teachers nor his grades particularly seriously. He had made her laugh often. Many lessons had been made reasonably tolerable only by his jokes. She had admired him because he was the only student who every now and then had dared to object to the rules. She suspected that he was not frightened of authority, not even deep down.

"He's too old for you," he said to her in a low voice when they met, gesturing at Paul with his head.

"It doesn't matter if a cat is young or old. As long as he catches mice," Paul replied. "An old Chinese proverb."

Wang looked at him amazed—Paul understood Mandarin!—then started laughing so hard he almost choked himself. Even Yin-Yin laughed in relief; there would have been no better way for Paul to win Wang's trust and respect.

"How are you?" she asked.

"Good," he said with his familiar impish smile, which had always left her wondering if he was being serious or not. "In the last few weeks I've lost all the money that I made in the twelve months before that on the stock exchange."

"How did you do that?" Yin-Yin asked, still suspecting that he was kidding.

"I was in Macao."

"You gamble?"

"We all do. Don't you have any shares? The whole country is in a fever of gambling," he said, laughing. "But tell me, how are you?"

"Not too good," Yin-Yin said.

"Have you also lost money, or it is love life troubles?" Wang asked, casting a mischievous look at Paul.

"Mama is very sick," Yin-Yin replied, telling him briefly about her mother's illness without mentioning the possibility of poisoning or the name Sanlitun.

"I'm so very sorry to hear that," Wang said in a serious tone. "And the doctors don't have the faintest clue what could have caused it?"

"No," she said quietly, noticing how torn she felt. Something in her resisted telling him about the poison in Mama's body.

A bicycle bell rang on the counter. Their food was ready. Paul got up and carried the tray with the soup and the dumplings through the empty rows of seats.

Wang looked at her intently. "Are you not feeling well?"

"I'm fine," she lied. "Just a bit tired."

Paul spoke up. "You must know Sanlitun?"

"The chemicals company?"

"Yes."

"Of course. It's one of the biggest companies in the province. Why are you asking?"

"Yin-Yin's mother was poisoned. There's so much mercury in her body that it's a thousand times more than the maximum level considered safe. There are more sick people in the village. We suspect that the poison is in the fish from a lake nearby. There's a Sanlitun factory by that lake . . ." Paul stopped there.

Wang had let a dumpling slide away from his chopsticks and fall into the dish of vinegar, splashing his own as well as Paul's shirt with black spots. Yin-Yin had never in her life seen a face change so dramatically. Wang had grown pale and looked as shocked as if someone had told him he was being arrested.

"Are you okay?" Paul asked, surprised at his reaction.

"I'm fine." He was a clown, but not a good actor.

"Wang, what's wrong?"

He put down his chopsticks and wiped his forehead with a handkerchief. His eyes wandered from Paul to Yin-Yin and back again. He leaned forward and whispered, "Are you a reporter from the West?"

Paul shook his head.

"Who are you then?"

"He's a very good friend of mine. You can trust him," Yin-Yin said.

"Have you known him long?"

"Yes, for a long time." She did not want to explain anything now.

Wang picked up his cell phone, which was lying on the table, switched it off, and took the battery out.

"Where are yours?"

Paul and Yin-Yin took their phones out of their pockets.

"Switch them off and remove the batteries."

"Why?" Yin-Yin asked, disconcerted.

"For safety," Wang replied curtly. Any hint of jokiness had vanished from his eyes.

"A few months ago I got a call from a friend and colleague in one of our offices in Hubei Province. There was some trouble with a Sanlitun factory there. They had channeled toxic wastewater into a river that supplied water for a pond where fish were farmed. All the fish died. I don't know how many tons of them. My colleague asked me to do a bit of research here. We have two factories in the Yiwu area, and the Sanlitun headquarters are in Hangzhou, only an hour from here."

He paused, as though he was trying to keep them in suspense.

"And?" Paul asked impatiently.

"I wasn't allowed to. Orders from Beijing."

"What do you mean you weren't allowed to?" Yin-Yin found it difficult to imagine that Wang would obey blanket orders like that.

Wang looked around the restaurant to make sure that the cooks were playing cards and that the two waitresses were sitting in front of the television before he continued speaking. "No one asks about Sanlitun. Period. On the Internet you'll find loads of positive stories about them in the financial news; they've exceeded their growth targets and revised their budgeted profits upward. Their market share is growing and all that stuff. Their share price goes up and up. You won't find anything else."

"Why is that?" Yin-Yin asked, amazed.

"The majority of the shares is owned by the state and the government of the province. The father of the company chairman was a close adviser of Deng Xiaoping. They are so well protected from on high that their factories aren't even inspected."

"How do you know that?"

"My colleague in Hubei told me. We have strict regulations about environmental protection and authorities who are supposed to supervise adherence to the regulations; that's all very well, but what's the use of it when everyone who has good contacts is able to get special exemptions? My friend told me that there were problems with Sanlitun factories in three more provinces. I heard from a colleague in the Beijing office that the *People's Daily* had received several dozen letters from readers complaining about the company. But those are all rumors."

"Can we talk to your colleague in Hubei?" Paul asked, speaking carefully.

"He's not talking to anyone any longer. He's been transferred to the head office in Beijing and now works in the basement. In the archives."

"Do you know a lawyer here who would take up the case?"

"In Yiwu? Very unlikely." Wang looked at Paul sharply. "Are you sure that you want to get involved with this?"

Yin-Yin turned to Paul as well. In his grave face she did not find the grim determination that she had expected. She saw faint lines around his mouth. She saw deep-blue eyes in which more than the shadow of a doubt lay.

"No," he replied hesitantly. "I'm not. Yin-Yin's father is understandably outraged and is considering taking the company to court. I—we—wanted to help him find a lawyer. Nothing more."

Wang thought for a moment, then took a pen out of his pocket. He picked up a napkin and wrote two telephone numbers and two names on it.

"The first one is an old lawyer in Yiwu and the other one is a lawyer in Shanghai. Both of them are unusual in their own ways. One of them may be able to help you. But you're not to breathe a word about where you got these numbers, not to anyone, promise?" He looked at his watch. "I've got to rush back to the office now."

He picked up his cell phone, put the battery back in, and switched it on. "Don't forget. Always take the battery out."

"Why?" Yin-Yin asked, although she knew the question betrayed how naïve she was.

"Because they can not only eavesdrop on every conversation via these things, but they can also switch them on remotely."

"Who?"

"Who's eavesdropping on me? All the jealous men whose wives I'm fucking!" he said, so loudly that the cooks stopped playing cards for a moment and the waitresses turned around to cast curious glances at him. He responded to their looks with a mocking laugh, said good-bye to Paul and Yin-Yin with a wink, walked out of the restaurant, and had disappeared into the stream of passersby within seconds.

Paul smiled at Yin-Yin. She read the name on the napkin and pushed it over to him. The lawyer in Yiwu was called Gao Jintao.

"Shall I ring him?"

"I don't know," she said uncertainly.

He switched his cell phone on again, but there was no more battery power. She passed him her phone, and he called the number in Yiwu. The connection was bad; it crackled and popped before breaking down altogether. He was able to make out what the lawyer was saying better the second time around. He was booked up. Paul gave him a brief account of a sick woman, a misdiagnosis, and polluted water. Gao interrupted him and told him that he had no time for them this evening but that they could go to his office at nine the next morning and discuss everything with him.

Paul gave Yin-Yin a questioning glance, but she felt unable to reply. He agreed to the appointment and ended the call. "Is that okay?"

She nodded, glad that the decision had been made for her.

"I suggest we book two rooms at the Grand Emperor Hotel, go and see him tomorrow, then travel to Shanghai after that. What do you think?"

"There are cheaper hotels in the city."

"It's on me, don't worry. It's not very expensive."

———

Yin-Yin went to bed feeling uneasy and was woken in the middle of the night by a sound that she could not identify. It sounded like someone carefully opening a drawer or a closet door. It was pitch-black in the hotel room; she had pulled the curtains so tightly together that no light came in; she had also put the alarm clock on the floor and covered it with a towel so that the red light from the time display did not illuminate the whole room. Sensing that she was not alone, she lay stiff as a board under the blankets, not daring to move, and listened, heard her shallow, tense breathing, and another person breathing too. Her heart was pounding with fright.

She held her breath and thought someone was moving in the

room. Who was it, and what did they want from her? She had no valuables with her, apart from the expensive watch that Sebastian had given her for their anniversary; it was lying on the desk. Or was this connected to the meeting with Wang and the phone call to Gao the lawyer? She heard a movement; a crack of the joints or something like that. She tried to remain still and considered her options. She could pretend to be sleeping and hope that the intruder would creep out again very soon without harming her; she could scream for help and hope that whoever it was would run off in fright, though he could just as easily attack her to keep her quiet. She could switch on the light, scream, and defend herself, or, depending on where the attacker was, try to get to the door and out into the corridor. She would be safe there. She felt the paralysis of fear creeping over her; she had to decide quickly, before she was completely overcome by panic.

Yin-Yin pretended to be turning in her sleep and rolled to the edge of the bed. She stretched a hand out to the nightstand, found the light switch, waited a second, pressed it, and stood up at the same time, screaming.

The room remained completely dark.

She heard the door being wrenched open and close again immediately. She tried to give chase, but banged her knee against the chair by the desk and jabbed her heel on the corner of the alarm clock, crying out in pain before she hobbled to the door. There was no one to be seen in the corridor. The key card for the room, which had to be slotted into a holder by the door to turn the power on, had been pulled out, and was lying on the floor; that was why the light had not come on. Yin-Yin put it back into the holder, closed the door, and looked around the room. The intruder had left no traces; her watch was on the desk and next to it was her cell phone, her notebook, and her small handbag.

Only then did she realize that she was trembling all over. She went into the bathroom and threw up. Then she rang Paul.

"Hello?" The sound of his sleepy voice calmed her a little. A couple of minutes later, he was in her room, wearing only his jeans and his undershirt.

"Are you sure nothing's missing?" he asked, concerned.

She sat on the bed cradling her knees close to her body, shivering.

"You probably interrupted him; otherwise he would have taken the watch," Paul said, beginning to tidy up by putting the alarm clock back on the nightstand, folding the towel, and taking it into the bathroom.

Yin-Yin nodded. "Do you think he wanted to steal something?"

"What else?"

"I don't know. I thought maybe it had something to do with our meeting with Wang and the appointment tomorrow morning."

He looked at her, surprised, then shook his head. "I can't imagine it's got anything to do with that. Who would be interested in what we're doing? Even if that were so, how would he have found out about the business with Sanlitun? Do you think Wang could have told someone?"

"No, I don't think so," she said, exhausted. If there was anyone whom she did not think capable of such betrayal, it was her old school friend the class clown. She had read somewhere that comedians were actually deeply unhappy people, and now she wondered if it was possible to misjudge friends. But she was tired, much too tired to follow that train of thought. Paul was probably right. It had been a common thief, whom she had managed to scare off before he stole her watch.

"I can call reception," Paul suggested. "I bet all the corridors have CCTV."

"Yes, try that."

He put the phone on speaker and asked for the duty manager.

"What can I do for you?" a sleepy voice murmured.

"My name is Paul Leibovitz and I'm in room 882. I'd like to know if all the hotel corridors are fitted with CCTV."

"Of course. Why are you asking?" The manager was suddenly wide awake.

"Do you record the images?"

"Yes. Why do you ask?" His irritation grew.

"Can I come down and look at the film of the previous half hour for the eighth floor?"

"Just a moment, please."

He heard voices in the background before someone put a hand over the receiver on the other side.

"I'm sorry, I've just been told that there've been technical problems with the CCTV. It hasn't been recording."

Yin-Yin felt nausea rising again; she took deep breaths in and out.

Paul put down the phone, kneeled down next to her, and put his arms around her. "If you like, I can stay the rest of the night here."

Yin-Yin wanted to say that it wouldn't be necessary, but the idea of being alone in the room again in a moment was intolerable. "Thank you," she said quietly. "I think that would help."

Paul brought the blanket over from his room, turned off all the lights apart from the one in the bathroom, tossed aside the scatter cushions on the two-seater couch, and made himself as comfortable as he could on it. She had offered him the bed; it was wide enough for two, but he had thanked her and refused. She turned onto her side, appreciating the feeling of safety that his presence gave her, and watched him in the half darkness until her eyes closed.

———

The lawyer Gao Jintao had his office on the first floor of an unremarkable building in Yiwu's "sock quarter." Paul and Yin-Yin walked through streets that seemed never-ending, with shop after shop selling only socks, which had clearly all been produced in Yiwu.

The stairwell was full of bicycles and boxes, and the doorbell did not work. Paul knocked on the door.

Gao opened the door just a crack and sized up his visitors thoroughly before letting them in. His office was a small, dark two-room apartment with piles of books, files, and papers on all the shelves, on all the tables and chairs, and spread out over most of the floor space, dotted with full ashtrays. It smelled of cigarettes and cold tea. Gao was a little man with salt-and-pepper hair, yellow teeth, and paw-like hands that seemed out of proportion with his small stature. He wore thick black glasses with dirty lenses and a faded Mao jacket, and was barefoot. Yin-Yin guessed he was in his late fifties. She checked that she had taken her battery out of her phone; Paul's battery was dead.

Gao cleared two chairs for them and invited them to sit down. He fetched three glasses and a Thermos with hot water, put a few tea leaves in the glasses, poured water over them, and sat down.

"What can I do for you?" he asked in his deep voice, lighting a cigarette.

While Paul explained what had brought them there, the lawyer watched him intently, swaying his upper body back and forth; he farted quietly twice.

Paul finished his account and asked, "Do you know anyone who would be willing to take this case on?"

At first Gao responded with a smile that Yin-Yin could not read. Was it meant sarcastically, or was he making fun of them?

"How do you like my office, young lady?" he asked abruptly. "It's nice but a little small, isn't it?"

She nodded.

"It wasn't always like this. I used to have an office with four rooms, a secretary, and a colleague who did research for me," he said in a tone of voice that implied that his visitors must surely know where he was heading with this story.

Yin-Yin and Paul gave him questioning looks.

"I had a car too. And a wife," he went on. There was no self-pity in his voice. "Until I agreed to defend three families whose land was taken away from them to build a new housing development on. They were poor farmers who came to my office one day. It was an open-and-shut case. The land seizure was so clearly against the laws of our People's Republic that I was convinced I would be able to help them. But I did not know our opponents well enough. That's always a terrible mistake to make, especially in our country. The other side had connections high up in the party in the province. We had no chance," Gao said, his voice still uncomplaining. "Have you ever been involved in a court case in China?"

"No," Paul and Yin-Yin said at the same time.

"Do you know about our legal system?"

"A little," Yin-Yin lied, although she had never in her life had anything to do with public prosecutors or judges.

Gao sighed. "Then I'll sum up the most important points in one sentence: the party takes precedence over the law."

"I know, I know," Paul replied impatiently. "But is that still the same today?"

"The same as yesterday. And the day before. The judiciary is not independent. Verdicts are passed by a commission in which party cadres play a decisive role. It's not like the West," he declared, turning to Paul. "The lawyers too are not independent, like they are in your country. The justice authorities grant the lawyers their licenses, and they take them back too. They took away my license when I refused to back down on that case, and wanted to appeal to the highest court in Beijing. Since then I can no longer represent anyone in court, but can only offer legal advice. And that is fortunate for you."

"What do you mean by that?" Paul asked, bewildered.

"Otherwise I would have to inform the authorities about our discussion. All registered lawyers in Zhejiang Province have received a directive to make an official report on any business to do with Sanlitun. Who visited you in the office? What did he want? What did you talk about?"

"Why?"

"I don't know. You're probably not the only ones who have cause to take them to court."

"How do you know about the directive?"

"From a lawyer friend."

Yin-Yin and Paul were silent as they registered this.

"Don't forget where we have come from," the lawyer said. "The concept of an independent judiciary does not play as major a role in Chinese thought and history as it does in the West. There was no legal system in this country twenty-five years ago. No lawyers, no notaries, no law degrees at the universities. Laws were barely written down. There were thousands of judges without any legal training. Now we have over two hundred thousand lawyers and over four hundred law faculties. The examinations to qualify as a judge or a lawyer are so tough that only ten percent of the applicants pass them. Go into a bookshop and you'll find shelves full of legal tomes; books on taxation law, real estate law, criminal law. Even guides to the law for people who can't afford the cost of a lawyer. So in that respect we have made great progress; ultimately, though, the progress we've made won't be of help to you." Gao sucked at his cigarette and looked at them. "Don't get me wrong. I'm quite sure that you've been victims of great wrongdoing and that you understandably want to see justice done. But you must be very clear about this: you will pay a price for it. No one can tell you beforehand how high the price will be. That depends on many factors, and this uncertainty is part of the system. Count on paying the highest possible price and then ask yourself if, when it's all said and done, it will be worth it."

He looked at them for a long time. "That is true for both of you."

"I am American and live in Hong Kong," Paul replied.

"So?"

"That is still not part of mainland China. Not yet."

"Are you sure? Are you telling me that you feel safe there because it is a so-called Special Administrative Region?"

"Yes."

Gao sighed again. "Do you have family in China?"

"No."

"In Hong Kong?"

"Yes, my partner." Paul was becoming visibly uncomfortable. He shifted from side to side in his chair.

"Is she Chinese?"

Paul nodded.

"You must be careful. That is all I am saying."

Yin-Yin sipped her tea; the warm glass in her hand felt good. The highest price? What could that be? She used to have a recurring nightmare in which a stranger broke all her fingers and her wrists so that she could never play the violin again. Would that be the worst punishment? Or was it to do with her life?

Paul's voice broke into her thoughts. "Do you really think that our lives would be in danger simply because we were threatening to sue Sanlitun for damages?"

Gao took his glasses off and cleaned them with the blue cloth of his Mao jacket before he replied. "Are our lives the most precious possessions we have? Or is it the way our lives are lived? You don't have to kill a man in order to destroy him. Take his work away from him. Take his family away from him. Take his friends away from him. Or the trust in his family and friends. Make him frightened. Anyone who constantly lives in fear is paying an extraordinarily high price, don't you think?" Paul and Yin-Yin did not reply, so Gao continued. "I don't want to discourage you. I just want you to know what's at stake."

"I doubt we're really—"

"Doubts are good," the lawyer interrupted. "Great wisdom comes from great doubts, that's what Confucius said." He laughed. "Apart from that, I cannot fail to mention that there have been incredible exceptions to the rule. Everything is about politics in this country, and sometimes you find yourself on the right side without knowing it. Who knows what forces may be working against Sanlitun in Beijing? You can only really feel safe here if you have nothing to lose, and there are not many people in that position. But you won't find a lawyer to represent you in our province. If you're lucky, you might find one in Shanghai." He opened a drawer, dug around in it, and pulled out a crumpled business card that he handed to them. The name on it was the same as the one Wang had written on the napkin for them. "Say that I sent you, then you'll get an appointment straightaway. And another thing: don't be fooled by your first impressions when you get there."

———

Yin-Yin and Paul decided to visit Da Long on the way to Shanghai, in order to tell him about their meetings with Gao and Wang.

There was an oppressive silence in the car. Yin-Yin's head was full of so many different thoughts that she did not know which she should concentrate on, which she should discuss with Paul first. Before her mother's illness, she had never experienced anything that had really caused her serious worry; until now, she had never felt threatened, or that her freedom was being restricted, but the memory of the lawyer's words and the intruder in her hotel room frightened her.

"Do you think Wang and Gao are exaggerating?"

"Maybe," Paul replied, deep in thought.

"Are you one of those people who have nothing to lose?"

"Fortunately not," he responded, smiling.

"Neither am I," she said.

"There was a time when I was one of those people," he added in a serious tone.

She looked at him, confused.

"I'll tell you about it one day."

———

A new VW Passat with tinted windows was parked in the village square, sunlight glinting on its shiny black paint. It was the kind of car that was rarely seen there. As Paul and Yin-Yin walked to her father's house, they passed two young men whom she didn't know, and who walked past without any greeting. An uneasy feeling came over her, and Paul dashed her a glance as if to say that he was feeling the same thing. They hurried toward her parents' home.

Yin-Yin had not seen her father behave in such a confused manner for a long time. He was sitting by her mother's bed, and responded to their greeting as briefly and casually as if they had been away for only a few minutes. He offered them tea and fetched dirty cups from the kitchen; instead of a plate of roasted sunflower seeds, he put a dish of empty shells on the table.

Paul wanted to tell him about Gao and Wang, but Da Long interrupted him as soon as he started speaking.

"I-I just had some visitors," he said.

"Who?"

"Two men from the Department of Health in Yiwu."

"What did they want?" Paul asked, surprised.

"They wanted to know how Min Fang was. Did you notify the authorities?"

Wang. Yin-Yin thought of her school friend immediately. He was a better actor than she'd thought he was. Why had he given them Gao's number if he was going to betray them? So that they would be seeing the lawyer while the officials interrogated her father alone?

"No, Papa. We didn't do that," she said.

"Wh-wh-who did, then?"

"I don't know. What did the two men say?"

"N-n-not much. Th-th-they wanted to know everything about Mama's illness. When and how it started. What she had been eating and drinking in the months before that. What the doctors said. What treatment she had received. I told them everything and showed them the paperwork from the hospital. They didn't even look at it, but put it straight into their case."

"You gave the documents to them?" she exploded. She had not meant to sound so upset.

Her father flinched and stammered a slow "Y-y-yes" that seemed never-ending.

"Did they examine Mama at all?" she asked more calmly.

"No. They didn't even go near the bed. They had no experience of sick people. They were not doctors."

"They didn't say anything about themselves, did they?"

Da Long thought for a moment. "N-n-not really. They asked about you and Xiao Hu. What you do in Shanghai, when you were last here. Where you were now."

"Do you know their names?" Paul asked.

"No. They didn't tell me who they were; or I've forgotten."

"Did they leave business cards or phone numbers?"

He shook his head.

"Did you tell them anything about mercury in Mama's body?"

"No. I only asked if her sickness might have something to do with the fish from the lake, because she had liked to eat it so much."

"What did they say to that?"

"They asked how I could have such a ridiculous thought, and said it was completely out of the question. The water was clean, they said, and the Golden Dragon factory produced only cough syrup and tea. Apparently the plant and the lake were inspected and tested two months ago. What do you think?"

Yin-Yin said nothing. Paul buried his face in his hands for a moment and took a deep breath. "Sanlitun factories are exempt from all inspections," he replied, telling Da Long the details of the conversations with Wang and Gao.

"Y-y-you mean they lied to me?" Da Long asked.

Paul nodded.

"J-j-just like they've always lied to us," Yin-Yin's father whispered, as though he were speaking to himself.

"Would you approach the lawyer in Shanghai for me?"

Paul waited before he replied. He drank a mouthful of tea, picked up a few sunflower seed shells, and crushed them between his fingers. Yin-Yin guessed what he was going to say, and she felt afraid.

"Yes."

"T-t-tell him everything you know. I want you to ask him if he will represent me." He gave his daughter a long look. "Y-y-you're worried, aren't you?"

"Yes."

"Don't be. I'm not afraid, and I have nothing to lose."

She wanted to say something, but she didn't dare to speak. He was her father. She could not ask Mama. It was his decision. She would not go against it, but there was a voice inside her that said he was wrong.

Only the dead have nothing to lose.

XII

———

I liked eating the fish. Anyone who has been hungry enough to chew a piece of bark is not picky about food for the rest of their life. You know that. Eel, catfish, crab; it hadn't tasted any different than usual. It was tender or tough, full of bones or easy to eat depending on the kind of fish and how old it was. I did not complain and I did not suspect anything. I was glad of every mouthful and never thought that death could be so furtive. Creeping up like that, making no sound underfoot, and with no odor at all.

The dead fish floated belly-up on the water. Sometimes there were more, sometimes fewer. The bones of the animal carcasses protruded from the ground like small talons.

Should that have been a warning to me? Two babies born blind and deformed. Two friends falling ill just days before me. Why didn't we put one and one together? We didn't dare. Because we believe what we have been told. Because we are good comrades. Always have been. Anything else would be too dangerous.

Besides, I was never very good at being suspicious.

I no longer hear every word that you say to each other, but I hear enough to understand what you plan to do. You want to go to court! You want to see those responsible punished! My beloved Da Long, what are you thinking? Has grief made you lose your mind? Have you forgotten where we live? If only I could speak again. If only for an hour, to bring you to your senses. Yin-Yin is right. Xiao Hu is right. No judge's verdict will make me well again. And you cannot win in the first place. We were *never able to win. We were able to outsmart them and we were able to try to slip away. But we could never win.*

We are a people suffering from memory loss. Either we don't want to remember, or we will not allow ourselves to remember. We are a country without a past, or with a past that lies so far back it seems unconnected to the present. No one today has been brought to justice for the mistakes, the suffering, and the deaths of that time. The past lies so far back that we all submit to the illusion that it no longer hurts. We are a country that only knows the present. And the future. As though we do not all stand on the shoulders of our forebears. As though a tree does not need roots.

Who will take any notice of a poisoned lake nowadays?

Of an old and useless woman?

Of a village in which the children are born cripples?

He who knows others is clever;
He who knows himself is enlightened;
He who conquers others is violent
He who conquers himself is strong

My dearest Da Long. Be strong and conquer yourself. Subdue your longing for punishment. For atonement. For understanding. For justice. I know that Laozi did not mean his words that way. But I can see no other meaning in them for you today. He who strives for the impossible opens the gate to calamity.

I don't have much time left. I can feel it. My strength is going. How tired I am. Is this what death feels like? How much I would have liked to sing these lines out loud once in my life. I discovered them too late. I wasn't allowed to listen to them before. Like so many other things. All the things they forbade us. All the nonsense we had to sing, read, listen to, and say. How they lied to us. How they misused the most precious thing we could give them, our trust. Has anyone been punished for that? And now you want justice for your sick wife!

XIII

They had reached the outskirts of Shanghai when Paul pulled the business card and the napkin out of his pocket and compared the phone numbers once again. They were the same, but it was only now that he noticed that they were prefixed with the area code for Singapore. He tapped the number hesitantly into Yin-Yin's cell phone.

"Hallo?"

"My name is Paul Leibovitz."

"Who are you? Where did you get my number?"

The voice was of a kind that made Paul wish he could hang up immediately. Sharp. Aggressive.

"I got it from Gao Jintao in Yiwu."

"Okay. What do you want?" the voice demanded.

"I need to make an appointment with you. As soon as possible, even if I have to fly to Singapore."

Silence.

"Where are you now?"

Every question sounded like an order. Paul shook himself. "In the car. On the way to Shanghai."

"Can you come to my office tomorrow at ten a.m.?"

"Yes. Where is it?"

"On the Bund. Number Two. In the building that used to be the Shanghai Club."

"There are two of us."

"No problem. Be there at ten sharp. I don't have much time."

Paul gave the phone back to Yin-Yin. She put it away, looked him in the eye for a moment without saying anything, sank back into her seat, and looked out the window. He looked at her profile. A strand of hair had fallen onto her face; she had tied the rest of it up into a topknot and put a chopstick through it. For the first time, he realized how young she was. Even though she was tired, there were no lines on her face, around neither the mouth nor the eyes. She had the body of a young and very beautiful woman who could have been his daughter. She looked exhausted and fragile; the melancholy in her face moved him. Paul thought about the last thirty-six hours, which they had spent nearly every minute of together. The distress on her face when she had told him about the death of her childhood friend's baby. Her laugh when Wang the class clown had said that Paul was too old for her. How she had trembled and not wanted to stay alone in her hotel room. He felt close to her, as though they had known each other for many years; he wondered if she felt the same way. He wanted to protect her, and would have liked to take her into his arms, but the fear that she would misunderstand the gesture held him back.

"Would you like to have a cup of tea at my place?" she asked suddenly, as the driver turned into Changle Lu, as though she had guessed what he was thinking.

"I'd like that." He wasn't sure if it was a good idea.

The car dropped them off at the corner of Fumin Lu. Yin-Yin bought a grapefruit, bananas, and a packet of watermelon seeds, and led him through a labyrinth of backyards and alleyways to her apartment. It was in the upper floor of a two-story building built in the 1920s. It was small, and Paul thought it was incredibly messy for a place that two young women lived in. Newspapers were strewn over the floor in the tiny hallway and socks and T-shirts were hanging from a laundry rack, with a plate of leftover noodles on top.

"I'm sorry. My roommate Lu isn't very tidy. She drives me crazy," Yin-Yin said. She showed him into her room, opened the window, and disappeared into the kitchen to make tea.

In her room there was enough space for an unmade bed, a small desk with a pile of papers, books, and fashion magazines on it, a bookshelf, and a music stand, which her violin case was propped up against. Her gorgeous cheongsam dangled from a hanger on the clothesline strung below the ceiling. Piled up on the only chair in the room were a dress and several tops. Paul sat cross-legged on the floor. The longer Paul looked at the chaos around him, the more he liked it. Twenty-five years ago the rooms he lived in would have looked the same. He heard Yin-Yin moving about in the kitchen. The clatter of mahjong tiles came from a neighboring apartment, and there was the distant monotone singsong of the man who collected old newspapers as he worked his way through the alleyways. The knife grinder followed in his wake, clamoring for attention. What a contrast to the quiet that surrounded him on Lamma.

Yin-Yin came in with the tea, sat down opposite Paul on the bed, and gave him a long look that he could not read. Paul could not remember the last time he had been with a woman alone in her apartment, and he felt unease creeping through him; the feeling that he did not belong there, but did not want to leave.

"Nice apartment," he said, to break the silence. He who was normally so comfortable with silence.

She smiled. Did she guess why he was feeling uneasy?

"You're a strange person," she said.

"What do you mean by strange?"

"Unusual."

"Is that a compliment?" he asked, flattered.

"More a realization."

"What makes you think that?" There was trace of disappointment in his voice.

"I don't know. The way you treat my father. The way you speak our language. The way you're helping us. Most of the foreigners I know run around wearing suits and are in China to do business. What are you doing here? What are you getting out of being so involved with the cause of Mama's illness?"

"Good question. Difficult to answer."

"Try."

"I like your father."

"That's not enough," she said, smiling.

"I find him incredibly brave. How he looks after your mother. How dedicated he is, and how calm he is as he goes about it. I felt both sorry for him and impressed by him. I'd like to help him. That's all."

"I don't think so. No one does something for nothing. That's the same in the West, isn't it?"

"Not for me. That's what's unusual about me," he said, hoping that she would catch the shade of sarcasm. Yin-Yin did not get his allusion. She shook her head quickly and sipped her tea.

After a while she asked, "How old are you?"

"I could be your father." The answer of an old man.

She rolled her eyes. "That's not what I asked."

"Fifty-three." Since Justin had died he had lost all sense of his age; it meant nothing. Now, in this room, in her presence, fifty-three sounded terribly old.

"Do you play an instrument?"

"No." As though he had to prove something to her, he added, "But I love music."

"I know." She looked at him until he dropped his eyes.

The clatter of the mahjong tiles. The singsong of the knife grinder. Birdsong. Every place has its own melody, Paul thought. You just have to take the time to listen to it.

After a long silence, Yin-Yin said, "You were going to tell me about why you were once one of those people who had nothing to lose."

The wrong question. The right question. "Because I had lost everything then."

The wonder in her face. There was worry and concern in her eyes, but they were the eyes of someone who had not been hurt deep in the soul. There was still so much youthful confidence in them that it almost physically hurt him to see it. It is not the passing of the years that makes us older, he thought, it is the wounds that life inflicts. The hurts and the losses. It was a look that made him feel old.

Older than he had ever felt, perhaps. At the same time it awakened a longing in him; for what exactly, he wasn't sure. For the unbearable lightness of youth, that he himself had never experienced? For the feeling that life was like an endless ocean shimmering with possibilities, which you just had to dive into?

"And now?" Yin-Yin interrupted his thoughts.

"I have a lot to lose."

"What?"

"Who," he corrected her. "We can only ever lose people. Everything else can be replaced or is unimportant."

"Who, then?"

"Christine."

"And who did you lose?"

"My son."

She said nothing for a long time. He was afraid that she would ask more questions, try to comfort him, or, worst of all, tell him about someone else who had lost his child, how terrible that had been, and that she could imagine how awful it had been for him . . . But Yin-Yin clearly felt that even a single word at this moment would be one too many; she bore the silence, which had lost all trace of tension, as she looked at her feet and clutched her teacup. Paul felt a vague disappointment at first, then relief. He thought about Justin and what he would say if he could see his father sitting on the floor in this untidy room. He would laugh at me, Paul thought. He thought about Christine and felt a bottomless longing for her. They had spoken on the phone every day, but only briefly, and the last few days had been so busy and intense that he had barely had time to think about her. Now he felt exhausted by his efforts, and realized that he looked forward to seeing her very much.

"You look tired. Would you like to go?"

"Yes, I think so."

"What do you mean, you think so?"

Paul smiled a little at himself. "That it would be better for me to go. I really am a little tired."

"I was afraid of being on my own."

"I know. Would you like me to stay?"

She shook her head. "My brother lives nearby. I'll go over to his apartment later."

"Where shall we meet tomorrow morning?"

"I'll pick you up at the hotel at nine thirty."

———

It was only when Paul was standing on Changle Lu that he realized how hungry he was. He had seen a few small food vendors opposite the supermarket, so he walked in the shadow of the plane trees toward Fumin Lu. It was shortly before twilight; cars, bicycles, pedestrians, and street peddlers were fighting for space in the overcrowded roads. Someone tried to sell him fake brand-name watches; another person tried to interest him in ballpoint pens. Belts, illegal DVDs. A woman followed him, hissing "Gucci, Prada, Wietong" continuously into his ear until he shooed her away by waving his arm decisively. Garish neon light lit up the fruit and vegetable stands, the tea booths, and the other street stalls. It made the faces of the stallholders look pale and cold. He walked past a massage parlor in which a couple of young women in pink dresses were staring at a television looking bored. One of them waved at him and he smiled back. In a gateway, an old man had hung a mirror on the wall, put a chair in front of it, and laid out scissors, combs, and razors neatly on a little table. He was reading a newspaper while waiting for customers.

Paul sat down in front of a soup-noodle stall that had set out folding tables and stools on the sidewalk. There was a delicious smell of meat broth, coriander, and garlic; a young man was kneading a grayish-white lump of dough, preparing noodles to order for each customer. He kneaded and shaped the ball, pulling it apart over and over again until he had a handful of long noodles that he then slung into a sieve and submerged into boiling water. Two young women who also worked for this stall squatted by his feet cleaning fish in the gutter, talking and laughing raucously; Paul could understand only snatches of what they said.

The soup tasted wonderful: spicy and hearty lamb and vegetables. When Paul shouted out his compliments to the cook, he smiled back, looking embarrassed. The awkward smile of someone for whom praise was a rare luxury.

The hum of life that surrounded Paul miraculously banished his tiredness. He felt a strong desire to go for a walk. He paid his bill, got up, and plunged into this world of alleyways, hidden court-yards, and plane tree avenues, in which wet underwear, stockings, and shirts hung on washing lines stretched across the streets and dripped down on the passersby; in which the smell of food wafted from every corner; in which he heard people who had eaten their fill burp and pass wind as he walked past their homes; the screech of quarreling; the snores of those sleeping. The whispers of the living.

The longer he walked around, the better he liked this place. The faded, monotone Shanghai of his memory, in which everyone rode a bicycle and wore the same gray or blue Mao suit, had turned into a restless, greedy city, filled with people who were searching, cast out from somewhere else. Full of nervous energy and full of courage. Full of people who had left their villages and towns, lured there in the hope of a better life. Shanghai reminded him of the New York of his youth. Or of Hong Kong in the 1970s, which he had loved, before the city had become a well-behaved faceless, glass-walled, air-conditioned zone, which smelled only of exhaust fumes rather than of people.

"Hungry for love," Christine had called him two weeks ago. Per-haps, he thought, she had hit on the right thing but had chosen the wrong word. Maybe after the years of isolation on Lamma, "hungry for life" would be more accurate.

Back in the hotel he rang Christine straightaway. In the last few days he had found it more and more difficult to deal with her annoy-ance and ill humor over the constant delays of his return to Hong Kong. She had not wanted to know much about the results of the lab tests and his suspicions on Thursday. Yesterday, he had told her about his conversations with doctors in Shanghai and that there might be hope for Min Fang if certain factors were in place; he also said that her brother had asked him to stay a few more days.

The longer the phone rang, the more nervous he got. Where was she? Why didn't she pick up the phone? Do you have family in Hong Kong? the lawyer had asked.

When he finally heard her voice, he noticed that something was not right.

"Are you well?"

"No," she replied, sounding weak. "I'm sick."

"What's wrong?" He did his best to remain calm.

"I threw up all night and I feel incredibly tired. It's been going on for days."

"Have you been to the doctor?"

"Yes. I went yesterday, and another time before that."

"You didn't tell me anything about that," he said accusingly.

"I didn't want to worry you," Christine said, before falling silent.

"Why aren't you telling me what the doctor said?"

He couldn't bear her. *I'm sorry to have to tell you.*

"Christine," he said. "Tell me."

"Nothing that you have to worry about. I have to take better care of myself. I'm overworked. That's all."

"Did you have a blood test?"

"Yes, of course."

"Is everything normal?"

"Yes, Paul. All fine."

"Do you have any bluish bruises on your body?" He had seen them on Justin but had not really paid attention to them. Bruises on a young boy—so what? They had been messengers from death.

"No."

"Nosebleeds?"

"No. Please don't worry. It's high time you came back," she said, with no hint of accusation in her voice.

"I know. Monday morning. On the first flight."

"Are you sure?"

"I promise."

"I need you."

"I need you too."

A little disquiet remained.

———

Yin-Yin picked him up at the hotel. She had brought him two small presents: a can of premium-quality green tea and a recording of her playing the violin for Schubert's quartet. She was in a good mood, having slept well, and was clearly glad to see him.

They crossed Suzhou Creek and walked down the Bund. Chen's office was at the other end.

Twenty minutes later, they were standing in front of number 2, a white neoclassical building built at the turn of the previous century, which had once been one of the most elegant addresses in Shanghai. A smart bronze plaque by the entrance. They climbed the stairs up to the third floor. Chen the lawyer opened the door himself. He was Paul's height but powerfully built, an impressive-looking figure who Paul thought looked more like someone from Wall Street than from China. Chen looked as though he spent many hours in the gym; he was wearing an elegant dark suit, a white shirt, black shoes, and rimless glasses.

He led them down a long corridor past a row of offices. It was Sunday, and there was no one else was around. His office had an impressive view of the river; the furnishings reminded Paul of the office of a British barrister he had once visited in Hong Kong: a heavy dark mahogany desk, a leather armchair, and two leather Chesterfield couches in a corner. They sat down; he did not offer them anything to drink.

"So, Gao sent you. How is he?"

Yin-Yin said nothing. They had agreed that Paul would tell the story and do all the talking to begin with, but Paul was finding it hard to reply. Sitting opposite, Chen seemed less aggressive than he had been on the phone, and his voice had lost its commanding tone, but Paul still found it difficult to get the measure of him. He sus-

pected that every question Chen asked was calculated to test them or trap them; every response had to be weighed up.

"Very well, as far as we can tell," Paul said vaguely.

"Does he still walk around barefoot in his office?"

"Yes."

"How do you know him?"

"A good friend recommended him to us."

"And he sent you to me because . . ." Chen waited for Paul to complete the sentence.

"Because he thinks only you can help us. At least, that's what he told us."

"It must be an interesting case. What's it about, then?"

Paul had barely mentioned the words "Sanlitun" and "mercury" before Chen interrupted him abruptly. "Shall we take a walk on the Bund?" he said, standing up. "Leave your things and your cell phones here. We'll come back to the office later."

They took the elevator down without exchanging a word, crossed the Bund, and walked by the water toward the Peace Hotel. On the promenade, they mingled with tour groups that were being directed by guides waving fans, and parents showing their children the Pudong skyline, looking proud. Tourists from the countryside, who could be identified by their shoes and their gray clothes, posed for photos with the skyscrapers in the background; young men walked around offering plastic toys, candied fruit, and lottery tickets for sale. There could hardly be a better place to have a confidential conversation.

A couple of barges were traveling upriver slowly; the sound of a horn from one of the ships made Yin-Yin jump.

After a while Chen said, "Now tell me what has happened." After Paul had finished telling him everything, the lawyer steered them toward a bench that had just been vacated, and they sat down.

"And Gao seriously thought I could help you?"

"Yes, he did," Yin-Yin said firmly. Paul could tell from her voice that she would not be satisfied with an I'm-sorry-but-I-can't-do-anything-for-you reply.

Chen sighed. "I'm a commercial lawyer. I advise companies on takeovers and property transactions. I started in criminal law but that's a long time ago now. What I do now is much more lucrative; I admit it."

"Why did Gao recommend you to us then?" Yin-Yin asked suspiciously.

"Because we're good friends. We went to college together. We were the top students of our year in the whole province of Zhejiang. After that we worked in the same practice for a few years, mostly on civil and criminal law. One day, two farmers came to my office. A party cadre had illegally confiscated their land without paying them compensation. That happened all the time."

"And?"

"I sent them away. Not long after I got a job offer from Shanghai to work in a commercial law practice."

"Didn't Gao have a similar case?" Yin-Yin wondered.

"Yes, but years later. To this day I don't know if it was coincidence or if someone was trying to test us. Gao took the case on. You have seen the consequences it had for him."

"He didn't seem defeated," Paul said.

"You're right there. Gao has a clear conscience. He's the only person I know who I can say that about. I admire him for that. Sometimes I do him little favors as a friend."

"What kind of favors?"

"I give him advice on complicated cases. Prepare the occasional document for him or get one of my colleagues to do some research on a case for him. He has no one else. Commercial law, you see, is profitable, but really quite boring in the long run. There are two souls beating in every heart. At least. Isn't that so?" he asked with a short laugh. "But I'm afraid your case is too much for me. If we found a court willing to hear the case, it would no longer be about protecting Sanlitun. It would be about protecting the government. The government of the province and, in the end, of Beijing," Chen said.

"Why?" Yin-Yin asked suspiciously.

"It would come to that with an environmental scandal like

this—or perhaps I should call it a crime instead. Sanlitun would not be held solely responsible. The officials in the city administration of Yiwu are also involved. The party cadres of Zhejiang Province too, right up to the capital. The censorship of the media is involved. The independence of our environmental protection authorities and our courts. It involves the corruptibility of civil servants and party functionaries. It involves the position of the Communist Party. You could say it involves everything."

A young boy tried to sell them plastic flowers. Chen shooed him away with an abrupt wave of his hand.

"I think what you're taking on is too much. If you want my advice, I would say you should let the matter rest."

"I expected a man like you to have a more original suggestion," Yin-Yin replied, disappointed. "My mother was a healthy woman a few weeks ago. Now she's lying in bed at home, unable to move. She groans and gasps. She grunts like a pig. She is blind. She is deaf. She shits and pisses in bed like a baby, and you're telling me to forget the whole thing?"

"Your mother won't recover regardless of the outcomes to any lawsuit."

"I've heard that enough times now," she said angrily. "What about the dead and crippled children?"

Chen said nothing for a while. Then he replied, choosing his words with care, "They too won't be brought back to life or made well. I'm sorry."

"And what about those who are not even born yet? Do you want to sit in peace in your office drafting contracts and advising companies, knowing that, only a few hundred miles away, healthy embryos are being turned into deformed ones simply because you're doing nothing? Could you live with that?"

Paul thought he couldn't be hearing right. Did Yin-Yin seriously mean what she was saying, or did she want to provoke Chen? What had made her change her mind to the opposite point of view?

"Young woman," the lawyer said. "Your idealism surprises me, and you will not like my reply at all. Yes, I could. If I offered you my help, under certain conditions, then it would not be because I had a bad conscience or on moral grounds; it would be because of other reasons that I will not tell you."

Two men crammed onto the bench with them. Chen stood up, saying, "Let's walk on a little."

They strolled to the end of the promenade. "I'll offer you this: your father can represent himself in court or submit a petition. Every Chinese person has the right to do that. I would be willing to draft a list of charges or a petition, and to advise him throughout the case, pro bono and on condition of anonymity, of course. Perhaps he'll be lucky and Sanlitun will offer to pay damages at the start of the case, in order to avoid bad publicity. Or . . ." Chen paused for a long time, as though he wanted to make sure that they were listening carefully to every word. "Or you could try to go to the media. I could also advise you if you choose to do that."

"That's impossible." Yin-Yin shook her head in disappointment. "Mr. Leibovitz has already told you about my friend at the *People's Daily*. He's not even allowed to make inquiries."

"I'm not talking about state-owned newspapers or television. I'm taking about the Internet. Write everything down. Take a photograph of your mother in which it would not be possible to identify her. Go to an Internet café and post the story and the photos online anonymously. Three hundred fifty million potential readers are waiting for you there. Indignant readers who have had or have heard of similar experiences. Angry readers who can become allies."

Paul watched as Yin-Yin flinched and stared at the lawyer, wide-eyed.

"A friend at work from Heilongjiang province told me about an interesting case not long ago. A factory in a small town had refused to pay for overtime worked. Several dozen workers staged a protest, including two young men, the Hu brothers. Without any warning, the factory guards started attacking them, and they beat up the younger brother so badly, on a public road, that he died that night. Although there were dozens of witnesses, the police and the authorities refused to investigate; they claimed that it had been an accident. The owner of the factory is an influential man in that town. That would normally have been the end of that. But a passerby had taken a video of the attack on his cell phone. The video appeared on the Internet two weeks later."

Chen held his breath for a moment before he continued. Paul saw that Yin-Yin was listening intently to every word the lawyer said.

"I don't know," he said, "if the censors overlooked it, if it spread too quickly, or if there was a political motive behind it. But the local government and the company were bombarded with angry emails from all over the country. Public indignation grew from day to day. After a week, it had reached such a level that the authorities had to react. The head of the factory security team and a few of his guards were arrested, as were several officials in the town council who had covered up for him. The attacker was identified and given a heavy sentence for manslaughter. The company, if memory serves, paid the Hu family damages of a hundred thousand yuan. That is the power of the Internet. We have no idea how it will change our country."

Paul and Yin-Yin were silent as they processed this.

"To be honest, I see that as your best chance." Chen looked at his watch. "I have to rush back to the office. Think about what I've suggested, and let me know what you decide."

They picked up their things from Chen's office. Yin-Yin had to go to a rehearsal, so they made arrangements to meet at a bar near the conservatory that evening.

Paul strolled alongside the Huangpu River toward the hotel. He took his time looking at the famous façades on the Bund: an unusual but impressive mixture of European architectural styles—neobaroque, neogothic, neoclassical, neorenaissance, with a little beaux arts and art deco. That was how the West had demonstrated its power in the past, and constructed a monument to itself. This row of buildings, over half a mile long, used to be the most famous sight in Shanghai. He realized that the tourists were turning their back on the Bund now. They were standing on the promenade and, almost without exception, looking across at the other bank of the river, at Shanghai's symbol of the twenty-first century, the towering skyscrapers of Pudong. The few visitors who were admiring the Bund were not Chinese.

———

They met in the Face Bar in the garden of the Ruijin Hotel, which was laid out like a park with several grand buildings in it; a British newspaper baron had built it for himself and his family in the 1920s.

Yin-Yin was already sitting on the terrace under a tree whose mighty branches, hung with lit lanterns, arched over her like an umbrella. They ordered two glasses of white wine.

"My brother's joining us later. Is that okay?"

Paul nodded. "Have you told him anything?"

She inclined her head as if to shake it.

"Did you mean to provoke Chen this morning?"

She looked at him in surprise. "What do you mean?"

"When you said that he would be responsible for the deaths of children if he did nothing. That was the gist of my argument, but you and your brother—"

She interrupted him. "That was a long time ago."

"Three days," he retorted.

"That's just what I said," she replied, smiling. "That's a long time in Shanghai."

"What's changed in that time?"

"A lot," Yin-Yin said. The laughter had vanished from her face. "Something inside me. I thought a long time about it this afternoon. It's a feeling that I can't put into words."

"Grief?"

She shook her head.

"Rage?"

"Not that either."

"Duty?"

"No, I wouldn't call it that."

"What then?"

"I've no idea. I see images: my mother in her bed. My friend

Feng. Her wonderful fit of giggles when we hid from my brother in the shed and he didn't find us. The tears that streamed down her rosy cheeks as she laughed. The way she carried my schoolbag when it was soaked through with rain and my arms and shoulders were so tired and achy from practicing the violin. The small green jade cat that she gave me as a talisman when I moved to Shanghai to study, which I lost shortly after. I see her in the hospital with her dead child in her arms. It's the feelings about the little things that help us to understand the feelings about the big things. Do you know what I mean?"

"I think so, yes."

"What would you call it?"

"Love," he said, without giving it much thought.

"What makes you say that?"

"I can't think of a better word."

Yin-Yin gave him an uncomprehending look. She wanted to object—he saw it in her body language, the way her back stiffened—but at the last moment she stopped and sat back in her chair, looking pensive instead.

The waiter brought the wine, peanuts, and a dish of olives. They clinked glasses in silence.

After his second sip of wine, Paul asked, "Is your boyfriend coming too? What's his name again?"

"Weidenfeller. Johann Sebastian. No, he can't make it."

"Have you spoken to him already?"

"Only briefly. He couldn't understand at all why we met with Wang and Gao in Yiwu. When I told him that we were having dinner this evening he got really annoyed."

"Why?"

Yin-Yin shrugged. "Sometimes I ask myself if I'm only in love with him for his name."

"Johann Sebastian? Do you find the name so beautiful?" Paul wondered out loud.

"No. But I love Bach."

Paul smiled.

"I don't even know what kind of relationship he has with his parents."

"Why does that interest you?"

"That's what's most important!" she said, astonished. "If I know how he treats his parents, then I'll know how he'll treat me in the future."

"If you think like that, we would never get married," Paul responded, amused.

"Is that up for debate?" she asked seriously.

How often had that happened to him? The Chinese did not get his humor; they never knew exactly when he was joking or not. "No," he replied, clearing his throat. "That was a joke."

Paul picked up his glass and clinked it against hers one more time. She took only a tiny sip.

"What do you think of Chen's idea about the Internet?" she asked, lowering her voice to a near whisper even though no one was sitting within earshot.

"I think it's a good idea. After everything that we've found out, it gives us the best chance of achieving something without taking a huge risk. I'm not sure if your father would be able to represent himself in court."

Yin-Yin chewed away at an olive as she thought. Her cell phone rang, but when she answered the call it was cut off. "I forgot to take out the battery again," she said, startled. "I think I'm starting to get paranoid about being followed."

"Oh yes, even paranoid people have enemies," Paul said, smiling.

"Is that meant to be reassuring?"

"No, just another bad joke. Sorry."

They saw Xiao Hu walking through the garden coming toward them. He was on the phone. He greeted them with a nod and walked away again.

"Ever since he became head of the legal department he's been ridiculously busy," Yin-Yin said, as though she had to apologize for her brother. "He's hoping for a promotion to the head office in Beijing."

Xiao Hu reappeared at their table shortly after, smiling. He was wearing a gray suit and a white shirt, and looked as though he had come straight from the office. But he seemed friendlier and more relaxed than at their previous meeting.

Yin-Yin told him what they had done and found out in the last few days. Her voice rose and fell to great effect several times as she talked, sounding indignant and angry, then pleading for his understanding in a gentle tone, and asking for his help.

Over the past thirty years, Paul had learned to read the faces of Chinese people; he did not understand why some foreigners claimed that the Chinese were inscrutable. Sad people looked sad. Happy people happy. Lonely people lonely. The expression of emotion in their features was merely a little more restrained, more proper, more subtle. Like so much else in this country. Shadows flitted over Xiao Hu's face; he blinked nervously and his lips thinned into two straight lines; he sank deeper and deeper into his chair. Yin-Yin was so worked up that she did not notice; when she finished her tale, she looked him in the eye expectantly and not without pride. The look of a little sister.

"You're both crazy," Xiao Hu said immediately. Paul could not tell if these words were uttered accusingly, despairingly, or in astonishment. "What do you plan to do next?"

Paul could see from Yin-Yin's face that she took her brother's question as a recognition of their efforts and as encouragement. "I think it would be best to take Chen's advice. I'll write something and put it on the Internet."

"Under no circumstances are you doing that," Xiao Hu said, sitting up straight.

Yin-Yin flinched. Little sister, big brother.

"Why not?"

"Because they'll get you."

"But I wanted to . . . I mean . . . anonymously . . . and . . ."

"Do you know how many officials are monitoring the Internet? Tens of thousands of them! They're everywhere. On websites. In forums. In blogs. Chat rooms. Email inboxes. There's no anonymity there."

"But Chen said . . ." Yin-Yin was close to tears.

"Chen has no idea. The story he told you about might have turned out that way. What about the others that didn't work out so well? When bloggers were sent to work camps, to psychiatric units, or to prison? They get everyone."

"Who's 'they'?"

"The party." He leaned over the table and repeated the words, whispering. "The party, which I'm a member of."

His sister sank back into her chair and fell silent.

A light breeze had risen and blew the lanterns above them this way and that. A leaf floated down and landed on the olives. Paul could see that Yin-Yin no longer had the energy to argue with her brother. What was Xiao-Hu thinking? He had put aside the cold detachment of his reaction a few days ago at the Thai restaurant; now the story had become his story too. In the flickering light of the lanterns, Paul could see that red spots had appeared on his neck.

"What do you suggest instead?" Paul asked carefully. He did not wish to provoke Xiao Hu.

"That I handle it."

"You?"

"Yes."

"How?"

"I have good contacts with a few party compatriots in Hangzhou. I'm going there in a few weeks for training. I'll ask around then. After everything that you've told me, I'm sure the authorities know about it already and have taken action. But they're hardly going to publicize it. If I'm not wrong, it's no longer out of the question that Sanlitun might be open to negotiations about paying some small damages."

Paul noted the doubt in Yin-Yin's eyes.

"Promise me that you won't do anything," Xiao Hu said sternly to his sister. "You wouldn't achieve anything and you'd endanger everyone: yourself, Papa, Mama. We'll see what happens when I'm back from Hangzhou. And not a word of this to Papa, understood?"

Yin-Yin nodded. She said that the day had been very long and that she was tired and would like to go home and get to bed. Xiao Hu seemed quite happy with that. He paid the bill, and they walked to Ruijin Lu together to get taxis. At Yin-Yin's insistence, her brother took the first taxi.

"I'll walk," Yin-Yin said when he had gone.

"Should I walk you home?" Paul offered.

"No, it's not far."

"What will you do?"

"Have a good night's sleep first."

"And then?"

Yin-Yin shrugged.

Paul took a pencil and paper out of his backpack and wrote down his email address and telephone number in Hong Kong for her. "Write to me or call if you need help. Or someone to talk to. If necessary, I'll come over again for a few days."

"Thank you." She pulled him to her and hugged him.

Feeling her body in his arms, Paul was shocked by how thin and fragile it felt.

"Thank you," she said again.

Before Paul could ask "What for?" she let him go, smiled in farewell, turned around, and walked down the street without looking back.

———

In the hotel, Paul fell into bed, dead tired. Even in the taxi he had noticed that the final remnants of energy were draining from his body like water in a sink that someone had pulled the plug out of. He felt nothing but exhaustion and a deep happiness that he would be flying back to Hong Kong the next day. The longing for Christine grew with every breath, as though he had suppressed the feeling for the last few days and it was seizing him with even greater force now.

Paul flopped across the wide mattress to get to the telephone. He could hardly wait to hear her voice.

She sounded sleepy but a little less weak. "Hurry," she whispered.

"Tell the pilot he should fly as fast as he can. I have to tell you something."

"Just say it. I'm listening."

"Not on the phone."

"What is it?" he asked, curious. "Come on."

"A surprise."

"What kind of surprise?"

"A big one."

"How big?"

"Big. Huge. Bigger than you and me together. It doesn't get any bigger."

XIV

Christine felt her knees buckle. Dr. Fu grabbed her under the arm in a reflex action and led her to a chair. She sat down and breathed heavily, registering what was around her only through a gray veil. A full waiting room, harsh fluorescent light, white-painted walls. Women flicking through magazines. The cry of a baby.

"There's no doubt about it," the gynecologist said in response to her question. "You're expecting a baby."

For a few seconds she thought she had lost consciousness. Not from shock, and not from fear either. Something within her had lost balance.

A baby? Her? Out of the question. A mistake.

She had not thought about having a baby for years. She was forty-three years old. She was expecting the menopause, not a baby. But what if it were true? If she were really pregnant for the fourth time in her life?

The first pregnancy had to be terminated. It had been a mistake, the result of a fleeting relationship. And she was young, nineteen years old. Only later, when she became a mother, did she begin to realize what she had done. The second time, she had brought Josh into the world. Shortly after his third birthday she fell pregnant again. She wanted the baby, but her husband did not. On no account. He had many arguments against it: his frequent business trips to China, her travel agency, Josh, whom she already had too little time for. Christine acquiesced—reluctantly. Later she found out that her husband already had a Chinese mistress on the other side of the border at the time, a woman who bore him a son not long after. That was why her child had not been allowed to live. The thought was still hard to bear today. For years she was haunted by a recurring dream in which she labored in great pain to bring a healthy baby into the world, her first, which she wished for more than anything in the world, but it vanished without a trace right after the birth. She looked for it everywhere, ran from room to room in the hospital in her blood-stained nightdress, clawed through all the closets in her apartment, ran through an MTR train in a panic in her dream, staring at every passenger, checking every shopping bag, until she finally sank to the floor crying in the last carriage and woke up bathed in sweat. She had wanted never to be pregnant again then, and had even briefly considered getting sterilized.

What if Dr. Fu was right? They would be old, very old, parents; the probability of birth defects was significantly higher. How would it work anyway? In her small apartment. The travel agency. Paul on Lamma. Sleepless nights, colic, teething. Her head was filled with doubts and questions, and just as Christine felt she might be buried beneath the weight of them, something miraculously tore her out of these thoughts, lifted her, and carried her away. A balance was restored, but it was no longer the same. In that moment there was neither fear nor worry, only a feeling she had no words for; it possessed her whole being and filled her with an almost unbearable sense of lightness. A human being was growing inside her. The size of a pinhead. A quirk of fate. A gift of happiness.

And what about Paul? The longer she thought about it, the less she could imagine that he could want to become a father again after Justin's death. She had never spoken about it with him. Sometimes she had wondered to herself what might have been if they had met ten years earlier. She would definitely have wanted to have a child with him. But she did not like those what-if games anyway; they didn't lead to anything. "What if?" was a question for people who had the luxury of time. She was not one of those people.

The thought of having an abortion without telling Paul anything about it crossed Christine's mind. At this early stage it would be a matter of minutes. He wouldn't even find out that she had been pregnant. She might have done it not so long ago. Pros and cons. The list of cons was unbearably long. To want a child or not. There was no *and*. With Paul, a secret abortion was unthinkable. She wanted to—she had to—tell him. If he said no, she would not object.

————

The flight from Shanghai had landed. Only a few more minutes.

His laugh. His look, which lifted her spirits so. How had she been able to stand a week without him? His arms around her made all the difficult thoughts disappear. A child. With him. How could she have had even a second's doubt?

When they were seated in the airport express train, he asked, "Now, tell me, what's the big surprise?"

Christine was so nervous she could barely breathe. She hesitated, pulled his head toward her, and whispered, "Not here."

"Where, then? Where are we going?"

"To Central. Then we'll take a taxi to the Peak."

"There, of all places? Have you thought this over carefully?" His voice sounded surprised and expectant but neither rejecting nor fearful.

She nodded. "Yes."

The taxi dropped them off at the end of Peak Road. Paul bought two bottles of water at the cable car station before they turned onto Lugard Road, a narrow footpath that snaked around the top of the mountain, with trees growing so densely on both sides that it was like a green tunnel in which the aerial roots of the trees touched the ground. It was a hot day, but not too warm at this altitude; the birds were chirping away and only a gentle murmur rose from the city. This was what she had had in mind.

Christine led Paul to the only bench that gave an unrestricted view of the harbor and of Kowloon.

"You're drawing this out," he said, turning and giving her a piercing look.

"I . . . I . . ." Christine faltered. *I'm pregnant. I'm expecting a baby.* She was afraid of saying one of those sentences. Words could sound so banal. "How much is one plus one?" she asked suddenly.

He thought. He pushed his sweat-soaked hair away from his forehead, keeping his eyes fixed on her; Christine had the feeling that she was watching someone thinking, puzzling over something. "One plus one," he repeated, "is . . ." Tears in his eyes. The short answer: "Three."

Christine nodded and felt her center of gravity start swaying once more. Like a suspension bridge with an overloaded truck going over it. Something could give way any moment and pull her into the depths. She was not able to make out what Paul's expression meant, what his reaction was. Was he happy? Was he frightened? Yes or no?

She felt defenseless, more at the mercy of another person than she had ever felt in her life, as though she had put everything she possessed in his hands. He took her in his arms; Christine did not know if he was crying tears of joy or sorrow. Her child. She did not want to lose another child. Not for the world.

"What are you thinking?" he whispered.

"If we're too old for a child."

"You mean, if it will be healthy?"

"Yes. No. We can test for that. I mean, whether it's terrible to have such old parents," she said, avoiding his gaze.

"There are many things that make parents hard to put up with. I don't know whether them being past the age of fifty or sixty is necessarily one of those things," Paul replied.

Was that a yes? Was he trying to tell her that he was glad? She did not have the courage to ask, so instead she said, as matter-of-factly as possible, "And how do you think it will go? I mean, the day-to-day of it?" Things to take into account. Practical thoughts. Perhaps she could hide behind them.

"That's not important."

"Why not?" she asked, unsettled.

"Do we want to make a list of pros and cons?"

"No. But we have to think about it."

"That's true. We have to know if there is enough space inside us."

"You're oversimplifying things," she responded.

"On the contrary. I'm asking the most difficult question first. Once we've answered that, we'll have the answers to all the others." He gave her a searching look. "What was your initial reaction?"

She continued looking down at the ground and hesitated before replying. "Disbelief."

"I mean, were you happy or not?"

Christine knew what he meant, but she did not trust herself to say the words.

"Yes or no? What did your heart say?"

There was a strange calmness in his voice, and the longer they talked, the stronger the energy that he radiated became. He had found his answer, and he knew hers. "We're old enough," he continued, "to trust our intuition. What else or who else can we trust?"

Only now did she have the courage to look at him. She saw the look on his face and asked herself how she could have doubted.

––––––

When they continued walking, Paul started talking about the times he had walked on the Peak with Justin. How they had imagined being able to fly, being birds pooping on people's heads. About how his son had such a thirst for knowledge, how he had lain on a bench with his head in Paul's lap, asking questions.

"Once he wanted to know if the world used to be in black and white."

She smiled. "What made him ask that?"

"We had watched the old Charlie Chaplin films. They weren't in color, of course, so he thought they were what the world was like. Another time he kept asking me if grown-ups sometimes felt happy for no reason like children did, or if they always needed to have a reason to feel happy."

"What did you say?"

"I don't know. I'm searching for it."

"For what?"

"Happiness for no reason."

"And? Have you found it?"

He tipped his head from side to side. "Happiness yes. But for no reason?" A wrinkle of the brow. "I'm afraid I'm not there yet."

Christine realized that her child would not just grow up with Josh as an older brother. Justin would be a part of her family, just as he had been part of their relationship in the last one and a half years. He belonged to it, just like the dead always belong, because they are a part of us. Some more so, some less so.

"Master Wong knew," Paul said suddenly in an unusual tone of voice. As though he were speaking to himself.

"What?"

"That you would get pregnant."

"You didn't tell me anything about it!" she exclaimed.

"No?"

Where did the awkwardness in his voice come from? "No, you didn't. What exactly did he predict?" she wanted to know.

"He said: *I will give life.*"

"You will give life?"

"Yes."

"Anything else?"

"No."

———

Three days later, Paul and her mother met for the first time. Christine had wanted to share her joy, so she told her about the pregnancy on impulse; her mother had insisted on meeting the father of the child. As soon as possible. Christine's mother refused to go into the city for the occasion, so they had arranged to meet at House of Supreme Harmony, a Chinese restaurant in the shopping center in Hang Hau.

Christine had been nervous about the meeting the whole day; she remembered the dinner at which she had introduced her ex-husband to her mother. It had been an excruciating two hours—torture. Her mother had disliked her future son-in-law at first sight. She had cross-examined him with questions, and he had answered politely, trying hard to make a good impression, to win her goodwill or at least her respect, but had received only a cold rebuff. Worst of all, Christine remembered how she herself had behaved. She had not dared to contradict her mother. She had grown more and more quiet in the course of the conversation, shriveled to a little girl as they talked about her as if she were a young child. She did not want to sit through another evening like that.

With her first disapproving glance, Christine's mother saw where the father of her second grandchild was from, or rather where he was not from. She had nothing against Westerners in principle, Christine knew that, but she believed that foreigners, regardless of where they came from, could not understand the Chinese way of thinking, or the culture, customs, and habits; she thought that there were fundamental differences in many respects, and that Westerners therefore had to be kept at a distance.

The House of Supreme Harmony was her mother's favorite restaurant; it was as big as half a soccer field and had red carpets and red-painted walls hung with fabric decorations in the shape of carp; there were gilded chandeliers and big round tables filled with families talking loudly, nineteen to the dozen. The floor was covered in food stains. Her mother thought that the more crowded and noisy a restaurant was, and the dirtier the carpet and table-cloths, the better the food was. Christine had long given up trying to persuade her otherwise. She usually didn't even notice the noise, or if she did, she put up with it patiently, but this evening the racket made her feel even more tense. Paul had tried to calm her nerves, and reassured her that he knew how to make a good impression in situations like these; it was not the first time he had been introduced to Chinese parents as a prospective son-in-law. That was not exactly what she wanted to hear, but it did make her feel a little bit better. She breathed a sigh of relief when she saw Paul enter the restaurant. He had been to the hairdresser; his gray curls now reached only to just above his ears, and he was freshly shaven and wearing a pair of black linen trousers and a white shirt.

He was holding a box of Christine's favorite pralines in one hand and a present for her mother in the other. They were little cakes in the shape of peaches—to the Chinese, this was a symbol for longevity, chosen with thought—and filled with lotus seed paste. Christine's mother placed the beautifully wrapped present on the table without even glancing at it. She looked Paul up and down briefly and sat.

"Paul, this is my mother, Wu Jie. Mama, this is—"

Wu Jie interrupted her daughter. "How much do you earn?"

"Mama!" Christine wished she could sink into the ground with shame. How many times had she told her mother, and reminded her, not to ask this question? Christine wanted to object, but Paul signaled to her with a smile that he had expected this kind of interrogation.

"The human being is a living treasure, but wealth is a dead one."

Oh, Paul, you could hardly have given a worse answer. Christine was afraid that he would go on to say that money meant nothing to him and that he lived very modestly from his savings since he had not worked for years because he was mourning his dead son. If so, the evening would come to an end before it had even really begun. Her mother would wait politely for the food, eat quickly, and make it clear that she wanted leave as soon as possible. She had lost her husband, her son, and her home; despite that, or perhaps because of that, she had worked until her body was worn out. How could she possibly understand Paul's withdrawal from the world?

Christine wondered how she could ever have agreed to the dinner. If only she could pretend she was feeling sick and leave the table for a moment. It was not a good idea for a Westerner to approach her mother with Chinese proverbs, and this particular one did not match her mother's experiences, absolutely not. People and treasure were two very different things to Wu Jie; they were not related to each other at all. Not in her life.

A mistrustful look. A brief glance that had nothing good in it. "With money, you are a dragon; without it, only a worm," she said contemptuously.

"You're right there," Paul replied. He had realized his mistake. In his friendliest what-an-honor-to-meet-you voice, he added, "That's why I would like to reassure you that I earn enough."

"Hmm," Christine's mother murmured, not sounding satisfied, as she drank her tea in slurps. She had pinned her thin gray hair back with two simple clips and was wearing a traditional red Chinese jacket with a dragon pattern. She gave Paul a suspicious look over the rim of her thick glasses.

Christine knew that for her mother the word "enough" did not occur in relation to money. Not because of greed, but because money was the only security that she trusted. Because money had enabled them to escape to Hong Kong. Because she was convinced that money could also grow wings for birds who could not fly.

"Enough for the five of us," Paul added. He had understood that his answer had been anything but satisfactory. "I have a house on Lamma and a broad portfolio of stocks that is performing very well."

She had not realized he was such a gifted liar.

"How much debt do you have against the house?" her mother wanted to know.

Christine tried to catch Paul's eye in vain; when he did not react, she pretended she hadn't heard anything, and flipped through the menu instead.

"None," Paul replied.

Wu Jie nodded, satisfied. "Do you gamble?"

He seemed to have expected this question too. "No," he replied calmly.

"Not at all?" she asked suspiciously.

"Apart from small bets on the horse racing at Happy Valley or Sha Tin, of course. But I wouldn't call that gambling."

Her mother nodded. She placed bets there too; she wouldn't have believed that anyone didn't do that.

"What do you work as?"

"I do research," he replied.

"Into what?"

"General research into principles."

A questioning glance at her daughter.

Christine had no idea what Paul meant. "General research into principles, Mama," she repeated in a tone as if to say that it answered all questions.

"And you earn money that way?" the mother asked, still filled with doubt.

Paul nodded calmly. "Please don't worry. I'll provide for the family."

Wu Jie looked at him carefully and said nothing for a while. "You're old and want to become a father."

"A man cannot expect to find both ends of the sugarcane sweet."

Christine wondered whether she should let Paul know that he really should stop spouting proverbs; she tried to find his knee under the table but he was too far away. To her amazement, a smile flitted across her mother's face.

"Your Chinese is remarkable. You know our pearls of wisdom well. Our food too?"

"He's an excellent cook," Christine interjected, hoping to change the subject.

"I cook a little," Paul said modestly. He had understood her intention; he picked up a menu. "Would it be all right with you if I ordered for us?"

Christine's mother inclined her head in assent.

Paul consulted with the waitress, perused the menu, and ordered steamed fish, stir-fried vegetables with sun-dried shrimp from Tai O, fresh oyster patties, tofu, and chicken feet.

Wu Jie nodded her head approvingly.

"When will you be marrying my daughter?"

"But, Mama! That's enough. I don't even know . . ." But Christine received only a dismissive wave of the hand in response. She wondered if she should start an argument, but her mother would not understand that. They were not sitting here to have a pleasant and enjoyable evening together. Paul was being interrogated to see if he was up to scratch as a future son-in-law, and Christine was a mere extra in her mother's drama. Of course Christine would decide for herself; she would have Paul's child and live with him even if her mother was against it. But Wu Jie's approval would make life easier. As long as she was alive, Christine was her daughter, with all the duties and restrictions that were part of the role.

"As soon as I have consulted an astrologer and have been given an auspicious date," Paul said, interrupting her thoughts. Christine cast him a look of gratitude, which he responded to with his wonderfully impish smile.

"You believe in Chinese astrology?" Wu Jie asked, surprised.

"Sometimes. But I think it can't do any harm."

Christine's mother laughed. That was the kind of pragmatic thinking that she liked. *We Chinese*, she liked to say, *have four kinds of religion: Confucianism, Taoism, Buddhism, and Pragmatism.* The last was her favorite.

"What do your parents do?"

"I'm afraid they have both passed away."

"How often do you visit their graves?"

"They are in New York, unfortunately. But of course I have a small altar in my house. I put fresh bananas and apples, my parents' favorite fruits, in front of it every day. I light a couple of incense sticks in the morning."

"Good, good," she murmured approvingly. "Did you have a good relationship with them?"

"An excellent one. I loved them very much."

"Do you have brothers or sisters?"

"No."

"Nieces? Nephews? Cousins?"

Paul shook his head.

"Uncles? Aunts?" Wu Jie asked, staring at him in disbelief.

"No, I'm sad to say."

Christine flinched once again. A man with no family. A lonely person. In her mother's eyes there could hardly be a worse punishment. That would either make her feel deeply suspicious—what had Paul done to deserve such a fate?—or very sympathetic. The expression on her face did not betray which way she was leaning.

"Do you play mahjong?" she asked, suddenly.

"Yes, I enjoy it very much, but I'm not very good."

The waitress brought their fish; within a few seconds, Christine's mother had put a large piece on Paul's plate and taken a helping for herself. Some of her fish disappeared into her mouth with a slurp; she chewed at it with enjoyment and spat a few bones out on her plate. Two waiters brought the chicken feet, the tofu, and the vegetables to the table. Christine's mother's gaze rested contentedly on one dish after the other.

Christine suspected that in her mother's eyes, everything of importance had been said. She watched her helping herself to the food with astonishingly deft movements, sitting slightly hunched over her plate, finally silent, deep in thought, sucking at a chicken claw with smacking noises. Despite the embarrassing questions her mother had asked, she felt full of respect and affection for her. Christine was not sure if Paul understood that, or could ever understand that. She owed her life to this brusque old woman with so little charm, who ate so noisily. Twice over. At least. Wu Jie had given birth to her. She had dragged her to the border and jumped into the sea with her. She had let Christine cling to her shoulders in the water when she ran out of strength. She had worked at the factory in Kowloon until her hands bled and her eyes and back were ruined, in order for her daughter to go to a good school. She had paid for the college fees in Vancouver with her meager savings.

Christine realized that it would be impossible for her to move to Lamma without her mother. The journey to Hang Hau was too long and troublesome. Her responsibilities as a daughter did not permit her to leave her mother there, not even for the sake of Paul and the child they were having together. He would understand. She hoped.

And her mother? One of the few proverbs that she remembered her saying was, "Some catch fish; others only cloud the water." She claimed that whether a person was one or the other was not to be decided by their words but by their deeds. And only time would tell on that count.

If Christine was interpreting her mother's behavior correctly, Paul had been granted that time.

XV

You will give life.
   You will take life.
   You will lose life.

The astrologer's words. Three simple sentences that he did not want to believe. What could the stars know about us? The first prophecy had come true; Paul wished he could shout, "And what about it?" But Master Wong's words went around and around in his head; they followed him no matter where his thoughts went. He had given life. Did that mean that he would also take life? Whose life? For what reason? It could be only by accident. Could he do anything to prevent it? And what did the third sentence mean? *You will lose life?* His own? The astrologer had not said that. Christine's? Their child's?

Paul could not sit still any longer. He walked to the stern of the ferry and looked at the murky water of the harbor, in which the harsh sunlight was reflected. From the door to the engine room came the thud of the diesel motor. There were three schoolboys in front of him, totally absorbed in pressing their Game Boy buttons. The Lamma butcher was leaning against the opposite railing and greeted him with a nod; there was a frozen side of pork in a wheelbarrow next to him.

Wong had told Christine that a man would enter her life. And that this man would not survive this year. If she were to give birth to a son, would he . . . How absurd; how ridiculous speculative thoughts like these sounded. He was embarrassed by them; he would never dare to speak these conjectures aloud. But still, they occupied his thoughts and made him feel uncertain.

The ferry docked at Yung Shue Wan with a hefty shudder; the wooden bollards creaked loudly with the pressure from the vessel. He walked slowly down the pier and bought fruit, vegetables, rice, and fresh tofu from Mrs. Ma, a bottle of wine from Mr. Li, and made his way toward Tai Peng. After a few steps he heard nothing apart from the twitter of birds, the rasp of the cicadas, a child's voice now and then, and the clatter of pots and pans every so often.

At home, he attended to his garden first of all. Since his return from Shanghai, he had not been able to spend time on it. The terrace was strewn with small twigs, leaves, and wilted petals. He had to prune the bougainvillea urgently, and pull a couple of dead stems away from the bamboo, as well as pluck the mottled brown leaves from the potted plants. He started to work, hoping that the sweeping, plucking, and cutting would distract him.

When he had finished his work in the garden, he cleaned the house thoroughly, had a simple dinner of soup, and went online to read the news and to check his emails.

Subject: testing
Received: 11:25

He did not recognize the sender. He wondered if he should delete the message without reading it, but after a moment's hesitation, he opened it.

testing!
hi paul,
just checking if our email connection works. have you arrived safely in hong kong?
would be glad to hear from you.
greetings from changle lu,
yin-yin

Paul had left Shanghai four days ago; he had to admit that he had not given Yin-Yin, Da Long, or Min Fang much thought since then. Christine's pregnancy left very little room for other thoughts. Paul felt too exhausted to write a long email. His reply consisted of a few pleasantries and a promise to write more soon.

The next morning he went up to Justin's room after breakfast. He opened the door carefully, as though he were afraid of waking someone from his sleep. Paul had kept the room all white: the wooden floor, the walls, the ceiling. There was a white bed in the middle with a white mosquito net over it; the net was swaying gently in the breeze. The sun cast the shadows of bamboo leaves on the walls. He stepped in and closed the door behind him. Silence. He noticed a fine layer of dust on the floor and the shelves. Would he be able to bear seeing another child playing between these four walls? Hearing it laugh? What to do with Justin's rubber boots and jacket in the hall? With the door frame which he had dismantled from the previous apartment and installed here, because the many markings on it showed how his son had grown?

To follow beauty into its hiding place, even when it was only a recollection that lay deep in the labyrinth of his memory, was so painful that he could hardly bear it. To forget would be betrayal. Forgetting was tantamount to death.

Paul suddenly doubted his own words.

Was there enough room inside him? Could a child grow up with a brother who was always present but also never there?

Paul did not have the answer, neither to this question nor to the many others that had presented themselves to him since he had found out that he was expecting a child. Was he too old to become a father once more, at fifty-three? Probably. How was it all to work on a practical level? He hadn't the faintest idea. Where were they to live? In Hang Hau, with four or five of them living in five hundred square feet on the twelfth floor? Unimaginable. Was there enough space in his house for the four of them, at least?

———

We are old enough to trust our intuition.

What had his inner voice replied? That he wanted this child; that it was a gift that he could not refuse. Not for anything. Despite everything. He had heard it immediately, loud and impossible to misunderstand: an irrational, passionate yes that stood in the face of all doubts and considerations.

When he went online that evening to read the *New York Times*, he saw a new message from Yin-Yin in his mailbox. Paul scanned the email.

Subject: ???
Received: 9:48

hi paul,
thank you for the quick reply. glad you are well :-)
i'm not too good, though. sleeping badly. playing badly. my mind is elsewhere. mozart and mendelssohn aren't taking it too well, nor is johann sebastian by the way (not bach! ;-))
went to see chen the lawyer again yesterday. couldn't get what he said about the internet out of my head. he encouraged me. the internet, he said, was like david's sling in the twenty-first century. no idea what he means by that, but it sounded good. he thinks that the risk to me is minimal if i go to a small internet café and make sure i stay anonymous. i mustn't tell anyone at all about it. no one should be able to tell from the posting who wrote it. what do you think? will it work? of course there's always a risk, there's no guarantee. tomorrow my brother returns from hangzhou. i'll wait and see what he says. will be in touch then.
yin-yin

The brevity of electronic messages was anathema to him. He printed out the email, read it thoroughly one more time, and wrote a short reply.

Subject: Encouragement

Hi Yin-Yin,

Thank you for your message. I agree with Chen that the Internet is your best chance. (Do you really not know the story of David versus Goliath?)

It shouldn't be a problem to keep what you write on the Internet anonymous. I'll help you with that, if you like. You can send it to me anytime and I would be happy to revise it, if that were even necessary.

I wouldn't hope for much from the discussions in Hangzhou. Don't let your brother put you off!

Look forward to hearing from you.

Warmest good wishes from Lamma,

Paul

Shortly after he had sent the email off, Christine rang to tell him once more how unpleasant she had found her mother's behavior and questions at dinner, and how sorry she was about it all.

He had found her mother neither rude nor hostile. He had seen a woman whom life had taken a lot from and given very little to, who was too old to bother with pleasantries. A mother who was concerned for her daughter and her grandchildren; he had found nothing to dislike in her brusque but honest manner. But under no circumstances did he want to share a home with her. She couldn't stay on in Hang Hau though; Christine wouldn't allow that. But to live under one roof with her? That would work for a couple of weeks. At most. She would have to move into a small apartment nearby or, better still, to Yung Shue Wan, at the bottom of the hill. It was a fifteen-minute walk to them from there. Uphill.

At the dinner, he had been astounded by Christine more than by her mother. The woman whom he loved, the forty-three-year-old single mother who owned a travel agency and supported her family, had turned in the blink of an eye into a good Chinese daughter who found it difficult to disagree with anything. He had seen from her eyes and her body language how embarrassing she had found her mother's questions, but the respect she had for her mother had stopped her from protesting, let alone asking her mother to be silent. Not in public. Not in front of someone who was not yet part of the family. A stranger. That was all he was that evening. The way the conversation had developed had reminded him of a fact that he had successfully pushed aside in the last few days: with the birth of their child he would become part of a Chinese family, regardless of whether he and Christine got married. He would be giving himself over to a dense tangle of duties and responsibilities, rules, and rituals from which it would be difficult to extricate himself. His happiness would depend on whether he was able to do that.

Two days later he found two emails from Yin-Yin in his inbox.

Subject: ???
Received: 0:59

hi paul,

just a quick email before i go to bed. my brother has returned from his party conference. he didn't accomplish anything regarding our case. apparently a few cases are being investigated at the sanlitun factories. he is annoyed and disappointed. he says we must be patient. we cannot do anything while there are still no results from the investigations. he still doesn't think it's a good idea to file a lawsuit or to put something on the internet. he says we can't win against the party. i say it's not that i want to win against the party. i'm not fighting the party at all, politics don't interest me. have never interested me. papa and i just want the people who poisoned the lake and who are responsible for mama's illness and the sickness of others in the village to be punished. he's always talking about the "new" china, i said to him, surely that can't just be about new buildings, new bridges, new highways, and new factories, can it? in the "new" china it must surely be possible for those who are guilty of crimes to be brought to justice. otherwise all this "new" stuff means nothing to me because it is so miserably similar to the "old." he grew quite subdued. i had never seen him that way before. i was right, he said (i have no idea when i last heard him say that), but we were not at that stage yet. at some point in the future it would happen, he was sure of it. did i really hear that? at some point in the future!!! justice is either important or it is not. if it is not, then i won't need it at some point in the future either; if it is, then why not today, here and now? he said he thought i had spent too much time with you, which infuriated me as though i couldn't have those opinions myself.

i'm going to sit down now and simply write down everything that we know, saw or heard and found out. then i'll send you what i've written and maybe you can add to it. as soon as it is ready i'll put it online.

by the way, I have postponed an audition for the symphony orchestra. i'm not in the right state of mind for it at the moment and i wouldn't get a third chance.

would be great to hear from you or see you in shanghai again.

feeling alone.

yours,

yin-yin

Subject: sanlitun text
Received: 3:44

hi paul,

i'm attaching what i've written about my mother, our village, and sanlitun. took longer than i thought, even writing it was painful. i'm so angry that it does me good to write it all down. showed it to my roommate lu. she is so horrified that she wishes she could send an email to sanlitun straightaway, to the mayor of yiwu too, and most of all to our prime minister wen jiabao or the whole politburo at once. please correct or add to the document as you see fit.

i am a bit nervous. i'm not a hero, definitely not. i just want to help my father. I say to myself: what could happen?

Yin-Yin

Paul sat on the terrace with a pot of tea and a bowl of lychees. He opened the attached document with a sense of misgiving, skimmed through it, and was reassured immediately. It was fantastic. All the facts and descriptions were correct and it was written in a matter-of-fact tone, yet the story of Min Fang's illness was so movingly told that even he was filled with rage all over again, even at this distance. He could not imagine anyone reading it being unmoved. He read it a second time, looking for places where Yin-Yin might have given clues to her identity; here too, she had done excellent work. It was clear to see that the writer of the piece knew the village well, but nothing else was evident. Yin-Yin's transformation since the first conversation he had had with her about the cause of her mother's illness was astounding. He marveled at the perseverance and persistence with which she was now driving things forward.

Paul went into the house, printed out the document, made a few changes, and replied to Yin-Yin.

Subject: Sanlitun crimes

Hi Yin-yin,

Congratulations. Your piece works, it more than works. it cannot fail to be effective. I've suggested some changes, which I'm sending you in the attached document. Even though you don't want to be a hero, you definitely have my respect. I find what you are doing remarkable.

Let me know if I can be of help to you in any other way.

I'm keeping my fingers crossed for you, and look forward to hearing from you.

Love,

Paul

The next day he had another two emails from Shanghai.

Subject: URGENT
Received: 0:56

paul,

thank you very much for your edits. i made all the changes you suggested. your chinese is really amazing. i'm going to pudong today. a friend of mine knows a teahouse there where it's no problem to get online and you won't leave any trace. there's always a risk. when i get scared i'll think of my mother and my father, that's what i did when i was writing the piece as well. i'm very excited. what will happen when i press "send"? it's the finality of it that shocks me. that will be that. do you understand what i mean, or do you think i'm being silly? are we the only ones affected or have there been problems like this in other villages? who will have the courage to comment on my story, to react to it in some way? i'll write with details as soon as anything happens.

think of me and wish me luck.

yours, feeling not at all like a hero,

yin-yin

Subject: DONE!
Received: 4:17

done! done! done! i just posted my piece: i feel free. no fear, just relief. i feel like my father: i have nothing to lose. even if they find out that i wrote the piece, what can they do to me? arrest me? lock me up? i am nothing but an insignificant little music student. i am not afraid.

will be in touch again soon,

yin-yin

No fear. Only relief. Paul was glad to read her messages, but at the same time, the more he thought about it, the more uneasy he began to feel. Yin-Yin had dared to tell the public her story; her piece was somewhere online, accessible to every Internet user in the world. Read by a few and then forgotten? Or forwarded from one Internet user to another? If so, over a few hours it could spread at the lightning speed that only this medium, with its incomparable power of magnification, was capable of. It was no longer in her hands, and there was no going back. He congratulated Yin-Yin once more on her courage and her fantastic piece of work, wrote that she was a hero on a small scale in his eyes, regardless of whether she felt like one or not, and asked her to be in touch.

He began his daily routine but anxiously logged in to his email several times before the evening, which he normally didn't do. His inbox remained empty.

The next morning he tried to call Yin-Yin on her cell phone but couldn't get through, so he left a voice message.

Three hours later, his telephone rang.

"Where is Yin-Yin?"

Paul was not sure whom he was speaking to. "Is that Mr. Weidenfeller?"

"Yes. Where is she?"

"How am I supposed to know that?"

"Because you've spent more time with her in the last ten days than I have," Weidenfeller replied in an agitated tone.

"I've been back in Hong Kong for a week," Paul responded, irritated. He did not feel like having a fight with a jealous man. "We haven't spoken to each other since then."

"Do you know where she could be?"

"Perhaps she's gone to her parents'?"

"No, I've rung their house already." Weidenfeller was gradually beginning to sound more worried than angry.

"How long have you been looking for her?"

"We were meant to meet yesterday evening. But she wasn't there when I arrived to pick her up. Her roommate saw her in the morning before she left the house; when she came back, Yin-Yin had gone. She had taken her laptop and her cell phone, and no one knows where she is. I even went to the conservatory. She hasn't been in touch with her brother for days." He said nothing for a moment, then added, in an almost pleading tone, "Might you have some idea where she is?"

"No," Paul replied, feeling uncomfortable.

"Tell me, when did you last hear from her?"

"When we said good-bye in Shanghai," Paul lied. If Yin-Yin had not told her boyfriend anything about posting her story online, she must have had her reasons. It was not for him to tell Weidenfeller. "Maybe she stayed the night with a friend who she's rehearsing with today. I'm sure everything will become clear in the next few hours," he said, even though he didn't think so.

"I hope so. Let me know if you hear anything," Weidenfeller said, giving Paul his cell phone number.

"Of course. Please do the same if you have news."

Paul made some tea, picked up his cordless telephone, sat in the garden, and rang Chen the lawyer in Shanghai.

"Paul Leibovitz here. Do you remember me?"

"But of course. Your girlfriend, Wu Yin-Yin, came to see me a few days ago and—"

Paul interrupted him. "She took your advice and posted a piece about Sanlitun and the fate of her mother on the Internet. There's been no sign of her since yesterday."

Silence.

"Did she do it from a public Internet café?" Chen asked after a long pause.

"Yes. As far as I know, she made a special trip to a teahouse in Pudong so that no one there would know her and she would leave no traces."

"Strange," the lawyer murmured quietly. "She was probably not careful enough about writing the piece, and betrayed her identity in it."

"No. I read it. It's very good, and doesn't give any clue to the identity of the writer. How could someone have found out that Yin-Yin wrote it?"

"I don't know. She must have made a mistake," Chen said, deep in thought.

"She sent me the piece. I thought it was—"

"She what?"

"She sent me the draft of the piece," Paul repeated, confused.

"How?"

"By email of course."

"Damn! How could she!" Chen exclaimed. "That was her mistake. Her emails were being monitored."

Paul groaned in shock.

"That is the only explanation. She must have aroused suspicion before. Did you have the feeling that you were being followed in Yiwu or in Shanghai?"

"No," Paul said. "But I wasn't looking out for that. Maybe the break-in was related?"

"What break-in?"

"An intruder broke into Yin-Yin's hotel room in Yiwu."

"Why didn't you tell me anything about that?" Chen said accusingly.

"I didn't think it was connected to our investigations. I thought it was a burglar in the hotel," Paul said apologetically. He stood up in his agitation and started pacing up and down his garden.

"How did you conduct your investigations in Yiwu? Apart from talking to my colleague Gao and this journalist? Did you make contact with any officials?"

"No. I looked up lots of information about Minamata disease on the Internet, about the symptoms and causes, and also stuff about Sanlitun."

"Were you using your own computer?"

"No. I . . ." Paul was barely able to finish his sentence. How could he have been so naïve? How could he have forgotten where he was? That first night he had even used the duty manager's computer. It wouldn't have taken long the next morning to find out what Paul had been using the computer for. And it was easy to make the connection between him and Yin-Yin. He had been thoughtless and careless. Yin-Yin was now paying the price for his negligence.

Chen swore quietly.

"Do you think Yin-Yin has been arrested?" Paul asked.

"That's what I'm assuming."

"But why? What could they accuse her of?"

"It could be many things. Inciting trouble. Endangering national security. Preventing officials from doing their jobs. Slander. Or, as is very common in such cases, the possession of state secrets. There's a three-year jail sentence just for that."

Paul sank down into a chair, knocking a teapot and a cup over. "That's ridiculous. None of those things can be true."

"Mr. Leibovitz, don't be so naïve," the lawyer replied in an irritated tone of voice. "The police don't need a reason at all to detain a person. The *laojiao* system allows it to lock up every citizen of this country for up to four years without trial by judge or the assistance of an attorney. The procedures of the criminal justice system do not apply in this case; the sentence can be imposed by any old police station."

"I know, I know," Paul said in a low voice. "But these laws came about in the time of the Cultural Revolution. I thought they had been abolished long ago."

"Lawyers and judges have been calling for that for years, but the lobbying by the security services has been too powerful. I just heard about a case in Henan Province where a farmer was arrested and the judge released him, but the police promptly rearrested him and sent him into forced labor for two years. Legally! Hold on a minute . . ." Chen's voice suddenly sounded muffled, as though he was holding his hand over the telephone. A few seconds later, he was back.

"Sorry, that was my secretary. Maybe we're worrying too much. I have some contacts in the police headquarters. I'll call them and be in touch with you again as soon as I can."

———

Paul dared not let the telephone out of his hand. He carried it from the terrace in the garden to the kitchen, the bedroom, and the bathroom as he went about his day. He took his phone with him when he went shopping in the village; as he was just checking how ripe the mangoes were at Mrs. Ting's, it rang.

"Bad news," Chen said, sounding serious.

Paul was gripped by fear. Whatever had happened to Yin-Yin, he was partly responsible. "What have you found out?"

"Nothing."

"Didn't you say you had bad news?"

"That *is* bad news. I called up two close contacts at the criminal investigation department who both owe me a favor, and they asked around, but even they couldn't tell me anything. That means that Yin-Yin or the Sanlitun case is regarded as so important by the police that only very few people are in the know. Or"—the lawyer paused for a moment—"or she was taken away by someone else."

"By whom?"

"If only I knew."

"Do you have any suspicions?" Paul asked carefully.

"No. The security services in Hangzhou or in Yiwu could have arrested her. Or Sanlitun's security personnel."

Paul's normally sturdy guts protested; he felt nauseated. "What— What can we— I mean, what, what should we do?" he stammered helplessly, feeling like an idiot.

"Wait. Search for her. I don't know."

The lawyer's bewilderment shocked Paul. "I'll come to Shanghai," he said impulsively.

"Hmm . . ." was Chen's initial reaction. After a pause, he added, "I don't want to stop you, but be careful. Look out for anyone watching you. For people following you. Or for people offering their services as a driver. You'll have to assume that your phone is being tapped and that your hotel room will be searched."

"Yes, of course. But can we still meet?"

The lawyer hesitated. "I'm afraid I can't help you any further at the moment."

"For a coffee, at least?" Paul asked, disappointed.

"Call me as soon as you're in the city and we'll see."

Paul looked at his watch. He had to speak to Christine urgently. If he didn't dawdle now, he could catch the two thirty ferry.

He called her and asked if she had time for a cup of tea. To his surprise, she suggested coming to Lamma to spend the afternoon with him and cook a meal together. It was very quiet in the office, so she wasn't needed, and she missed him.

He bought the ingredients for one of her favorite dishes, gong bao chicken with peanuts, and went to meet her at the ferry. Her smile when she saw him. Christine seemed to float as she ran toward him. Even though there was not even the hint of a curve to her belly yet, Paul had the feeling that the pregnancy was making her younger and ever more beautiful from day to day. He took her into his arms, but she seemed to notice from the way he held her and kissed her that something was not quite right.

"What's happened?" she wanted to know, giving him a piercing look.

"Yin-Yin has probably been arrested."

There was no reproach in her look, more the disappointment of a person who had seen misfortune approaching and had hoped right up to the last moment that it would not arrive. "I want to get to your house as soon as possible," she said, taking his hand.

At the house, Paul made some iced tea from scratch, put a deck chair on the terrace for Christine, fetched a chopping board, a sharp knife, the chicken breasts, garlic, spring onions, and ginger, and sat next to her. The air in the garden was still, warm, and humid; Paul loved weather like this. Christine, on the other hand, looked pale and exhausted.

"Should we go inside instead?"

"I'd love to, if you had an air conditioner . . ." She gave a tired smile. "Tell me more about what you know."

Paul peeled the garlic and ginger and told her about his conversations with Weidenfeller and Chen.

"It doesn't sound as though the lawyer wants to have very much more to do with this business."

"No." Paul cut the chicken breasts into small cubes and the spring onions into long strips. "No, he doesn't." He tried not to let his disappointment show.

"Who else could help her?"

"I don't know." He wiped the sweat off his brow.

"Come let's go into the house. I'll put the fans on."

Christine perched on the bar stool by the kitchen counter and relished the cool air from the fan on her warm body. Paul put salt, soy sauce, Shaoxing rice wine, a teaspoon of potato flour, and a little water into a bowl, stirred the mixture well, and then marinated the chicken in it.

"And now you want to go to Shanghai," she said after a while. It was not a question, more a statement.

Paul looked up in amazement. "How do you know that?"

"I know you. You have a bad conscience because you feel responsible."

He nodded mutely.

"You think that you encouraged her to defend herself, to put herself in danger, and now you're abandoning her at the very moment that she's in trouble."

"Isn't that right?" he asked uncertainly.

"Yes."

"Really? Do you think so?"

"I don't think that she could have gone so far without you."

Paul prepared the sauce pensively. He poured light and dark soy sauce, Chinese rice vinegar, sesame oil, a little sugar, flour, and chicken stock into a bowl, and mixed it well. Christine set the table.

He lit the gas stove and warmed some oil in a wok. When it was hot enough, he threw a handful of dried chilies and Sichuan peppers in, and tipped the wok from side to side until they were crispy.

"It smells wonderful already," Christine said, escaping back into the cool airstream from the fan.

Paul added the chicken to the wok, then the rest of the ingredients. Concentrating on cooking did him good; the smell of the frying garlic, ginger, and spring onions relaxed him. To finish the dish, he added the sauce and the peanuts. Shortly after that, the steaming dish of gong bao chicken was on the table; the cubes of chicken were coated with a thin layer of light-brown sauce, with dark-red chilies among them—it looked delicious.

Christine served the warm rice from the rice cooker. They sat in silence opposite each other, then Paul suddenly reached across the table and gave her a kiss. "Thank you."

"What for? You cooked the meal."

"For everything."

She helped herself to two pieces of chicken and put them into her mouth. "Did you know," she asked, chewing away with enjoyment, "that this dish was called something else during the Cultural Revolution? It was called 'quick-fried chicken cubes.'"

Paul shook his head. "Why?"

"Because it's named after a Qing dynasty official."

He nearly chocked. "I suspect there can't be many countries in which even the names of dishes can fall into political disfavor."

Christine balanced a peanut between her chopsticks and put it in her mouth. "What do you want to do in Shanghai? You surely can't think that you'll be able to find out who is responsible for her disappearance?"

"No, probably not. I want to talk to Weidenfeller and Xiao Hu and discuss what we can do. And I want to go to Yiwu to talk to your brother. I don't know how he'll react when he finds out what has happened to Yin-Yin. I'm afraid his son won't be very much help."

"That's true."

"You don't object?" he asked.

"Would that change anything?" Christine was smart enough not to expect an answer to her question. She continued: "I'm not comfortable with it, but you always say that I mustn't worry."

"And you mustn't. In the worst-case scenario they'll deport me and send me straight back to Hong Kong."

"For the first time, I'm actually feeling something akin to responsibility for my brother's family. I'm grateful that you're helping." After a short pause, she added, "When will you go?"

"Tomorrow."

"Have you got my grandfather's amulet on you?"

Paul pulled it out from under his white T-shirt. "Always."

"Should I come with you?"

"You? While you're pregnant? Absolutely not. I'll be back in three days anyway."

XVI

The drive had taken around two hours, she guessed, maybe more. They had handcuffed and blindfolded her and put her in the back of a minivan. She could tell by the sound of the sliding door.

She had heard rumors about "dark houses," a whole system of them spread around the country, where people could disappear for years without an obvious reason, secret prisons used by the secret police. But she had never given it much thought. Now she was in a basement room, cold and uncomfortable. Two chairs, a bed with a mattress but no sheets, a small closet, a lightbulb hanging from the ceiling, a dirty toilet in a corner. There was a tiny window high up.

Yin-Yin heard people coming down the floor, voices. The door opened.

She had promised herself she would stay calm.

Two men walked in, closed the door, locked it. One was handsome and young, probably her brother's age. They were not in uniform but rather in worn suits. The other man was older, with a grim face and a scar on one of his cheeks. She noticed his unusually large hands. He looked intimidating.

"Sit down," he said, pointing to the bed.

Yin-Yin hesitated. For the first time it occurred to her that they could physically harm her. Two men, one woman, alone in a room. A bed. There was nobody nearby to help her. No matter how loud or how long she would scream.

"I. Said. Sit. Down."

Reluctantly she obeyed.

"Who are you?" she wanted to know.

"None of your concern," he replied.

"I did not do anything wrong." She sounded more intimidated than she had intended to. As if she had made a mistake. There was nothing to justify or apologize for.

"Who do you think you are?" he yelled without warning. "What is right or wrong is not decided by you. It is decided by the authorities. By the party. Do you understand?"

Yin-Yin said nothing, turned her head, and stared at the wall.

"Do you understand?" he repeated with a sharp, terrifying voice. She started to tremble.

The man came closer. "Look at me. I am asking you something."

Yin-Yin did not move. She closed her eyes, prepared for an assault, a slap or worse. He would hit her in the face. The other man said something quiet she did not get; the older man waited a few seconds and then stepped back.

"We have a few things to talk about and we expect you to cooperate. It is in your own interest." The young voice was surprisingly soft, almost gentle.

She opened her eyes, relieved, and looked at him. A hint of a friendly smile on his face.

"You are a musician, right?" he asked in a cordial tone.

"Yes."

"An artist."

She nodded, not sure what he was aiming at.

"Who is your favorite composer?"

"Schubert. Mozart." She did not think these names meant anything to him, but she was relieved to talk about music. "And of course Beethoven."

He gazed at her for a while without saying anything. "Is it true that you suffer from mood swings?"

"No," she replied confused.

"Never?"

"I am sometimes unhappy, because I am not sure if I've got

enough talent as a musician. I work hard and I am never satisfied with the results. If you want to call that mood swings . . ."

"Never satisfied? Must be depressing."

"Sometimes."

He looked around as if he were searching for something. "You missed," he said finally, "a few classes last fall."

"I was not feeling well."

"Why not?"

"I had some issues."

"What issues?"

She shrugged.

"Some people told us you are mentally unstable."

"Who said that?" Yin-Yin asked, surprised.

"Teachers. Students. Lu, your roommate."

"They are all lying."

"We found sleeping pills next to your bed."

"I rarely use them," she protested. "It is because of my Mom's illness . . ." She stopped and suddenly understood what they were getting at. Declaring her insane and putting her in a mental institution would be a legal way of getting rid of her. She could spend years in a psychiatric ward without ever being evaluated by an independent psychiatrist. The whole purpose of this conversation was to remind her of their power.

There was more than a hint of a pleased smile on his face. He knew she had understood.

"To change the subject: Whose idea was it to put all those things online?"

"Mine."

"Yours? According to your brother's and father's cadre files, you have never been interested in politics."

"I am not. This is not about politics," she answered him back. "This is about justice, about—"

"Everything is about politics," the older man interrupted her angrily. "We can put you in jail for the rest of your life."

"What for?"

"For whatever we want!" he shouted.

His colleague gave him a sign to calm down.

There was silence in the room. Prison or mental institution, as long as they wanted, for whatever reason they wanted. It was the plain truth, and Yin-Yin felt something crumble inside her.

"Are you part of a foreign organization?" the younger one wanted to know.

She shook her head.

"Who was helping you?"

"Nobody."

"Are you getting money from abroad?"

"Why are you asking these questions? Can't you imagine that a Chinese woman my age has the courage to act on her own?"

"I can't imagine somebody so smart doing such stupid things. Why are you ruining your life? Imagine never being able to perform in public again . . . No orchestra would be prepared to take you."

Count on paying the highest possible price and then ask yourself if, when it's all said and done, it will be worth it.

"Think about your family."

"I do. That's why . . ." She did not finish the sentence.

"You did not think it through, smart-ass," the older man said suddenly. "Who will care for your mother if something happens to you or your father?"

"What should happen to my father?" she asked.

"Da Long could be"—the man paused for a moment—"arrested, for instance."

He was right: She had not thought it through. She had considered only what they could do to her, but never imagined they would use her sick mother to blackmail her. "What do you want from me?"

"Answers. Names."

She looked at them for a long time and took a deep breath. There was no way back.

"My name," she said very slowly, "is Wu Yin-Yin. The answer is justice."

Maybe it was her tone, maybe the men were just getting tired of her, maybe it was their usual strategy for an interrogation, but both made aggressive steps in her direction.

"You are making one mistake after another," the younger one said without a trace of gentleness left in his voice, "and your whole family will pay for them."

They left and came back the next morning. The same questions and answers over and over again.

After a few days they took her to another building, a kind of guesthouse for a business or for the district authorities, locked her up on the sixth floor, and put guards outside her door, who brought her meals three times a day, never saying a word. A bigger, brighter room with a bed, two chairs, and a large closet. From the locked window she could see fields lying fallow and factories and houses in the distance.

The most difficult thing was not knowing. And the helplessness. Imprisoned without charge. Nobody hinted at what crime she had committed, exactly. What they planed to do with her. How long she was to stay in this room. Days? Weeks? Months? They had taken away all power over her own life, and she could bear it only by exercising the utmost self-control. She had to limit her emotions to what was absolutely necessary.

A kind of hibernation of the soul.

XVII

Xiao Hu lay in bed with his arms and legs spread out wide. He closed his eyes and counted to eight, breathing deeply as he did so, feeling his lungs expanding and filling with oxygen; he held his breath for a moment and then started counting again, letting the breath sigh out of his body. He was meant to do this breathing exercise two dozen times every morning and evening; it was important not to think about anything while doing it, his colleague—who had been practicing yoga regularly ever since a trip to India a few months ago—had warned him. It was an old meditation exercise that was supposed to help prepare for the day ahead, create strength, and enable him to work with full concentration. Xiao Hu was skeptical. He found it difficult not only to lie still but also to breathe peacefully and unhurriedly. The air seemed to want to enter and leave his body quickly and automatically. It was even more difficult for him to think of nothing. He tried to fix his mind's eye on an image, but regardless of whether he thought about the Jin Mao Tower in the light of the setting sun or his new Bose sound system or a woman's breasts, it lasted mere seconds before one thought after another coursed through his head again.

He had been doing these exercises for two weeks now but had not seen any improvement in his ability to concentrate; as a result, he'd decided to give it two more weeks—if nothing changed, then he would stop doing them.

After the final breath, he stretched with relief, felt for his spectacles on the nightstand, and stood up. His iPhone showed that it was 5:15 and displayed four new text messages, which he scanned: greetings from friends in America and Canada. He drew the curtains open; a narrow red stripe on the horizon announced the dawn. Xiao Hu's gaze wandered through the living room, with its open-plan kitchen. He had deliberately furnished the apartment sparsely: a narrow Ikea couch in front of a flat screen TV on the wall, a small dining table with four chairs, a low shelf for the sound system and a few books, that was all. An excess of space. For someone who had lived in 160 square feet of space with his parents and sister when he was a child, who had not even had his own bed and who had shared a kitchen, dining room, bathroom, with five other families, there was no greater luxury.

He switched on the espresso machine, pulled on his sportswear, turned on the television, got onto the exercise bike, and pressed the Medium Sweat button. It started with a fifteen-minute warm-up, during which Xiao Hu watched the morning news while pedaling lightly. The incline grew steeper. He had to pedal energetically; he felt his heart pounding and the first pearls of sweat on his brow, then the damn impulse to cough rose again. A gray-brown cloud of smog had been lying low over the city for days, obscuring the tops of the skyscrapers; he felt as if it was coming through the chinks in the imperfectly sealed windows into his apartment. The poor-quality air had made his asthma worse and worse in the last few years. He managed with some effort to suppress a coughing fit.

Xiao Hu thought about his sister and her disappointed face when he had told her about his conversations at the party conference in Hangzhou. He had tried everything and achieved nothing. During a break in a meeting, he had spoken to a district chairman from Yiwu, but he had waved him away. The two employees of the province governor, whom he knew well, had also not wanted to be told anything about Sanlitun. A sensitive subject. No press, no comment, even internally. Instructions from Beijing. There were rumors about problems in some factories but no one knew any details. Their advice: stay away.

The urge to cough grew stronger. He took a deep breath and expelled a hard, dry cough that hurt his chest and throat. Xiao Hu coughed and spluttered more and more violently until even his head hurt and he had to get down from the bicycle. He had done eighteen minutes—pathetic—or just about half the mountain setting.

Xiao Hu had a shower, ate a warmed-up croissant, and left for the office. In his calendar, he had a meeting with the head of his department at ten o'clock and lunch with a fellow party member from Hunan Province at one p.m.

Just before noon, Weidenfeller rang, in a panic about Yin-Yin's whereabouts.

Xiao Hu did not know when he had last had such a shock. Maybe it was when he was little. Once, when he had not been able to swim, he had fallen into a pond and had sunk in the water for several endless seconds until his father had pulled him out with a strong grip. The fear that had overcome him as he gasped for air and had felt only water fill his mouth. The panic with which he had flailed his arms, looking for something to hold on to: a reed, a plank, a hand. That was what he felt like now. He felt a piercing sensation in his guts, a pain that immediately spread through his whole body. He sensed that something terrible had happened, that Yin-Yin had done something that was not just foolish, but something from which there was no going back, and that she was sinking deeper and deeper. It was impossible to foresee the consequences, but this time there would be no hand to pull her out. For a moment, he felt as though he was losing control over his own life.

He tried not to let any of this show. He calmed Weidenfeller down and reassured him that they would have news that afternoon. He would make a few phone calls and soon find out where Yin-Yin was. He called a close contact in the mayor's office, for whom he had recently secured a lucrative life insurance deal at a special rate, and asked him where his sister, Wu Yin-Yin, born on December 19, 1978, in Panzhihua, Sichuan, was.

The man rang him back ten minutes later and said he hadn't been able to find out anything.

His cell phone was reminding him with monotonous beeping about his next appointment. Yin-Yin had to wait. This lunch was too important to cancel at short notice.

Xiao Hu had reserved a table by the window in a small restaurant on the Huangpu riverbank. The party functionary from Hunan was around his age, pleasant, and very ambitious, an up-and-coming district secretary whom Xiao Hu had met at a conference in Beijing the previous year. Since then, the man had been to Shanghai several times; they had enjoyed a few evenings out in restaurants and karaoke bars. On his last visit, the man had offered to sell him an empty piece of land in a suburb of Changsha, the provincial capital, that would be designated as land for construction in the next year; the decision had been made by the district government, but had not yet been officially announced. The value of the land would multiply twenty or thirty times overnight—it was a sure thing. But Xiao Hu was hesitant. The party functionary expected something in return, of course, but had not given any indication as to what that might be. If Xiao Hu was not able to return the favor, he would be beholden to him, and he was determined not to place himself in that kind of debt, no matter how tempting the opportunity was. He either had to find a diplomatic way of turning down the offer or put the district secretary off until the man indicated what he wanted in return from Xiao Hu. But even then he would not feel comfortable with the deal. Until now, he had managed, for the most part, to avoid getting tangled up in the tightly woven mesh of favors, gifts and reciprocal gifts, bribes, obligations, secret talks, and agreements within the party that blanketed the whole country. It was not easy: if he were to reject the proposition, word would get around and make most of the party cadres mistrust him. No one, and he was no exception, could afford to be the odd one out in the party. The nail that sticks out is hammered in, as the proverb went.

The lunch went as he had anticipated. They talked animatedly about the rising stock market index, about the booming property prices in Shanghai, about the chances of Yao Ming becoming the most valuable player in the NBA that season, about the pluses of the

new VW Passat, and only at the end did the man from Hunan casually mention his wife's sister. A gifted young lawyer whom Xiao Hu
simply had to meet. She wanted to move to Shanghai, and needed a
job urgently. And she wanted to buy an apartment too. China Life
had invested in several building projects and surely had excellent
contacts to the building companies . . .

The party functionary did not have to say more. Xiao Hu nodded; he had understood; he promised to give it some thought.

On the way back to the office he felt even more anxious than
before. He rang his secretary and asked her to cancel an unimportant meeting at three p.m., citing an unexpected appointment.
He walked down the river promenade, heading to Starbucks for
an espresso. The air quality was worse than it had been the day
before; he coughed violently and was glad when he reached the
air-conditioned café. A job in his department and buying an
apartment at a discount: both of these things were not very difficult for Xiao Hu to arrange. His company was always looking
for new young lawyers anyway. Would it be reprehensible of him
to employ the young woman from Hunan? It was a good deal, no
doubt about it, but it depressed him nonetheless. He was one step
further in a direction that he did not want to go in. To many party
functionaries it would sound naïve, dishonest, or incomprehensible, but he had not become a member of the Communist Party of
China to get rich, even though he had nothing against the wealth
he had acquired.

He had been happy and proud when they had asked him to
join the party while he was at college. What an honor. From the
one hundred and sixty-four law students in his year they had invited three people. Three! The Communist Party of China was not
a sports club that anyone could join or leave at will. Only the best
were good enough for the party; it was composed of the country's
elite. He had not had a moment's hesitation, even though he knew
his parents would have their reservations. At the time, he simply
ignored them, submitted his application, and studied into the night;
he was one of the first to step into the library in the mornings and

one of the last to leave in the evenings; he graduated with the highest possible grade, hoping to bring honor to the party.

He passed the obligatory probation period without a hitch, and the initiation ceremony was short and simple. He wrapped the red party book in transparent plastic film that very night. He got an unimportant job as a lawyer in the city administration of Shanghai and was promoted after six months. Xiao Hu suspected that there was someone keeping an eye on him and championing him, without making himself known. From then on his ascent was swift. Training, conferences, seminars. The teachings of Mao. The teachings of Deng Xiaoping and of Jiang Zemin. The role of the Communist Party in the media and the judiciary. It had not occurred to him before that to seriously question it. Politics in the last thirty years had been too successful for that. Of course there were always cases in which he had a different opinion from what the official party line demanded, but these were never on fundamental issues. He saw corrupt party members whom he would have taken firmer measures against, had he any say. He saw the gap between rich and poor grow wider, but was this the party's failure? His friend the neurologist Zhou claimed that anyone who was not rich now had themselves to blame. Anyone who didn't make it now would never make it. After the Cultural Revolution the whole country had started from practically zero, and anyone who did not make use of the many chances that came his or her way practically every day was simply too stupid. Everyone had the choice.

Xiao Hu had a second espresso. He thought about Yin-Yin, and his doubts grew. He understood the rage and disappointment she felt when they had last seen each other. He shared those feelings. Whatever his little sister had written in her Internet post, whomever she had accused, whatever she had called for, that did not justify taking her into custody and probably subjecting her to a long and torturous interrogation. He would have understood if she had received a police summons or a serious warning from the security authorities, but not more than that. Now she had ended up in a system that Xiao Hu knew about only theoretically from his studies; she was subject to the authority of the state and had very few rights as a suspect. With luck they would at some point allow her to contact a lawyer or her family, but until then, days, perhaps weeks, or, in the worst case, months could pass. They could send her to a psychiatric unit and no one would object; no one would defend her. What law had his little sister broken?

He really ought to be grateful to her, he thought. She was fighting the fight he wouldn't or couldn't. He was not sure which. Even though he would never say that out loud. He went back to the office, completed his work listlessly, and left for home early.

The next morning, shortly after eight, he received a call from the Shanghai head office of the Communist Party. He was to be there at ten. Lu Guohua, a high-ranking functionary from the office of the party secretary of Shanghai, wanted to see him.

Shocked, Xiao Hu thought about the offer he had been made by the man from Hunan. Had he fallen into a trap?

What was it about, if he could ask?

Family matters. Urgent family matters.

Not a reed. Not a plank. Not a hand.

————————

The department of the Communist Party that he had been summoned to was in an office block on Beijing Xi Lu; it was a faceless gray building with a giant Chinese fan waving on its roof. Young party members in ill-fitting suits were walking in and out, and there were dozens of bicycles in front of the building, like in the old days.

Xiao Hu asked for Lu Guohua at the reception. Room 555.

The corridor on the fifth floor was a long, poorly lit tunnel, at the end of which was Lu's office. The doors to the left and the right were closed. Xiao Hu's footsteps sounded loud, as though he were walking though an abandoned building. He held his breath for a moment before he knocked and entered. Took a deep breath. He had lain awake half the night and tried to prepare himself for this meeting.

Family matters, the woman on the telephone had said.

What could be in store? Was his sister in the room waiting for him? Possible, but not likely. He'd figure a way through. What should he be afraid of? He owned three apartments and was financially independent, at least for the next few years; if push came to shove, he would easily find a well-paid job in the private sector. He was a worthy member of the party and had done nothing wrong.

He knocked twice and listened.

"Come in."

The room was large and bright, and there was no sign of his sister. In an alcove there was seating for official visitors, a couch upholstered in red satin, and two armchairs with white arm caps. There was a piece of elegantly written calligraphy on the wall: "Seek truth from facts." This was a slogan that Xiao Hu had quoted many times in essays he had written for the party. It was said to be by Deng Xiaoping, though others said Mao was the source; apparently, Confucius had also spoken words to that effect. The room was uncomfortably warm, and smelled of cigarette smoke. Either the air-conditioning was not working or they liked it warm. Xiao Hu cleared his throat.

The official who was waiting for him was sitting at the other end of the room. Xiao Hu recognized him from several party events; he was one of those who worked closely with the first party secretary in the city. A short, thickset man with deep wrinkles in his forehead and a dark-brown mole on his chin. He was wearing one of those ridiculously large pairs of glasses with thick black frames, in the style that the former party chief and president Jiang Zemin had brought into fashion, which had been worn by every second party cadre during Jiang's time.

On the desk were a computer screen, two telephones, and several half-filled ashtrays. Lu read from a folder, looking up only fleetingly.

"Wu Xiao Hu?" A dark, forbidding voice.

"Yes."

Lu indicated a chair in front of his desk.

Xiao Hu sat down.

The functionary closed the folder and sized up his visitor for a moment without saying anything. Narrow, dark-brown eyes that rested on him; a gaze that Xiao Hu could not get the measure of.

Not friendly.

Not hostile.

A look in which curiosity mingled with the cold self-confidence of those in power. The longer the silence went on, the more uncomfortable Xiao Hu felt.

"How long have you been a member of the party now?"

"Ten years and nine months," Xiao Hu replied. Not a word too many. Only reply to what he was asked.

"I've read your cadre file. Incredible. We are satisfied with you. You are among the best in all subjects. Your analyses and self-criticisms are impressively clear. Well done."

"Thank you."

"The party needs people like you. You have a promising future before you." He paused and lit a cigarette without offering his guest one. "I've heard you would like to work at the Ministry of Justice in Beijing."

Xiao Hu nodded.

"Why not? But here in this city we have very interesting and influential positions that need to be filled too," Lu said, a smile flitting over his face. "We're looking for an experienced lawyer to join the staff of the party secretary of Shanghai. Would that not be something for you?"

The question confused him. He had come there imagining the worst; he had expected an unpleasant conversation, an interrogation, a severe warning about his sister's behavior. Now Lu was considering him for one of the most interesting positions that Xiao Hu could imagine for someone of his age and with his qualifications. Had he been invited to this office for an interview? It must be a trap, he thought. A test. A game whose rules he could not discern at the moment. He must not show any weakness, must not say anything that anyone might use against him one day. He gave a little cough. "It's a huge honor for me to even be mentioned in this context."

Lu seemed content with this reply. He leaned back in his chair and blew smoke into the air pensively.

"Are there things in the party that you don't like?" he asked. When he saw the look of confusion on Xiao Hu's face, he added, "I can think of a few things."

How naïve did the man think he was? He had not studied the history of the Communist Party of China in order to reply with a list of mistakes and failures now. Too many people had fallen for this trick before him, had had the courage to voice criticism, and paid for it with many years in labor camps. Short sentences. Neutral statements. Offer nothing that could be seized on to attack.

"The party has been ruling for over fifty years. It has achieved great things in difficult times. It's impossible not to have made mistakes too in the course of things," he answered evasively.

"Such as?"

Xiao Hu thought for a moment about what President Hu Jintao had criticized his own party for in his speeches of the last few weeks and months.

"The path to a harmonious society is long, and—"

"What exactly?" Lu interrupted him. "You're testing my patience."

Xiao Hu could feel himself getting warmer; the cigarette smoke could trigger an asthma attack any moment. He needed fresh air urgently, but did not dare to ask the man to open the window. Where had his resolutions gone? He had one threatening him, but his feeling of trepidation was growing nonetheless. He did not want to talk about the party; he wanted to know where his sister was, what they were accusing her of, and how he could help her. He made an effort to conceal his anxiety, sitting upright, ramrod straight, with his hands on his lap. He felt them grow damp.

"That means that we cannot leave anyone behind on the path to socialism the Chinese way." His body relaxed a little; he remembered similar statements from a speech made by the prime minister.

"You mean that there are too many rich people and too many poor people in China today. Do I understand you correctly?"

Sweat ran from his armpits down his torso. The urge to cough became even worse. Was Lu on the left or the right of the party? One of the conservatives or one of the reformers? Xiao Hu was so agitated he could no longer remember what this functionary's repu-tation was, and what the right answer would be in this case.

"I wouldn't say too many rich people, but certainly too many poor people, isn't that right?"

Lu threw a packet of cigarettes onto the desk in disappointment. "What does 'isn't that right' mean?" he asked in annoyance. "Of course there are too many poor people. Far too many. You surprise me. I expected a clearer statement from you."

Failed the test, Xiao Hu thought, knowing that this was only the beginning. This damn cough; he tried to suppress it, swallowing, pressing his lips together, pressing his tongue to the roof of his mouth, which sometimes helped, but now everything seemed to make it worse. Xiao Hu turned away, held both hands to his face, and coughed as if his lungs would burst. Lu observed him impas-sively and waited for the coughing fit to pass.

"How are your apartments doing? How many now?"

It took Xiao Hu a few seconds to understand the question.

"Three," he replied, still coughing. "They're rented out."

"Didn't you want to sell them?" The smugness of that voice.

"No, I don't speculate with property," Xiao Hu said, knowing that Lu was not interested in the answer. He simply wanted to unsettle him, show him that he knew everything about him, that it was pointless to hide anything from the party. He was not issuing threats; his hints were enough, and he knew it.

Instead of responding to this, the party cadre looked at his hands and pulled his fingers one by one until the knuckles cracked. "There's been a tragedy in your family. Your mother is seriously ill," he said abruptly.

"Yes," Xiao Hu confirmed, in a flat, exhausted voice.

"What happened?"

The next trap. If he knew about Min Fang's condition, he knew every detail of her suffering. Lu simply wanted to hear how Xiao

Hu described the situation, what words he would use, whose side he was on.

"The doctors," he said, "have diagnosed brain damage. She is lame, blind, and dumb. There's no hope of recovery."

"Is it true that certain members of her family are laying the responsibility for her illness on external factors? To be precise, on a chemical company?"

Xiao Hu nodded mutely. This was the moment he had feared. The moment in which he had to take a stand. "There are signs—" he began hesitantly.

"What kind of signs?" Lu interrupted.

"That my mother had eaten poisoned fish, and that the lake that the fish came from is contaminated. We seek truth from facts." He had never before found it such an effort to get a couple of sentences out.

"Who is 'we'?" Lu ignored his allusion.

He did not want to betray her. Big brother. Little sister. He was responsible for her. *Promise me that you will care for Yin-Yin when we are no longer here,* his mother had often said. Why was his sister not sitting next to him now? A glance would be enough for him to know that he was not alone. Just like before, when Da Long raised his voice in anger at the children. United even though they were so different.

"Who is 'we'? You and your family? Or only your family?"

Lu had backed him into a corner with his questions and statements, but now he was showing him the way out of the trap; the door was wide open. Xiao Hu struggled for breath. "We, that is, we— I mean, to be precise: my sister."

Lu passed three pieces of paper to him across the desk. "Did she write this piece on the Internet?"

Xiao Hu scanned the first page. "I don't know."

"What do you mean, you don't know?"

"I've never seen it, ever," he replied in a low voice. "What makes you think that my sister . . ."

"Who else could it be?" Lu growled. "Did you know about it?"

"No." He was a terrible liar.

"She's blaming the Sanlitun chemical firm in a public statement. She's libeling them. She hasn't gone through the relevant authorities; she is accusing them of serious misconduct." His voice grew sharper with every sentence. "She's accusing them and calling for a public trial. She's refusing to accept scientific findings."

"Where is my sister?" Xiao Hu said it in such a quiet voice that he had to repeat himself twice.

"I cannot tell you that. But I can tell you quite precisely what will happen to her if you do not help her. Sanlitun will take her to court for libel and damage to its reputation. The company will set very high claims for damages. Your sister will be paying them off her whole life. Whatever she possesses will be seized. Her violin, for example. Do you want that to happen?"

Xiao Hu felt his hands shaking; he could barely breathe. He thought about Yin-Yin. About the mercury in his mother's body. About the vacant look in her eyes, which had been able to gaze so tenderly before. Lu was waiting for a reply.

"No," he whispered.

"Apart from that, I've heard that your father is considering suing Sanlitun. Is that right?"

He nodded dumbly. No fear left.

"What's going on in your family?" Lu shouted. "The police will take him away for interrogation. That could take a long time. Hours. Days. Weeks. Who will look after his sick wife during that time?"

Xiao Hu knew that this was his last opportunity to take a stand. He could object. He could talk about the other sick people. About dead cats. About the laboratory tests. About Wang the journalist. The longer he said nothing, the more clearly he felt the moment of dissent slipping away. As if someone or something was taking the decision away without giving him a chance to consider things properly and weigh the pros against the cons. As if a cold sense of calm was suddenly spreading through him. Xiao Hu had the feeling that he had slunk out of his own body for a moment and was observing the scene from above. Everything grew more and more distant. Lu.

The disgusting, smoke-filled office. His sister. The village. The people. It was as though he were sitting in the back of a car that was moving away from it all. He turned around, looked out of the rear window, saw Yin-Yin waving with his parents next to her. Da Long looked serious and Min Fang was crying. He watched them become smaller and smaller until they finally disappeared altogether.

"I can only put it down to grief," he heard himself say.

"That isn't appropriate for a party member with your ambitions."

"I know," someone inside him whispered.

"Take care of it," Lu ordered. "Talk to your father. He has to write a letter to your sister. She must apologize to Sanlitun and all the authorities that she has attacked. It would be unfortunate if you were to be disadvantaged by the irresponsible behavior of your family."

Lu stood up, walked over to the sideboard, switched on a kettle, waited for the water to boil, and poured it into two mugs with tea leaves. He put a mug in front of Xiao Hu on the desk without saying anything and sat down again. "I've spoken to a few party comrades at Sanlitun," he suddenly said in a conciliatory tone. "They were moved by the tragic fate of your mother, and they told me how they could help. The company is prepared to pay your parents a sum of fifty thousand renminbi in order to make life easier for them. It's a generous gesture, but of course it is not an admission of any fault whatsoever."

"And?" Rice grains do not fall from heaven.

"In return, Sanlitun expects your family to sign an agreement that they will never, now or in the future, bring charges against the company or make any claims on it for damages."

Xiao Hu thought about it. Fifty thousand renminbi. It had become difficult to determine the relative worth of sums of money in China. What should he measure it against? The amount was at least double the annual salary his father had last earned as an engineer. Yet it was no more than what Xiao Hu had earned in a day on the stock market recently. If Sanlitun was responsible for his mother's illness, it was a mockery. Fifty thousand renminbi. Better than nothing. The price of a human life. There were cheaper ones.

"That's a very generous offer," he said in a voice that sounded like his own, yet was horribly alien to him at the same time. It was as though he was seeing and hearing himself on a movie screen. "I'll talk to my father. May I see my sister?"

"No. She's not in Shanghai."

"Where is she?"

Lu merely shook his head.

"Tell me how she is, at least."

"Talk to your father. We expect a reply in two days."

XVIII

A glance from the border official. A young face. Unlined, rosy-cheeked, indifference in the eyes. It was taking an unusually long time to get through immigration this time. The woman at the next counter had gone through already, even though she had arrived after him. Paul didn't know what to do with his hands; he tried not to let his nervousness show, gazing with deliberate calmness at the long lines of people and trying to give the uniformed official a relaxed smile that was more of a grimace, which was studiously ignored. Paul had imagined the worst-case scenario over and over again on the flight: they would stop him from entering, interrogate him, and send him back to Hong Kong on the next flight. The man returned his passport without saying a word and nodded.

The taxi ride to the city center took almost two hours. Christine had booked him into the New Asia Hotel, a large-budget hotel that was popular with Western tour groups. She thought he would attract less attention among all the foreigners.

Approaching the Nanpu Bridge, they got stuck in an impossible traffic jam caused by an accident. The driver switched on the radio, looking for music that he liked, but ended up listening to a show in which listeners called in to talk. The subject was cosmetic surgery. One caller wanted to lengthen her legs, and was asking how many centimeters was possible, and if she could still play badminton after the operation. The next caller said that he had paid a small fortune for his wife's breast augmentation, but she had left him two months later for another man. Now he wanted to get his money back; after all, he didn't want her new lover to benefit from it. Was there any legal recourse for him?

———

The hotel was on the north bank of Suzhou Creek, not far from the Bund.

The receptionist flicked through his passport repeatedly. It looked like she had never seen an American passport before. When she disappeared into a back room with his paperwork, he started to worry.

After she returned, he asked, "Is there a problem?"

"No. Everything's fine. I couldn't find your reservation," she said in a flat voice, as Paul scrutinized her body language for any sign that she was lying.

He took his things up to the room and rang Chen.

"Mr. Leibovitz, where are you?"

"In Shanghai, not far from your office," he offered, hoping their proximity would make a meeting possible.

"I'm sorry, I've no time at all."

"Perhaps later?" Paul tried not to let his disappointment show.

"No, I'm tied up the whole day."

No time, Paul thought. There was no such thing. Time was ultimately a question of priorities. "That's too bad. What about tomorrow?"

"I'll be in Beijing. But I have news for you. Yesterday evening I spoke to my colleague Gao in Yiwu. He said you absolutely have to see that journalist Wang in Yiwu again. He has very good contacts in the city and probably knows more than he told you the first time you met. Gao rang me again an hour or so ago and told me that Wang had been incredibly angry when he heard about Yiwu's disappearance. He thinks Wang can help you. If he wants to. Do you have his number?"

"Yes. But do you really have . . ."

"No."

After he put down the phone, he sat in his room feeling at a loss for some time. The room was so small that barely anything more than a bed, a desk, and a closet fit in it; if his suitcase had been any bigger, he would have had to open it on the bed. The window looked out onto a lit well. The air-conditioning rattled like an old diesel engine. He would be able to stand being in there only at night; he would rather spend the afternoon wandering the city.

The taxi drivers hanging around the front entrance of the hotel swarmed around him immediately. No, he didn't need a driver. No, no cheap-cheap massage for him either. Paul walked onto a small bridge over the river, stood in the middle, and leaned over, looking at the murky water. It was a very warm late-spring day. The air was worse than it had been over a week ago; gray-brown clouds of haze and exhaust fumes shrouded the tops of the skyscrapers of Pudong.

His cell phone hummed, and Paul jumped as if a stranger had started talking to him from behind. A text message. On the screen were the words XIAO XIN. Little heart. No explanation. No name. He knew what the Chinese words meant. They could be a friendly greeting from an acquaintance or a veiled warning. Who could have sent it to him? Yin-Yin? Most unlikely. Xiao Hu? Paul called the number of the sender.

"Hello." A deep male voice, unfamiliar to him.

"Did you just send me a text message?"

Silence.

"Who are you?" Paul asked urgently.

Silence. Loud, steady breathing.

"Who are you?" he repeated.

No reply.

Paul ended the call. Less than a minute later, the second text message came: XIAO XIN.

How did the sender know his cell phone number, and that he was in the city? He thought about Yin-Yin. She was the only one who could land him in serious difficulty, if she claimed it had been his idea and that she had been following his instructions. But he trusted her, naïvely or not . . .

On the way to the Bund he crossed over to one side of the street, then back again several times, convinced he was being followed. The promenade by the river was full of people; he sat down on a bench and sized up everyone who walked past. How ridiculous, he thought. How was he to know if someone was following him or not? He was not a detective and was not able to distinguish a mere passerby from a spy. The mere thought made him feel even more uneasy. Besides, a nervous person would attract much more attention than a calm one.

A new text message: XIAO XIN.

He bought a Chinese SIM card with a new telephone number from a convenience stand and called Christine. All through the flight, he had thought about her and the life that was growing inside her. Arriving in Shanghai, the telephone call with Chen and the "xiao xin" messages had distracted him, but now he realized once again how much he missed her.

"What's this telephone number?" she asked, unsettled.

"I bought a China Mobile SIM card. It's cheaper." A white lie. He didn't want to worry Christine; she couldn't help him right now. "Are you okay? Are you taking care of yourself?" Stupid questions. He heard phones ringing in the background and the voices of her colleagues.

"Yes, as much as I can. You sound very tense."

Paul told her about the conversation with Chen.

"What will you do now?"

"I'm meeting Weidenfeller and Xiao Hu later. Tomorrow I'll go to Yiwu and talk to Da Long and Wang. I'll be back with you the day after tomorrow."

"Have you thought about what would happen if Yin-Yin said it was all your idea and that you, not she, had written the piece?"

"Christine! What makes you think that?" he exclaimed sternly. It was least easy to forgive someone else for voicing one's own faults and fears.

"It just occurred to me," she said apologetically. "Why are you getting so worked up?"

"No, I hadn't thought about that at all," he said with a bad conscience.

"Paul, take care of yourself. We need you."

Sometimes a word was enough.

He took a side street back to the New Asia Hotel. In the room, he slotted the security chain into place, took off his sweat-soaked clothing, and stepped into the shower. The hot water felt good. Paul realized how tense his shoulders and back were; he closed his eyes and stayed under the warm spray of water until the small bathroom was filled with steam. He stepped out of the shower, reached for a towel, and then got such a shock that he nearly slipped and fell. Two large Chinese characters were showing in the steamed-up mirror above the sink: "XIAO XIN."

He pricked his ears. Nothing more than the drone of the old air conditioner came from the room. Paul opened the bathroom door very slightly; the security chain was in place as before. Someone must have come to his room while he was taking a walk and drawn the characters on the mirror with a finger. They gradually disappeared, and fat drops of water trickled down the mirror. Paul dried himself quickly and crawled into bed. It was a long time before he stopped trembling.

Xiao xin. Little heart.

They had been correct there, though they hadn't meant it that way. He had a small heart. One that was filling with fear. One that ought to be braver than it was. One that was large only in its neediness and its longing for love. He wanted to go back to Hong Kong. He was no hero.

He thought about moving to another hotel, but he would have to show his passport there as well. His details, like all foreigners', would be passed to the authorities, and whoever had found him in the New Asia would track him down in the Hilton or the Jinjiang too. He got dressed and gathered his passport, flight ticket, cash, credit cards, notebook, and pen. He had to hurry. Weidenfeller had invited him to his apartment for a drink, and then they were to go on to dinner with Xiao Hu at a restaurant in the French concession.

He took a taxi to the Okura Garden Hotel, walked through the lobby, left the building through a side entrance, and walked down

Maoming Lu until he reached Grosvenor House, a redbrick art deco construction from the 1930s, one of the loveliest addresses in the city then and now.

Yin-Yin's boyfriend lived on the tenth floor; he greeted him at the elevator with a firm handshake and a serious look on his face. Paul couldn't remember the last time he had shaken hands when greeting someone.

Weidenfeller was taller than Paul had remembered. He had broad shoulders, light-blue eyes, and short, cropped hair that made his face look energetic and severe. It was a severity that did not go with his soft, slightly nasal voice. Paul judged him to be in his late thirties. He was wearing a suit with a white shirt and a tie, and he was perspiring. He had clearly only just come home himself.

He led his guest into the living room, a large space with a high ceiling and white walls, furnished with a mixture of modern furniture, art, and Chinese antiques. A painting of the Forbidden City that looked like a photograph hung over two white leather sofas, and there was a flat screen television opposite tuned to CNN news with the sound turned off. In the middle of the room was an old Chinese closet and dresser whose dark-brown polish shone in the light. The dining table and chairs were behind a six-section wooden partition with various dragons and scenes from a wedding carved into it.

"Beautiful place."

"Thank you."

"Where did you get the antiques?" Paul asked, impressed.

"I used to travel a great deal, and bought them in the provinces. Are you interested in jade?" Without waiting for a reply, he opened a display cabinet in which several dozen pieces of jade lay. Little dragons, tigers, dogs, and oxen in blue, orange, pink, and lavender, along with amulets, rings, and mouthpieces for opium pipes.

"These are the most beautiful pieces in my collection," Weidenfeller said, picking up a light-green rectangular piece. It was a dragon with large jaws and a curled tail, as large as the palm of a hand. "This was a belt buckle. It's from the Tang dynasty. Over a thousand years old."

Paul nodded, even though he was not particularly interested in jade. Perhaps he had been too quick to judge Yin-Yin's boyfriend. At their first meeting he had seemed typical of one of those corporate types who worked in China for some time in order to earn as much money in as little time as possible, and lived in Beijing or Shanghai without getting to know the rest of the country, which they weren't interested in anyway.

"Would you like a drink?" Weidenfeller asked, putting the jade away. "Whiskey? A gin and tonic? A martini, perhaps? Or a beer?" He opened a cupboard that concealed at least two dozen bottles of hard alcohol, and poured himself a large whiskey.

"No, thank you. Maybe later," Paul said. "Or maybe I will have something. A cold beer, if you have one."

"I wouldn't have offered otherwise," his host said, disappearing into the kitchen for a moment. "A German Beck's. I hope that's all right with you."

Paul sat down on the sofa and looked at Weidenfeller. He was perched on a stool cradling his whiskey; he took a large gulp of it and stared at the wall. He was breathing heavily. As though he was suddenly remembering the reason for Paul's visit.

After a while, he asked, "Have you found out anything?"

"No, not yet, unfortunately. I'm going to Yiwu tomorrow—"

"This is your fault," Weidenfeller said, interrupting him abruptly. "I hope you know that."

Paul sighed heavily. He had feared an accusation like this and had resolved not to even engage in a discussion on this point. "Listen, I don't want to argue with you."

"You inspired Yin-Yin, without thinking it through."

"She's a grown woman. She knew what she was doing," Paul retorted, annoyed. He did not intend to justify himself.

"Stop your smart-ass talk, for God's sake," Weidenfeller said bitingly. "It's always the same with goddamn do-gooders like you. You get involved in something without having the faintest idea about it. Create all kinds of chaos and claim at the end that you were just acting for the best. You make me sick."

"You're mistaken," Paul said. "I've known this country for over thirty years and—"

"Don't give me that old spiel. For over thirty years? That makes things even worse. You clearly seem to have understood nothing. China is not Europe. China is not America. Different laws apply here. We have to respect them, whether we like it or not. We're guests here, and we have to behave accordingly."

"I know you're very worried. I am too," Paul said, trying to calm him down. "But a crime has been committed here. That can't mean nothing to you."

"What we think about it is irrelevant. Why can't you understand that? The way crimes are dealt with here is a matter for the Chinese, not for you. If they decide to execute petty criminals and let the serious ones off scot-free, it's their affair. If they poison their air, their fields, their rivers, it's their business. At some point the people will have enough of it and fight back."

"Or maybe not."

"Or maybe not, that's right. But even then it's not your business, Herr Leibovitz. I've lived in China for years, as you know. I'm doing fantastic business here and have never had problems. None, at least, that we haven't quickly found solutions for, be they official or not. Do you know why? Because I play by the rules. Because I don't meddle with things."

Paul realized again why he had disliked this man at first sight. He felt belittled by the cold logic of this kind of argument. The reasoning did not convince him, even though all he had to counter it was a feeling.

"I don't know what you mean," Paul said. "I didn't post the piece on the Internet."

"On the Internet?" Weidenfeller gave him a confused look.

"Yin-Yin wrote down the story of her mother and the results of our investigations and posted it on the Internet anonymously. Didn't she tell you about it?" Paul could see how his final sentence offended his host. Weidenfeller swallowed a few times and his lips trembled uncontrollably.

"No, she didn't tell me. But she obviously told you," he replied quietly. "And yet you did nothing to prevent it?" He stood up, walked over to his bar, turned his back to Paul, and poured himself another whiskey. He emptied his glass in one gulp and filled it again. "I don't understand it," he muttered to himself. "I don't understand it."

Neither of them said anything for a long time.

The sound of the doorbell broke their silence. Paul got a shock. "Are you expecting anyone else?" he asked suspiciously.

"No," Weidenfeller said, surprised. He went to the door.

Paul got up and followed him. They heard the elevator moving, stopping at one of the lower floors. The sound of male voices could be heard from below. They heard the doors closing and the elevator coming closer, stopping with a jerk. Xiao Hu stepped out of it. He was pale and had dark rings under his eyes. "A meeting got canceled so I got away from the office earlier," he said half apologetically when he saw their astonished faces.

"Why didn't you call first?" Weidenfeller asked, a little unnerved.

Xiao Hu shrugged. "Am I disturbing you?"

"No, not at all. Come in. What would you like to drink?"

"Whiskey on the rocks. A double."

Weidenfeller poured the drink in silence; he was so quiet that Paul could hear the crackle of the ice cubes when the warm whiskey flowed over it.

Xiao Hu collapsed onto the other sofa, his gaze wandering from one to the other of them. "My sister has done something really stupid."

"I know," Weidenfeller said shortly. "Leibovitz has just told me. And you won't believe this: he knew about it beforehand."

Xiao Hu looked at him in disbelief. Paul nodded.

"You knew what my sister planned to do?"

Paul nodded once more.

"And," Xiao Hu said, speaking slowly and enunciating every word carefully, "you allowed her to go ahead with it?"

"What was I supposed to do?" It had slipped out. A sentence that sounded like a betrayal of Yin-Yin, as though he had had even the slightest doubt about whether she had been doing the right thing. They were really succeeding in making him try to justify himself.

"You could have told me about it, for one thing," Xiao Hu said sharply.

"Why?" Paul said in anger, more at himself than at the two men. "If Yin-Yin had wanted one of you to know about it, she would have told you, wouldn't she?"

"You're a self-righteous asshole," Weidenfeller spat out.

Xiao Hu looked at him thoughtfully. Paul was not sure if he was considering the logic of his argument or if he agreed with Weidenfeller. He took a big gulp of whiskey, looked at the ice cubes in the glass, waited a moment, and then emptied the glass with a second swallow.

"Another one?" Weidenfeller asked.

"Yes, please. Thank you." Yin-Yin's brother cleared his throat. "This morning I found out that my sister has been arrested." He looked at them in turn, took a deep breath, and sighed loudly. "Sanlitun wants to press charges against her for libel and damage to its reputation. They are demanding compensation."

"You . . . You can't be serious," Paul stammered. "*They* want to sue *us?*"

"Not you, Mr. Leibovitz," Xiao Hu replied in a stifled voice. "My sister. That's a significant difference."

"And one he hasn't grasped," Weidenfeller interjected. "That's the problem."

Yin-Yin's brother continued without paying any attention to him. "The case will probably be heard in Hangzhou or Yiwu. She would have no chance. She would be ruined for life."

Paul buried his head in his hands. He was dizzy. For a moment he felt as if he were sitting in a small boat being rocked from side to side by high waves. He couldn't believe what he was hearing.

"There is a way out, if we don't make any mistakes," he heard Xiao Hu say. "A senior party official has intervened on her behalf at my request. The company is prepared not to press charges and even help my parents with some money. In return, Yin-Yin must withdraw her accusations and my father must not pursue the case any further."

"That's a mockery; that can't be true," Paul said. His heart was pounding with rage.

"But that's the way it is, regardless of whether you think it's right or not," Xiao Hu said.

All three men sipped their drinks almost in synch and gazed silently at each other.

Yin-Yin's brother broke the silence. "I'd like to ask you for a favor."

Paul could see how difficult these words were for him. "What can I do for you?"

"You have to talk to my father."

"Me?"

"Yes. According to what Yin-Yin has told me, he thinks highly of you. I don't have a good relationship with him. We hardly speak. He doesn't trust me. He would listen to Yin-Yin, but she can't do anything now."

"What should I say to him?"

"You have to convince him that he absolutely has to accept the offer from Sanlitun; there is no other way. And he must write a letter to Yin-Yin and tell her to do the same."

"You can't expect him to do that," Paul blurted out. "Is he supposed to thank the criminals who crippled his wife for their magnanimity?"

"Not thank them. But my family must sign an understanding never to ask for further payments for damages or compensation in the future."

"He can't do that. You can't ask him to do that."

"What choice do we have?"

Paul got up, paced the room in circles a few times like a caged animal, and went to stand by the window. Shanghai by night lay before him. A restless sea of lights and neon signs advertising perfume, beer, and computers. Construction sites lit up bright as day, with dozens of cranes rising from them. On the roads below he saw the endless stream of cars and pedestrians passing. He grew nauseated.

The offer from Sanlitun was not only cynical, it was, in a deep and true sense, evil; he could not think of a better word for it. How on earth was he supposed to convince Da Long to agree to a deal in which he had to betray his own family? He found it impossible to imagine what he would do if he were in the same position.

He felt the two men behind him watching him. He turned around and said quietly, "I can't do it."

"Why not?" Xiao Hu asked calmly.

"Because, because . . ." Paul was lost for words.

"You want to help my father, don't you?"

"Yes."

"And my sister."

"Persuading him that we have no choice would be a great help."

"Do you know what you're asking me to do?"

"I'm asking you to do what is best for my family."

"We . . . We have so much incriminating evidence. The laboratory tests. The other sick people. Sanlitun can't just . . . I mean, no court . . ." The words tumbled out of Paul's mouth without thought, not directed at anyone. He shook his head slowly. "It won't work."

"Why not? Do you mean for him or for you?"

It was a perceptive question, which he didn't have a reply to straightaway. "I saw how deep in despair he was. I saw how he fought for your mother's life. He asked me to help him find a lawyer. I promised to do that," Paul said, avoiding the question.

"You don't know my father."

"What I have seen is enough for me. I don't need to know more."

"You think he wants justice?"

"Yes, of course, what else? People should be brought to account for what they do. What else would you call that?"

"My father's sense of justice is not highly developed. I can assure you of that."

"What . . . What do you mean by that?" Paul asked uncertainly. He had no idea what Xiao Hu was hinting at.

"I'll tell you. Then you'll understand why my father and I don't get along. Are you sure you want to know?"

"If it will help you."

"Not me. You," Xiao Hu said, exasperated. "Do you know how my grandfather died?"

Paul shook his head.

"He committed suicide during the Cultural Revolution. He jumped out of the window. Out of fear of the Red Guards."

"I'm very sorry to hear that," Paul said. "What does that have to do with your father?"

"When we were children he told us it was an accident. Our grandfather had lost his balance hanging the laundry out in front of the kitchen window." Paul said nothing, so Xiao Hu continued. "Later on, he acted as if he was taking me and Yin-Yin into his confidence and told us that we were old enough to know the truth about the death of our grandfather. He said that the party was responsible for his death. It had persecuted him unfairly during the Cultural Revolution and had his life on its conscience."

"Isn't that right, since he jumped out of the window because he was frightened of the Red Guards?"

"My grandfather was an intellectual. He read forbidden publications that he hid under the kitchen floorboards at home . . ." Xiao Hu paused, as though he wanted to make sure that Paul understood every word. "Only his wife and his son knew about them. My father was the one who betrayed his own father to the Red Guards."

Paul lowered his eyes. "How do you know that?" he whispered.

"It's in his cadre file. A friend of mine in the party put it on my desk a few months ago. My father denounced his father at several meetings. He told them where the books were. I've read statements from the meetings."

Da Long had delivered his father to the Red Guards. Paul thought about Christine. About her mother. About the almost forty-year-long silence in the Wu family. About wounds that never heal. That was why mother and son had never searched for each other. How would Christine react when she heard about this? Did she have to know?

"How old was your father then?"

"Fourteen. Why?"

"That's very young, don't you think?"

"Old enough to know what it means to tell the Red Guards what is hidden under the kitchen floor," Xiao Hu replied angrily.

"Are you sure? Many children denounced their parents back then. School pupils did the same to their teachers, and college students to their professors. Your father obeyed Mao's orders. Why are you laying the blame on him but not on the party? The party created the conditions for children to betray their own parents."

"The party has admitted that mistakes were made during the Cultural Revolution. My father has not. He deceived us. Lied to our faces. I will never forget that."

Paul looked at Xiao Hu. Red spots were showing on his neck; he was clearly one of those Chinese people who could not tolerate alcohol, and reacted to even a small amount with a rash. He looked tired and pale, but life had barely left any traces on his features to date. Paul did not know what else he ought to say to this young man. Should he remind him that it was pure coincidence, and not merit, that led to him being born in 1974 rather than fifteen years earlier? That he, by Chinese standards, belonged to one of the luckiest generations in this country for centuries? A generation that knew nothing but growth and a gradually increasing standard of living, who had so far been spared the terrible decisions that their parents had had to make. Who could say with any certainty how he would have behaved during the Cultural Revolution? Whether he would have been a victim or a perpetrator, or both?

Paul was not sure who was speaking to him here. The grandson who grieved for the circumstances of his grandfather's death? The son who was hurt and disappointed because the father he had looked up to was also a traitor? Paul could have understood grief, but not the self-righteous indignation that he heard in Xiao Hu's voice. Did he have to remind him that he belonged to the same party that was responsible for a system that had locked his sister up; that people had to face difficult decisions like the one Da Long and Yin-Yin now had to make?

"Anyone who stays unharmed has not lived," he said at last.

"Don't you have anything more to say than that?" Xiao Hu asked, surprised and annoyed.

"No."

"I don't understand you." There was more than a hint of resignation in his voice.

"You don't have to."

"Will you speak to my father anyway?"

"Yes. I'll explain Sanlitun's offer, or threat, to him quite clearly, and what the consequences of a refusal will be. He must decide for himself. Does Da Long know about Yin-Yin?"

"I haven't told him."

"Can he be sure that she will really be released if he agrees to the conditions?"

"Yes."

"Are you sure?"

"Of course," Xiao Hu said unconvincingly. The red spots were spreading on his face.

Paul flagged down a taxi on Huaihai Zhong Lu and told the driver to let him off at nearby Zhapu Lu. It was too early to go to bed, and he felt uneasy at the thought of being alone in the room. He was thirsty, and wanted to be among people.

Zhapu Lu was a lively road full of restaurants, karaoke bars, shops, and kiosks. Red lanterns were strung in front of the buildings, and loud music streamed out of the bars. The air was filled with the smell of cooking, rice wine, and cigarettes. Paul stood in front of a street stall stacked with several bamboo baskets, each as large as a wheel, which were sizzling and steaming away. He looked around to see if he was being followed, but no one seemed to be taking any interest in him. A stocky woman with red cheeks was standing behind the bamboo baskets, selling steamed buns filled with sweet pork. He bought one; it was so delicious that he bought another two immediately. A couple of feet away, a fly-by-night trader was selling pirated

CDs and DVDs of the latest Hollywood films from a folding table.

Many of the food stalls had put tables and chairs on the street. Paul found a stool on the pavement at a fish stall. He sat down next to the fish tanks and a running faucet and ordered a beer. Directly across from him on the other side of the road was a hair salon, a traditional Chinese massage parlor, and a beauty salon. Paul could see the young women sitting behind the large windows. Some of them were watching television, looking bored, and the others were doing each other's hair. One of them was painting her fingernails.

He drank his beer in a few gulps and ordered another. A Porsche four-wheel-drive vehicle made its way through the pedestrians; everyone moved aside without grumbling. Two young women in tight black dresses were standing in front of the hairdressers. They were about eighteen; twenty at most. They smoked their cigarettes, watched him, and finally beckoned at him. Paul acknowledged them with a thin-lipped smile and shook his head.

In his mind's eye, Paul was remembering his first trip to China: people wearing blue-gray uniforms, no cars on the streets, ration cards. Bicycles, bicycles everywhere. Faces full of suspicion and curiosity. How much this country had changed in the space of one or two generations. The lives of most Chinese people were getting better year after year; what would happen when the economy stopped growing? When falling stock markets wiped out the savings of millions of people? Would this country stay peaceful, or would the Chinese tendency for mass movements create new victims? After all, Paul thought, the Communist Party of China was only in power because of a succession of political campaigns. The Anti-Rightist Movement. The Great Leap Forward. The Cultural Revolution. After that, the slogan "Get rich, comrade"; since then, money was the only thing that mattered. What could be next?

In his room, he did not see any further signs of an intruder. He put the security chain in place, propped a floor lamp against the door so that it would fall over if anyone tried to come in, and jammed the back of a chair under the door handle so that it would not be possible to push the handle down. He wanted to ring Christine and tell her everything, but he didn't dare to. Who knew if someone was listening? He wrote her a short text message instead:

> Darling
> I wish I were with you. Missing you is hard.
> In touch properly tomorrow. Sleep well.
> Take care of yourselves.
> With love, Paul

He took two aspirin to alleviate the effects of the alcohol, undressed, and, despite the thronging thoughts and the noisy air-conditioning, fell asleep immediately.

———

Paul woke when someone rattled the door handle. The floor lamp crashed to the ground with a loud thump. The sound of breaking glass. For a moment he thought he was dreaming, then he jerked himself onto his side, turned on the light, and jumped up.

"Who's there?" he shouted, tense.

"Housekeeping." A reedy woman's voice.

He looked at the clock: 9:12.

"Later. Come back later," Paul said, sinking back onto the bed. He had overslept. He was supposed to have been picked up at nine a.m. by a driver whom Weidenfeller had organized for him through his company.

He went into the bathroom and had a quick shower, sticking his head out of the shower curtain every few seconds to look at the bathroom mirror. The steam formed evenly over the mirror without showing any words.

The driver was waiting for him in front of the hotel. He was a friendly young man who nodded understandingly when Paul asked him not to drive too fast.

The journey to Yiwu seemed unbearably long to Paul. He called

Wang the journalist, who replied in hurried snatches of speech. They arranged to meet that evening in the lobby of the Grand New Era hotel, where Wang would reserve a room for him.

When they got off the highway, he called Da Long.

Da Long answered in a tired voice that brightened somewhat when he recognized Paul, who said that he would be with him in about half an hour.

Paul wanted to focus on seeing Da Long again, but found it difficult to gather his thoughts. He'd tell him about Yin-Yin's arrest but had no words of advice or comfort, only the vague hope that Wang might be able to help them, even though he couldn't imagine how.

———

Paul slowed down as he approached the house. Sweat was running down his neck, and strands of hair were sticking to his forehead. The air there was less humid than in Shanghai, but just as warm. He opened the heavy wooden gate hesitantly. The hinges creaked loudly, drowning out the roar of the highway for a moment; the metallic sound hurt his hears. The courtyard was full of laundry drying: towels, cloth diapers, and bed linen, flecked with brown and yellow stains that could no longer be washed out. The water dripping from the laundry had covered the dry, dusty ground with a crazy pattern. The sound of a violin concerto came from the house; Paul thought it was Mozart.

Da Long sat on the steps to the verandah with his legs spread wide, his elbows propped on his knees, smoking. He got up and walked toward him, mustering a brief, tired smile. The sight of this small man touched Paul just as it had the last time; he resisted the impulse to reach out to hug him and hold him tight.

"G-g-good to see you. Have you eaten?" he asked, seeming as helpless as he had when he had met his sister.

"Yes," Paul lied. He didn't want to put him to any extra trouble.

"W-w-ell, surely you can manage a little more. I have some noodles from yesterday and vegetables and tofu from this morning."

They went into the dim house, which smelled more strongly

than on his last visit. Paul would have preferred to stay out in the courtyard and eat on the verandah. He walked over to Min Fang's bed, and Da Long followed him.

She looked even more painfully thin than she had ten days ago. Her mouth was half open and her cheeks had collapsed; her head lolled back on her neck as though she were trying with all her might to look behind her; her eyes were fixed on the ceiling. One leg stuck out from under the blanket, dry and stiff as a board, with shrunken folds of skin hanging from it. Paul could feel the pressure of tears in his eyes. After seeing this, how was he supposed to bring himself to tell Da Long about Yin-Yin's arrest and the price of getting her released?

"Sh-sh-she is barely still there," Da Long said, gripping the bed frame. "Y-y-yesterday she choked again and almost suffocated in my hands. And she's getting bedsores. I don't know what to do." The helplessness in his voice.

He disappeared into the small kitchen and returned with two bowls. He set plates and chopsticks and put teacups, a teapot, and glasses on the table. In one of the bowls was a kind of salad with pieces of tofu, grated melon, cucumber, green beans, and sprouted soybeans; in the other were some cold noodles in a spicy sesame sauce. Everything was delicious. Paul could not understand how Da Long could conjure up such delicacies from so little.

"Christine sends her greetings," Paul said, because he did not know what else to say.

Da Long sucked at some noodles, which disappeared into his mouth with a loud smacking sound. "I-I-I didn't expect to see you again so soon."

A polite way of asking, *Why are you here?*

Paul sipped his tea and looked across the table. Da Long was bent over his plate, looking at him over the top of his glasses. He was waiting for an answer, and Paul was losing his nerve. His hands felt numb, and he felt the urge to cough without being able to do so.

Da Long guessed that something was wrong. He chewed slowly, and when his mouth was empty, he pushed his plate into the middle

of the table, sat back, and waited. When Paul still did not say anything, he asked, "Did you see Yin-Yin in Shanghai? I haven't heard
from her for a few days."

Paul took a deep breath, ran his fingers through his hair, shifted
from side to side on his stool, folded his hands on the table, and
propped his chin on them.

"Wh-wh-what's happened?" he heard a voice say in the half
darkness.

"Da Long, I'm sorry—"

"Is she dead?" Da Long interrupted him, his voice trembling.

"No. Yin-Yin has been arrested."

Da Long crossed his arms across his chest and rocked his upper
body back and forth gently; his gaze passed Paul and lost itself
somewhere in the room. Time stood still. Paul had expected an
explosion, an outbreak of rage, outpourings of hatred, mocking
laughter, but not this silence.

"She's been arrested?"

"Yes."

"By whom?" A voice that betrayed no emotion.

"Probably by the police in Hangzhou or Yiwu. We don't know
for sure."

"Why?"

"She wrote a piece about Min Fang's illness and its causes and
put it on the Internet. She included our investigations. She named
names. She called for those who were responsible to be punished."

"Did you know about it?"

"Yes," Paul replied, watching Da Long closely. His face had taken
on the quality of a mask; it did not show any reaction at all; the dark-
brown eyes were fixed on something in the distance, unblinking.
Even his full lips had not compressed themselves into a thin line.
He looked as if he had withdrawn himself to a distant place, which
Paul's voice, but not the meaning of what he was saying, could just
about reach.

"Who else knew about it?"

"No one, as far as I know."

"What are they threatening to do to her?"

Even this question was asked without showing any feeling. If only he would shout and scream, Paul thought. Or jump up in horror, pace the room, thump the table, cry; anything would be better than this awful paralysis.

"Nothing yet, officially. Xiao Hu has found out that Sanlitun wants to press charges against her and claim damages for libel."

Da Long rocked himself from side to side mechanically.

"Xiao Hu has intervened on her behalf. He's managed to get Sanlitun not to press charges. The company is even willing to give you all some money."

"Wh-wh-what do they want in return?"

"They want Yin-Yin to withdraw all her accusations and apologize. You have to refrain from any attempt to take legal action against Sanlitun. Now and in the future."

"What will happen if I don't do that?"

"I can't tell you that. Xiao Hu thinks that Yin-Yin would have to go to jail for a few years and be financially ruined."

The violin concerto had ended; the muffled roar of the highway could be heard from outside. Min Fang breathed noisily.

"Da Long?" Paul asked carefully, when he couldn't stand another minute of Da Long's silence. What was going on inside him? What was he thinking?

Silence.

"Perhaps there might be another solution."

Still nothing.

"I mean . . . I've arranged to meet Wang, Yin-Yin's former classmate, later on today. You may remember that we met him on my last visit to Yiwu, Yin-Yin and I."

Silence.

"I've been given to understand that he might have something that could help us." As Da Long was still saying nothing, Paul simply continued speaking. He didn't care what he said, he said whatever came to him; he talked and talked simply to not have to bear the silence. "Of course, I don't know what that could be. A witness?

Maybe. Why not? I mean, Wang is a journalist, after all; he knows the area well. He's a local reporter; they always have the best contacts. I know that from my own experience, after all; that's how they make a living. Why shouldn't he use them for us? He must have been in love with Yin-Yin before and wants to help us now. He seems a very decent guy. What do you think? All on condition of anonymity, of course. We don't want to create any difficulties for him. Or he could give us the names and numbers of his contacts who could help us. In Beijing, perhaps. I . . . I could go there tomorrow and talk to them. No problem. I can't promise anything, of course not, how could I, you know how it is. Anything's possible. It's not that we can't do anything, we . . ." Paul paused for breath. "Da Long?"

Silence.

"Da Long, can you hear what I'm saying?"

He did not react.

Paul could not stand being seated any longer. He got up and walked around the table, intending to touch Da Long, to hug him, to do something to lessen the pain, but he didn't dare to. He put his hand on Da Long's shoulder but pulled it away again immediately. There was no comfort. Paul had experienced this himself; anyone who still attempted to comfort a person in such moments rather than bearing this silent loss of consciousness was thoughtless or cowardly.

Paul took a few steps toward Min Fang, but stopped in the middle of the room. His gazed wandered through the room. A few rays from the low-hanging sun were coming through a tear in the curtain and falling on the bed; dust motes danced in them. A soiled sheet lay below. "Da Long," he said in a broken voice, "can I do anything for you? Say something." No reply. He walked back to the table and crouched in front of Da Long, hoping he would look at him. He wanted to look him in the eye, but Da Long was looking straight ahead; his gaze was lost in the dimness. "I'm going now," Paul said, loudly and clearly. "To Yiwu. I'll come again tomorrow morning. Is that all right with you?"

There was no point. He was talking to someone who had been

robbed of the power of speech. He wanted to go, but for some reason he did not dare to turn his back on both of them. It was as though he feared that they would dissolve as soon as he let them out of his sight. So he walked backward to the door in small steps.

"Da Long, I . . . I . . ." The limits of what could be said. He had hardly ever felt them like this. "I . . . I'll be back tomorrow."

———

Wang stepped into the lobby of the Grand New Era Hotel with a black briefcase tucked under his right arm, which he held on to with both hands. He was almost half an hour late, and he looked worn out. He had dark shadows under his eyes and a tense, almost frightened, expression on his face; there was no sign of the playfulness Paul remembered from the last time. When their eyes met, he gestured to him with his head to come with him, and turned on his heel without waiting, disappearing into the revolving doors. Paul hurried to follow and caught up with him in on the street after a few feet.

"Where are we going?" he asked, out of breath.

"To a friend's place. Not far from here."

"To Gao the lawyer?"

"No. That would be too dangerous."

They walked side by side in silence, turned off the main road into a small, dark alley that stank of public toilets, crossed a wider street, and entered a neighborhood full of garishly lit shops, their windows full of nothing but toilet brushes and toilet seats. They stepped into one of the bigger shops, whose walls were covered in toilet seats: gold, pink, black, transparent, round, rectangular; some were heart-shaped. Paul had never thought they could come in so many different shapes and colors. A sales assistant sat in front of a computer looking at share prices. She looked up briefly, nodded a silent greeting at Wang, and continued reading. They walked past her, disappeared behind a curtain, made their way through a storeroom full of boxes, cartons, and toilet seat covers, and climbed up narrow, winding stairs to the first floor. They found themselves in an office stuffed so full with paperwork, files, catalogs, and toilet brushes that there was nowhere to sit. Wang cleared some space on two chairs, put the briefcase on the desk, and removed the battery from his cell phone. Paul did the same, sat down, and waited in anticipation for what would happen next. He had met Wang only once and knew almost nothing about him, but now he had no choice but to trust him. He wondered for a moment if he had been lured into a trap, but discarded the thought immediately. He did not need to be led to this hidden office in order to be frightened more than he had already been, or threatened.

"Have you heard anything from Yin-Yin?" Wang wanted to know.

"Only that she's been arrested and that Sanlitun wants to press charges against her for libel. Unless—"

"She takes everything back, apologizes, and her father refrains from taking legal action against the company," Wang finished his sentence.

"You know the latest already?" Paul asked, surprised.

"No, but I know our country."

Wang picked up the briefcase and opened it; it was filled to the brim.

"I told you last time we met that I worked on a story about Sanlitun some time ago, and then had to stop my investigations when my boss ordered me to. Do you remember?"

"Of course."

"What I didn't tell you was how far I got in my investigations. I had an informant at Sanlitun." He pulled a pile of folders and papers out of the briefcase. "These documents prove that the company knew exactly what it was discharging into the water. At least three provinces are involved. Five lakes or rivers. Four factories. Five villages. Several hundred people, probably thousands. Everything has been recorded. Measurements of the industrial effluent. Laboratory results. Internal memos. Written reports. Instructions to employees."

Paul looked from Wang to the papers he was holding and back again. "Where did you get them?"

"From someone I know who worked at Sanlitun until recently, and who needed money very, very urgently."

Paul picked up one of the folders and leafed excitedly through it at random.

"I can't do anything with this now," Wang said. "I wanted to keep it all for a time when I would be allowed to write about a case in which a company was poisoning the environment and covering it up like this. But we can't wait that long. If you take this material to Hong Kong and give it to the press, it will make headlines. Maybe even international ones. What do you think?"

Paul nodded wordlessly.

"That will put pressure on the authorities here. A good lawyer in Shanghai, Chen, perhaps, would then be able to get a good outcome for the family."

"You trust Chen? He was very abrupt on the phone today . . ."

"Chen is okay," Wang reassured him.

"I thought," Paul said, "that no judge would be willing to . . ."

"Not officially, of course. This material here creates serious problems for Sanlitun, and it would be prepared to make concessions if canny negotiations were made. I can assure you of that."

"Should I take all of this with me?" Paul asked, still disbelieving.

"Yes. And not a word to anyone about whom you got the documents from. Not ever. You know what China is like. You know what that would mean for me."

Paul nodded again. "But I wonder . . . I mean, why are you taking this risk? Why are you helping . . ." He was not able to finish his sentence.

Wang shrugged. "If only I knew," he said, with the ghost of an ironic smile on his face. "A journalist has to put up with a lot. I've grown used to . . . well, I wouldn't call it lying, but keeping quiet about the truth. When I heard that Yin-Yin had disappeared, I knew what they planned to do with her." He paused for a moment, pensive. "Maybe it's the last straw." He put the papers back in the briefcase and gave it to Paul. "Don't let this out of your sight. Put it under your pillow at night. Take it with you to the toilet. For all intents and purposes, it's life insurance for Yin-Yin."

Paul was surprised at how heavy the briefcase was. He wanted to get back to the hotel as soon as he could so that he could look through the documents in peace.

"It's probably best if you stay in your room this evening," Wang suggested. "How will you get back to Shanghai tomorrow?"

"I have a driver and a car. I'll stop to see Da Long on the way. I'll speak to Chen in the afternoon, then fly back to Hong Kong the day after tomorrow."

"On no account can you say anything about this on the telephone as long as you're in China."

"Don't worry about that."

Wang got up. "I have to get back to the office. I'll bring you back to the hotel first."

They walked back the same way they had come, as silently as before. Paul clasped his arms around the briefcase; he was too deep in thought to talk. If what Wang said was right, he was holding material in his hands that he would have dreamed of having when he had been a journalist. The daily papers in Hong Kong would love to have it, certainly *Apple Daily* and the *South China Morning Post*. The *Asian Wall Street Journal* would be interested, as would the *International Herald Tribune* and the BBC. Their reports, if not the ones before, would see to it that Yin-Yin was set free and that Da Long was paid compensation. He just had to make absolutely no mistakes now; he wanted to get Chen's advice as soon as possible.

Wang said good-bye in front of the Grand New Era. Paul was suddenly in a hurry because he needed the toilet urgently. The restroom in the lobby was closed for cleaning, and the elevator was taking too long, so he took the stairs up to the second floor, walked down the corridor, and hurriedly swiped his key card through the slit above the door handle. He had to do it a second and a third time before the green light finally showed. He pushed the door open, put the card in the slot next to the entrance to keep the electricity on, went straight to the bathroom, and put the briefcase down next to the sink. He heard a sound, and before he realized what had happened, the light had gone out. Someone had pulled his card out of the slot and cut the power.

It was so dark that Paul could not make out even the outline of the toilet, the shower, or the door.

"Hello?" He wished his voice sounded steadier.

Instead of a reply he heard heavy breathing only a few feet away from him. There was a stink of garlic. Paul felt his heart pounding in his throat; he stretched his arms out and tried to orientate himself and get to the bathroom door in small steps; he was frightened that he would grab ahold of a face or a human body any moment.

A cry out loud; a piercing pain on the forehead and the nose. He had bumped into the door frame. He licked his lips and tasted blood.

"Be careful, Mr. Leibovitz. Don't hurt yourself."

The voice came from his room; the man was sitting either at the desk or on the couch next to it. He spoke Mandarin with an accent that Paul identified as coming from Beijing and the surrounding area.

He felt his way out of the bathroom by following the wall until he was standing at the entrance to the bedroom. The heavy curtains had been drawn so the room was in total darkness; even the digital clock display on the television had been covered. The big bed had to be to his right, a few feet away, and the sideboard with the mini-bar was opposite, behind that was the desk, and next to it was the seating area with the couch. He heard the sound of several people breathing.

"It would be best if you stayed where you were," said the voice from the darkness. It did not sound unfriendly; it almost sounded concerned. "I don't want you to injure yourself."

Paul felt himself growing a little calmer. "Who are you?"

"A friend."

"Then turn the light on."

"A friend who prefers to stay unknown." When Paul did not reply, he added, "A friend who is trying to keep you from doing a stupid thing."

"What stupid thing?"

"Bringing things into the public that do not belong in public."

"Who says—"

A voice that did not give the impression that it would accept any opposition interrupted him. "A friend who knows what the consequences would be. Consequences that you can't even foresee."

"What do you want from me?" Paul asked, intimidated.

"The documents that Mr. Wang gave you."

"Why didn't you take them from him?"

"Because we weren't sure he had them. Apart from that, we don't want to interfere with the freedom of the press."

Paul could hear that the stranger found his own comment amusing. "What will you do with the documents?" he asked.

"That's none of your business."

Paul hesitated. What choice did he have? He had no idea how many people were in his room. The garlic lover had probably blocked off the door to the corridor. He could scream for help but would probably be overpowered before anyone heard him.

"These documents . . . I can't . . . they're extremely important," he stammered.

"That's why I want to have them," the voice replied calmly.

"Where have you come from? Beijing?"

"You're asking too many questions."

"Who has sent you?"

"Once again, that is nothing which should concern you."

"Sanlitun?"

"Perhaps. Perhaps not."

"Who else could have any interest in these documents?" Perhaps he could engage the man in conversation and win some time.

"Many people. 'The net of heaven is broad / The mesh is big / But nothing escapes it.' Laozi knew that."

"I don't know what you mean," Paul said.

"The provincial government in Hangzhou could also be interested in these documents. The mayor of Yiwu. A competitor of Sanlitun's, certainly. What do you think? Or the environmental authorities in Beijing. I can think of others. Do you know the favorite color of the Chinese?"

"Red," Paul whispered in reply.

"I see you know our country," the stranger said with a mocking laugh. "Red brings us luck. But our favorite color is gray. Everything is gray in this country. We are the masters of the gray zone. We know it well. Everything is possible. Nothing is impossible. Things are seldom what they first appear to be here. Sadly I have no time to take this conversation further. Maybe another time. My colleague at the door will now switch on a flashlight for a moment. You will fetch the documents from the bathroom and throw them onto the bed. Then you will lie down on the right-hand side between the bed and the wall, flat on the ground, facedown, and you will not move. When we have left the room you will count to a hundred and back again before you do anything. If you are clever, you will count to two hundred. If you're as smart as I think you are, you will act as if nothing has happened and will not leave the room for the rest of the day. Do you understand me?"

"Yes."

He was no hero, and this was not a movie in which he would manage to escape with a few kicks and punches. He felt his way back into the bathroom; the light was just sufficient for him to avoid bumping into the door frame again. As soon as he was back in the room with the documents, the man turned the flashlight off. Paul heard the briefcase land on the bed with a slapping noise.

"Very good. Now lie down."

Paul went down on his knees and crept into the space between the bed and the wall; his heart was beating so hard that it hurt his chest, and he felt as if he couldn't breathe. He heard several men stand up and saw the glow of a flashlight. They picked up the brief-case and left the room a few seconds later.

He stayed lying in the darkness for a long time, motionless. The pounding of his heart gradually calmed down and his back began to hurt, but he still did not stand up. The game was over. He gave up. He wanted to go back to Christine. He was no a match for the masters of the gray zone. He longed for a black-and-white world. *Xiao xin.* Little heart. At some point his cell phone rang. Paul raised himself and crawled along the wall down to the entryway to the door. He got up, opened it, picked up his room card, and slotted it into the holder to switch on the light. The phone displayed a missed call: CHRISTINE.

It took him all his remaining strength to act as if nothing was wrong when he called her back. Fear and tension were certainly not good for a pregnant woman, and she couldn't help him anyway; apart from that, he was convinced that their conversation was being tapped. In his tense state, Paul did tell her about the accusations being made against Yin-Yin, and that nothing could be done at the moment, but he would visit Da Long once more tomorrow and then get a flight back to Hong Kong in the evening or by the following morning at the latest.

Christine didn't suspect anything. She was so preoccupied with herself and her pregnancy that although she reacted to the news of Yin-Yin's arrest with alarm, she continued to tell him about things at the office and about dinner with her mother and Josh. Paul was barely listening; he felt cold, so he turned the air-conditioning off and switched on the heating, filled the bath with hot water, and paced up and down between the desk and the bed. When the conversation finally ended, he undressed and got into the bath. But he found the narrowness of the bath and his own nakedness intolerable, so he got dressed again. He listened for every noise, and his skin crawled at the thought of spending the night alone in the room. For a moment, he wondered if he should go and sit in the lobby. Instead, he switched on all the lights in the room, turned on the television, and put the volume so high that it could surely be heard in the corridor. His hands and feet were cold, and he felt as if he were freezing even when he had covered himself with two blankets. When the winners of the football match shouted for joy and sank to their knees after the deciding goal, Paul started to cry. The tears streamed down his cheeks; he turned on his side, hugged a pillow, and cried until he fell asleep in exhaustion.

———

The driver dropped him off in the sandy village square. Paul asked him to wait rather than to drive on to the nearest town. It would not take long; an hour perhaps, at most. He had tried to call Da Long many times that morning to tell him he was on his way, but his calls had gone unanswered.

Paul hurried through the narrow streets; he had to stop himself from breaking into a run. He wanted to get the conversation over as soon as possible and then get away from there. He did not know what to say to Da Long, how he was to make it clear to him that they were facing a force that they had to bend to, that he had been wrong, that he was sorry he had thought otherwise.

The laundry in the courtyard had been taken down; it lay piled in a bamboo basket on the verandah. The ground had been swept clean: there was not a leaf, not a twig, not a cigarette butt to be seen.

"Da Long," Paul called out. No reply. "Da Long?" he said in an uncertain voice. "Da Long," he said again, louder this time.

Only then did Paul notice that neither the door nor any of the windows was open. Da Long could certainly not hear him. He climbed the steps up to the verandah, knocked, and tried to open the door. It was locked. He tried to peer through the windows, but the makeshift curtains hanging in front of them had been pulled tightly shut. He couldn't find a single gap to look through.

"Da Long?" His cries grew more urgent. He looked in the shed and he walked around the back of the house to the kitchen, but that door was locked too. Paul walked back to the front door, kneeled down, and tried to look through the keyhole. He couldn't see much in the dim light. A chair, part of a table with something on it. Paul couldn't see what it was from the position he'd assumed. He walked around the courtyard one more time, looking for traces in the sand left by men's boots or by the rolling of a trolley bed, for scraps of paper or any sign that Da Long might have left behind. Paul saw nothing apart from fine brown, evenly swept sand.

XIX

He had spent his life being protected by her love. Thirty-nine years, seven months, and twelve days.

They had spent every one of those days together. Their children had laughed about it in secret. He knew that. They thought their parents didn't need much from life. Maybe they were right. Maybe it was a sign of being easily pleased and simpleminded to be unable to imagine living without the other. Or maybe not. Min Fang thought the opposite was true. She thought it was the most demanding of all things to expect to find happiness with just one person.

The protection of their love. It had kept him from despising himself. The long shadow of an autumn day, humid and much too hot. The clatter of young people on wooden steps. A dark-red liquid seeping from a mouth and trickling over cobblestones, draining away in a gap between them, but leaving traces forever.

You were a child. You didn't know what you were doing. Her words. Spoken so often and with such conviction that Da Long believed them in the end. But what to do with the child? It was not another person; it was strange and mysterious, but it was a part of him. How well could a person live with a traitor within him? Who had the courage and the strength to forgive himself? Not to suppress it, not to forget it. To forgive himself. With her help, he had managed. Partly. What she couldn't take away from him was the deeply felt shame at having done something wrong at a decisive moment in his life. This shame would haunt him to his final hour.

He got up, walked over to the bookshelf, and looked for a book. Two hours had passed since his wordless farewell to Paul, and Da Long had no idea what he had done in that time. He must have sat at the dining table numbly, unable to think straight. Now he was gradually stirring, and he needed advice. He could not talk to Min Fang, or to Yin-Yin. He searched out the dog-eared old copy of the *I Ching*. He and Min Fang had often consulted this book of oracles over the years, and read out passages to each other for comfort or support, just as others turned to Buddhist, Confucian, or Christian writings for the same. Thousands of years of Chinese wisdom spoke forth from the *I Ching*; it had been a help to him in many difficult life situations.

He took the book down, sat next to Min Fang on the bed, looked at the contents, turned to hexagram number thirty-six, and began reading aloud: "'Ming One—Darkening of the Light.' In times of darkness, be careful and hold back. Do not needlessly attract powerful enemies by acting without forethought."

Da Long lowered the book. Had she turned her head toward him, or was he imagining it? Was she trying to give him a sign?

"Min Fang?" He looked at his wife. Her stiff limbs sticking out from under the thin blanket. The twisted hands. The half-open mouth from which no more words found their way to him. He leaned over and looked in her eyes. Dark brown. Fixed gaze. He moved her head slowly from side to side, hoping that her eyes would follow him. No reaction in her pupils. "Min Fang? Can you hear me?"

My dearest Da Long—I turned my head, perhaps a finger's width. I have no strength for more than that. If only I could at least look you in the eye. Just one more time. I understood every word. You know what they are doing. You have always known. They are forcing us to do things that we should not do. Things that will make us one with them and betray all that is beautiful. I don't know of any way out. If I could end my life myself, I would. But I can't; I need your help to do it. I can't even kill myself anymore. How should I make myself understood? If only I could move my hands. Pick up a pen and write for you what I want to say. Or sing it for you. Hum it. Breathe it.

I can't do any of that. I'm a prisoner. Useless. If I were no longer here, you would not have to press charges against anyone on my account. If I were no longer here, you could move to Shanghai to be with Yin-Yin. If I were no longer here . . .

———

She did not move; he must have been imagining it. Da Long read the lines a second time.

In times of darkness, be careful and hold back. This was not a piece of advice he knew what to do with at this time. Was he needlessly attracting powerful enemies? Powerful, yes, but needlessly? What should he do? Sign a piece of paper saying that his wife was ultimately responsible for being in the state that she was? What a thing to ask. What a disgrace. It was blackmail: cold, calculated malice. What choice did he have? He could not write such a letter even if he had wanted to. Everything in him revolted at the thought. But at the same time, he had no doubt that they would make good their threats and take Yin-Yin to court. It was like playing a game of Go with no hope of winning; the opponent was backing him into a corner, one move after another. He was hemmed in, his white pieces were surrounded, the ring around him grew tighter, it was impossible to break free, no matter how often he looked at the board, or from which angle he did so.

———

The river that separates life from death is a shallow one.

Tell me, Da Long, can a person love someone more than they love themself? Is that our secret? We remained true to ourselves by staying true to our beloveds. Where does that lead us now? We have to part. I'll go first, and you'll follow me. Later. I'll wait for you. Patiently. Set me free. Let me go.

———

Da Long looked elsewhere in the *I Ching* for words that could help him. "'The times are difficult,'" he read out into the silence, in a loud voice. He watched Min Fang out of the corner of his eye at the same time to see if she was not giving a sign to him after all. At least a little one. "'You must hurry on restlessly without fixed abode. If you do not want to make compromises within yourself but wish to stay true to your principles, a lack is the result.'"

Were these the words that he had been looking for? *You must hurry on restlessly without fixed abode.* In times of darkness. But where to?

There was no place to head to for shelter, nowhere to aim for. They had only this one house. Just this one life. He had the feeling that he had come to the end of a long march. A wanderer whose path had taken him to the outermost edge of the cliff at the end of a peninsula. The sea roared beneath him. There was no going back.

Of course Xiao Hu was right. Whoever it was who put him under pressure now, whether it was Sanlitun or the authorities in Yiwu or Hangzhou, had all the power, and he had nothing but his own stubbornness. Pigheadedness, some would call it. How difficult was it to sign a piece of paper? It would set his daughter free and wouldn't make Min Fang's condition any worse—quite the opposite. With compensation payment, he could try to improve her care. What was there to object to?

Da Long turned to number forty-seven and cleared his throat.

"'Kun—The Oppression (The Exhaustion). Times of adversity are the opposite of success. But they can lead to success if they befall the right person. If a strong person encounters hardship, he remains cheerful despite all danger, and this cheerfulness is the foundation for success later on. It is the constancy that is stronger than fate. He who allows himself to break under exhaustion will certainly not have success.'"

Da Long read the lines again, and then once more. *He who allows himself to break under exhaustion will certainly not have success.* "Min Fang," he said. "Am I like that? A broken person? Not a strong one? No, no longer. Maybe I've never been one. I know you would say that wasn't true if you could. But a strong person would never have told anyone about secrets that lay hidden under the kitchen floorboards. A strong person would have seen through the lies back then and not years later. A strong person would have looked for his mother and his sister. Wouldn't have been accused of wrongdoing by his son. Min Fang, forgive me. I don't know what I should do. It's too much for me. They are destroying us, and I don't even know who *they* are. Who is holding Yin-Yin under arrest? Who has stipulated these conditions for us? Who are we defending ourselves against? Why don't they dare to come out of their hiding places and show their faces? We thought that the dark times belonged in the past, thought we lived in a new age. Just because the cities had new faces. Because cars had replaced the bicycles on the streets, because our children could go to college, because of a thousand big and small things, we let ourselves be deceived by appearances. Willingly surrendered ourselves to the tempting promises of a new era, an era in which we had no place. Now I have no more strength. Can you understand that? What a question! I'm sorry, I'm confused. What was I saying? It's the loneliness that makes me talk this way. I miss you so. Why can't we simply disappear? Just steal away from here. Dissolve into thin air, like the smoke from the incense sticks on the altar to our ancestors."

Why don't you read on? You'll find the answer you are looking for in the next few lines. I know 'Kun' by heart. We read it together. Several times. We were familiar with adversity. We were often oppressed. "When the water has flowed out of the bottom of the lake, the lake must dry up and become exhausted. That is fate. At such times, there is nothing a person can do but accept his fate and stay true to himself. But that is the deepest level of our actual self." We have come to that, Da Long. To the deepest level. You and I. We didn't seek it out. I didn't ask for the poison in my body, and you didn't ask to have a sick wife. The deepest level is not a comfortable place. It's not one we stay in gladly. Anyone who climbs down this far is stronger than he imagined. Not everyone can bear to meet his actual self.

You have the strength. I have never heard you complain since I fell ill.
Not once. You clean me up at night. You clean me up in the day. You put
up with my stink. You have accepted it, your fate. Do not despair.

———

Hurry on. Restlessly. They could not stay here. It was no place for
her. Da Long closed the book and buried his head in his hands.
Accept his fate and remain true to himself. How was he to do that?
There was one option, but he flinched at the thought of it. He
could kill both of them. A few weeks after Min Fang fell ill, he had
thought about it for one long, agonizing night, but discarded the
idea the following morning. Only people who no longer had any
hope willingly ended their lives. He was not one of those people yet.
Apart from that, he did not presume to act for his wife, and he did
not want to leave his children on their own. Now things were different. An important condition for Yin-Yin's release would no longer
apply if her parents were dead. As far as the other condition went, he
could not help her; only she could decide if she was to withdraw her
accusations or not. He hesitated as he weighed everything up. The
thought of leaving Yin-Yin alone caused him the most pain. But she
would be thirty years old before too long. She would get married and
have a child herself at some point. Min Fang was of no more use to
her. How long could he care for Min Fang? What would happen if
he himself fell ill? Before Min Fang died. It was only a question of
time before she became a burden to her daughter.

How was a decision to die made? In a few hours or even from
one moment to the next, because we no longer see a way out? Or
did it stretch itself out over weeks, months, perhaps years, without
our being aware of it? How did a person get tired of life? Da Long
had no answers to these questions; he was not a person who had
given much thought to how he would die. He had hoped to spend
as much time as possible with his future grandchildren and not to
suffer at the end. He had wished to die quickly and with Min Fang
at his side. The thought of circumstances arising in which he would

take his own life had not occurred to him before. Now he actually felt relief at the notion.

How could he do it? He had to make sure that neither of them survived and that they did not suffer any pain. With a knife? He could never manage to slit Min Fang's wrists, to do physical violence to her. Da Long looked through the container of medication: painkillers; pills for cramps; not enough to kill them both. If they had both been in good health, they could have lain down on the railway tracks, but they were too far away; he would never manage to carry her all the way there. Rat poison? One of the pesticides stored in the shed? He had read that farmers who committed suicide that way died agonizing deaths.

Da Long had another idea. He got up, walked slowly through the room, and looked around him carefully. Too big. Too many windows. Too many doors. It was unsuitable for what he had in mind. He had another thought, and went into the small, narrow kitchen, which had room for only the stove, the old oven, the sink, and a sideboard. One window. Two doors. He looked at the window and traced the cracks in the wooden frame with his long fingernails. The frame was old and cracked all over; the door leading outside was the same. Nothing that couldn't be fixed. Da Long fetched a pair of scissors, towels, blankets, and sweaters and started to cut them up into strips and stuff them into the cracks in the door and window frames. Carefully, he wedged material into the smallest of crevices with a screwdriver and put more layers over them. He opened the door to the courtyard and stuffed thin cloths between it and the frame so that it took him all his strength to close it again. He stuffed pieces cut from a dishtowel into the keyhole.

Da Long, where are you? What are you doing? I can hear you moving around in the kitchen; I can't make out what you're doing from those sounds. You're not clattering pots and pans. You're not washing dishes. You've been gone so long and you know how I don't do well without you. I never have. Come to me. Sit on the bed again. Tell me what you're doing. Tell me something. Read to me. I need to hear your voice. I need you.

———

He returned to check on Min Fang every now and then, gave her water, and held her hands, which seemed colder than usual. For a moment he was overcome by doubt: Was he allowed to do what he was doing? Was he allowed to raise himself to a position of mastery over life and death? He could not ask his children for advice or his wife for her agreement. Was he allowed to decide for her? For himself, he had no doubt. He was free, at least in this respect. Da Long bent over his wife and kissed her forehead, her mouth, and her neck. He pushed her gently to one side and lay next to her. He took the book from the nightstand, turned to hexagram thirty-three, and read:

"'Dun—The Retreat. The circumstances are such that the enemy forces, helped by the times, are prevailing. In this case, to retreat is the right thing, and it is through withdrawal that success is gained. Success consists of conducting a retreat in the right way. Withdrawal is not to be confused with flight. Retreat is a sign of strength. Do not waste the right moment so long as you are in full possession of your strength and wits.'"

———

Only now do I realize what you have in mind. Are you sure? Have you thought through everything? It's not in your power to go back on this. I wish you would let me go alone. You are too young. You are in good health.

———

Twilight had fallen outside. Da Long got up, went outside, sat on the steps, and lit a cigarette. It was a mild and pleasant evening; there was no lovelier month than May. Not as hot and humid as the summer, but no longer as cold as the winter, when he felt more and more pain in his bones every year. A bird cheeped on the shed roof over the roar of the highway in the background. He heard a freight train pass in the distance.

Was there an alternative? Of course, he thought, there was always an alternative, but it was not one that he wanted to choose. He was tired, incredibly tired. *When the water has flowed out of the bottom of the lake . . .*

When the bird fell silent, Da Long got up and tidied the house. He mopped the floor, took the laundry off the line, and piled it up carefully. He picked up the cigarette butts and swept the courtyard thoroughly. It should not look like they had left the house in a rush, even though that would have been impossible anyway, with Min Fang's condition. They were not fleeing. They were retreating, and if a retreat was conducted in the right way, it was a sign of strength. That was what the *I Ching* said. That was what Da Long thought.

He looked in the closet for the white nightgown that Yin-Yin had brought back for her mother after a trip to Beijing a few years ago. The long sleeves were decorated with frills, and there was a ribbon and beautiful mother-of-pearl embroidery on the front. Min Fang had laughed, embarrassed, when she unpacked it, and said that she was too old for it, but Yin-Yin had contradicted her with vigor. And then Min Fang had indeed worn it, so often and for so long that she finally put it away in the closet because the material was getting thin and she was worried that she was wearing it out from wearing it and washing it too many times. He sniffed it, hoping to find a trace of her scent on it, but it smelled only of laundry detergent and the closet. How big it seemed now on her emaciated body. It was difficult for him to pull it over her stiff arms and legs. In the end, he used the scissors to widen the neckline at the back. He combed her thin gray hair and fastened it with a hair tie. Min Fang had liked to wear her hair that way. He wiped her face; he had cut her finger- and toenails only a few days earlier. *The person of superior character retreats in a spirit of goodwill and withdraws cheerfully.*

Da Long put his arms under his wife gently and carried her to the couch. Then he picked up the heavy mattress and carried it through the room into the kitchen. It fit exactly into the space between the wall and the stove. He moved the stereo into the kitchen, set it next to the sink, and turned it up.

He heard Min Fang grunting for breath and hurried to change his clothes. He pulled on a clean pair of trousers and his favorite jacket, of brown corduroy, which Min Fang had patched the elbows of so often.

Da Long carried his wife into the kitchen, laid her on the mattress, and put a pillow under her head. He was filled with a sense of ease that he had not felt for months. He walked through the house one last time. The front door was locked, and the makeshift curtains hanging over the windows were drawn tightly shut. On the table he had put a letter, with the *I Ching* on top of it, opened to hexagram thirty-three: "When one sees the way ahead so clearly, free from all doubt, a cheerful mood sets in, and one chooses what is right without further thought."

He went into the kitchen, closed the door, and pushed the towel against the bottom edge. Propane was heavier than air; it would flow from the canisters like water and drift along the floor at first; that was why the doors had to be especially well sealed at the bottom.

He turned the music down until it could no longer be heard. Min Fang had always hated it when he stopped a piece abruptly with the press of a button instead of gradually fading it away. He played the CD of Yin-Yin playing Schubert once more from the beginning.

Da Long lay down next to Min Fang and turned her on her side so that her right arm was lying over his head and his left arm was under hers. They lay there for a while without moving. His heart was beating wildly in agitation and he could feel that hers was too. Gradually they calmed down. He took his time, as though he was waiting for their bodies to be in tune one more time before they took their leave. He reached out behind him and opened the canister. The gas streamed out quietly, with an even hiss. He moved nearer to his wife. Stomach to stomach. Nose to nose. Her warm breath in his face. Her wonderful, beautiful, strong body. Her breasts, which had nourished two children. Her laugh. Her singing. Her happiness in small things, which he had had to learn. That was Min Fang before the poison. He would fall asleep with her in his arms. It was growing dim. The world was sinking. His eyes shut. In the protection of her love.

————

Time to sleep. Without fear. To go, without regret. Without grief. Free. Thanks to you.

You're closing your eyes. I can't see it; I feel it, rather.

Your heart is beating more slowly; the pauses between the beats are getting longer. Will you go before me? Wait for your wife, take me with you.

Dying in the evening is not a bad thing, Confucius said.

Here we lie. Deep in the red dusk. How wary we are of wandering. Hand in hand.

Is this perhaps death?

XX

Xiao Hu gazed at his parents, or, to be precise, at what remained of them: two handfuls of grayish-black ashes in plain dark-brown wooden urns. He had actually wanted their remains to be kept in just one container, but had been told that was not possible for legal reasons. That was why he had had to take two urns home with him. They stood open on the dining table in front of him now. There was a faint smell of a fire gone cold in the room, or perhaps he was imagining it.

Xiao Hu gripped his father's urn with both hands, stood up, and started carefully uniting his ashes with his mother's. A tiny, fine cloud of dust rose from the urn and settled in a thin film on the glass table. For a moment Xiao Hu did not know what to do. He could not possibly wipe the remains of his father off the table with a damp cloth. Finally, he took a credit card out of his wallet, scraped the ashes carefully into a little pile, swept them onto a piece of paper and let them trickle into the urn. He closed the urn, held it uncertainly in his hands, and began to shake it, hesitantly at first, then more vigorously. His parents had died the way they had lived, Xiao Hu thought; they could be at peace only in a single container. He put the urn on a shelf next to the television, put down an offering of an orange, his mother's favorite fruit, for each of them, lit a few incense sticks, and bowed several times. He wanted to keep them with him until he and Yin-Yin had decided whether they wanted to scatter the ashes or keep them. It was a question he had not given any thought to yet. Two weeks ago, death had not been a subject that had particularly moved him. Neither his own nor that of others. He felt too young to think about his mortality, and he had been spared the loss of loved ones until then. Now two deaths had hit him at once, and with a force that Xiao Hu himself was surprised by.

They hadn't even left a farewell letter. Not a line. After Paul Leibovitz had called, Xiao Hu had driven to Yiwu immediately. Before they called the police, he and Paul had searched the house together, but they had not found anything. Only the *I Ching* lay open on the table. The thirty-third hexagram: "Dun—The Retreat. The power of the darkness is in ascent." What did that mean? In that moment, his father seemed as mysterious to him in death as in life.

"The person of superior character retreats in a spirit of goodwill and withdraws cheerfully. The retreat is easy for him because he does not need to do violence to his convictions by choosing to withdraw . . . The situation is not ambivalent. The inner act of detachment is a clear-cut fact. Thus does one have the freedom to leave. When one sees the way ahead so clearly, free from all doubt, a cheerful mood sets in, and one chooses what is right without further thought. A clear path like this always leads to good."

Xiao Hu had read these lines in the dimness of his parents' house, but he had not understood a word. He had often seen Min Fang and Da Long consult the *I Ching*; he knew that they valued its advice; later, he had referred to it himself, but he found it difficult to get anything from the coded messages of this book of oracles, with its old-fashioned language full of metaphors. What did his father mean to say to him and Yin-Yin with these words? That he and Mama had gone gladly, or in good spirits, to their death? Was that supposed to comfort their children? How could their death lead to anything good? What did "the power of the darkness" mean? It had not played any role in his life so far. The power of light, yes. The power of ascent. The power of positive change. The power of everything-is-possible-there-are-no-limits. Not the power of the darkness.

His father had not been one to wear his heart on his sleeve. He had been reserved with strangers and had often remained silent even with his children. But for him to have taken his life without taking leave from them, without any words addressed personally to them, was something Xiao Hu could not grasp. He was annoyed and hurt by it. What on earth would his sister say?

He had had a premonition. The entire morning. When he saw Paul Leibovitz's number light up on his cell phone screen, he had barely dared to answer the call. The hoarse voice. "Xiao Hu, I'm sorry . . ." Silence. Seconds that seemed endlessly long and hard, in which he sensed disaster before it was spoken.

He had gotten through the days after that. Gone to work, chaired meetings, organized the cremation, accepted the brief condolences of his colleagues. At the same time, he had felt as though he had been standing outside himself, as though he were living the life of another person.

Since the cremation two weeks ago, he had felt worse and worse with each passing day. He slept badly and barely ate anything; at night, he woke up drenched in sweat and he felt exhausted as never before in his life. Finally, he called in sick without really being able to say what he was suffering from. He first cited stomach trouble, and then delayed his return to the office with a series of other excuses.

He spent the first two days in an almost comatose state in bed, existing between worlds, sleeping, then lapsing into a strange dozing state, floating, waking for short periods before gliding back into the dimness. He had a vague impression of the sounds from the street— car horns, traffic, bicycle bells, voices—which seemed to be coming from another reality. He heard cell phones, noises at the door to the apartment, whispers, and calls, and did not know if he was imagining it all. He dreamed peculiar things: about talking fish, flying cats who ate only bananas, and about his mother, who was suddenly better but could no longer speak, only croak. Like a toad.

When the noise grew too loud for him, he got up. He got dressed and walked aimlessly through the city. He spent hours in cafés, restless like a person waiting long past the appointed time. He could not imagine what his father's last thoughts had been. Had he died

feeling bitter? Despairing? Or had he done it with a light heart because, this way, he did not need to do "violence to his convictions"?
Was that the hidden message? The longer Xiao Hu thought it over,
the more he felt, despite his grief, respect for his father's consistent
behavior in rejecting the request that the party, Sanlitun, or whoever
it was, had made of him. He admired his courage; it made him feel
respect for his father again, a respect he had thought was forever
lost.

The loneliness was terrible. He felt it particularly at night. The
usual stream of thoughts and plans that had otherwise filled his
head had been subdued. An odd peace reigned within him, one that
he had felt only in rare moments before. The pain and the grief were
stronger than he would have thought possible, given that he had
been estranged from his father and had already wrapped his head
around his mother's demise; they had barely exchanged a word for
months. Perhaps it was the finality of it that had taken him un-
awares. The things not said, the questions not asked. All things that
he had neglected in the past few years, thinking that there was still
time to address them if he felt the need to.

Xiao Hu felt strangely vulnerable. He was not sure if it was due
to the death of his parents or to the arrest of his sister. Soon three
weeks would have passed, and he still did not know what had happened to her. Vanished without a trace. Xiao Hu had once thought
things like this happened only to poor farmers in remote provinces
who did not know how to defend themselves, but never to the sister
of a middle-ranking party cadre in Shanghai. Three weeks without
any contact from her—they'd never let that much time lapse without some kind of communication. He had made telephone calls and
invited party comrades out to dinner, had used all his contacts, had
even spoken to his boss, who knew people in the ministry of justice
in Beijing. His boss had promised to look into it; two days later, he
had simply said that he had gotten nowhere. No explanations, no
apologies. Xiao Hu had tried to reach the party secretary who had
questioned him and set him the ultimatum. No luck. After the death
of his parents he had been convinced for a few days that it would

be just a matter of hours until he saw his sister again. Whoever was keeping her under arrest would surely relent after such a loss.

The power of the darkness.

Xiao Hu knew the rumors about secret prisons in which people who had petitioned the government directly in despair were held, supposedly for days, weeks, or months. Farmers whose land had been seized without any compensation or for far too little in payment. Migrant workers who were cheated of their wages by factory owners. Women whose husbands had been abused by the police. Citizens who had no hope of achieving their rights through legal recourse. They traveled to the provincial capitals or straight to Beijing to appeal for justice at the office that had been specially built for such cases. This was a tradition that had its origins in the Ming dynasty, when subjects had made the dangerous journey to the capital to plead for help from the imperial authorities against corrupt officials. The Communist Party had incorporated this right in the constitution after the revolution, but Xiao Hu knew that it existed mainly on paper. Anyone who tried to exercise it had to reckon with harassment or worse. Nevertheless, he had not wanted to believe the rumors about the secret prisons.

Every day that passed without him hearing anything from Yin-Yin made him feel more and more uncertain.

It was his fear for his sister, his feeling that he had to do something for her, mixed with a growing rage over the injustice that was being done to her, that led to him formulating a plan during those few days when he was lost to himself. It did not come overnight. It did not occur to him from one hour to the other, but slowly, almost imperceptibly. He had been sitting in a café in Changle Lu when the idea occurred to him, a thought so outrageous that he thought it actually might work.

He wanted to continue what his sister had begun. If the death of his parents was not sufficient cause to set her free, if his contacts made no difference, then only public pressure would do the trick, and in China, that could be achieved only via the Internet. Paul Leibovitz had sent him Yin-Yin's piece by mail from Hong Kong.

He wanted to add to it and publish it on the Internet again, but do it more cleverly, without leaving any traces. No emails on the subject. No Internet searches from his computer. He would get rid of his laptop, so that if they searched his apartment no one could seize it and find the deleted information on his hard drive. He would make a list of more than three-dozen websites, Internet forums, chat rooms, and blogs, and post the piece on them under an assumed name and address. He knew what key words and expressions the Internet police looked out for; he would avoid using them and hope to slip past the authorities that way. For a couple of hours, at least, perhaps even a few days, if he were lucky. That could be enough time, he thought, for it to spread widely enough, to reach a critical mass that would make it difficult for the official censor to intervene.

Yet he hesitated. He distracted himself in cafés with magazines and at home with the television, and found himself developing the plan on long walks. He stood in the darkness in front of the building Yin-Yin had lived in and stared up at her unlit window. He held conversations in his head with his mother, who reminded him of his responsibility as an older brother. He was seized by a restlessness that made it more and more impossible for him to sit quietly in his apartment. He paced back and forth between his kitchen and his living room, read random pages of the *I Ching*, and discovered, much to his surprise, more and more sentences that piqued his interest: "The persistence of the lonely person places high demands." He turned to another page. "Getting used to what is dangerous can easily lead to it entering one's own nature. One knows it and gets used to evil. Thus does one lose the right path, and disaster is the natural consequence."

Xiao Hu shook his head. He had not gotten used to evil. He had not even been aware of it.

"If you are truthful, you have success in your heart, and what you do will succeed."

Truthfulness in the heart. One of those old-fashioned phrases that had made him not take the book seriously before. Now it sounded almost like an echo to him. Truthful. What did he have to do now to be truthful? What was important to him if he forgot about everything around him, if he did not let himself be distracted, if he peeled away layer after layer from himself like an onion and went right to his innermost nature? Yin-Yin. Little sister. Big brother.

A clear path like this always leads to good. That was the last sentence that his father had left him.

Xiao Hu read the hexagram on retreat over and over again; the more he read it and the more intently he engaged with it, the more he understood the advice that his father had found within it, which now applied to him too. He had to withdraw. From everything that he had learned in party training. From colleagues and friends. From his desire to be transferred to Beijing. *The inner act of detachment is a clear-cut fact. Thus does one have the freedom to leave.*

He realized that a retreat was not the same as the end. A retreat had many faces; it could merely be a detour on the march forward. Properly used, withdrawals were not capitulations, but weapons. *When one sees the way ahead so clearly, free from all doubt, a cheerful mood sets in . . .*

The situation was unambiguous.

Xiao Hu thought about whom he could meet that evening. He picked up his iPhone and scrolled through the more than five hundred contacts in it. He knew countless acquaintances, colleagues, and friends from the party whom he could get in touch with to chat about cars, women, property, and stocks and shares. None of them was a friend he could ask for advice about his plans, someone who would encourage him. Maybe Zhou. Yes, he had spent a lot of time with him after buying two apartments from his wife the previous year. Since his parents had died two weeks earlier, they had only spoken once, briefly; every time Xiao Hu called, Zhou was at the hospital, playing golf, or out at dinner, and promised to ring back.

"Hey, Xiao Hu. Sorry I haven't called. Been too busy."

He felt uncomfortable hearing the embarrassment in his friend's voice. "I know. No worries. Am I disturbing you?"

"No. What's up?"

"Nothing in particular. I wanted to ask if you guys were free this evening."

Zhou hesitated before replying. "Hmm. This evening is no good."

"Tomorrow?"

"Not good either. Maybe next week."

"Okay. When?"

"I . . . I don't know what my shifts are yet. Best if I call you at the beginning of the week."

Xiao Hu hated poor excuses. "Zhou, is everything all right?"

"Of course. Why shouldn't it be? Why are you asking?"

"Just asking."

It was as if he had an infectious disease. He wondered if he was on some kind of list of people to be avoided. Did Zhou know something? The doctor was also a member of the Communist Party, though a passive one, but perhaps he had heard news by chance from within the party, through a patient or a relative, that Xiao Hu himself was not aware of yet. Or had he simply sensed that his friend's fate was wending its way toward something undesirable and was therefore keeping his distance? Did he think that the double suicide was not the end of Xiao Hu's problems but only the beginning?

Xiao Hu ended the call, disappointed, went to the kitchen, made himself a double espresso, and fetched the letter from Paul Leibovitz, which he had hidden behind the coffee can. He pulled the copy of Yin-Yin's piece out of the envelope, read it thoroughly once more, and made notes in the margin. His sister wrote wonderfully well; it was another talent that he envied her for. His version would sound nowhere near as elegant, precise, or passionate.

He flipped open his laptop and created a document incorporating his changes. He described Yin-Yin's mysterious disappearance and the circumstances that had led to his parents' suicide, and added a new conclusion: How much was a person's life worth in China? How could people defend themselves against injustices done to them by the state? Could there be a "harmonious society" as long as the law and justice that the party was also subject to did not prevail?

He called on all readers to protest by email to the authorities in Hangzhou and to Sanlitun. To demand that Yin-Yin be released. To call for an investigation into the deaths of Mr. and Mrs. Wu—even though he did not have high hopes of many readers doing so. The risk was too high. There was too much fear.

Or was he wrong? He knew the power of the Internet could not be underestimated. It had changed China, but how quickly, and in what way? Had it given courage to the cautious, or only to those who were already brave? The story that the lawyer Chen had told his sister about the role of the Internet in the police investigations in Henan Province was an unusual case, but not the only one. Xiao Hu had recently heard of another instance, in which a security camera in a parking lot had filmed a party secretary molesting an underage girl. When her parents had tried to press charges, the police had refused to investigate. The film footage mysteriously found its way onto the Internet a few days later. The fury and bitterness it unleashed among bloggers and in chat rooms was so huge that the authorities had had to arrest the man. The story of Sanlitun and the village was significantly more explosive than that of a pedophile party cadre. It just had to be online for long enough.

Of course, suspicion would fall on him immediately. They would look into who had all the details of the case, and very quickly conclude that it was him. He was aware of what lay ahead of him: interrogations for hours, perhaps days. Threats and false promises. But Xiao Hu believed he was strong enough.

The state security forces would likely not succeed in proving that he was guilty of anything; his faultless party file spoke in his favor, after all. If anything, the death of his parents gave him a courage that he had not had at his last interview at party headquarters.

He put the document on a USB stick, which he would later put in the trash, and made his way to the area around Jing'an Temple, where there were quite a few Internet cafés. After that, he intended to go to the Xujiahui area of town and then later to Pudong, to cover his tracks.

The first café was in a shopping mall. It was small and filled with cigarette smoke; at most of the terminals were young people playing computer games. No one looked at him. He put his USB stick into a computer. Everything had to be done quickly so that no one could catch a glimpse of the text by accident. Xiao Hu marveled at how calm he was. Only after logging in, but before pressing Send, did his index finger hesitate for a few seconds. And not because he doubted.

He was sending more than a document. He was taking his leave. And within it lay, as always, a beginning too.

The freedom to leave. What a precious thing.

XXI

He woke from a bang on his door. The clock on his nightstand showed 5:27 a.m. They are here, he thought. Already.

Another knock, loud and hard.

"Let me in," a voice demanded.

Xiao Hu was terrified. He turned on the light, got up, and put on a T-shirt and pants in a hurry.

"Open the door."

"One second. I will be right there."

Bang. It sounded like they would shatter the wood any second.

He rushed to the entrance, but looking through the peephole, he saw no one. They must be hiding in the dead corners close to the wall, he thought. He held his breath and listened. It was quiet.

"Hello?" he said. "Who is there?"

No answer.

"Hello?"

Xiao Hu did not dare to open the door.

Suddenly he heard a loud scream from the apartment next to his. It was the young couple fighting—a man was angrily complaining about being shut out; the woman must have locked her husband out and just let him in again.

Xiao Hu was too anxious to go back to sleep. He made himself an espresso, heated up a *pain au chocolat,* and tried to work out. After a few minutes he had to get off his exercise bike, as his heart was pounding too hard.

A knock on the door in the middle of the night. It was the way they would get him, he imagined. Or they would come to his office, storm into a meeting, and arrest him.

As Xiao Hu left the garage on his way to the office, he was sure somebody was following him. A motorbike stayed right behind him. He made a detour and took the Nanpu Bridge instead of the tunnel. The bike disappeared long before he reached the bridge.

He was under no illusion: as soon as the authorities became aware of the documents online, he would be a prime suspect. They would monitor his every movement, his every call.

When he walked into his office he noticed immediately that something was different. His secretary did not dare to look at him, his colleagues avoided his gaze. They already knew. The head of his department canceled a meeting with him on short notice. There was a more urgent board meeting he had to attend to, and in the evening he had to fly to Beijing unexpectedly. Were they already discussing his fate?

All morning Xiao Hu sat in his office, staring out the window instead of at the two computer screens, unable to concentrate on work or even make a phone call. He had felt so calm and strong the day before, knowing that he was doing the right thing. *A clear path like this always leads to good.* But the path was murky now, the inner act of detachment more difficult than he had imagined.

The power of fear.

Suddenly his secretary came in and brought him a freshly brewed herbal tea. He still looked pale and sick, she said. The tea would help him feel better, but he had to take care of himself. If there was anything she could do for him, he should let her know.

Her kind gesture confused him. Maybe he was just paranoid.

He left early, and when he turned onto his street he saw two black Audis with tinted windows parked in front of his building. He drove by, turned back onto Ruijin Lu, and kept driving. After a while he made a U-turn, driving aimlessly, thinking what to do next. He had no place to go, no place to hide. His friend Zhou and his wife were an option, even though he had been less than welcoming lately.

But he was desperate to talk to somebody. He drove to People's Hospital No. 1 and parked in front of the main gate. It was shortly after five p.m., the time when Zhou usually left work. He turned the music on and waited. After half an hour, he saw Zhou's Audi leave the compound. He got out and waved; Zhou stopped.

"What are you doing here?"

"I had a meeting not too far and thought I would stop by. Do you have time for a drink?"

"Now?" His friend sighed.

Xiao Hu nodded.

"I am pretty busy," he said. "Maybe just a coffee—there's a Starbucks around the corner."

They sat at a small table among busy shoppers.

"How are you?" his friend asked.

"I am all right," Xiao Hu lied. "What's up?"

"Not much. Going on vacation next week."

"Where?"

"Thailand."

They fell silent for a while.

Zhou leaned forward and lowered his voice: "I have something exciting for you. A friend of mine is working at Dragon, the real estate developer. He said the company is hugely undervalued. They will announce a landmark deal in the next few days. Think about it."

"I will," Xiao Hu said absentmindedly. "How is your wife?"

"Good. She bought a new BMW last week. Great car. Didn't you order a new one as well?"

"Yes. I'll get it next month."

"Which series? A five or a seven?"

"Five."

They fell silent again, had a sip from their vanilla Frappuccinos, and looked around, avoiding eye contact.

Meeting his friend had been a mistake, Xiao Hu thought. It made everything worse. He did not want to talk about cars and stocks. He did not care about rising or falling share prices. Not anymore. But what else was there to talk about? Did he expect Zhou to ask about his sister's whereabouts? His parents' suicide? Not really. He could not share any of his anxieties, neither with him nor with anybody else. The petty conversation made him realize how much he had to rely on himself now.

They got up after ten minutes and left, their cups still half full.

For the next few hours he drove around the city. He took the batteries out of his mobile phone, as his sister had once advised him to do, though he had ridiculed her for it at the time. He passed by his apartment building and saw that the Audis were gone, but a black Volkswagen looked equally suspicious. Xiao Hu made sharp, unexpected turns, drove fast on the inner-city highway, switching lanes frequently, just to make sure nobody was following him.

When he'd almost fallen asleep in the car, he checked into the Grand Hyatt at the Jin Mao Tower. It always had many international guests, and he felt safer among them, even though he knew it would not make any difference. If the authorities wanted to arrest him, they would do so wherever he was.

His room was on the eighty-second floor. He opened the curtains and looked at the city beneath him. Lights, billboards, illuminated skyscrapers, elevated highways, cars, stretching to the horizon. The face of a new China, the fabric of the Chinese dream. The skyline had filled him with pride only a few weeks ago. His sister had been right: it was nothing but a façade.

He felt lost like never before.

XXII

Yin-Yin heard a steel bar fall into place, and someone put handcuffs on her. Then there was only an oppressive silence. She looked around her. Her prison was small and round, a kind of sphere or diving bell made of metal, in which she could not even stand upright; she could have touched both walls at the same time if she had been able to stretch her arms out. Harsh sunlight came in through two portholes. She pressed her nose against one of the cold windows and saw nothing but a deep-blue sky.

She crouched on the floor, pulling her knees close to her chest and resting her head on her hands. A loud jolt startled her. Yin-Yin felt as if she were in an elevator, going up. The sphere began to swing back and forth, like a pendulum. Yin-Yin jumped up, banged her head, gave a little scream, swore, and peered through one of the portholes. She saw a pier and a giant crane on rails with a long, rusty arm; she was hanging from this arm in her prison. On the quay below her she could see black automobiles with tinted windows and men in suits talking animatedly to each other. They looked up every now and then at the steel ball dangling over them. Then they laughed. There was another jolt, followed by a piercing rattle, the sound of a massive anchor chain falling into the sea. The sphere was gradually lowered.

They want to drop me in the harbor, Yin-Yin thought. She screamed with all her might. The metal sphere crashed into the sea, and the water surged up around it. Yin-Yin drummed her fists against the steel walls. One last brief look, then she disappeared under the surface of the water and was sinking even further. The sunbeams disappeared as she sank down to the bottom. All was lost. It grew darker and darker. She screamed and screamed.

"Yin-Yin. Yin-Yin." It was Lu, her roommate. "Wake up, wake up. You're dreaming."

Lu's hand on her shoulder fetched her back from the bottom of the sea. The familiar smell of her room. She blinked and took some time to open her eyes properly. The harsh light was blinding; she turned her head to one side to get away from it.

"Are you okay?"

Yin-Yin nodded.

"Should I put on some music?"

"No, please don't. Just some talk radio."

"A particular station?"

"Any."

The sound of a human voice was enough. During her imprisonment she had often not exchanged a word with anyone for a whole day; at some point she had begun to sing and talk to herself. Since then, she had found silence difficult to bear. Four weeks had passed since her release, but Yin-Yin had still not listened to a single note of classical music. She refused to, and kept postponing the moment without knowing why.

"Call me if you need me," Lu said, and switched off the light.

Yin-Yin stared at the ceiling. The five o'clock news burbled away; she was waiting for the sounds of morning. Neighbors making their way to work, parents telling their children to hurry up. Old Mrs. Rong next door, with her deep, hacking cough every dawn. The first light of day entered the room, painting black patterns on the walls. She was exhausted but fought with all her might against falling asleep again. The nights, when all the memories came back and she had terrible, wrenching dreams, were worse than the days. She thought about getting up so she wouldn't fall asleep again, but she was too tired. She tried to turn her thoughts to something pleasant: a concert, a new dress, the score of the Kreutzer Sonata, but the notes blurred before her eyes; her exhaustion overcame her.

When she woke, it was already past nine. Lu moving around in the kitchen, the smell of fresh coffee. There was a long day ahead of her. She had decided to leave China, for a few weeks or months; she was not sure. A former classmate who was studying at the Juilliard School in New York had invited her to visit, and Yin-Yin was toying with the thought of applying to the school too. She had booked a flight via Hong Kong, to visit Paul Leibovitz and her aunt. The flight left at two o'clock, and she had neither packed yet nor tidied her room.

Her brother was taking her to the airport. They sat in silence in the car for a long time. She did not feel like talking, and he had given up asking her questions. Not like the first few days after her release. *Where were you? Did they beat you? Threaten you?* He couldn't leave her in peace. *Can you remember any names? Faces?*

No, she couldn't. No, they hadn't tortured her. Not her body, at least. No. No. No. He shouldn't worry about her. She was fine. Considering. No matter how hard he tried, Xiao Hu found it difficult to understand her silence. *Say something, Yin-Yin*, he said, when his questions led to nothing. *Just tell me what happened.* He wanted to write down what she said; the more details, the better. He wanted to hear what had happened to her, thus hoping to lessen her burden.

The things you could not talk about, you had to keep your silence on. She could not say anything. She was not there yet. Not for a long time yet. She held everything at a safe distance: her brother; Johann Sebastian Weidenfeller, whom she had broken up with right after she had been set free; her violin; the symphony orchestra. Even Mozart, Beethoven, and Schubert.

She had dared to come out of her hiding place—or had been forced out of it—only once: when she had scattered her parents' remains. A small heap of gray ashes. Inconceivable. They had stood on the beach looking at the grayish-brown East China Sea and opened the urn. A moment of weakness. When she saw how some of the ashes trickled into the water and dissolved there while the rest were lifted into the air by the wind, carried away, and blown in all directions forever.

Then she had rested her head on her brother's shoulder and cried. Not sobbed, just a few tears before she had herself under control again. She had learned that in her five weeks of captivity: control, not to lose control.

Xiao Hu interrupted her thoughts. "Will you call me if you're ever not well?"

She nodded.

"If you need help?"

"Yes."

"If you like, I can come and visit you," he offered, though he guessed she might stay away for a long while. "I have time now."

"I know, thank you." She was sorry that she couldn't really share with him how she felt. She had him to thank for her release, and she was proud of him. He really had risked everything, and it was thanks only to a combination of unreliable factors such as luck, coincidence, and the political expediency of the moment that he too had not been arrested and that they had not both vanished into labor camps or a psychiatric ward. Shortly after her release, Xiao Hu had handed in his notice to China Life. He had told his sister that he too needed a rest, though, unlike her, he did not know yet exactly how he would be spending his time. He would look through offers from head-hunters in due course, or set up his own law practice. Yin-Yin looked at her brother's profile. From this angle he looked like their father, which she liked. He was now her only immediate family. So near. So far. He meant well, and had generously given her the money for her trip. But she still needed distance. Even when saying good-bye. He hugged her, and she did not resist.

Could one be a stranger to oneself?

The power of darkness.

———

Paul Leibovitz was nervous. Yin-Yin could tell from the way he kept looking at the display board, from the way his gaze flickered all over the hall.

She was not sure how she would greet him. Initially after her arrest, she had seen him as an ally; the thought of him, his encouragement, his confidence, had given her strength in those first few days. At times she had even gotten the crazy idea that he would get her released. After a week, disappointment and rage took over. Everything was his fault. He was safe in Hong Kong; he had more liberties. How naïve she had been. Now he was abandoning her. But those feelings passed too. What remained was an indefinable feeling of annoyance that she herself had yet to put her finger on.

When he finally spotted her, an uncertain smile flitted across his tense face.

He hugged her awkwardly.

"How was the flight?" No one was safe from pleasantries.

"Good."

"Have you been to Hong Kong before?"

"No." She had already told him that in an email.

"Are you hungry?"

"No."

He picked up her suitcase and led her to the Airport Express. He stopped twice on the way to show her the impressive construction of the roof and told her a little about the architect and how the airport had come to be built, in only eight years . . . complete with highways . . . two suspension bridges . . . a tunnel through the harbor . . . a masterpiece.

Yin-Yin stopped listening, wondering what was wrong with him. He was behaving like a guide. How could he think that these things would be of interest to her now?

She wanted to stay three days, but she absolutely did not want to stay in a hotel on her own. Since her aunt's apartment was clearly too small, Paul and Christine had offered for her to stay with them; his house was big enough. Now Yin-Yin doubted that it was a good idea.

At first they sat in uneasy silence on the train as they glided almost noiselessly through a landscape of water, green hills, high-rise buildings, containers, and cranes.

"Have you heard that three more Sanlitun managers were arrested yesterday?" Paul asked.

"My brother told me about it," she said casually.

"Isn't that great?" When she did not respond, he added, "Even lots of Chinese papers are now carrying detailed reports on this story."

She nodded.

"Did you know that it has all made headlines internationally?"

"No. Actually, yes. Xiao Hu said something about it." What did he want from her? For her to embrace him in happiness? To be grateful to him? She was not interested in all that. More than a dozen managers and officials had been arrested. Three factories had been closed, at least for now. Lakes, rivers, and fields were apparently being thoroughly tested. Everyone affected by the pollution would have recourse to damages. Discussions were under way as to the level of compensation. The storm of protest on the Internet had swelled in a few days, and the official censor had stood by without taking action, for whatever political reasons it might have had. It either wanted to make an example of Sanlitun, which Xiao Hu suspected, or the pressure from the public had been so great that the authorities had no longer dared to ignore it. Or perhaps the case was simply ideal for the government's environmental protection campaign. Television broadcasters and state-owned newspapers were all allowed to run reports on the case. Despite this, she did not feel proud, nor did she have any sense of triumph.

Her parents were dead.

Yes, she was free again, but for how long? The end to her imprisonment had seemed as arbitrary as her arrest. No one had told her why she had been suddenly taken back to Shanghai. No one answered her questions. No one took responsibility. There could just as easily come a day when there were men standing outside her door again, forcing her to go with them. They had let her go, but they had not returned her sense of security.

The inner act of detachment. Thus does one have the freedom to leave. She had detached herself, but she did not know what from. She felt like driftwood floating on the sea. The freedom to leave. She had chosen it without any idea of where the path would lead her.

Paul sensed that she was not interested in his questions. He looked at her, and when their eyes met, he did not look away. "I'm glad to see you," he suddenly said in a familiar tone of voice, which she remembered from Shanghai. "Please excuse all the nonsense in the airport earlier. I'm"—he searched for the right word—"I'm a little tense."

"Why?" She was not feigning ignorance.

"Because I'm sorry about what happened."

"Was it your fault?"

He gave her a thoughtful look.

"It's a question, not an accusation." She did not want to be misunderstood.

"I was careless."

"You were."

"I never have thought it would go so far. I . . ." A questioning look. As though she could finish the sentence for him. "I completely underestimated the situation."

"Are you saying that we should not have done anything?"

"No, that's not what I mean, not after everything both of you have achieved. But I was too careless. I want to apologize for that."

Yin-Yin nodded, leaned her head back, and closed her eyes.

"How did they . . ." She heard his hesitant voice. "I mean, was it . . ."

She could tell that he wanted to ask the same questions that her brother had. She could not share the experience, not with him either.

"I don't want to talk about it."

They sat next to each other in silence for a while.

"Do you believe in Chinese astrology?" Paul suddenly asked.

"Yes, of course," Yin-Yin said, surprised. "Why do you ask?"

"Because I went to see a fortune-teller some weeks ago; he prophesied that I would give life this year. That has come true."

"And?" She did not understand what he was getting at.

"He also said that I would take life. Hasn't that come true, at least indirectly, with the death of your parents?"

Yin-Yin thought for a moment. "In a way, yes," she said, and tried to smile. "Couldn't you have told me that earlier? Do I have to watch out now? Did he predict anything else?"

"No."

His cell phone rang. Christine. She was not feeling well, had severe nausea. She apologized for not being able to come to Lamma, but hoped to make it tomorrow.

"What would you like to do?" Paul asked after he had spoken to Christine. "Should we have something to eat in town, or should I get some food and cook for you at home?"

"Can you cook?" she asked, surprised.

"Christine says I even cook very well."

"Then let's cook. But not Chinese."

"What, then?"

"Something special. Maybe Italian?"

The confusion in his eyes amused her. "Italian? I can't."

"German?"

He laughed out loud. "No, not a single dish."

"Then I'll cook."

"You? What?"

"Spaghetti with spicy tomato sauce. A student from Rome taught me. They call the sauce *il classico* there, I think. It tastes great."

They went to a supermarket and bought Italian pasta, canned tomatoes, onions, garlic, carrots, olives, fresh basil, Parmesan cheese, and, Paul insisted, a bottle of wine from Tuscany.

She enjoyed the ferry journey to Lamma, and liked arriving on the island even more.

Paul became short of breath pulling her suitcase up the hill.

The first thing Yin-Yin noticed in the hall was the child's raincoat and rain boots.

He took her up to her room; it was on the second floor and was painted all white; two red lanterns hung from the ceiling. She had never seen such a clean and tidy house.

She looked out the window at the garden in bloom.

"It's lovely here. A little paradise."

"Thank you. Would you like something to drink?"

"Yes. And I'm getting hungry."

In the kitchen, she sliced onions and garlic, fried them in olive oil, and added three sliced chilies. Paul opened the bottle of wine.

He passed her a glass, and they clinked glasses without saying anything.

Yin-Yin put the tomatoes in the pan, turned the flame up, and stirred the mixture. The red sauce was soon bubbling vigorously, and some of it fell outside the pan with a dull plop.

Paul sat at the bar and watched her.

"Sorry I'm making a mess of your stove."

"Doesn't matter."

She stirred some more, washed the basil leaves, and cut them into fine strips.

"You've grown too thin," he said.

"Is that bad?"

"It depends. Are pounds the only thing you have lost?"

A strange question, that she had not yet asked herself. "What else?"

"I don't know," he replied. "I haven't been imprisoned for five weeks."

"No, you haven't," she said tensely. They were walking a thin line. Yin-Yin did not want to answer lots of questions, even if he was asking them more subtly than her brother had. What had she lost in that small room, apart from weight? Trust? Probably, but in whom or in what, she did not know. A carefreeness that her father had sometimes scolded her for? Possibly. Her belief that things would turn out right? Her mother's illness had already robbed her of that.

"Maybe I've also gained weight?"

Paul gave her an earnest look. "Gained weight? In what way?"

"Not on my physical body," she said in a tone of voice that made it clear that she did not want to continue this train of thought.

He sipped his wine pensively. "How long will you stay in New York?" he asked, changing the subject.

"I'll see. Two or three weeks. Maybe longer. I think I'd like to study at the music school there."

"What are you looking for there?"

"I'm not *looking* for anything. I'm *visiting* a friend." Was she not expressing herself clearly, or was he trying to provoke her? "What strange questions you ask."

"I'm sorry. I don't want to annoy you. I . . . I . . . just want to know how you are, really."

"You can see that for yourself." How was she supposed to reply to his questions when she did not have the answers yet herself?

Yin-Yin turned the gas flame down so that the sauce would not burn.

"I have something for you," he said, standing up and going upstairs. When he returned, he was holding a slightly crumpled envelope. It was addressed "To Wu Yin-Yin." Her father's handwriting. It was glued shut and had a red seal on it.

"Where did you get this?"

"It was in your parents' house on the table, under the book."

She stared at the envelope in disbelief. "My brother said there was no letter of farewell."

"I was in the house for a while before him, and I put it away without telling him about it," Paul said, a little embarrassed. "It's addressed to you. I'm sorry if you feel that was wrong."

She took the letter from him, sat down, hesitated, and wondered if she had the strength. Her left leg shook violently—as a result of her imprisonment, her limbs sometimes started twitching uncontrollably.

With her heart pounding, Yin-Yin opened the envelope.

To limit her emotions to the minimum necessary for survival.

My darling Xiao Bai Tu!

She lowered the piece of paper. *Xiao Bai Tu.* Little White Bunny. Her childhood nickname. Bunny is no more, she thought. Bunny is dead.

What are we thinking in our final hours? Of our children, what else? You are all that will remain of us. You live on—through

*you we have outwitted death. The thought of leaving you
and your brother alone made me question my course of action
for a moment. But you are old enough. You don't need us any
longer; on the contrary, we would have grown to be a burden.
Are already one. If I had not had the idea of trying to press
charges, you would not be imprisoned in a secret place now. Your
suffering is my fault. I can only ask you for forgiveness. Mr.
Leibovitz has told me what you did. I admire your courage and
am very proud of you. You did the right thing.*

*I have not always been so brave in my life. I did something
terrible once, and have never had the strength to tell you about it.*

Yin-Yin stopped reading. Whatever it was, she asked herself if
she wanted to know. She looked at Paul as though he could answer
this question.

"What is it?"

"My father. He . . . He wants to tell me a secret." She paused. "I'm
not sure I should read on." She put the letter down on the table. Did
Paul know what this was about?

"It must have been very important to him for him to tell you
about it," he said. "Otherwise he wouldn't have taken the time to
write this to you in his final hours."

Was she allowed to go against the wishes of her father? This letter was meant for her regardless of whether she liked the contents
or not. She picked up the letter and continued reading.

My silence was a big mistake. I know that now, but it's too late.

*Darling Xiao Bai Tu, your father was a weak person. I
allowed myself to be misled. I did not fight back. It was the time
of darkness, and I took it for a time of light. I was not the only
one, but that is no excuse. It never is. I betrayed my father. I
led the Red Guards to our house. He leaped from the window
because of me. His death is my death. What horrors can conceal
themselves in words. I have only said these things once in my life,*

*to your mother. She forgave me. Without the protection of her
love I would not have survived. Now I am going with her.*

*It hurts me that I will not live to see whose love will protect
you and Xiao Hu.*

*Your brother knows about all this. Not because I told him
but because he read it in the party files. Till the end, he could not
forgive me for it.*

*Perhaps you're asking yourself why I never had the courage
to talk to you both about it. I can't answer that question. Shame
was one reason. Regret. I tried many times, but couldn't bring
myself to do it. I can only ask for your understanding and for you
to look kindly on this.*

*With love,
Your Papa*

She read the final sentences twice, thrice, suddenly felt Paul's
hand on hers, and looked up. "Do you know what it's about?"

He nodded. "I think so. Before I went to your parents' house,
Xiao Hu told me about how your grandfather died."

So many questions and thoughts were whirling through Yin-
Yin's mind that she found it difficult to keep track of them all. Why
had her brother not told her? Neither before the death of their parents nor after? Were there other family secrets that she knew nothing about? How would she have reacted if her father had spoken to
her about it? With accusations? By distancing herself from him?
She couldn't imagine that. Who was she to lecture him on anything?
How old must he have been? Twelve? Thirteen? A child!

The letter changed nothing about her love for him. He was the
person who had held her hand when she learned to walk; who had
taken turns with her mother to watch over her at night when she
was sick; who, along with Min Fang, had encouraged her to study
music. Whose belief in her had seemed inexhaustible. To her, he was
the same strong, silent, and loving father as he had ever been.

Paul looked at her, his blue eyes full of concern, and asked in a thoughtful voice, "What are you thinking?"

Yin-Yin gave a short sigh. Western people, she thought. They asked strange questions. Johann Sebastian had clearly not been the only one. She hated the question. *What are you thinking?* If she had wanted him to know what she was thinking, she would have told him. "What am I thinking?" she repeated. "That I'm hungry."

She folded the letter, put it back in the envelope, and stirred the thick sauce. Paul stared at her in disbelief. "You can put the water on for the pasta," Yin-Yin said. "The sauce is almost ready. Where's the sugar?"

He set the table in silence. She waited to see if he would make another attempt. But Paul had understood that she did not want to talk about her parents or about her time in prison. So he told her about growing up in New York, about his first trip to China, and about how he had met Christine. They talked about music and looked up Yin-Yin's friend's place in Manhattan, where she would be staying, on Google Earth. It was on the corner of Avenue B and Tenth Street.

It was late. Paul said good-night. He was exhausted, she could see it, and he too wanted to go to bed. Yin-Yin sat alone at the kitchen bar and wondered what she should do. Sleep was out of the question. She was afraid to go for a walk in the dark. She wanted to stay indoors; there was something comforting about this room; she felt safe in this house, perched on top of a hill. It had started raining. Fat drops of rain hit the windowpanes. She walked into the hall and looked at the pair of child's rain boots. The yellow raincoat in the closet. The marks on the door frame.

The long and difficult path to letting go.

Back in the living room, she flicked through Paul's record collection and realized that they had very similar tastes. Yin-Yin wondered if she would dare to listen to classical music again for the first time since she had been freed. What did she feel like? The violin? No. Schubert lieder? Mahler? No to those too; singing would remind her too much of her mother. The piano would be best. Schubert? Bach? Beethoven?

She decided on the *Well-Tempered Clavier*. As she took the CD out of its case and put it in the stereo, she was incredibly nervous, as if she were doing something forbidden. She would soon find out whether she could bear it or not.

The first few notes were no more than a memory. Still very distant, as though someone were speaking to her in a language that had once been familiar but that she had forgotten. With every prelude, every fugue, more memories returned. She sank into the couch and absorbed the sounds. After two hours with the grave and profound Bach, a carefree Mozart took her by the hand and led her through the night. With him as a companion, the fear diminished more and more until it had disappeared.

The magical power of music, its mysterious strength. It was like a key that opened something within her; that was why she loved it. Because it went to the depths of a human being and was totally unstoppable. Because the times of darkness could not harm it. Because no one could lie to himself or herself in its company. Mozart, Yin-Yin thought, was always reliable. Like a friend.

Finally, she dared to move on to Beethoven. The composer she had the most respect for. Not only because she admired his musical brilliance, but because of the feelings that his music roused in her. She had to be careful with Beethoven; even when she had felt much more stable than she did now, there had been times when she could not listen to him in the past, and she had felt able to play his music even less often than that. She put on the *Moonlight* Sonata. A shudder ran down Yin-Yin's back. She swallowed. This was why she had become a musician. Because she had not been able to hide from compositions like these. Because they demanded the utmost participation with the soul.

Just like life.

The piano notes brought forth tears: liberating tears that did good; tears that she could not hold back, did not want to hold back. Yin-Yin realized that this was not a second moment of weakness, but one of the first instances of strength.

The situation was unambiguous. The power of darkness was now waning.

The night had almost ended when she opened the sliding door to the terrace and stepped out into the rain. It was wonderfully warm and powerful, and soaked her T-shirt and trousers in seconds. She closed her eyes and opened her mouth. She felt the rain on her body, the fat drops falling so fiercely on her skin that they felt like needles pricking; the water ran down her face in rivulets. The sound of the piano came out from the house to her. She had not felt such lightness for a long, a very long, time.

XXIII

It would be a lovely evening, a very special one. Christine had put a lot of thought into how her mother and Yin-Yin should meet. Dinner together at home? She didn't feel comfortable with the idea; it would give their meeting a kind of everyday normality that did not suit the occasion. On Lamma, with Paul? No, not that either. She was afraid that his presence would unsettle her mother and distract her. She decided on the Dragon Grill, the best Chinese restaurant in the whole of the Tseung Kwan O district; she reserved one of the private dining rooms normally used for family celebrations and business lunches and dinners. Grandmother and granddaughter were meeting for the first time, and she wanted both of them to get to know each other in peace so that they could find a connection without being drowned out by the noise of eating and drinking around them. She preordered her mother's favorite dishes—steamed tofu with Chinese ham and winter mushrooms, duck stuffed with eight treasures—as she wanted her mother to feel happy that evening. Christine could not imagine what she might be thinking. For forty years she had thought her son was dead, and had now found out that he had just died and that she had two grown grandchildren. Christine thought about Josh, her son, who was not as old as Da Long had been when her mother had last seen him. Just imagining being separated from him tomorrow and never seeing him again was quite unbearable.

It would not be an easy evening.

Three women, three generations; one family, no common language. Her mother would speak Cantonese to her and Mandarin to her granddaughter. Christine would speak English, which her mother hardly understood, to Yin-Yin. One of them would constantly be requiring another one of them to translate.

Christine had not been able to go to Lamma during the day, so she picked Yin-Yin up at the ferry point. She got a shock when she saw Yin-Yin approaching. Her skin was pale and her face had grown thin; there were shadows under her eyes. She looked past Christine as though she were a stranger.

"Yin-Yin?"

She stopped in surprise, as though it was a coincidence that they were meeting here. "I'm sorry, I didn't see you. When I listen to music I get completely distracted," she said, removing the headphones.

"Don't worry about it." Christine could not take her eyes off Yin-Yin. The traces left by her imprisonment.

"Do I look so terrible?"

"What makes you say that?" Christine asked uncomfortably.

"The way you're looking at me."

"No, no, you just look a little tired." Not a good start.

They took a taxi to Hang Hau. Christine felt her shoulders growing more tense by the minute, and a hint of pain at the base of her skull, the early sign of a headache. She singled out a few points of interest during the taxi ride, including the old airport, and told Yin-Yin about the many nature reserves in the city. Her niece listened politely.

"My mother is very much looking forward to this," Christine said, feeling that she wasn't sounding very sincere.

"So am I," Yin-Yin said in the same tone of voice.

"I've got a packet of her favorite candy here. Coconut candy and pralines from Hainan island. You can give them to her if you like. She'll be happy to receive them."

"Thank you. But I've brought a photographic book on Shanghai for her." It did not sound like she wanted to give her both the book and the candy.

"That . . . That's much nicer, of course," Christine said, embarrassed. "I'll give her the candy, then."

The restaurant was on the third floor of a shopping mall. Wu Jie was waiting for them. She sat bent over on a chair, staring into space. Instead of the new red jacket that Christine had given her a few weeks ago, she was wearing a worn old vest top; a hairpin had come loose, and strands of gray hair were falling in front of her eyes.

"Mama, this is Yin-Yin." Christine was so nervous that she found it difficult to breathe.

Wu Jie pushed the hair out of her face and looked at her granddaughter for a long time, as though she was looking for similarities to her son. She stood up, supported herself on the arm of the chair, greeted Yin-Yin with a few simple words, and sat down again. Yin-Yin replied politely and gave her grandmother her present. Wu Jie looked at the book briefly and put it aside. "Thank you."

They took their places and several waitresses surrounded them immediately. They unfolded napkins, poured tea, and brought little dishes of peanuts and eggs with ginger and mustard to the table. When they had left the room, an oppressive silence set in.

Christine began to doubt her choice of venue. The room was beautiful, but much too big. Three of them were sitting at a table that could accommodate at least twelve people, and for her mother's tastes, the tablecloth and the floor were probably too clean and the waitresses' uniforms not flecked with enough stains from the food.

Yin-Yin said something and her grandmother answered briefly. Yin-Yin gave an embarrassed smile and asked something else, which she received an abrupt reply to.

Even though Christine did not understand what her mother was saying, she could tell from the tone of voice that it was not going well. She was familiar with this way of communication: the curt tones and surly replies; the absolute minimum. She had gotten used to it over the years; it was not meant to be unfriendly, the way it seemed from the outside, but to Yin-Yin it must have seemed almost hostile.

"Yin-Yin is a musician," Christine said.

"No one in our family is musical," Wu Jie said firmly, as though there was still some doubt as to whether this was really a relation who was visiting them.

"Her mother was a music teacher and she sang," Christine said quickly, not translating what her mother said for Yin-Yin at all.

"I see. Does a musician earn money?" Wu Jie wanted to know, as she gave her granddaughter a skeptical look. Christine translated.

"A person won't grow rich from it, but it's enough to live on." Wu Jie nodded absently.

Yin-Yin tried to start a conversation. She asked questions and her grandmother answered without looking up, until Yin-Yin finally fell silent.

"What did you say?" Christine asked.

"I asked her how her health was."

"And?"

"Bad, she said."

"What else?"

"Whether she was happy in Hong Kong. She said it would be terrible if not. After forty years!"

Christine thought about an old Chinese proverb that a teacher of hers used to quote: Mountains and rivers are easy to move, but a person's nature is difficult to change.

It can't be changed at all, she thought now. Not at all. Not in her mother's case, at least.

Four young waitresses brought the rice, tofu, and vegetables. A waiter put the duck on the table, carved it with a celebratory flourish, and showed the women the treasures inside: lotus seeds, chestnuts, two kinds of mushrooms, ham, dates, gingko nuts, and sun-dried scallops. Christine had, as always, ordered too much, but it all smelled delicious, and her mother beamed for a moment. The waiter served them and they started eating in silence.

Christine tried to start a conversation again. She asked her niece about Xiao Hu, about Yin-Yin's plans for New York, and the audition for the symphony orchestra. She translated the replies into Cantonese.

Her mother gnawed at a duck bone, helped herself to steamed

tofu, spat gristle out onto the tablecloth, and did not seem interested in Yin-Yin's replies. She had never been a communicative person. At least, not with words. But her silence right then made Christine more and more uncomfortable with every passing minute. Why didn't she want to know anything about her granddaughter? Did she have nothing to say to her? Why was she so silent?

Her mother had behaved in the same strange way two months earlier when Christine had finally told her about what had happened to Da Long. For reasons that she herself did not understand, she had delayed telling her mother that she had met her brother in China. First she was too tired, then her mother was not well, then Christine was afraid it would be too much for her, then came the news that she was pregnant, and then finally she had to tell her everything at once. Da Long had survived the Cultural Revolution! Had become an engineer. Had married and had two children. Now he really was dead. Christine had been so emotional that her voice had trembled and she had kept hesitating as she told her mother all this; she had only managed it all with difficulty. Her mother, on the other hand, had listened to everything without saying a word. Only nodded now and then or murmured something she couldn't make out.

Mama, what's wrong? she had asked.

Nothing, Wu Jie had said. Her reply had made a shudder ripple through Christine's whole body. Nothing. Untouched.

She thought about her unlived life. About unshed tears. Things not said. Sorrow not shared.

Christine had hoped that the granddaughter would make the grandmother speak, that Wu Jie would ask after her son, that Yin-Yin would talk about her father. But they did not once mention the name that connected them both.

She missed Paul. He would have relaxed the atmosphere and made it more lighthearted with his questions and with his sense of humor. She searched her mind for things to talk about, but everything that occurred to her had a shadow cast upon it: Min Fang, Yin-Yin's childhood, her own in Hong Kong. So they praised the food instead and talked about tea, mahjong, lucky numbers, and Chinese astrology.

The dinner was over in just under an hour. Wu Jie was keen to leave.

The farewell at the MTR station was brief; they would meet tomorrow afternoon one more time, but now they were taking trains going in opposite directions.

Christine brought her niece back to the ferry point.

"I'm sorry. My mother can sometimes be a little gruff."

"That's fine."

"I don't know why she was so distant. Even when I told her about Da Long's death, she reacted very calmly, almost coldly."

"Maybe she can simply never forgive him."

"Forgive him?"

The two women's gazes met. *You don't know?* one pair of eyes said. *What are you talking about?* said the other.

"Didn't your mother tell you anything?"

"No, about what?"

Yin-Yin looked around the train carriage uncomfortably, trying to hint that this was not the right moment to talk about family secrets.

"Forgive what?" Christine said impatiently.

Her niece leaned over to her and said in a low voice, "The death of her husband. It was no coincidence that the Red Guards stormed your apartment that day. Your father had been betrayed to them as a counterrevolutionary."

The door being kicked in. The fear of death in her parents' faces. Her father on the windowsill. A black crow unable to fly. Where was her brother? Why didn't she ever see him in this image? A horrible realization rose within her. She hoped it was not true.

"Did Da Long . . . ?"

Yin-Yin nodded.

Looking for something to hold on to, Christine grabbed her niece's hand. "How do you know that?'

"I only found out yesterday. My father wrote me a farewell letter. Paul found it and gave it to me. It's in the letter."

She did not want to cry. Not on this train. Not in front of Yin-

Yin. She saw a little girl in front of her, one with braids, big eyes, a blue school uniform, and long, thin legs. One who had spent too many hours alone in one hundred square feet, who had longed for her father and for a big brother, who had borne silence for years, and who had had to be much too brave for her age.

All because of a few books hidden under the kitchen floor! Because her father had read Confucius! Two-thousand-year-old writings that were now taught in the schools again. Because a fourteen-year-old had been careless, impertinent, or wanted to seem important.

She felt that she was looking at her life as if it were a great big jigsaw puzzle with important pieces missing. She was now holding one of them. When she added it, another picture would emerge; a lot would be explained, but the reasons would still not be clear.

Her mother's pain. Was it not for the missing son but for the traitor? Perhaps she had arranged for him to be sent to the country-side so that she and her daughter could escape to Hong Kong without him. Had they fled not the Communists but their own family? So many questions that she would never get answers to. Blanks that had inserted themselves into her life.

How close had mother and daughter been? Why had she never managed to share her sorrow? They had lived together for over twenty years, and yet they knew so little about each other.

"I'm sorry," Yin-Yin said, sliding closer and putting her arm around her aunt. "I thought you knew . . ."

"Do you have the letter with you?"

"Yes."

"May I read it?"

Yin-Yin hesitated.

"Please."

Yin-Yin took it out of her bag and gave it to her. Christine opened the envelope. She had a vague hope. Perhaps he had thought about his sister too. Not much, a couple of sentences—oh, even a few words would do. She unfolded the letter carefully and read it. Not a word about her. Not a line about her mother. Why was he asking his children for understanding and forgiveness, not those whose lives had been so drastically affected by his actions? Without his betrayal, her father would have lived, and she would not have had to grow up in the tragic fragment of family that was left.

"Where is the letter for me?" she asked almost sullenly. "Where is the letter for my mother?"

Yin-Yin put the envelope away. "There's . . . He . . . Don't forget what circumstances he wrote this under—"

Christine interrupted her. "You don't need to defend your father. He had many years to write us a letter." She did not want to argue, and she could feel that every further word said would only make her more furious. Instead, she was overcome by a deep sadness.

After a long pause, Christine asked, "Does Paul know about it?"

"Yes. Xiao Hu told him about it in Shanghai."

They got off the train at Central and walked silently to the ferry terminal. She did not want to explain herself. Why hadn't Paul told her anything? She presumed he had wanted to protect her.

They said good-bye at the pier with a quick hug. Christine watched her niece walk up the swaying gangway, headphones in her ears. How she had changed in the weeks since they had first met. China years, she thought. Now she too had lived through China years. She waved briefly and watched the ferry until it was gone from view beyond the pier.

She hated saying good-bye to people, whether at the ferry terminal, the train station, or the airport. The loneliness of being left behind, the emptiness and the sudden silence that enveloped her, was so difficult to break out of. Christine sat down on the steps leading to the pier and took out her cell phone. She had to hear Paul's voice. A few words would be enough.

"Talk to me," she said.

"What's happened?" he asked, worried.

"Nothing." She swallowed her tears. It was not the right moment.

"You don't sound well."

"Just talk to me about something," she repeated in a tired voice. "I need to hear your voice."

"I love you."

"More."

"You are the heart of my happiness. You are my rose, my love. You are everything I have. More?"

"Yes."

"You're hungry for love."

Christine could see his smile. "Aren't we all?"

"Some more than others."

She could have ended the call there. She didn't need more than that. "Paul, I love you. More than anything. Don't ever leave me."

"Never. You sound so sad."

"I am."

"Why?"

"The dinner."

"Didn't it go well?"

"No. It was very difficult."

"Why?"

Christine hesitated. She didn't want to talk about her brother's betrayal now, or about why Paul had not told her about it. "You know what my mother is like. She can be very difficult. I didn't get the feeling that she was especially interested in her granddaughter."

"And what about Yin-Yin?"

"She tried her best."

"I'm sorry. I know how important it was to you."

"It's my family," she said, hoping he would understand what she meant.

"I know. But it's growing, and the new members will be more talkative, I promise."

"I sense that," she said, wishing she could take the next ferry to Lamma.

XXIV

He had just switched off the light when his cell phone rang. CHRIS-
TINE was displayed on the tiny screen. They had talked earlier that
evening. Christine had wanted to lie down because she was feeling
nauseated and her limbs were aching; she had promised to call again
tomorrow. She had turned down his offer to come to her apartment.
It wasn't that bad.

A stranger's voice on the phone. Paul knew immediately that
something was wrong. Tita Ness. Sorry, who? It took him a few seconds to realize who it was. The Filipina maid. She was very agitated,
and he had trouble understanding her. Mrs. Wu. Not good. On the
way to hospital. Bleeding. Very sudden. Kwun Tong Hospital. Paul
looked at his watch: 11:17 p.m.

The last ferry from Yung Shue Wan to Central was leaving in
thirteen minutes. Almost no chance, he thought immediately, then
he started moving without thinking. Slipped on his underwear,
grabbed a shirt and pants from his closet, dressed, and ran out of
the house. It had been raining. The tiles on the terrace were wet.
He slipped and fell, got up, and kept running. He took the short-
cut down the steps, bounding down them four or five at a time.
He lost his balance at a landing and crashed backward into a trash
can, which fell over with a loud clang. He hurried on down to the
village, where he heard the bell signaling the closing of the gates to
the ferry. He ran past Green Cottage like a man possessed, and past
the Island Bar, shouting for them to wait for him. *Wait! Wait!* When

he got to the post office he heard the low rumble of a ship's motor in reverse gear. When he came to a stop on the pier, the ferry had turned around and was on the way to Hong Kong.

The next ship left at 6:20 a.m. Apart from medical emergencies, when acutely ill or injured persons had to be evacuated from the island by helicopter, it was the only way to leave the island. He was trapped. Paul wondered if it was possible to swim to Hong Kong. The East Lamma Channel at Pak Kok was a little more than a mile wide, but the current was strong, there was a lot of shipping traffic at night, and the weather was poor. There had been a strong wind blowing all day, and it had gained in strength that evening. He looked at the water and saw white crests on the waves in the light cast from the pier. He couldn't swim in that. His only chance was to find a private boat that would take him over.

Paul tried to reach Christine on the phone, but neither she nor Tita Ness answered. He ran to the Island Bar, where there were still a few people, British and Australians who had lived on the island for a long time and knew him by sight. When Paul explained why he needed to get to Hong Kong as quickly as possible, silence fell in the bar. No, none of them had a boat. But the bartender knew a fisherman who had a small motorboat that was moored in the harbor. He lived around the corner, just up the steps, in the upper part of the village.

The fisherman had already gone to bed. He opened the door grumpily. He was a head shorter and few years older than Paul. He looked suspiciously at the barefoot stranger who was drenched in sweat and whose gray hair was sticking to his face. At this hour? He shook his head.

Paul offered him a thousand Hong Kong dollars.

No.

Two thousand.

The old fisherman sized him up more thoroughly but shook his head again.

Three thousand.

At least he was awake now. He stepped out of the door, looked at the dark sky, the palm leaves swaying in the wind, and the churning sea. In this weather? No.

Five thousand.

No.

Ten.

Can you swim?

Paul nodded.

Did he have the money with him?

Paul said no. Explained, appealed, showed his Hong Kong ID card. Promised. Ten thousand. In cash. Tomorrow evening, latest.

The man gave a long sigh. Okay. Ten minutes, at the pier.

Paul ran back, only now noticing how cool it was. His bare feet were cold; he could hardly feel them. In the bar, someone asked him if they could lend him more clothing; he got a windbreaker and some shoes that pinched his toes.

The fisherman brought a faded yellow life vest with him and tossed it to Paul. Then he climbed onto a tiny square raft and paddled out to his boat, which was fastened to a buoy sixty-five feet offshore. He untied the rope, fiddled with the motor, pulled a strap a few times until the motor sprang to life with an unsteady rattle, and picked Paul up from the breakwater.

It was an old wooden boat, barely fifteen feet long, and wide enough for only one person. In it were two oars for an emergency, a fish trap, a net, bamboo poles, Styrofoam markers, and a plastic pail.

To balance the weight better, Paul sat at the bow. The fisherman passed him a powerful flashlight to search the black waters for big pieces of driftwood. They ducked as they passed underneath the pier and kept as close to the shore as possible. Despite that, the boat began to bob up and down. Paul knew that this was only the beginning; it would get worse when they rounded the tip of the island at Shek Ko Tsui and crossed open water in the channel between Lamma and Hong Kong.

He thought about Christine, and tried to calm down. What might have happened? There were only two weeks left to the due date, so this was not a matter of a preterm delivery with all the complications and risks that implied. The pregnancy had progressed with no particular problems until now, apart from frequent morning sickness and water collecting in Christine's arms and legs. She had been able to carry on working until yesterday, and had spent the summer and the fall preparing for her new life. She had rearranged Paul's house, given notice on his future mother-in-law's small apartment in Hang Hau, and found her a new one in Yung Shue Wan. As soon as Christine had found a tenant for her apartment, she, Josh, her mother, and the baby would move to Lamma.

The regular prenatal appointments had not given any cause for concern. According to the results of the early diagnostic tests, the baby was healthy. Nevertheless, the astrologer's words still haunted him.

You will give life. You will take life. These first two predictions had come true. Not a day passed in which he did not think of the third prediction, even though he had grown calmer in recent weeks, when the doctors had reassured him that the baby was now able to survive a preterm birth.

You will lose life.

Paul saw the blinking of the beacon marking the tip of the island. They would be traveling alongside land for about a hundred yards more. Now fifty, thirty . . . Paul turned and tried to look the fisherman in the eye. He was standing upright at the stern, with his legs spread wide, one hand on the motor and the other holding a cigarette that had gone out. Ten more . . . five more . . .

The first broadside crashed into them with full force, making the whole boat shake. The water pounded the side of the boat relentlessly in dull thuds. Paul put the flashlight away and clutched the sides of the boat with both hands in order not to be pitched overboard. The fisherman too was now sitting down, and holding on to the stern of the boat. The spray had completely drenched both men in seconds. Fat, salty drops of water ran down their faces. The wind was coming from the northwest, chasing dark clouds over the night sky illuminated by the city. Paul, who had always thought himself seaworthy, felt as sick as a dog. Waves crashed into the boat over and over again, and it slowly began to fill with water. The fisherman shouted something at him, but was drowned out by the noise. He spat out a few curses in Cantonese and pointed at the pail. Paul tried to hold on to the boat with one hand and use the other to bail water out of the boat. Suddenly the boat pitched upward so steeply that he fell backward and his back crashed into the side of the boat. Their boat was at a dangerous angle. Paul crawled back to the bow on all fours. The fisherman was shouting something again, but it was carried away in another direction by the wind.

From one second to another, the storm abated, and the sea grew a little calmer. They had made it into the shadow of a container ship that was moored offshore by Lamma. Their boat was heading straight for the black side of the ship, which rose in front of them like a sea monster that seemed never-ending. Paul shuddered as he saw how small they were compared with the freighter. They traveled through calmer waters for a few minutes. Paul bailed water out of the boat with both hands, as quickly as he could. The fisherman slowed the boat down a little, as though he wanted to draw breath before making the great leap across the East Lamma Channel. They had barely passed the container ship when they took a sharp dip. The wind was now blowing at them straight on, just like the swell, which was much greater than it had seemed from land. Paul looked at the lights of Hong Kong in front of them. The high-rise buildings appeared so near, and yet impossibly distant at the same time. If they capsized, they would not be able to swim the distance in this storm, neither to Hong Kong nor back to Lamma. Their only hope would be to be seen by a ship and be rescued.

Two large ships were approaching from port and starboard; they would have to cross their paths. For a moment, Paul wondered if they could do it, or if they should turn back instead. Once more, he tried to catch the fisherman's eye, but the man ignored him. He had eyes only for the two freighters, and he seemed to be calculating a route that would bring them through the two vessels. They headed toward the ship approaching from port side. Paul couldn't see a gap, only walls of steel towering over them. The captain must have thought they were blind or crazy; he had sounded his horn three times, sending it echoing in the night. Soon they were so near that Paul could even see small patches of rust on the side of the vessel. They reached the eddy around the stern, turned ninety degrees, and with another daring turn, the fisherman had them on course again. The second freighter appeared directly in front of them, and the swell around its bow hit the side of their boat at an angle. Paul fell forward onto his stomach and felt a sharp pain in his head.

He stayed facedown, and heard the fisherman shout, but did not move. The boat was beginning to fill with water frighteningly fast again, so Paul began to bail water again from a prone position. Faster, he heard the old man scream, faster, faster! After a few minutes, the waves grew less powerful. Paul lifted his head and saw Green Island at what he estimated to be six hundred feet distance. They had reached the wind shelter of the island.

The fisherman set Paul down at a small jetty by Kennedy Town; he would spend the rest of the night in the harbor. As arranged, Paul gave him his ID card for security, thanked him, and ran to the road. There must be a taxi, even at this hour. His shoes were tight and soaked with water; he pulled them off and ran on barefoot.

The first taxi driver stopped, saw what state his prospective passenger was in, and drove on. The second did the same. The third wanted to know if Paul had come from a shipwreck. Something like that, he said, and asked the driver to take him to the hospital in Kwun Tong by the quickest route possible.

Paul curled up in the backseat, shivering all over. The trembling did not get any better, even when the heating in the car was turned up so high that the driver started sweating and rolled down a window. Paul was trembling not just from the cold. The fear was worse. Nothing must happen to Christine. She was everything that he had left. He wanted to tell the doctors that if they had to decide between saving the life of the mother or the child, they should save Christine.

The clock showed that it was just past two in the morning when they reached the hospital. The trauma and emergency unit knew who he was talking about immediately. The pregnant woman with the bleeding, whose waters had broken. She was on the maternity ward, third floor. Before they could say anything else, Paul had disappeared up the stairs.

The labor ward was busy even at this late hour. Women and men in green and white uniforms hurried down the corridors, and no one took any notice of Paul's strange appearance: a tall Westerner, breathless, in a white shirt and white pants, so wet that his clothing clung to him, barefoot, holding a pair of shoes dripping water. He heard loud groaning coming from a room, and the soothing voice of a nurse; from another room came the piteous screams of a newborn.

He found Christine in the next room. She was lying in bed dressed only in a white nightgown, with no cover, with a drip by her side. She was hooked up to a cardiogram that was monitoring the baby's heartbeat and her contractions. Her smile when she saw him. She was pale and sweating. Her lips were cracked. What was wrong with her eyes? Either they had given her medication, or the exhaustion had drawn a veil over her gaze. He took her hand and kissed her on her forehead, her eyes, her mouth. My darling. My little one. Are you all right? Is everything okay?

A nurse came in, looked at him in surprise, and wanted to know who he was.

The father, Paul said. The young woman gave Christine a questioning look and she nodded in confirmation.

Your wife is doing well, the midwife said. The baby's heartbeat was normal and the contractions were still weak. The waters had broken, but there was no cause for concern. The doctor would carry out a caesarean section soon. He was just busy with another birth at the moment.

No cause for concern. The wrong words.

Christine realized that. She pressed his hands. Paul pulled a chair up to the bed and sat down. He wanted to be strong for her, but he felt only how weak he was. After Justin's death, he had really thought that there would never be anything else that he need be afraid of. Now he was learning otherwise.

"Rest," he said, in a low voice.

"Why are you so wet?"

"I've been swimming."

She laughed and closed her eyes. Suddenly she clutched his hand and bit her lips, raised herself, groaned, and sank back onto the pillow.

"Can I do anything for you?" he asked with concern. He could not remember any of the many breathing techniques that they had learned in the prenatal classes.

"Stay by my side, that's enough," she said. "You mustn't be worried."

"I've been trying to convince myself of that during the pregnancy. It's not that simple."

"Trust in Master Wong."

"Why him especially?" Paul had tried to sound casual, but Christine lifted her head, amazed at the fear in his voice.

"Because all his predictions come true."

"Please, please no."

"Why not? He prophesied that you would give life."

"Yes. And?"

"In a few minutes it will happen. What could go wrong? Apart from that, he would have said."

"What?"

"If something were to happen to me or the baby."

"Don't say that," Paul said.

"Do you still not trust in the stars?" she asked. "People need something that they can believe in, don't they?"

"I— I don't know," he said. "I can't say that I believe in them. But I can't say that I don't believe in them either."

She smiled again. "You're much more Chinese than I thought."

He saw the next contraction coming in her face. Only now did he become aware of the strange noise that filled the whole room. How could he not have heard it before? A mysterious pounding. A completely unique sound, one that reminded him of a horse galloping. Fast and relentless. For a long moment, he did not know what it was. It was his baby's heartbeat. He could hear the heart of his unborn son.

Paul listened. What magical strength this sound transmitted.

What kind of person was behind this heartbeat? A fearful one or a brave one? A tender soul or a coarse one? What secrets would he come to the world with? Every life was a promise. Every life was a gift.

———

Paul continued sitting next to Christine in silence. He stroked her face and her belly. She groaned quietly. At some point two midwives and an anesthetist came in and prepared her for the operation. They raised her and sat her on the edge of the bed, and the doctor put a long, very fine needle into the epidural space of her spine to numb the lower part of her body. Paul looked away. One wrong prick of the needle, too far to the left or the right, and Christine could end up wheelchair bound. Extremely unlikely, of course. Statistically speaking.

He walked alongside Christine, holding her hand as she was wheeled down the corridor and into the operating room.

He had to let go at the entrance to the operating room. The obstetrician asked if he wanted to be present for the operation. That would be fine, but he just had to change out of his wet clothing first, which was not a bad idea anyway, and put on a cap, a face mask, and hospital scrubs. Paul followed the obstetrician into a room, undressed, and pulled on the scrubs. Then his courage left him. The fear of being overcome by panic during the operation was overwhelming.

You will lose life.

Whose life was he to lose? Christine's? In Hong Kong, there was practically no risk of a healthy woman dying in childbirth. His son's? A caesarean section was the safest method of delivery for a baby; again, the figures showed that nothing would likely happen. How much could statistical averages and graphs be relied on when it came to a life? Not much at all.

The worst feeling was the powerlessness, the feeling of having to look on helplessly while his fate was being decided. How often he had held conversations with himself in the months before Justin's

death, begging that someone might save his child, that a super-
natural force might make everything right after all. He had tried to
pray. He had made sworn pledges—to sell his apartment, to build
a temple, to fund an orphanage in the Philippines—if his son were
healed. He had done everything, but not found a god within himself
to whom he could turn.

Paul collapsed onto a bench and waited. Through the door, which
was ajar, he could hear the voices of the doctors and nurses. To his
amazement, he felt that he was becoming calmer for the first time
that night.

His son came into the world eighteen minutes later.

Paul listened to the animated voices in the operating room, but
could only hear fragments. Blood loss. A mystery.

Paul followed the doctor. "How is my wife?" he asked. "How is
my wife?"

"She's fine. You can go to her," one of the doctors said.

Christine lay on the operating table, her body covered with a
green screen, with her white legs sticking out at the bottom. Paul
went to the top end of the table. She was conscious and her forehead
was covered in tiny beads of sweat. She reached for his hand. He had
never seen her smile so beautifully before.

The obstetrician was suddenly by their side. He was very sorry.
It was difficult to explain. Their baby had had a twin. It was not
possible to establish on the spot whether it was a boy or a girl, a
fraternal or an identical twin. They had just found the remains of it
in the placenta with the afterbirth. It was incredible that no one had
noticed it in the scans before, but that sometimes happened. The
second fetus must have died early, at only a few weeks' gestation. It
had probably not been a healthy fetus. Or perhaps the mother's body
had been able to nourish only one of the fetuses, so it had rejected
the other one. If that were so, one baby had been sacrificed so that
the other one could live. Perhaps that was some comfort.

You will lose life.

"Is our son healthy?" Paul asked.

"Yes, of course. He's doing well," the doctor answered lightly, brushing away his concern. He brought him to a side table where a midwife was weighing and measuring the baby.

Paul looked with his heart racing at the naked, blood-smeared infant. The pale skin, almost bluish in some places. The wrinkled little hands. The wide mouth and the eyes screwed shut. A miracle weighing 7.3 pounds and measuring 19 inches in length, fragile and vulnerable. The midwife checked his temperature, wrapped the baby in a towel, and laid him in Paul's arms. How light he was. And small. His head fit comfortably in his father's hand.

"You can come with me to wash the baby for the first time, if you like," the midwife said, leading him into another room. She filled a plastic basin with water, checking the temperature a few times until it was right. "Is this your first?"

Paul was unable to say anything. He shook his head.

"Then I won't have to show you anything."

She helped him unwrap his screaming son from the towel and watched as Paul laid the baby's stomach on his right hand and slowly dipped him in the water feetfirst.

The midwife had done this for Justin, but Paul had watched every move carefully. The long-faded memory was suddenly alive again.

With his left hand, he trickled water over the baby, washing his back, his little arms, and little legs.

A handful of life.

The warm water calmed the boy, and his angry cries of protest gradually stopped.

Paul laid him on a towel, dried his little body carefully, and put a diaper on him. His son opened his eyes for the first time and looked at him. He had his mother's dark hair and his deep blue eyes.

"Does he have a name already?" the midwife asked.

Paul nodded. "David."

"No Chinese name?"

"Not yet. We want to ask an astrologer for advice."

"He'll be hungry soon. Come, let us bring him to your wife."

Paul covered the baby in a blue-and-white-striped blanket and carried him with light steps down the corridor.

Christine was lying alone in a room with two beds. She looked pale, but her eyes brightened when she saw them approach.

"Your son needs you," the midwife said, laying the baby on Christine's chest. The baby began drinking from her breast in mere seconds.

Christine looked at her baby and her husband in turn, over and over again. "What are you thinking?"

"What strange questions you ask," Paul said.

"I just want to know how you're feeling," she said, smiling weakly.

Paul got the reference. He smiled back. "You're much more Western than I thought." He was indescribably tired, and felt pains in his whole body, especially at the back of his head. He pushed his fingers through his hair and found dried blood on his hands. "Do you think I could lie down on the other bed for a bit?"

"Join us on this one," she said.

He gave the narrow bed a dubious look. "Is there room?"

"For you, yes," Christine said, moving a little to one side with great effort.

Paul squeezed into the narrow space next to her and put his arm under her head. He took a deep breath and buried his nose in her hair. Despite the hospital and the operation, she had not lost her wonderful smell.

His son sucked away noisily. "He's really hungry."

"Aren't we all?"

Paul remembered the beating of his son's tiny heart and understood that he no longer had to search for the answer to Christine's question: *What do you believe in?* The answer lay in his hands. He believed in the strength of this heart. Of every heart. In hope. In promises. In magic. He believed in the greatness, the tenderness, and the uniqueness of every being. In the love that everyone was capable of giving. It was quite simply and plainly a belief in life, with all its tragedies and beauties.

ACKNOWLEDGMENTS

This book is a work of fiction. The events and characters are the products of my imagination. The ideas for the book came from the countless journeys that I have made to China since 1995. I was inspired to write this story by the many conversations that I had there and in Hong Kong, where I lived for a time, with friends, acquaintances, and strangers. I feel deeply indebted to the people who helped me on my travels and in my research, for their trust in me, their openness, and their support. Special thanks go to Zhang Dan, who has made such an effort, with bottomless patience, to explain her country and her culture to me. I'm also indebted to Lamy Li, Clara and Derick Tam, Bessie Du, Wang Cai Hua, Emily Lee, Zhang Yi, Dan Yi, Dan Yiu Kun Yat, Fang Xingdong, Qian En Wang, Maggie Chen, Richard Chen, Graham Earnshaw, Clemens Kunisch, Dr. Gerhard Hinterhäuser, Alwin Bergmann, Dr. Reinhard Kruse, Dr. Ekkehard Scholz, and Dr. Joachim Sendker, who all helped me in one way or another with my research. I would also like to thank my parents for their help, and my sister, Dorothea.

My son, Jonathan, helped me with his penetrating questions and with his ideas. And in the end, I have benefited from the trust, the discipline, and the experience of my wonderful editor, Hanna Diederichs.

I would like to thank my agent PJ Mark for his encouragement and the passionate way he helped to turn my dream into reality. Writing a book is a lonely thing to do, publishing a book is teamwork. Therefore I am very grateful to everyone at Atria, especially Dawn

Davis, David Brown, Hillary Tisman, James Thiel, Carly Loman, Isolde Sauer, Douglas Johnson, Joshua Cohen, and Susan Bishansky.

I owe my biggest thanks to my wife, Anna. She was involved in every stage of this manuscript coming into being, and read every chapter with a critical eye. Her advice, her comments, questions, encouragement, and, above all, her love, have made this book possible.

ABOUT THE AUTHOR

Jan-Philipp Sendker, born in Hamburg in 1960, was the American correspondent for *Stern* magazine, and its Asian correspondent, based in Hong Kong. He is the author of *The Art of Hearing Heartbeats,* an international bestseller, *Cracks in the Wall,* a nonfiction book about China, and the novels *A Well-Tempered Heart* and *Whispering Shadows.* He lives in Potsdam, Germany, with his family.

ABOUT THE TRANSLATOR

Christine Lo (previously known as Christine Slenczka) is an editor in book publishing in London. She has also worked as a translator in Frankfurt and translated books by Juli Zeh and Senait Mehari from German into English. Her most recent translation is *Atlas of Remote Islands* by Judith Schalansky.